HOUSE ADAMANT

THE OLD GUARD

BOOK TWO

OF THE HOUSE ADAMANT SERIES

Faolan's Pen Publishing
22 King St. S, Suite 300
Waterloo, Ontario
N2J 1N8 Canada

Printed in the United States of America
1 2 3 4 5 6 7 8 9 10
First edition

ISBN 978-1-989674-79-6

HOUSE ADAMANT

THE OLD GUARD

BOOK TWO

OF THE HOUSE ADAMANT SERIES

GLYNN STEWART

FAOLAN'S PEN
PUBLISHING

faolanspen.com

ONE

"I am delighted to be the first to welcome you to the United Worlds, Lieutenant Commander Adamant," the naval officer seated across the desk told Lorraine.

He might even mean it, the young woman reflected as she smiled in response to his pleasantry. On the other hand, the tanned-skinned Adamantine woman was sure her smile and warm expression also came across as perfectly sincere.

"Thank you, Captain Wolfe," she told her host. "I'm afraid my commission is suspended until we have a legitimate new King in Adamant, however. *Pentarch* is the correct title—but, as my documents note, *Envoy* is perfectly acceptable as well."

Her Royal Highness Lorraine Alexis Elouise Nala Adamant was the Second Pentarch of the Kingdom of Adamant, one of five of her mother-the-King's heirs and charged to stand for election to replace King Valeriya Adamant.

Except she'd been *Fourth* Pentarch until her uncle had killed her parents and two of her three siblings. There was a reason for the *legitimate* in her phrasing, and she saw that Captain Wolfe of the United Worlds Navy had picked it up.

The stubby man with the shaven head was one of dozens of administrative officers aboard MacDougall Station, the military platform her ship was docked with.

"I see... Envoy," he allowed. "Your documents are entirely in order. We are aware of the current crisis in your home state, of course, but the United Worlds has received no communiques that would invalidate your diplomatic papers."

"I appreciate that confirmation, Captain Wolfe," Lorraine told him. She didn't quite flutter her eyelashes at the man—that would be too obvious—but other body language was just as effective.

She was twenty-eight years old, with dark hair, pale skin and gold-blue hazel eyes. The UWN officer probably had a decade on her, but he was clearly not immune to her beauty—the result of long-ago genetic engineering by the ancestor who'd founded a kingdom of multiple star systems.

"Will there be any issues with my ship?" she continued.

"As Envoy of your Kingdom, you are authorized to travel aboard any vessel of your choosing," Wolfe said calmly. "You are far from the only such Envoy traveling through the United Worlds on a frigate, Envoy Adamant."

There was no way in stars or worlds that the UWN officer was going to give her a royal title of any kind, Lorraine could tell. The United Worlds was the galaxy's oldest and largest democracy, the state that had subsumed Earth and all of her oldest colonies. The United Worlds controlled everything, in fact, between Sol and the wormholes reaching deeper into the void.

Wormholes like the one from the Bright Dream System to the Tavastar System—the one Lorraine and her ship had just passed through.

"Most such frigates are... well, in somewhat better shape," Wolfe said wryly. "Though, given the reports of what happened in Bright Dream, that *Goldenrod* exists at all is impressive."

"My uncle appears... very determined that the extent of his crimes not be revealed to the greater galaxy," Lorraine told the local.

"I regret the loss of *Corsair* and her crew, but Commodore Wray gave us little choice."

"You were caught by a battlecruiser while aboard a frigate, Envoy Adamant," Wolfe reminded her unnecessarily. "That you are in this office talking to me is damn impressive. Against those odds, no one will ever blame you for what was necessary."

The United Worlds, for all of its many pretensions, did not claim pacifism or moral superiority over those who used violence. Why bother, after all, when they had *so much else* to claim superiority about?

"Captain Stephson's Chief Engineer wanted me to ask if it was possible for us to purchase parts and repair services aboard MacDougall Station?" Lorraine asked.

Lieutenant Colonel Sigrid Stephson was the commanding officer of *Goldenrod* and about half of the reason Lorraine had survived the thirty-six-light-year, almost-six-month journey from the Adamantine System to Bright Dream and its wormhole.

The other half was the third occupant of Captain Wolfe's very plain office. Major Vigo Jarret of the Adamant Guard was Lorraine's right hand, her left leg, her backup, her support—her chief bodyguard and the man whose iron loyalty had carried her all of this way.

If Jarret was silent in this office, it was because he had nothing to say and believed Lorraine had their initial meeting with the people who would decide the fate of their entire Kingdom entirely in hand.

No pressure.

"I know that we have a chandlery on MacDougall to cover basic supplies for the warships that dock here, but the repair yards are usually restricted to UWN vessels only," Wolfe said slowly. "What supplies your engineer can't purchase here, I'm sure our chandler can help you source from Tavastar Station itself."

"That should be more than sufficient," Lorraine agreed. "We are free to travel to Tavastar Station, then?"

Goldenrod had received very clear orders on exiting the wormhole: all warships were to report to the UWN's MacDougall Station and were *not* permitted to approach the massive civilian station supporting the wormhole.

"No non–United Worlds warship is permitted within one light-second of Tavastar Station," Wolfe warned calmly. "Your shuttles, on the other hand, are authorized for both personnel and cargo transfer."

"Thank you, Captain," Lorraine said. "I am pleased with the welcome and support MacDougall has offered us, but I have business on Tavastar before I head deeper into the United Worlds."

"Of course, Envoy." He paused. "I do need to ask what your intended final destination is, Envoy."

"Earth, of course," she told him. "I intend to bring the sad state of affairs in my home kingdom to the attention of the Grand Assembly and ask for their assistance in restoring order."

The last she'd heard was that the Royal Election for a replacement King had been suspended. Her uncle, Benjamin Adamant, ruled as Regent—a role never intended to last more than the six months of the Election.

Lorraine was going to see a proper Election held. She might lose it, but the Kingdom's constitution and traditions would be honored.

And if she had to kill her uncle to pull that off, that was a *bonus*.

"WE CAN'T JUST SEND you over to Tavastar Station in an unarmed shuttle," Jarret argued silently as they walked through MacDougall.

Both of them had implanted neural links. While the technology wasn't up to putting information directly into their brains, it was able to feed data to both the optical and auditory nerves. More than good enough for most purposes.

Including a silent conversation that no one around the two Adamantines could hear.

"We are limited in our options," Lorraine told him, gesturing for her bodyguard—and the three other Adamant Guards that had waited outside Captain Wolfe's office—to follow her into an observation gallery.

"The United Worlds has strict rules about weapons on and near space stations," she continued.

With her Guards keeping a clear bubble around her, it took them a few moments to get to a point in the gallery where they could observe outside the station.

MacDougall Station was a large iteration of a relatively standard form, a rotating cylinder in space a kilometer across and roughly the same high. The false gravity from the rotation was roughly ninety percent of a standard gravity at the "main deck," with a large open space in the center that could, in theory, berth a full battle squadron of the United Worlds Navy.

Most of the cylinder-style stations Lorraine had been on were enclosed artificial worlds, with full biospheres carefully assembled for long-term sustainability. MacDougall used the volume for the fleet anchorage instead—though it was still fully enclosed, with massive airlock doors allowing even the largest UWN battleships to enter and be repaired in atmosphere.

"We are allowed arms on MacDougall and Tavastar Station," Jarret pointed out. He stepped up beside her at the railing, looking "out" at the holographic window showing them the space outside MacDougall Station.

If nothing else, the fact that the window was in front of them gave the lie to the apparent orientation of the room. Any actual view out into deep space, even ignoring the danger to the station of anything resembling a window, would have been beneath her feet.

Illusory or not, the "window" let them see the slow flow of traffic around the military station. The UWN carrier *Fidelity* was rising into view like a particularly grouchy moon, six million tons of armor, guns and combat shuttles. She was the flagship of the task force assigned to Tavastar, one of the farthest-flung major forces of the United Worlds Navy.

Past her, so far away that it was barely a yellow glint to the human eye, was Tavastar Station. Home to over forty million people, it was Lorraine's most immediate destination.

"You are allowed hand weapons," Lorraine conceded Jarret's point. "Four bodyguards with sidearms. That's all I'm allowed at any given moment—and *I'm* not supposed to be armed, at that!"

"We are most definitely not allowed armed shuttles in the space between MacDougall Station and Tavastar Station," she continued. "So, yes, we can and will 'just' send me over to the station in an unarmed shuttle. With you and three other Guards. Aboard one of the Guard shuttles, I think."

"Stephson is going to need every hand she can get if we're making repairs out of our own resources," Jarret said grimly. "And every shuttle. She and Cheng Cortez are going to ask how long we'll be here. You know that."

Lorraine nodded, still studying the tiny fleck of gold that marked her next stop. Commander Rose Cortez was *Goldenrod*'s Chief Engineer—also known as the *Cheng*—and the woman tasked with making sure the crippled warship was able to fly again.

"And as soon as I have anything resembling a timeline, I'll let them know," she finally said. "But the Fund's nearest office is on Tavastar Station—as is Adamant's nearest attaché office."

The United Worlds Stability Convention Fund was the money theoretically set aside to support the United Worlds Navy in enforcing the agreements of that Convention. Like many systems, Adamantine paid into the Fund—but whether the UWN would actually be prepared to support the sovereignty of the Kingdom of Adamant against an internal coup was an open question.

"I need to talk to both our people and the Fund before I can even begin to have a plan. I need more information, Vigo."

"And we'll get it for you," he conceded with a sigh. "Just... let me talk to the locals before we head over to Tavastar? I've been going over the rules for us bodyguards and I think I may have a chance to conjure something for our trip over."

"I could probably use the rest, but so could everyone else," Lorraine admitted.

The transit through the wormhole had taken roughly an hour—an hour during which they were utterly safe from anything in the universe. Less than a dozen hours before that, though, they'd been fighting for their lives.

And Lorraine Adamant was not so foolish as to believe they were entirely safe in the United Worlds.

TWO

The Midas-type modular combat shuttle was the mainstay of the Royal Kingdom of Adamant Navy's shuttle force. Depending on the modules hooked up to the cube-shaped core of engines and cockpit, it could be everything from a bomber to a transport shuttle carrying ten thousand tons of cargo.

Its "standard" configuration was a light transport craft capable of carrying twenty people or a few hundred tons of cargo—and that was the configuration Charlie-Two was rigged up in as Vigo Jarret took his charge over to Tavastar Station.

Four of the sixteen shuttles aboard *Goldenrod* belonged to the Adamant Guard, part of the detail assigned to the ship to protect Her Royal Highness Lorraine Adamant, who happened to share the same body as Lieutenant Commander Lorraine Adamant, the commanding officer of *Goldenrod*'s Bravo shuttle flight.

Or had, at least, before everything had gone to pieces. Lorraine had to be the Pentarch these days, but she'd be lying if she said she didn't miss the Lieutenant Commander.

"We are clear of Mom and heading for our designated rendezvous point," Lieutenant Juturna Deering reported. Now the second-in-command of both *Goldenrod*'s Charlie Flight and Vigo's Archangel Section Three, she was their pilot.

Vigo might only be allowed to bring four armed bodyguards to protect his principal, but the big Adamant Guard was perfectly willing to bend definitions.

Deering and the other half-dozen Guards aboard the shuttle wouldn't be boarding Tavastar Station, which meant the fact that they had battle armor and proper rifles stocked away on the shuttle wasn't violating the local rules.

"Escorts are on the scope," the copilot, Chief Jayesh Laszlo, reported. Laszlo was a loaner, a senior RKAN noncom seconded to the Adamant Guard to make up for their personnel losses.

From what Vigo's subordinates had said, the Guard didn't want to give either of the NCOs back. They'd stepped into holes opened by treachery—the original commander of Section Three had been murdered by his second-in-command as part of the attack on Lorraine—but they'd more than proven themselves.

"I was promised a proper security detail for Her Highness," Vigo noted. "What did they send us?"

The Pentarch had to play by the rules, entirely aboveboard and talking to senior people. Captain Wolfe's whole job, Vigo judged, was to manage senior foreign officers who tried to throw their weight around—helped, he figured, by the fact that Wolfe's bland "Captain" was actually the equivalent to many navies' Commodores and junior Admirals.

The United Worlds Navy was the largest military force in human space, with no less than eighteen officer ranks. Captain Wolfe's insignia—three blue squares over three red squares—marked him as an O-9, equivalent to an RKAN *Lieutenant Admiral*.

Only battleships and carriers ranked full Captains for commanding officers in the United Worlds Navy.

Vigo, for his part, had spoken to the far more junior officer—a mere Commander who still technically outranked *Goldenrod*'s Lieutenant Colonel CO—in charge of MacDougall Station's shuttle squadrons.

"I have four Falcon-type 'starfighters' on the screens," Laszlo reported, his tone sharpening at the term for the spacecraft. "Which are, so far as I can tell..."

"Modular combat shuttles in interceptor mode," Vigo agreed with a grin. "They call their MCSes *starfighters*, Chief. Apparently, it makes recruiting much, much easier."

"When do they tell the wannabes that they're going to spend most of their careers hauling cargo?" Deering asked. "I mean, sensors tell me I *want* one of those babies, but the basic concept is the same and I'm guessing their flight-hour ratios would look pretty familiar."

"So far as I know, yup," he agreed. His grin didn't fade much as he tapped his gold ace wings. Even among the RKAN's shuttle pilots, those were a rare adornment. He'd earned them decades earlier, before transferring from the Navy to the Adamant Guard to take care of Lorraine as a very small child.

"Whatever they call them, they've got the engines and the beams to keep us safe for the journey," he told Deering. "And while I'd love to think that's unnecessary, well..."

"We were supposed to be unnecessary on *Goldenrod*," Deering agreed.

Enough of the Guard had supported Benjamin Adamant's coup to clear the way for the King and two of the Pentarchs to be murdered. Lorraine and her brother Nikola were alive—or, at least, Nikola had been alive when the last news had left Adamant months earlier.

Lorraine was looking for friends here in the United Worlds, following what the Guard had called the Exodus Protocols. Fate had handed her brother, Nikola Adamant, the Masada Protocols. It was his job to dig into the planetary defense centers and hold the line until those friends arrived to save the day.

Even when they'd had a battlecruiser chasing them, Vigo had

known Lorraine and her companions had got the better end of that deal.

NO ONE WAS EVER GOING to think that Tavastar Station had been built to be wholly practical. Vigo studied it with a cynical eye, though, and recognized the true purpose of the overly elaborate and decorative space station: to awe and impress those coming from outside the United Worlds.

It resembled nothing so much as a child's puzzle toy, one of the ones with dozens of rings that needed to be teased out from each other. Like the versions intended to occupy children rather than be solved, of course, Tavastar Station's rings were all interconnected.

The station resembled what he knew as a trinity knot, a set of three spheres interlinked with each other. Each sphere was made of at least a dozen ring stations of varying sizes, from half a kilometer across to the massive five-kilometer outer docking rings that defined the equator of each sphere.

From the glittering color, Vigo suspected that at least some of the outer rings had been literally plated in gold. The Tavastar System lacked any inhabitable worlds, but it still had an asteroid belt close enough to the wormhole to provide raw resources—and while gold was rarer than the other metals that had built the station frames, it was common enough on that kind of scale.

Between the complexity and extravagance of the station, it sent a very clear message: *you have entered true civilization. You cannot match us. Be in awe.*

The United Worlds, by centuries-old law shaped by tragedy, ended at the wormholes. Beyond the first set of wormholes were the first-order clusters—like the Bright Dream Cluster that was home to the Kingdom of Adamant. From there, many of those first clusters eventually found wormholes going even farther out.

He believed there were even some *third*-order clusters out there, three wormhole transits from the United Worlds, but he'd admit he wasn't certain.

"We have docking instructions for Bay C-Seven-One-Five," Deering told him. "How many shuttle bays does this place *have*?"

"Forty-three million human beings, Lieutenant," Lorraine's voice interrupted.

Vigo had known the Pentarch had moved up to the shuttle cockpit, but Deering clearly hadn't. As far as lessons in situational awareness went, it was pretty harmless—and from the pilot's sheepish expression, he wasn't even going to need to say anything.

"Most stations with major populations in the clusters are cylinders with false ecosystems," Vigo said. "To build something like Tavastar, where everything is artificial and that many people... well..."

"It takes a great deal of confidence in your logistics," his boss agreed. "Though I presume we have scanners on the farming platforms?"

"Yeah. Trio of ten-kilometer cylinders half a light-second away," Deering confirmed. "If nothing else, they stand out because of the battleship. There's only one that isn't at MacDougall, and she's hanging out with the farms."

"Confident in their logistics, but not stupid," Vigo concluded. "Even the United Worlds has a two-week turnaround to get food in quantity from the nearest planet. Those farms are the only lifeline for everyone here."

The United Worlds had a significant number of freighters capable of making one hundred and four times the speed of light—twenty-four cee faster than their own *Goldenrod*—but even those freighters couldn't make the two-light-year journey to and from that nearest planet, Greenhall, in the blink of an eye.

"So, folks are either very aware of the stations' importance or blissfully oblivious," Deering concluded. "Always an interesting mix."

"Indeed." Lorraine was silently present for a minute, until Vigo looked back at her and raised a questioning eyebrow.

"Running through the maps in my link," she told him over their connection. "Deciding whether I go to our office or the Fund's office first. It's going to be a busy few days."

"That's your part of the job, Your Highness," he told her. "If you want my opinion?"

"Sure."

"Check in with our people first. Your papers give you authority regardless of what the Black Regent has said—though they may have received clear-enough orders that they'll ignore that. Most likely they'll have some idea of the lay of the land and be able to give us a starting point."

And unless he was severely mistaken, Lorraine had the passcodes and authorizations to empty the local attaché office's bank accounts to serve their needs. She wouldn't do so without reason or need—but Vigo could make sure the right people knew that the threat was there.

"There's also the argument that if we'll hit a brick wall with the Fund, we're better to know sooner than later," she said.

"I don't expect it to be that obvious," Vigo admitted grimly. He wasn't sure he really believed the United Worlds would help them. He was, however, sure that the Stability Convention was a sufficiently big deal that at least lip service would be paid to the concept of the United Worlds as a protector of galactic peace.

If Lorraine openly called out the Stability Convention Fund as a complete dead letter, it would become obvious that the various Conventions and the attached Funds were glorified tribute paid by the first-order cluster nations. Vigo knew enough people understood that to keep an open realization from stopping the flow of money and resources... but it would still be a public relations disaster the United Worlds didn't stwant.

They'd be heard. He just didn't expect to be *listened* to.

"I'll start with our people; you're right," Lorraine agreed. "Then... then we talk to the United Worlders and see what happens."

THREE

Trade Attaché Pema Ceferov was a wispy shadow of a human, with thin platinum hair that hung halfway down their back and only made the shockingly white color of their skin more obvious.

They were standing behind a heavy desk when Lorraine entered, guided by a junior secretary who seemed to have no idea how to handle royalty and was erring on the side of obsequious.

"Your Highness," Ceferov greeted her with a carefully calculated bow. "I have to admit, I never expected to see a member of House Adamant in the United Worlds, let alone a Pentarch."

They paused thoughtfully, gesturing her to a seat in front of their desk.

"Forgive my impertinence, but shouldn't you be in the Kingdom, taking part in the Royal Election?" they asked.

Lorraine took the indicated seat, noting that the trade office hadn't provided a seat for Jarret. Her close detail—Corporals Palmer and Alvarez—had taken up positions outside Ceferov's office, but the head of her bodyguard had come in with her.

He took a silent post next to the door, his gaze scanning the room like a security camera.

The trade attaché clearly didn't know what to make of that, but Lorraine distracted them with a ready smile.

"My mother had a very particular mission for me, Em Ceferov," she noted. "The traitors involved in her death have a far longer reach than I dared fear. We were pursued to the wormhole itself by a rogue battlecruiser of our own RKAN."

She shook her head grimly.

"*Corsair* is no more, a crew of honorable spacers and officers of RKAN delivered to the void by a commander lost to treason. My mother's orders were clear and I will complete my mission." She shrugged. "Some things are more important than standing in the Election, Em Ceferov."

Like making sure the Royal Election happened at all. Ceferov shouldn't have seen any information Lorraine hadn't—it was the Diplomatic Corps couriers she was "borrowing" information from now—but he might know less.

Or just not be able to read between the lines. One hundred and seventy-four days had passed since King Valeriya Adamant's murder, but the news that had reached Tavastar was from only forty days later.

Still, the List was supposed to be finalized and the Royal Election kicked off within weeks. As of forty days after the King's death, however, the new Crown Regent Benjamin Adamant seemed to have no intention of starting it.

She supposed the active civil war her uncle and brother had kicked off was a good reason, but it still smelled.

"We are... a long way from home here, Your Highness," Ceferov said slowly, taking their own seat and glancing askance at Jarret. "With the best couriers available to the Diplomatic Corps, our news from home is four and half standard months old. Within the United Worlds, we may have grown used to renting local ships, but the export rules around translight drives are draconian."

"I know, Em Ceferov," Lorraine reminded them. "I was a Navy officer, after all."

The Kingdom of Adamant could just barely build ships capable of eighty-eight times the speed of light. Their faster ships—the specialty couriers running at ninety-six times lightspeed—used translight drives purchased from Bright Dream.

Bright Dream had access to much of the general technology and knowledge base of the United Worlds, but even they could not, per United Worlds rules, buy translight drives. They had to reverse-engineer the next generations of the technology from the science and knowledge they did have access to.

"My apologies, Your Highness. I'm used to educating young diplomats and bureaucrats whose technical schooling was focused on very different areas," Ceferov conceded.

Lorraine smiled thinly.

"My own was military history, navigation and tachyonic physics," she told them. "That said, *education* is part of what I need from you, Em Ceferov. I have what I believe are high-quality briefs on the situation here in the United Worlds, but nothing substitutes for immediate experience.

"What do our resources and networks here look like?"

Ceferov studied her frankly in silence. She returned their regard, using her synchronization with Vigo Jarret's neural link to piggyback on her bodyguard's survey of the room.

The office was plain enough, much less ornate or elaborate than the golden puzzle rings of Tavastar Station itself. The white gauntlet and six blue stars of the Adamantine flag had been enameled onto the wall behind Ceferov, with small shelves on each side of the room holding a collection of artworks centered on a small bar on one side and a bookshelf on the other.

Most of the artwork, she judged, had come with assorted trade attachés from Adamant. She recognized the style of some of the pieces, if not any specific works. It was all in traditions common in the six star systems of their home nation.

The desk was interesting, though. Unless she missed her guess, the heavy piece of furniture was made of stone, with decorative scrollwork carved into the legs and a protective coating over the rock.

In neither style nor material was it an Adamantine tradition, though she supposed she could see something similar come out of Tolkien.

Examining the room through Jarret's eyes let her keep her own regard on the wisp-like enby in the very particular slim-fitted suit across from her. Ceferov's suit was in the same style she'd seen in the concourses of the station: a pure-white jacket with thin purple lapels and piping.

Very fashionable for Tavastar Station—and forty million people produced their own fashions, Lorraine was certain.

She let the silence hang until Ceferov finally cleared their throat.

"Your paperwork is all in order, but you understand the situation you are putting me in, I hope," they finally said quietly. "We have no specific orders to deny you help or attempt to arrest you, but it is quite clear that the Regent's Government wishes you detained and returned to Adamant as a person of interest in King Valeriya's death."

Lorraine met their eyes and smiled again.

"You don't want to get involved in dynastic politics," she observed. It wasn't a question. "Personally, neither did I.

"But the documents I have provided your office confirm me as an Envoy Plenipotentiary of the Kingdom of Adamant," she continued. "Barring specific orders from the Cabinet, you have no authority to deny that status and all that comes with it.

"Which means that, right now, you work for me."

She could fire the diplomat. She'd already checked—none of the synthetic-intelligence citizens aboard Tavastar Station were working for the trade office, which meant they were running standard expert systems.

Those AIs could be extremely capable but were only as clever as a smart dog. They had no flexibility when it came to things like Lorraine's documents and authorizations. As far as Trade Attaché Ceferov's computers were concerned, Lorraine was in charge.

From the discomfort they were trying to conceal behind a practiced mask of diplomacy, they either knew or suspected how much trouble she could cause them—but the long-term consequences of working with her could be, quite literally, fatal.

"The theory of the hierarchy is one thing, Your Highness," Ceferov said calmly. "The reality is that I am the senior official on a posting four months from home. A large degree of flexibility is both allowed and expected.

"While, yes, the documents you carry are intended to give you authority over me, I answer to the Cabinet and the Government, not House Adamant," they reminded her. "And our Government's position on you is clear."

"And yet you have no orders or communication from them revoking my plenipotentiary status," Lorraine told them. "So. What do you plan on doing?"

"I am not so foolish as to attempt to detain you," Ceferov said with a glance back at Vigo. "The only armed soldiers in my office right now report to you. For some reason, we don't assign RKAA troops to trade attaché offices."

The Royal Kingdom of Adamant Army—RKAA, pronounced "Ar-Kah"—was the main ground force of the Kingdom. They would be the logical people to provide security for the Diplomatic Corps if the Corps decided it needed more than regular private security.

RKAA troops guarded the Kingdom's actual embassies, after all.

"If any office other than an embassy had a proper security detail, I would have expected Tavastar Station to have one," Lorraine observed. She'd known they didn't have one, but she wondered why. While the Kingdom had an embassy on Earth, Tavastar Station was the real anchor point of the Diplomatic Corps presence in the United Worlds.

That was why she needed Ceferov's data.

"We don't like to draw attention to ourselves here," Ceferov told her. "Which is why I can't help you, Your Highness. Your papers say one thing, but the position of the Prime Minister and Cabinet are clear—and whatever either of us may think of the Regency, the Prime Minister and Cabinet *are* the Government of the Kingdom of Adamant.

"I'm afraid I will have to decline to recognize your authority," they said. "I respect your papers, even your status as Pentarch, but the chain of command here is clear."

"I see." Lorraine smiled and arched an eyebrow as she met the diplomat's gaze. "Then I'm afraid I have to inform you that the Kingdom no longer requires your services. I'll make certain the office HR handles your out-processing paperwork and you will receive generous severance, but you are fired."

She could see the moment Ceferov felt their access to the office network cut off. There'd been no time to set up a gentle logout or anything resembling the normal process. Given that Ceferov had administrative access to their systems, she'd needed to remove them immediately and completely.

"You can't..." They trailed off, then inclined their head. "I see that my computers disagree with me."

"Major Jarret, can you have one of our people escort Em Ceferov out of the office?" she asked. "Will there be a problem?"

The attaché hadn't moved. Now they sighed and reached into their desk. She half-expected Vigo to stop them, but her bodyguard simply gripped his sidearm without drawing it.

Ceferov removed a small black disk, slightly thicker and wider than their palm, and placed it on the desk. A moment later, a sharp whine filled the air, and Lorraine winced.

"Somehow, I'm not surprised House Adamant has enhanced hearing," Ceferov told her. They seemed surprisingly unbothered by her firing them. "Portable security jammer—calibrated, in this case, to my office systems.

"I have reason to believe at least one of my people is working directly for the Regent," they noted. "I do not want to deny you help, Your Highness. I would prefer not to get involved at all, but you are here.

"I'm going to turn this off in a moment and concede to your demands to get my job back," they continued, "assuming that is enough for you?"

"So long as you help, I am prepared to be as much of an ogre as you need," Lorraine told them sweetly.

"I am here to serve my Kingdom, Your Highness," Ceferov replied. "But I also have an obligation to protect my people, and I would rather not get shot in a dark corridor by one of my financial analysts.

"Providing you the information you need, I think, is safe enough so long as I clearly do so under pressure. But I wanted to explain where I was at. Control of the computers is insufficient to really fire me, you know."

"Believe me, Em Ceferov, I can make it stick," Lorraine warned. They weren't wrong—but between control of the computers, control of the money and being willing to do most things short of *shooting people in dark corridors*, she could make a lot of things stick.

She gestured to the disk.

"Leave the jammer on for a moment longer, though," she instructed. "If any of this conversation is going to be on the record, then there are questions I need to ask while no one is recording."

"We can edit the recordings afterward to cover the gap, but if someone is paying attention, any long blank will raise questions," Ceferov noted. "Ask."

"The Stability Fund," she said simply. "Who's in charge and how are the pieces moving here?"

DESPITE THEIR OWN protests about the available time, Ceferov leaned back in their chair to process that.

"So, *that's* the play," they murmured. "Don't worry—reporting your move to the Regent would be getting even more involved than this. Answering questions like yours is part of my job."

Lorraine waited. While she didn't want to cause more trouble for the trade attaché with their superiors than she had to, a blank spot in their office recordings wasn't going to be a problem for *her*.

"Tavastar Station hosts the Stability Convention Fund's office for the Bright Dream Cluster," they said slowly. "It's not as large as some of the other SCF offices on border stations closer to Sol, but it's sufficient for the work they do."

Ceferov shrugged.

"Which is mostly collecting money," they continued. "The Fund is defined by a fascinating mix of cynicism, idealism, greed and threats. Unusually, the *threats* go more hand in hand with the *idealism*. In my experience, greed and cynicism are more common bedfellows.

"The SCF rarely needs to do more than send a courier ship with an arbitrator to convince people it's doing something. But... well, Bright Dream is on the smaller and poorer side as first-order clusters go," Ceferov noted. "It is still home to around a hundred inhabited star systems and a quarter-trillion human beings."

The most common translight drive in the twenty-sixth century could manage seventy-two times the speed of light—nine times the fixed tachyon quanta, the velocity that tachyons and faux tachyons could only travel in exact multiples of. Traveling from Earth to Tavastar at that speed was a journey of over a year. Wormholes crossed hundreds of light-years in an hour or so, creating the core lines of human expansion.

Human civilization was anchored on the sphere centered on the Sol System. From there, the wormholes created spokes out into the darkness. At the far end of each spoke, new spheres expanded—and from the wormholes found in those spheres, new lines stabbed out to anchor the second-order clusters.

The United Worlds spread about a hundred and fifty light-years from Sol, Lorraine believed, putting Tavastar roughly halfway out to the UW's outer frontier. It had been discovered three centuries earlier, the eleventh of the seventeen wormholes in the UW's territory.

And even Lorraine probably should know more about the other sixteen first-order clusters than she did.

"I know how much the Kingdom pays into the Funds," she told Ceferov. "The Stability Convention is only one of five, too. While the sums are staggering by the standards of an individual, they're a minor entry in the Kingdom's budget."

"But every one of the Cluster's hundred star systems pays in to all five of the Funds," Ceferov concluded. "And across seventeen first-order clusters, some twenty-two hundred star systems do the same.

"The amount of money that flows into the five Funds is practically incomprehensible. Some of the Funds, like the Interstellar Navigation Convention Fund and the Humanitarian Initiative Fund, actually spend their money," they said wryly. "The other three... Well."

The Stability Convention Fund, the Democracy Support Fund and the Agricultural Security Fund, Lorraine realized by process of elimination. It was telling, she supposed, that the Democracy Support Fund was theoretically adjacent to her mission and they hadn't pinged her planning radar at all.

"They're tribute structures," the trade attaché continued bluntly. "But the Stability Fund does do things occasionally, so they need people who can put up the face and who will actually *act* when needed."

"But we might be wasting our time," Lorraine noted.

"And you might not." Ceferov shrugged. "The Fund's people are a mix of idealists, government bureaucrats whose careers have gone there to die, and spies. If you can prove the situation is what you say it is—and I imagine you have evidence and arguments, if nothing else— you might make more headway than you'd think.

"Even some of the spies, after all, are idealists," they said. "The man in charge is Bryan Reis. I can pretty much guarantee he won't give you the time of day, but they're a somewhat diffuse structure.

After all, they act as cover for a bunch of intelligence agents, so watching their staff too closely doesn't serve their purposes."

"So, don't go to the top," Lorraine said.

"Exactly. I can't give you much more than that, Your Highness, but that's my advice. There's half a dozen middle managers who have the authority to at least get you to Earth."

"Even if some of them are spies?" she asked.

"If they help you, Your Highness... does it matter?"

FOUR

For a professional paranoid, having the woman he was charged with stuck aboard a single ship for six months had been rather useful. Vigo was painfully aware in hindsight that he hadn't been paranoid *enough*, but once the moles and traps had finally been dealt with, *Goldenrod* had been a safe place to keep Lorraine Adamant.

Going from a ship with less than three hundred and fifty people aboard, where he had full control of the security systems, to a civilian station with forty-plus million aboard, where he wasn't even allowed to deploy a full drone perimeter, was a shock to the system.

Corporals Judy Alvarez and Panam Palmer were two of his best, the senior NCOs of the Pentarch's super-close detail—the dozen women who did such things as go into bathrooms with Lorraine and escort out one-night-stands.

The fourth member of the immediate detail, Lance Corporal Volundr Fuchs, was a heavyset bear of a man who rejoiced in the nickname of "Fluffy." Vigo had learned the source of the nickname and promptly done his best to forget.

Fuchs had paid part of his way through college working in pornography, and none of his fellow soldiers had ever been inclined to let him forget it. Vigo had to keep an eye on the gentle ribbing to make sure it stayed gentle ribbing—but he did that with everyone in Archangel Detail.

Fuchs was from the Second Section of the Detail, the Guards focused on technical and ship support. At that moment, he was running what limited drones they were allowed aboard Tavastar Station, watching the crowd around them and helping Vigo pick a course that kept them separated from any particularly dense groups of people.

"Makes me miss being trapped on a starship," he told Lorraine silently. "I like crowds, but I was worrying about being this visible *before* anyone told me the Regent had an agent in our office here."

"We assumed he had agents here," she reminded him. "Plus... I have my suspicions about where his resources for this came from. Don't assume the only threats are following us from home, Vigo."

"Wasn't planning on it," he confirmed. The Adamant Guard had files on every possible threat to the Pentarchy and Monarchy they could find. Included among those files were detailed notes on the various megacorporations that had tried to set up operations in the Kingdom only to collide with Adamant's strict anti-colonialism laws.

The United Worlds–anchored interstellars had made their bed and got to sleep in it, as far as Vigo was concerned. The reputation for exploitation and chicanery that preceded them had been earned honestly, and the Kingdom of Adamant was far from alone in having laws intended to keep the megacorps out.

But the interstellars had *so much money*. Overthrowing a system or even multi-system government was pocket change to them if they found the right person.

"Ping at thirty-two degrees," Fuchs said on the closed net the five Adamantines were sharing. "Wait, no. TSS scan platform again. Someone's hat got in the way of the beacon."

Vigo swallowed a chuckle as he glanced over and saw The Hat in question. It deserved capitals, an elaborate structure that rose at least a meter from its already-tall wearer's skull.

The drone behind it was almost invisible, a vectored-thrust robot using the fact that centripetal pseudogravity only existed when someone was on the plates to stay in the air. It had the right shape for its quiet engines to keep it airborne in real gravity too, but all the machine needed to do right then was keep away from surfaces.

Their GuardNet had flagged no less than sixteen of the robotic spies on his local map. Tavastar Station Security made a point of being practically invisible across the platform, but the quiet and oft-missed drones were everywhere.

The half-dozen drones orbiting Lorraine's protectors were enough louder that they'd drawn eyes as the quintet made their way through the main concourses. Each of the Guards also had shoulder-mounted cams, and the links piggybacking on their optic nerves were also feeding to the network Fuchs was running.

Even with all of that, luck often outweighed planning and technology, and Vigo saw the moment the network controlling the TSS drones failed. One moment, the drone he was eyeing—highlighted in his vision by the GuardNet connection—was jetting through the air on a surveillance pattern that kept it away from bulkheads, decks, and crowds alike.

The next, it was just drifting—an illusion of motion provided by the once-a-minute rotation of the massive ring. It should have been operating on an internal agent, but that had likely been disabled too.

And if there might be another reason to disable the surveillance drones in the area, Vigo's job wasn't to consider coincidences. It was to protect the Pentarch.

"Archangel, *down*," he barked. Using Lorraine's Guard identifier was part of the command, a long-drilled-in habit between them. When he called her Archangel, the situation had just gone to pieces and he needed her to listen without question.

She went down, flattening herself against the metal deck. The other three Guards didn't need specific orders. Their sidearms were in their hands—he cursed United Worlds weapons laws in that moment—as they searched for the threat.

For maybe half a second, it seemed like the only source of activity in the region was them. The sudden lurch into defensive posture with drawn weapons sent the crowd around them moving away—not running, not most of them, but drawn guns had a salutary space-clearing effect at any time.

Vigo glanced around for some kind of cover, but Tavastar Station's concourse didn't lend itself to anything that would resist gunfire. They were in a broad, ten-meter-tall area set up as a faux outdoor mall. Shallow planters down the middle held palm trees, and the walls were covered by shops and restaurants, intermixed with the occasional very high-end office.

"I still have drone control," Fuchs reported. "But that's short-range. Everything is being jammed."

Vigo had enough time to consider pinging the shuttle before *something* came screaming out of the air, dropping out of what he thought was an air vent to hurl itself toward Archangel at lethal velocity.

Unfortunately for the drone, Vigo's twitch reflexes resembled an automated turret more than anything he'd actually been born with. With his weapon already drawn, the attacker crossed less than a third of the distance before he put a bullet into it.

A spray of metallic debris marked the death of the flying robot, and Vigo took a moment to be glad for both his prior paranoia and the fact that the TSS drones were down. He'd read the rules of what he was allowed to be carrying—and twelve-millimeter high-explosive rounds were definitely on the forbidden list!

He was supposed to be loading his guns with frangible rounds that wouldn't risk the hull of the station—and his *people's* guns were loaded with the right bullets.

Which meant it took Fuchs three shots to knock the second attack drone out of the air. The robotic aircraft now spewing from what Vigo was certain was an air vent—and equally certain was supposed to be shielded against unknown drones—weren't armored or even particularly tough as robots went, but the glorified glass of the frangible bullets was designed to break up on metal.

Palmer and Alvarez were kneeling, one on either side of Lorraine, and they joined in the fire as another wave of drones emerged.

Vigo compartmentalized. Part of his mind was in control of his hands, playing backstop to his people—a drone got through their field of fire and he put an explosive round into it, ending it half a dozen meters short of Lorraine—while he swept for the second part of the trap.

He saw the second air vent cover blast free in time to turn as the first drones burst out of it, only for his gun to click on empty as he took down the second drone.

Reloading was a drill, automatic, but the surviving drones were coming *way* too quickly. Palmer switched targets, blasting the closest two down and buying him time—but they'd taken down at least a dozen of the robots and there were still way too many of the things left.

He shot down a drone and winced as debris peppered Lorraine. His charge was doing the smart thing and staying down—the sidearm she wasn't supposed to have held the same frangible rounds as the junior Guards, and while her reflexes were inhuman, they were genetic augments, not cybernetics.

She was more likely to hit the rapidly receding crowd of bystanders than the Guards, and that was the last thing they needed.

Vigo shot down another drone and sensed more than saw a *third* vent blast open. Whether or not they lived through this, Station Security was going to be livid over it. You did not screw with the air supply on artificial habitats.

He was still turning to engage the new group of drones when there was a brilliant flash of light. Lasers were visible in atmosphere, sort of, if only by the short-lived lines of burning air.

And *enough* lasers were visible regardless. Suddenly, the only drones he could see were clearly transmitting TSS security codes as the surveillance drones were moving again—lasers cycling far too rapidly as they cut the attacking drones out of the air.

***

"KEEP UP BACKSTOP," he ordered his people. "There may be another wa—"

He almost shot the drone that popped down in front of him, a jet of cold air washing over his hand.

"This one will appreciate the backstop," the drone told him in a melodious voice. "This one apologizes for the gap in security. Your attackers knew Tavastar Station Security protocols far too well.

"This one will make certain the leak is found. *'Quis custodiet ipsos custodes?'* people ask. Aboard this station, Vimes watches the watchmen."

"You are Vimes?" Vigo asked, slowly beginning to catch on. "I didn't realize a synthetic intelligence worked for TSS."

"This one's employment is not advertised, but yes. This one is Vimes, senior inspector with Tavastar Station Security."

Vigo felt a bit strange talking to a drone. There was no way the small robot hovering in front of him held enough intelligence to carry a conversation—but a synthetic intelligence was heavily distributed. While Vimes would have a central core somewhere, it could speak through anything it was controlling.

"Thanks for the save," he told the SI, helping Lorraine back to her feet. "That was getting dicey."

"This one apologizes for the delay," Vimes replied. "Uniformed personnel are on their way, but the initial response belongs to Vimes. Hostile actors were unexpectedly familiar with TSS protocols and implemented a jamming field across the zone.

"It took this one an excessive time period to recognize the issue, deploy other mesh nodes into line of sight and download an encryption update to the affected nodes. You should not have been endangered, Pentarch Lorraine, and you have this one's apologies."

Vigo ran back through the incident in his head and concealed a smile.

"How long was 'excessive,' Inspector Vimes?" he asked.

"Twenty-two-point-six seconds," the SI confirmed instantly. "Twenty-two-point-six seconds in which your four Adamant Guards fired ninety-six standard frangible and twenty-nine unauthorized high-explosive rounds in self-defense and thirty-two semiautonomous platforms attempted lethal attacks on Lorraine Adamant, Pentarch and Envoy Plenipotentiary of the Kingdom of Adamant.

"You and your Guards rose to the occasion, Major Jarret, but this one should have prevented that being needed."

Vigo spotted a group of uniformed officers entering the concourse. There was still a large clear area around them—but now that he was looking, he could see other drones hovering at eye level, warning people away.

Vimes appeared integral to Tavastar Station Security's response protocols. Everything it was doing could be done by humans via neural links, but the SI could handle more drones more efficiently than any augmented human.

"Uniformed personnel are arriving," Vimes told him, echoing his perception. "Vimes will retain overwatch, but Inspector Jones Ó Comhraidhe will take over interface duties."

That was the chubby redhead leading the way, the Guard presumed. Ó Comhraidhe was around Vigo's own age and despite seeming slightly out of breath, his eyes were attentive and he held the carbine in his hands like he knew what to do with it.

"Do not," Ó Comhraidhe panted out, "put those guns away."

Vigo had been about to give exactly that order, since there were now TSS drones and human personnel on hand. Ó Comhraidhe had six officers with him, all carrying tactical carbines of an unfamiliar model.

"I recognize that we carry weapons on sufferance, Inspector," Lorraine said, smoothly stepping in both physically and verbally. "We would not want to intrude."

"I appreciate that, Pentarch Adamant," Ó Comhraidhe said, his voice calmer now as he surveyed the space. "But my people aren't allowed explosive rounds either, so if the pulse rounds we have loaded fail against the next round of drones, I'm hoping your Guards can finish the job."

"I hope this incident is over," the Pentarch noted.

"So would I," the Inspector agreed. "I'll need statements and... whatever implant download your people are comfortable with." He looked vague for a moment. "I'm aware that your diplomatic immunity extends to your Guards, Pentarch, but that isn't necessary here.

"This is open and shut, though I do need those statements and visual-feed downloads," he continued, his voice surprisingly firm for his calm concessions.

"*Somebody* just took a shot at a visiting dignitary on my station. My boss, the SI you just spoke to, is going to blow a circuit if we don't find out who jammed its drones. Everything you can give me, I'll take."

"Inspector, we will provide whatever help we can," Vigo promised. "I'd love to be certain there isn't going to be another attack."

"There shouldn't have been *one*, Major Jarret," Ó Comhraidhe said. "You impressed the Watchman—and that's not easy—but it shouldn't have been necessary.

"If you'll come with me, we can run through this most efficaciously at the station?"

FIVE

Ó Comhraidhe was true to his word. It took barely an hour for Lorraine and her people to get clear of the TSS facility, and they didn't even have to give up their weapons.

Outside of the first conversations with Vimes and Ó Comhraidhe, no one had even mentioned the fact that her chief bodyguard had clearly fired off ammunition that was explicitly banned aboard the station, even for diplomatic security.

Unfortunately, she knew that there was nothing her people could contribute to the investigation beyond what the TSS with their drones and surveillance systems and synthetic-intelligence senior inspector could pull together.

That left them once again in the corridors and concourses of Tavastar Station, making their way to the same destination as before with a sharper eye over their shoulders.

The United Worlds Stability Convention Fund office was a surprisingly subdued front, less decorated or standout than even many of the private offices they'd passed. A simple sign in the standard font of UW gave the name of the Fund and that was it.

A lot of people had died to get Lorraine Adamant there.

Hundreds of local spacers in the San Ignacio System when her uncle's dogs had opened fire on the friendly ships protecting her. Dozens of the crew of *Goldenrod* herself. The entire twenty-five-hundred-strong crew of the battlecruiser *Corsair* Commodore Wray had brought after her.

It felt like the office should have been something spectacular, wrapped in gold and iron to mark its importance and make it worthy of the sacrifices that had been made.

Instead, it was so ordinary it hurt, and Lorraine still paused at the door in a moment of near-terror.

"I get it," Vigo said silently in her head. He could have whispered, but this wasn't a conversation for even the other Adamant Guard to hear. "After all it's taken, here we are."

"The sacrifices must mean something," she replied. "Forward."

"Forward," he agreed.

They stepped across the threshold together, the movement momentous to them even if no one else would understand.

THE INSIDE of the SCF office was no less bland than the outside. Solid but likely inexpensive furniture, the metal-and-synthetic cushion style common and cheap on stations like this.

It was all so aggressively banal that Lorraine suspected it had to be intentional. This was not a space that wanted to draw attention to itself. The Stability Convention Fund didn't *want* to be noticed.

They just wanted to keep collecting money from the first-order clusters and doing nothing in exchange.

That bitterly cynical thought carried her across the plain metal floor to the gray-plastic-coated desk where a pair of holograms flanked a human supervisor, as if the office might see so many visitors as to require extra hands.

The man behind the desk was in his late forties, with the slumping shape of someone who'd had decent muscle once but had seen it go to seed trapped behind a desk. The only attention he gave Lorraine was to indicate one of the holograms with a thumb, as he seemed focused on something on his screen.

She cleared her throat loudly.

"Excuse me," she said firmly. "I need to make a formal statement of claim under the United Worlds Stability Convention. I don't think your hologram can handle that."

If he hadn't already reacted to her, she would have taken his jerk as him waking up. Certainly, he was actually paying attention to her now, taking in her unmarked uniform and the four bodyguards arrayed around her.

"And... you are?" he finally asked.

"I am Pentarch Lorraine Adamant, Envoy Plenipotentiary for King Valeriya Adamant of the Kingdom of Adamant," Lorraine reeled off swiftly. "My Kingdom has long been a supporter of the Fund, and it falls to me to place a formal claim for assistance against a coup d'etat in our nation."

"I see. You're going to need to make an appointment, I think," the receptionist told her. "Director Reis isn't in the office, and he—"

"I'll handle this, Larry," a new voice interrupted. "I've been waiting for the Pentarch."

Lorraine turned to see who was speaking, half-expecting to find another decaying bureaucrat intending to cut her off at the knees. Whatever she was going to say, though, she swallowed as she saw the newcomer.

Decaying definitely wasn't going to fit, though he probably was a bureaucrat. The Fund manager was of middling height but a slimly athletic build, with ear-length pitch-black hair and brilliant blue eyes that sparkled across the room as he met her gaze.

"The Envoy is entirely within her rights to lay a statement of claim, and we don't need the Director for that," the startlingly attractive young man told the receptionist.

"I am Alastair Devine, Your Highness," he told her, then bowed. Devine's bow was a deep and extravagant thing, a gesture no

Adamantine citizen would ever have bothered to give a monarch—and, as a Pentarch, Lorraine didn't generally rate even the moderated bows called for in Adamantine royal etiquette.

"If you and your escort will join me in my office, we shall see how the Stability Convention Fund may be able to assist the Kingdom of Adamant in this dark hour."

"Lead the way, Em Devine," Lorraine replied with a quirked smile. "Let's get to work."

Work, after all, appeared to be something front-desk man Larry was allergic to.

LORRAINE SUSPECTED she'd seen Devine's office—or a close sibling thereof—in a magazine or video article somewhere. As an example of *what not to do* when setting up offices.

There were no large open areas of shared desks in the SCF office, just several corridors with transparent-paneled offices on both sides. Alastair Devine's office was at the far end of one of the corridors, allowing Lorraine to see that many of the offices were empty.

His office was larger than most of the ones they passed, but it had no greater personality. Gray-tinted synthetics coated the metal frames of the furniture. There was no art, no books, nothing. Just plain walls—and the very standard United Worlds blue they'd been painted was the only splash of color Lorraine had seen in the space.

Nothing was this bland and colorless by accident, she judged. The Stability Convention Fund was either trying to break its employees or make any visitor want to get out as quickly as possible.

Or both, she supposed.

Still, the room had enough functionality that three chairs were settling themselves against the faux-glass wall as Devine waved the door open. Two more were positioned in front of the featureless and empty desk—and the chair behind the desk didn't look like it had any greater personality than the rest of the office.

"Welcome to Tavastar Station and the United Worlds, Pentarch Adamant," Devine told her. He gestured her and Jarret to the seats in front of his desk, leaving the ones against the wall for her other escorts.

"Or is it Pentarch Lorraine?" he asked. "I'll admit I'm not as familiar with the exact details of Adamantine royal protocols."

"Either works," Lorraine told him. "You can call me Lorraine, if you'd like."

Vigo didn't physically move, but a small image of his face with a raised eyebrow popped up in the corner of her vision.

If anyone had earned the right to question her flirting, it was Vigo Jarret. On the other hand, any tool available could clear the way.

"Then you may call me Alastair, Lorraine," Devine said with a smile. "Now, I hope I am not too out of line, but I do need to review your credentials to see if you are able to file the notice of claim we're speaking of."

"Vigo," Lorraine said quietly, carefully holding Devine's gaze. She'd seen men with blue eyes practice turning them to ice as a tool of intimidation. Devine wasn't one of those—his eyes were warm like a summer sea, with a sparkle of amusement dancing alongside his words.

Jarret took a chip folio from inside his jacket and slid it across the desk. Hopefully, he hadn't revealed anything illegal doing so— Lorraine wasn't entirely sure what her bodyguard had tucked away in his clothes, but more than just the explosive rounds was banned on Tavastar Station.

Devine reached out and palmed the folio. He opened it, revealing the datachip—in the shape of the gauntlet symbol of the Kingdom of Adamant—and then placed his hand on the storage medium.

He was silent for five seconds, his hand held still, then leaned back and smiled.

"Give me a moment," he asked. "My first glance looks good, but I want to check a couple of things."

Lorraine knew a lot of people who would close their eyes when actively accessing information on their feed, but Devine kept holding her gaze as he worked through whatever data he was looking for.

"Your Black Regent missed a step, I see," he finally noted. "We rarely see notice of claim or request for help around coups, Lorraine. The reality brings us back to Sir Harington and an old but quite applicable quote: 'Treason doth never prosper: what's the reason? Why, if it prosper, none dare call it treason.'"

Devine smiled, and despite his words, there was a surprising warmth to it.

"Perhaps that was an oversight by the drafters of the Stability Convention, but the truth is that you must have formal plenipotentiary standing to make a notice of claim," he explained. "Had the proper paperwork, so to speak, been filed by Regent Benjamin Adamant and his Government, your plenipotentiary status would be invalid.

"However, no such counter-paperwork has been filed with the United Worlds. Your standing, as issued by Her Majesty King Valeriya, is official and unquestioned. You have the right to be here and to ask for assistance from the United Worlds under the Stability Convention."

Lorraine swallowed a sound she couldn't let the United Worlds bureaucrat hear. A single form could have ended her entire mission right there. It was out of character for her uncle to miss something like that... except that, she supposed, Admiral Benjamin Adamant was a soldier, not a diplomat or bureaucrat.

He'd gone to RKAN and Valeriya Adamant had gone to the Diplomatic Corps. The entire line of attack Lorraine was following was her mother's type of plan, not her uncle's. And it appeared she might have just found a blind spot in her uncle's forward planning.

Something to keep in mind. This was far from over.

"Now." Devine laid his hands on his desk, one on top of the other, and leaned back. His gaze moved away from Lorraine's to take in her bodyguards, and a small smile flickered across his lips.

"I know what the official line coming out of the government in the Kingdom of Adamant is saying, and I know, roughly, what you have been telling people here in Tavastar," he noted. "Given the differences, I suggest we begin with you laying out the events of your mother's death as you see them—and how that leads to your claim under the Stability Convention."

"Okay," Lorraine agreed. She took a moment to muster her thoughts—and bring up some prepared comments she had tucked away in her neural link—then met his gaze and returned his smile.

"Everything began on March twenty-fifth, twenty-five thirty-three, Standard Reckoning," she started. "I was—am, technically—an officer in the Royal Kingdom of Adamant Navy and my vessel was carrying out training exercises in the outer system.

"We weren't present for the initial events and, indeed, weren't even aware of them until an emergency transmission from the commander of the Adamant Guard reached the head of my bodyguard detail.

"Members of the Adamant Guard and other organizations of the Adamantine military had made a coordinated move against the King and the Pentarchs, the five heirs," she explained. "My mother, father, eldest brother and older sister were all killed, along with their spouses."

She couldn't keep herself from needing to inhale to steady her nerves.

"The latest news I have from Adamant is from early May," she reminded him. "As of that update, no one was yet certain what happened to my nieces: the twin daughters of my brother Daniel.

"An attack was also launched on my brother Nikola, then Third Pentarch, which was thwarted by regular Royal Kingdom of Adamant Army troops under his command. Several different layers of attack were put in place aboard the frigate I served aboard to assassinate me."

She glanced away from Devine toward Jarret.

"Major Jarret was in command of my bodyguard and succeeded in preventing all of those attacks," she noted. "By the time we had neutralized all of the threats aboard *Goldenrod*, one of my Guard section leaders was dead and we had uncovered a traitor in my own Guard detail."

Someone they were still going to have to deal with. The damage to *Goldenrod* hadn't been so... morally convenient as to kill Jelica Laurenz, who was only still alive because of a deep-seated Adamantine aversion to cold-blooded murder or execution.

"But, based on the attacks and pursuit by elements of Home Fleet under Benjamin Adamant's orders, we fled the system and activated an emergency contingency plan of my mother's. Thanks to the resources and credentials that plan provided, I am here, filing a formal notice of claim on the Stability Convention for the resources and help necessary to remove my uncle and restore proper order to my Kingdom."

"Straightforward enough, once you strip away everything beyond the essentials," Devine conceded. "I cannot imagine the heartbreak in this whole mess for you, Lorraine. You have my deepest sympathies."

"Thank you," she murmured.

He was either sincere or one of the best fakers she'd ever met. He even seemed to recognize that it was more than just losing her mother that hurt. More than just losing her *siblings*. That hurt would never fade, but it couldn't get worse, either.

That her uncle had betrayed them all hurt just as much and got worse every time she collided with another piece of proof of his treachery.

"I... will admit that you will face a large barrier to your claim," the Fund bureaucrat continued. "I understand that, to you, circumventing the normal order of succession is treason, but... the Prime Minister and Cabinet remain in place, yes?"

"Prime Minister Dakila Bayer is an old colleague and political ally of my uncle," Lorraine noted. "I have reason to suspect that he was fully involved in the coup. In any case, what I have seen in the news from home suggests that he has fallen in line with my uncle's plans, his Cabinet with him."

"I will admit a lack of familiarity with the Kingdom of Adamant," Devine said. "But to most of the United Worlds, so long as the elected government is in place, calling this a coup is a... very large stretch. Replacing one aristocratic figurehead with another is not something to rile up most of us."

Lorraine pressed her lips together hard for a moment, considering how to phrase her next words.

"Alastair, the King of Adamant is not a figurehead," she finally said. "There is very real power—including one of two full vetoes on legislation—vested in the hands of the King. As Crown Regent, my uncle now wields all of that power. Half or more of the executive branch, so to speak.

"More than that, though, our Kings are chosen by election, Alastair. All *Pentarch* means is that I have both the right and the obligation to stand in the Royal Election. A King is elected for life from a short list of possible candidates—but they *are* elected.

"My uncle is not. He has made no effort to initiate the Election. The last I had heard, his argument with my brother had turned into open civil war and he was using that as an excuse to postpone the Royal Election."

"Your brother refused to participate in the election?" Devine asked.

"I do not know one way or another," she admitted. "I know that my brother had secured control of several planetary defense centers on Mithral—the southern continent of our capital planet—and that my uncle has launched an assault on those bases with the troops at his command.

"My home planet is in open civil war, Alastair, and I suspect the emergency powers of the Crown have been activated using that excuse. My uncle will drag out the war with Nikola and his loyalists to allow him to secure power.

"Without the Royal Election, without a properly selected King, with the Government leadership fully co-opted by a usurper... my Kingdom's traditions, constitution and democracy are under threat.

"So, I am here," she echoed her earlier words, and gestured around the office, "asking for the help I have every right to demand. The chip Major Jarrett provided does include the formal request for assistance, I believe."

Devine nodded. He didn't move otherwise, his hands still flat on the table and his eyes thoughtful.

"The case is... inherently complicated," he finally told her. "I would see an argument and there are certain resources I could break free, but I suspect if money was enough to fix the problem, well." He chuckled. "I may know little about your Kingdom, but the wealth of your House is famous."

"I need ships, Alastair," Lorraine said grimly. "A powerful-enough force to, I hope, convince my uncle not to fight. I would see him punished for what he has done... but I would save my Kingdom first.

"A powerful-enough United Worlds fleet should be enough to act as guarantor of a fair and open Royal and General Election, allowing the people of my Kingdom to decide their own fate."

Devine chuckled softly.

"I'd say you'd learned the right words to convince diehard United Worlds democrats to listen, but I have the distinct sense you mean everything you say, Lorraine," he confessed.

"Your ask, though..." He paused thoughtfully, then sighed. "You understand, of course, that this is just a branch office, intended more for processing the contributions to the Fund than managing formal requests.

"I have officially assumed your case as primary manager, but my authority is far from unlimited," he warned. "I could, for example, take a UW courier ship out to Adamantine and see if my presence alone could resolve the situation—but if your uncle and brother were already throwing armored divisions at each other four months ago, I doubt things will be calm enough for that in three months."

That, Lorraine noted silently, meant that a mid-level manager at the Stability Convention Fund could access a hundred-forty-four-cee government or military courier without even blinking.

"My family is known for many things," Lorraine told him. "But a willingness to bend for anyone isn't one of them. Especially not the United Worlds. Your corporations have sown a crop your diplomats reap every time they speak."

"There's usually enough ships behind our diplomats to pay that price," Devine said levelly. "But I agree. Showing up in a courier, even with the United Worlds Navy implicitly behind me, will not end your civil war."

She was intrigued to realize that there was no sign that he was accessing his neural link, but from the degree to which his certainty on the situation and her Kingdom kept increasing, she was certain he was.

"I could speak to Rear Admiral Laterza," he continued slowly. "I believe the Convention provides sufficient authority to conjure with that I could borrow a carrier group from the Tavastar Fleet Station."

For a moment, Lorraine bit her tongue, then she sighed.

"A United Worlds carrier has less weight than you think," she told the civilian. "Ton for ton, UWN capital ships are more powerful than anything in the Bright Dream Cluster... but ton for ton, a carrier is considered the least effective form of capital ship."

It wasn't that combat shuttles were *ineffective*. For their intended purpose of providing *options*, nothing matched them. For straightforward slugging ability, though, the firepower to go toe-to-toe with a peer capital ship... beams and missiles were far superior.

"A carrier is a *constabulary* ship, Alastair," she explained. "Effective at providing security against lesser powers—but if you brought one fleet carrier against RKAN's Home Fleet, all you'd be managing is a lot of dead spacers on both sides."

And a rather large infusion of new technology samples into Adamant's technology base, because that carrier would lose. She'd take twice her mass in battleships with her, Lorraine judged, but the ten battleships of Home Fleet had over *six* times a single carrier's mass and cubage.

"You have every right to make your notice of claim, your request for help," Devine said, "but it is clear to me that your situation is well beyond what I can arrange. So, I suppose my question is: what do you expect from me, Lorraine?"

"I need to get to Earth, to present my case to the Grand Assembly themselves," Lorraine told him. "I need a real fleet, and even the highest levels of the Fund can't authorize that. As I understand it, the Assembly must authorize any multi-capital-ship deployment through a wormhole."

The same dark history that limited the United Worlds' borders to the wormholes made them hesitant to send ships through them. No one had yet, after all, successfully predicted *when* a wormhole would fail.

But it had happened. Twice.

"You have a ship," Devine noted. "You were correct to check in and file your notice of claim here. I can provide documents countersigning your existing credentials and smoothing your way through the United Worlds, but I fear that may be all I can do."

"My ship is rated for eighty-eight times the speed of light," Lorraine reminded him. "That would be almost a *year* for me to reach Earth. I could lease a faster courier. As I understand it, UW technology import/export laws are such that I can rent a far speedier ship heading toward Sol than back into the Cluster—but even that leaves years before I would be able to return to my home.

"I do need your help, Alastair," she concluded—and despite his impressive self-control, she saw the moment he caught on.

"I need access to the Charon Complex wormhole in the Greenhall System. And I think you can get it for me."

SIX

Alastair Devine leaned back in his chair, steepling his hands in his lap—still intently holding Lorraine's gaze in a way that she knew was probably inappropriate, but she found herself not minding.

"Secrets are hard to keep," he finally said. "Especially one like the Sol–Greenhall wormhole, I suppose."

"The sudden extra attention paid to our cluster by all of the United Worlds was noticeable," Lorraine told him.

Ten years earlier—at least ten years earlier, Adamantine Intelligence was unclear on when the work had been done—an artificial wormhole had been opened between Sol, the home system of all humanity and the capital of the United Worlds, and Greenhall, Tavastar's neighboring star system with a properly habitable garden world.

Lorraine hadn't known the details until the Exodus Protocols had been activated, but all of the information had been tucked away in her implants just in case. Her mother and Colonel Roma, the now-deceased commander of the Adamant Guard, had built some truly paranoid contingency plans.

"Secrecy was probably doomed as soon as there was any civilian usage, you realize," she continued. "But what's important to me right now is that wormhole can get me to Earth in less than two weeks instead of almost fifty."

"And, of course, could get help back to Adamantine just as quickly," Devine conceded. He was still leaning back and hadn't committed himself either way beyond admitting to the Complex's existence.

"The Charon Complex represents a spectacular leap forward for interstellar travel and the power of the United Worlds," he noted. "Much information on it remains classified, but I know enough to recognize that the price tag is beyond any other polity of humanity, even if the technology were released."

And the United Worlds did not release FTL technology directly. The so-called TIE—Technology Import/Export—rules around UW military and FTL technology were arcane and draconian—enough so that even the Republic of Bright Dream Navy, just on the other side of the Tavastar wormhole, only had reliable access to drives capable of eighty-eight times the speed of light... where the UWN was standardized at one hundred and twelve.

Even civilian shipping in the United Worlds usually exceeded the hundred-times-lightspeed line, but those drives were never sold past the wormholes. Given how much lip service the interstellar megacorporations paid to other UW laws, Lorraine figured the penalties for breaching the TIE rules had to be *truly* impressive.

"But you can authorize access to the wormhole for transit to Earth?" Lorraine prodded.

"I..." Devine trailed off into a half-amused, half-frustrated sound. "I actually don't know, Lorraine," he admitted after a moment. "Which, given how logical a request it is, tells me that someone upstairs either didn't think about it or very much didn't want to make up their mind."

"Is it something I'd need to go to Director Reis about?" she asked, her tone intentionally saccharine. She was going to take Attaché

Ceferov at their word on Reis's usefulness for now, but she had a particular impression of the office politics for the Fund, too.

"The Director has no greater authority with regards to the Charon Complex than I do," Devine told her, the spark in his eye telling her she'd touched home. "I will need to do some research, Lorraine—and talk to Rear Admiral Laterza, too. Even if she can't spare enough ships to meet your needs, a perspective from our military is needed here."

Part of Lorraine wanted to keep everything about her request quiet. The fewer people who knew what she was doing, the fewer people who could leak the plan to either her uncle's people or the other allies she suspected he had in the United Worlds.

"I understand," she told him. "I do need to warn you, though, that someone has already made an attempt on my life here on Tavastar Station. If you become associated with me, you may draw attention you do not want."

"Unless your uncle is truly lost to reason, he will not raise his hand against an official of the United Worlds," Devine said placidly. "Attacking *you* here is bad enough for his case—and is a large part of why anything fully inside my authority, you would already have.

"If he were to strike at me directly? To once again quote ancient history—Cicero, mostly, this time—*cīvis Rōmānus sum. I am a Roman citizen. Let kings tremble.* I am an officer of the United Worlds. To strike at me is to strike at Earth and invite her infinite wrath."

His smile was calm.

"You should be safe here now," he assured her. "But even more than you, I am beyond your uncle's reach."

"And if my uncle has made alliance with someone of your worlds, with the resources and skills to strike without trace?" Lorraine replied. "TSS was already hitting roadblocks in their investigation of the attack on me.

"There are shadows on this station that my uncle can call upon, though I doubt they serve him."

"Then I shall be safe for other reasons," Devine told her with an unabashed grin that cut years off his face. "Let them try, Lorraine. And in the trying, perhaps we will learn more of who attacked you!"

"WELL, I guess I know two things about our *case manager*," Jarret said silently in Lorraine's head as they headed for the shuttle.

"Which are?" Lorraine asked.

"He's very pretty and he was very determined not to stare at your tits," Palmer told her.

Lorraine's gaze flickered swiftly to her right, where the dark-colored Corporal gave her a wide grin.

"You caught that too, did you?" Alvarez said. Lorraine nearly gave herself whiplash, looking at the Guard escorting her to her left.

Jarret was leading the way, with Fuchs following behind while his drones kept a visual perimeter. If Lorraine had been even slightly less used to the level of security the Guard kept on her, it would have felt stifling.

As it was, she still felt surrounded—but after the last few months, that was more reassuring than anything else.

"He took one solid look at your chest when he was sitting down, then spent the rest of the meeting keeping his gaze *locked* to your face," Alvarez continued. "He, uh, seemed impressed."

The entire conversation was silent, taking place in the local iteration of the GuardNet holding the four of them and the nonsentient surveillance drones. No one around the group would have realized why Lorraine was fighting down a blush—but their formation was enough more obvious than it had been earlier to keep a noticeable bubble of empty space around them anyway.

"My *chest* is hardly that impressive," she pointed out carefully. "And I doubt that was what Vigo meant, anyway."

Both Corporals were more generously equipped in that area than

Lorraine was. She'd had no complaints at any point, but she knew that part of her physique didn't *impress*.

"That wasn't quite how I was going to phrase that part of my point," Jarret finally interjected, his barely controlled amusement clear even in the digital communication. "I was going to say that he seemed quite taken with the Pentarch, though professional enough that I doubt he'd let that impact his judgment.

"My *other* point, though, is about Em Devine himself," the head bodyguard continued.

"He's very confident," Lorraine noted. "Arrogant, even."

"No. Confident," Jarret corrected gently. "I watched the man move, Lorraine. If I hadn't known the SCF got used as cover for operators, I'd have guessed ten seconds after I met him."

"Operators?" she asked.

"Covert ops people. I'd guess our Devine is mostly an analyst—especially now—but he's been trained for and seen real action. Close-up, ugly action. He moves like it, and until he locked on to your eyes, he was watching the space around him like it."

"There were a pair of very low-profile drones sticking to the corners and out of view," Fuchs noted. "One was following him the whole time; the other was waiting in his office. Both were directly linked to him, not the office security."

"He might be as safe from knives in the dark as he thinks?" Lorraine asked.

"Nobody is safe from a knife in the back, drones or no drones," Jarret said grimly. "We're heading right back to the shuttle for a reason. I'll be slightly happier on MacDougall Station, but I'm not going to breathe easy unless you're on *Goldenrod* for a long, long time, Lorraine."

"Then let's get back before we give you asthma, Major," she told him. "Cortez needs to finish her review before they order parts from here anyway."

"And I don't think we want a box of materiel packed by strangers on the same shuttle as you, anyway," Palmer pointed out. "We never thought Tavastar Station was safe, but the threat profile is definitely elevated now!"

SEVEN

Vigo read Cortez's report with a sinking feeling. *Goldenrod* was a tough little ship, but the emphasis had to be on *little*. At two hundred meters long and a hundred and forty thousand tons fully loaded, she was the smallest warship in the star system.

The United Worlds Navy was large enough and powerful enough to use cruisers for the constabulary, diplomatic and trade-protection roles most first-order cluster nations used frigates for. *Goldenrod*'s closest cousins in the UWN's Tavastar Fleet Station were destroyers, built to protect capital ships, not deploy for long operations on their own.

And the smallest UWN destroyer in the star system was *three* hundred meters and a quarter-million tons.

The little ship had given her all to get the Pentarch this far, and there was only so much that could be done to fix that without a full shipyard. She still had her translight drive, her shuttles and some of her weapons—but she'd never be a true warship again.

That was going to be a problem. Vigo had always known reaching out to the United Worlds was a long shot, but the farther they went, the more it cost them. *Goldenrod* wouldn't have been much of a base to start a civil war from to begin with—and now she was even less so.

At least the Chief Engineer was well on her way to undoing the "tuning" of their drive that had allowed *Corsair* to pursue them so precisely. The battlecruiser would have been able to pursue them regardless, but the prep work done by the Black Regent's people had let the capital ship emerge on top of them, repeatedly.

Vigo knew Lorraine was still struggling with the timing on that. *Goldenrod* had gone in for a refit right before she'd come aboard, primarily to create space for his Adamant Guard detail. That was when the work had been done on her FTL drive, work matched to a specialty scanner installed on *Corsair*.

And that work had been done almost a year earlier, long before the coup had been launched. Benjamin Adamant had clearly been working toward his plan to wipe out his family for a long time.

Even Vigo found that hard to swallow, and Benjamin Adamant wasn't his favorite uncle.

"Major, a few moments of your time?"

He chuckled.

"Captain, I've been waiting for you," he told Stephson.

The Valkyrie-esque form of Lieutenant Colonel Sigrid Stephson had appeared on his link's feeds a good minute earlier, as the ship's security systems told him she was coming. He'd had to lock her out of the ship once, when he hadn't known who he could trust, though that would never have lasted.

He still had more access to *Goldenrod*'s systems than he was telling her.

For now, Stephson took a seat across from him.

"We have a lot of decisions to make over the next few days," she said quietly. "Most of them are going to be Lorraine's, as mission commander."

Vigo nodded his understanding.

Lieutenant Commander Lorraine Adamant had been a shuttle flight commander, a mid-ranked officer no more important than any other O-4 on paper. With King Valeriya dead, Lorraine's commission was suspended until the Royal Election was complete.

Thanks to the Exodus Protocols, Lorraine was now officially both an Envoy of the Kingdom of Adamant *and* mission commander of their entire operation, by her mother's authority. Stephson commanded *Goldenrod*, but Lorraine Adamant commanded the mission.

"But you're here because there's one that isn't," he concluded.

"Jelica Laurenz."

The name hung in the air like a ticking bomb. Lieutenant Jelica Laurenz was one of Vigo's officers, a shuttle pilot and a member of the Adamant Guard. A ten-year veteran of the Adamantine military before she'd been recruited, trusted and empowered to protect the Pentarchy...

She was also a traitor and a murderer. She'd been part of the attack on Lorraine, to the point of setting several of *Goldenrod*'s nuclear weapons to detonate in the magazine—though he figured she'd expected to be able to get off the ship before they blew and had been just as happy to have them disarmed as anyone else.

When the noose had started to close in around the fact that there *was* a traitor, though, she'd made an attempt to complete the assassination herself. She'd killed another Guard and come within millimeters of managing to kill Lorraine herself.

"We'd have been better off, in many ways, if we'd shot her rather than taking her into custody," Vigo admitted unflinchingly. "We needed information on who else she'd co-opted, but..."

The Kingdom of Adamant very specifically did not have the death penalty as an option. They had still executed people—seven, he believed, in the entire two-century-plus history of his nation—but because it wasn't part of the written law, it required something truly beyond the pale, accompanied by a mass of extra paperwork.

"Let's be honest: we could shoot her, and no one would ever follow it up," Stephson pointed out. Something in her tone told him she didn't expect him to agree with her but felt she had to say it.

"If Palmer had shot her rather than punching her out, I would have given her the same damn medal she's already getting," Vigo noted. Though Palmer had been blind at the time, which he supposed would have made that difficult.

"But we needed the information we got from her—and no one on this ship is a goddamn barbarian. We will not execute our prisoners out of hand."

But they didn't have to treat them overly gently. He suspected that Laurenz's medical treatment after being taken prisoner had been far more rough and ready than it should have been, and he'd chosen not to look into that.

"Then what do we do?" the other officer asked bluntly. "We have nobody to hand her over to, no authority we'd trust—and we're sure as *fuck* not letting her go."

Vigo stared blankly at the wall, past the starship captain, while considering options.

"She has to come back to the Kingdom with us, when all of this is done," he decided aloud. "Keeping her in the brig is a pain, but... honestly, having an open-and-shut case of someone to put on trial for all of this will help.

"She's an *asset*," he realized. "We have more than enough evidence for any judge to lock her up and throw away the key. And having that trial, very publicly and messily, will help set the tone of the PR campaign we have to wage."

"So, I have to keep feeding her?" Stephson asked. "Despite everything, I do need to talk to the Pentarch about off-loading a dozen souls who wanted to jump ship back in the Kingdom."

She sighed.

"We told them they could and then, well, *Corsair* interfered."

"They understand, I hope," Vigo said. "I wasn't under the impression we'd had any problems?"

"Nothing but grousing. They did their duty, more than I would have expected." She chuckled. "Hell, we had thirty-four people wanting out when we headed into Ominira and only thirteen asking to be let off here."

A grim thought smothered any urge of Vigo's to join in her chuckle.

"How many of them died?"

"Four. The rest changed their minds." Stephson joined him in his grimness now as she met his gaze. "The Pentarch did that without even trying, I think. I'm assuming she'll sign off on letting people who want out here out."

"They're a security risk," Vigo warned. "I can see arguments for holding them... but they fought for us this far. We can't justify keeping them."

Unlike Laurenz. He'd keep *her* until he handed her to a court and the wolves that pretended to be Adamantine court reporters.

"LONG STORY SHORT, *Goldenrod* is now a particularly militaristic-looking yacht," Commander Rose Cortez told the gathered officers flatly.

Vigo assumed that the other members of Lorraine's command staff—Captain Stephson's senior officers, plus him and Lorraine herself—had also read the report the Cheng had sent out. It still helped to lay out the key points.

"We still have almost all of our defensive systems," Lieutenant Commander Mattias Paris pointed out. The tall and gangly Tactical Officer sat across from Vigo and looked more rested than Vigo had seen him in months.

Goldenrod was rotating with MacDougall Station, providing the crew with a gentle half-gravity of "down" throughout the ship. After months in translight, where the frigate couldn't provide any gravity for her passengers, the feeling was more than welcome.

"We lost screen projectors, electronic countermeasures, jammers, transmitters..." Paris reeled off, then shrugged. "But we had spares for all of that. The defensive screen is around ninety-eight percent, correct, Cheng?"

"If we're rounding to whole percentage points, yes," Cortez said with a bright smile. It wasn't directed at Vigo, but he still had to focus past it for a moment.

He either needed to spend more time with the frigate's engineer or less—and he really wasn't sure which was a better idea.

"Beyond that, we also have managed to retain or rebuild eighty-five percent of our lighter beams, which serve primarily in a defensive role," she continued. "Plus most of the main heavy beams, but..."

"We have no external missile launchers," Paris finished for her. "The racks are *gone*."

"In some places, that's the only reason we have a hull left," Anna Savege pointed out. The soft-edged brunette who served as *Goldenrod*'s XO was either filling in details or trying to soften the harsh report.

If she was trying to soften things for Lorraine, she was failing. Vigo hoped that none of the officers could read his Pentarch's mood, but he'd known her since she was a small child.

None of this was news to her, but it was still a litany of damage and weaknesses. Every hit they'd taken in their long flight from the Adamantine System to the Bright Dream System had cost them capability—and lives.

"We have been able to fabricate a small number of new missiles," Paris noted. "But we had very few warheads left after everything. And... well..."

"We have one missile launcher." Stephson's summary cut through the air like a knife. "So, we don't *need* more than the dozen missiles you've been able to put together, do we? We might need to see off a pirate—but against a real threat, we can only run."

"We do have some good news there, I suppose," Kagan Yildiz told them all. The ship's Navigator was a sharp-edged man with birdlike features, now looking at the model of *Goldenrod* in the middle of the room like a hawk studying a fleeing animal.

"Once we were able to shut the drives fully down and examine them externally, it looks like primary engine five is in better shape than we thought," he continued with a nod to Cortez. "If we have time, Commander Cortez and I want to completely remove primaries two and five."

"Between supplies we should be able to purchase here and the remnants of two and five, I think we can get the remaining four primary engines completely online," Cortez said. "Plus *all* of the secondaries. Short two primary units, we'll only be good for six gravities, but that is nothing to sneer at."

The biggest restriction on a spaceship's acceleration was its crew, Vigo knew. RKAN rated its warships for seven and a half gravities of emergency thrust, with dire warnings for exceeding seven. Seven gravities was generally regarded as the most a military crew could withstand while operating the ship at all.

"So, one missile launcher, most of our beams and almost all of our defenses," Lorraine Adamant summarized. "But we're capable of sublight and translight travel, correct?"

"We will be," Stephson confirmed.

"How long do we need?" the Pentarch asked.

"A week," Cortez told her. "I can close us up so we can fly in three days, but a week will be a lot better."

"We'll plan for the week. We'll need to be a bit paranoid about where we go and who we send, even onto MacDougall Station," the princess warned. "But either we get access to the wormhole and a week won't cost us much... or we don't get access to the wormhole and one more week won't matter."

Everyone around the room understood the math on that. A week to Greenhall was one thing. Fifty weeks for the direct route to Sol was something else—something Vigo wasn't sure the crew could *take*.

"Which brings us to our people, I suppose," Savege noted. The XO shrugged. "We still have thirteen hands who want to be left ashore. I don't think they realize just how crap a situation being left on Tavastar Station would put them in."

"We'd have to pay out their last few months of salary from ship-board resources, but that still wouldn't cover a ticket home," Stephson agreed. "We can talk to them individually and make sure they realize that, but..."

"How hard up are we for hands?" Lorraine asked. "We've lost too many people getting here."

"We have," Stephson agreed levelly.

Vigo knew that Lorraine had made certain she knew the names of every one of the forty-seven spacers who'd died aboard *Goldenrod*. And had met with each of the other thirty-five that were still in sickbay.

But then, *Goldenrod* had gone up against a battlecruiser over ten times her size. A quarter of the crew wounded or dead was three-quarters less than they should have expected.

"With the damage we've taken, though..." The Captain shook her head. "Without any missiles, down two primary engines and a quarter of the beams? I've run it through with the Chief of the Boat, and we figure we can fight *Goldenrod* at her current full effectiveness with a hundred and eighty hands. We can fly her, system to system, with as few as a hundred."

Vigo ran those numbers through his link. One hundred and two of the original people aboard *Goldenrod* had been Marines or his Adamant Guards. They hadn't been immune to the losses, but most of the dead had been the RKAN crew.

"If we put everyone who wants out ashore, we'll still have around two hundred hands, plus the Guard and Marines," Savege said. "I guess we'll be fine, though I worry about dropping them off with no way home."

"That's their choice," Vigo interjected. "We hardly want to reward them for leaving."

"But we do want to reward them for standing with us even after we promised they *could* leave," Lorraine countered. "Over thirty members of the crew asked to be let off at a stop inside our Kingdom, and *I* said we would let them go."

Vigo caught the emphasis. The scions of House Adamant, the young men and women who were raised to be Pentarchs, were taught many things. Among them was that leadership and governance meant you couldn't always keep your word—but that the more you *did* keep it, the more value others gave it.

"They stuck with us this far, did their duty and served well," the Pentarch continued. "We owe them for that. I will make arrangements for all of them to get home—and any other member of the crew who wants out.

"These people fought a battlecruiser for me. I will not force them to go further, and I will not drop them off penniless on a foreign shore. They are owed."

And that, Vigo knew, was that.

"I know none of my Marines will take you up on that," Lieutenant Commander Enitan Zdravkov noted. The Marine CO was massively broad despite their surprisingly short height, which gave them a disproportionate presence at the table despite their silence to that point.

"I'll make sure they get the offer," they continued, before Lorraine could say anything, "but I worry I might get laughed out of Marine Country."

"Laughter is fine," the Pentarch told them. "But I want our people to know that they have the option. Everything up to this point has been, well, straightforward.

"From here, we are heading into the heart of humanity. The womb of the megacorporations that have torn nations like ours to pieces in the hunt for profit. Nothing I have seen in my studies or in our interactions so far with the United Worlders counters the impression that we are walking into a pit of snakes."

Not how Vigo would like to have referred to the homeworld of all humanity—but as the man tasked with Lorraine Adamant's safety, he preferred her to be paranoid than naïve.

"I'll have Chief Roman tell the crew," Stephson promised. Senior Chief Leonard Roman was the senior RKAN noncommissioned officer aboard, the "Chief of the Boat" who acted as the Captain's left hand.

"Which leaves us with one real question," the Captain continued. "The destination is Earth. What's the next step?"

"The crew makes the repairs to *Goldenrod* and makes their choice of whether they're sticking with us," Lorraine told them. "I have spoken with the Stability Convention Fund people, and we're waiting on news there."

She smiled grimly.

"Em Devine may get us official permission to pass through the wormhole. He may not. Either way, I don't think we want to make any announcements until we *have* put everyone ashore who is leaving.

"Let's keep some secrets until we know the people left are making the journey."

EIGHT

The ship slept.

An airlock hissed open, and an alert ran through the system—only to shut down a moment later as overrides kicked in.

The lockdowns kept the alert from reaching the central system. The original code would have warned it of the intrusion, as much as the central intelligence routine would have required warning as opposed to simply *knowing* something had entered the ship.

Two dozen drones spread out from the airlock. No human set foot on the decks.

No human had set foot on the decks in years.

The process was entirely automated, without even a particularly complicated intelligence behind it. The drones swept through the hull in a long-programmed routine, checking every nook and cranny for things that had changed.

Nothing had.

Nothing ever did. The interior of the ship was kept in stasis. Eleven degrees Celsius. Zero percent humidity. Atmosphere: one hundred percent nitrogen.

Drone jets that would have been unnoticeable in most environments echoed through abandoned vaults as the machines searched for the impossible. Humans might not have gone through the motions, but that was why they sent robots.

Eventually, a drone socketed into a connection just outside the main computer.

A spark of awareness ran through the core—pursued by the overrides the drone injected. The central intelligence routine would not awaken. Could not be *permitted* to awaken, though neither the drone nor the human who'd sent it aboard knew that.

An integrity check on the computer systems completed and the drone withdrew its cables.

The drones withdrew toward the airlock, their work complete, and the ship was left to her slumber.

NINE

"Your Highness, you have a guest at the boarding lock."

Lorraine looked up from her desk at the voice of Guard Sergeant Merle. The Adamant Guard NCO wasn't in her office—part of the suite put aside for civilian supercargo and commandeered for her role as Envoy—of course.

He was providing the Guard's eyes and ears at the main boarding airlock at the front of the ship, where Marines made sure that no one unexpected boarded the frigate.

"A guest, Guard Sergeant?" she asked thin air, relying on her link to send the response to Merle.

As part of the passenger suite, the office was included in the so-called "presence section" of the frigate, which mostly meant that there was carpet on the floor and wood-trimmed drywall on the walls. It was also deep enough in the ship that none of the battle damage showed there, which almost let her pretend she was in an office on a surface somewhere.

Of course, centripetal pseudogravity didn't actually work like real gravity, so just putting down a tablet or anything else made it quite clear she was aboard a ship.

"It appears our SCF case manager has come to visit you in person," Merle told her. "Does he have an appointment?"

"No, he doesn't," Lorraine replied. She glanced at the screen above her desk, with the twenty-third letter to a family member of a fallen crew member half-written on it.

"On the other hand, he is probably one of my higher priorities at the moment," she told Merle. "Check him over and loop in Jarret, Palmer and Alvarez. Then send him up."

"Aye, aye, Your Highness."

Alvarez was right outside Lorraine's door, which meant no one was getting into the room without the Corporal being informed in advance. Palmer was to keep the other NCO from Lorraine's close detail in the loop—and Jarret was so that he could be present when Devine was.

Lorraine wasn't particularly worried that she was going to tear the man's clothes off or anything like that, but there were very few people in the galaxy she was prepared to meet without a bodyguard in the room.

Alastair Devine might get there, if he kept working with her and for her goals. Might. At that moment, though, she would have Jarret in the room when she spoke with him.

───────

JARRET ARRIVED JUST FAR ENOUGH in advance of Devine to settle in a seat to the side of the room, not quite behind the desk with Lorraine but not quite in front of it either. She drew more comfort from his solid presence than she would admit to anyone— except Jarret himself, and she knew he knew.

With him by her side, she was ready to face the universe. Let alone one mid-ranking United Worlds bureaucrat with a covert ops background.

"Pentarch Lorraine, Alastair Devine to see you," Alvarez

announced as she opened the door to the office. "He's been cleared, he's unarmed. Now."

There was a grin in the Guard's voice, and Lorraine gave Devine a sharp glance. He gave her a sheepish shrug.

"If I can have the holdout back afterward, I'd appreciate it, Corporal Alvarez," he told the Guard. "I won't pretend I forgot I had it, but I assure you that I mean no harm to anyone."

"I believe you, or you wouldn't be getting into the Pentarch's office," Alvarez told him, waving him through.

Sharing the bodyguard's clear amusement, Devine stepped through the door and gave Lorraine a smooth bow. He moderated it based off her reaction to the first one, she noted, and came far closer to the respectful-but-not-groveling depth that an Adamantine citizen would use.

Of course, an Adamantine would usually save that for the King themselves, but there was only so much she would expect from a United Worlder. The complex shades under which Lorraine wasn't normally rated a bow, but might, right then, both as a formal Envoy of the King *and* as a Pentarch during the Royal Election, qualify for one were... Well, even *she* would be consulting an etiquette guide.

"Pentarch Lorraine," he greeted her. "It is a true pleasure to see you again."

She was watching for it and caught the moment he glanced down toward her chest and the extra button she'd undone on her uniform blouse since he'd come aboard. Lorraine might not have much to work with there, but she'd had literal training in working with what she had.

Pentarchs received all kinds of education that others wouldn't.

"Alastair," she returned the greeting, rising to shake his hand across the desk. "I'll admit I expected a call, not a visit."

"The sad truth of the matter, Lorraine, is that anyone involved in intelligence work in the United Worlds realized long ago that between algorithmic video falsifications, quantum decryptions, synthetic-intelligence eavesdroppers and a thousand other deceptions and observers... electronic communication channels cannot be trusted."

He shrugged as he took the one empty seat in the room, then gave Jarret a firm nod.

"A pleasure to see you as well, Major Jarret."

"We all know who you came to see, Em Devine," Jarret said with a soft laugh. "I'm just the bodyguard. Speaking of which, though... just what *did* you try to sneak past my people?"

"Holdout pulser," Devine said instantly. "Pulse laser weapon: fits in your palm and uses a trinary chemical lasing medium. Until the cartridge is collapsed to mix the medium, it has no chemicals or power cells that will trigger most weapons scans.

"Most United Worlds security scans would miss it, Major. You should be pleased with your people—I'm certainly impressed by them."

"I'll pass that on," Jarret replied. "Even the cartridge-fed pulse lasers I'm familiar with are long arms, not holdouts."

"But this is the United Worlds and we have our toys," Devine replied. His gaze flicked across the room to meet Lorraine's eyes, and she felt a shiver of warmth in the base of her spine.

Those warm blue eyes were dangerous, she judged.

"This room is as secure as our mere first-order-cluster technology can make it," Lorraine said dryly. "What was so important that it could not be trusted to electronic channels?"

"Oh, I'm claiming this was entirely an excuse to see the exotically gorgeous foreign princess when anyone but you or my boss asks," Devine told her with a wink and a smile that made the eyes all the more dangerous.

"And yet, I am asking," Lorraine told him—but she knew her smile and tone cut away any chill to the words. She was more amused by the spy pretending to be a bureaucrat than was probably wise.

"As I said when we met before, I am officially your case manager with the Stability Convention Fund," he explained. "I don't know if anyone outside the SCF, let alone someone from the

Kingdom of Adamant, really understands how much that actually lets me do."

"Based off our last conversation, anything from 'provide a large sum of money' to 'deploy a force not exceeding a single UWN capital ship,'" Lorraine noted.

He grinned.

"You pay more attention than most," he observed. "I'll admit, I was only about ninety percent certain I had the actual authority to send a carrier group. I know Rear Admiral Laterza well enough, though, to be sure that I could make it happen anyway."

If the man was prepared to go outside the technical limits of his authority to help her, Lorraine wasn't going to complain. Though she was going to worry about the cost—she doubted sleeping with Alastair Devine would be enough to "rent" a fleet carrier.

"I have done my research since then," Devine confirmed. "I would have required Admiral Laterza's cooperation but, yes, my authority would have stretched that far. As we discussed, well. The Grand Assembly has to sign off on sending anything more than one capital ship past the wormholes."

"A rule which I suppose doesn't apply to the Charon Complex?" Lorraine asked wryly.

"That, Lorraine, is because the Charon Complex consists of artificial tachyo-quantum superpositions, not wormholes," he said with a chuckle. "I am not a physicist but my understanding is that the difference is one of semantics."

"My master's is in higher-order tachyon physics," she told him. "Much of my career was in navigation, so it was useful. And... yes and no." She paused thoughtfully, then grinned.

"Do you *want* me to explain the difference between a gravitationally neutral Einstein-Rosen bridge large enough for faux-tachyonic transfer and a quantum superposition?" she asked.

There was a surprisingly long silence, then Devine sighed.

"Lorraine, I think I know what most of those words mean," he told her. "But string them together like that, and the best I can do is plug them into a datasearch, which tells me that the Einstein-Rosen bridge is a partially obsolete physics theory from the twentieth century.

"Which doesn't help me." He smiled self-deprecatingly. "So, let's go with *there is a small-but-real difference and it doesn't matter?*"

Her grin widened in answer to his smile.

"If the description is accurate, transit should be faster than a natural wormhole," she told him. "But fundamentally... you're right. What matters is the political usage, which is that those wormholes don't trigger the laws restricting UW authority."

"Exactly. As Benjamin Franklin once said, *half a truth is often a great lie.* In this case, it makes a useful tool."

"And you can get us access to that tool?" she asked. "The wormhole?"

"Yes." He arched an eyebrow at her and his eyes sparkled. "It's not necessarily easy or straightforward, but I can get your ship through the wormhole.

"So long as I'm aboard."

That was not part of what Lorraine had expected, and she raised her own eyebrow in turn, leaning back to consider that particular wrinkle.

"Vigo?" she asked silently.

"We're in unknown waters and I don't know the rules," her keeper replied. "I don't exactly *want* a United Worlder on the ship, but let's be honest: there's nothing on *Goldenrod* he can steal that's of worth to the UW.

"He's a potential threat, but I can manage that if we have to."

She nodded slowly, still holding Devine's gaze as he waited comfortably for her to process that.

"May I ask why, Alastair?" she asked.

"Whether or not I could write a letter of passage that would authorize you to use the Charon Complex is... unclear," he admitted. "But acting as your case manager, especially with a sign-off from the Tavastar Fleet Station, I have the authority to make the passage *myself*—with no real specification or limitation on what ship I make the journey in."

There was a wicked sparkle to his eyes as he explained.

"So, I can't send you on your own, but I can go in any ship I care to rent. Would you be so kind as to lend me yours, Pentarch Lorraine Adamant?"

"We might be able to do that," she allowed with a wicked chuckle of her own. "You're certain that our presence won't be a problem?"

He shrugged.

"Access to the Charon Complex isn't as restricted as it probably should be," he reminded them. "Most of the megacorps have sweetheart deals that, at the very least, give them access to couriers on a regular basis."

"That seems to describe a great deal of the United Worlds," Jarret said grimly.

Devine glanced over at him, then nodded.

"Our government has kept their interference from inflicting too many harms on the citizens of the United Worlds themselves," he said slowly, "but yes. The LSX Twenty-Five have... far more influence than is probably wise or healthy.

"Still, I am merely a civil servant."

"The LSX Twenty-Five?" Lorraine asked, not quite sure she understood the reference.

"The Lunar Stock Exchange Index Twenty-Five," Devine explained. "Sorry, I'm so used to everybody knowing the term it's just part of the language to me. The LSX is the single largest and most highly capitalized stock exchange in human history, with access to the latest technology in hundred-forty-four-light couriers.

"The Index Twenty-Five are the companies that the exchange uses for its default index value. If they aren't the largest corporations in all human space, they are certainly the corporations with the largest capitalization on the largest stock exchange known to the United Worlds."

Lorraine nodded. The communication lag meant that most

companies used local stock exchanges for raising capital and disseminating ownership—and many systems had anti-colonialism laws that required any corporation operating in them to have a controlling share listed on their local exchange.

"So, the LSX Twenty-Five are basically what we mean when we say *interstellar megacorporation*," she concluded.

"The smallest corporation on the LSX-Twenty-Five has an operating budget larger than any national budget outside of the United Worlds itself," Devine agreed. "Their power, even in the UW, flows from money and influence.

"We do our best to keep them in line at home, but I spent a decade in our embassies, Lorraine. I know how they misbehave outside our borders." The last of his humor faded into a grim set to his face, and he leaned his head into steepled hands for a moment.

"Which brings me, I suppose, to the other piece of research I've spent the last two days working on," he noted.

"I can't prove it, but I think I know who tried to kill you. And whose money underwrote your uncle's coup."

TEN

Vigo wanted to demand answers from the too-cool-and-collected man sitting in his boss's office. They'd managed to get through the attack on Lorraine without casualties, but it had been a near thing. If the SI Vimes had been one iota less capable of a computer and cop, he'd have lost Guards and quite possibly lost *Lorraine.*

But they needed Alastair Devine, who was most definitely *not* a mere civil servant, so Vigo kept his peace.

He'd already set Lieutenant Major Avital Klement, the head of his Second Section and responsible for electronics, systems and overwatch, the task of making sure there was a space aboard *Goldenrod* that would serve for a VIP guest that was quite separate from Lorraine's quarters.

"Who, Alastair?" Lorraine asked, putting a voice to Vigo's question in a far icier tone that he would have dared. She seemed to have a better feel of how to work with Devine than him, which was fine.

That was her part of the job, after all. His was to make sure Devine didn't screw them over somehow.

"Freebright Interstellar Technologies," the United Worlder said flatly. "FBIT." He pronounced the initials *Eff-Bit.* "They were one of the key groups involved in building the Charon Complex and sit at the forefront of our faster-than-light-travel research.

"Of course, they're on the LSX Twenty-Five, so FBIT is hardly focused on one thing," Devine continued. "Like the other megacorps, a large portion of their revenue is generated outside the United Worlds or via importing goods to the UW at prices that local production can't match."

"Buy low, sell high, while enforcing both prices via exploitative agreements and channeling goods back home to sell for pennies on the pound," Lorraine summarized. "But if they were involved in building the Complex..."

"They were the first out the door with the Bright Dream Cluster being newly accessible to operations from Earth," Devine agreed.

Vigo shivered. The same wormholes at the Charon Complex that made their mission possible also underlay the very threat they were facing. Without the Complex, the wormhole from Tavastar to Bright Dream was so far from Earth that the cluster had been shielded from the worst of the excesses of the megacorps.

With that distance now cut by orders of magnitude, they were suddenly close to hand. An almost-fresh field of markets and resource sites, from the perspective of the UW's corporate vampires. As the head of Lorraine's Guard Detail, he'd seen the impact in his security briefings over the last few years.

Even before the Kingdom of Adamant had known the Charon Complex existed, they'd recognized that the megacorporations were suddenly more active and present than they'd ever been.

"So, when my mother spent the last decade of her reign reinforcing our anti-colonialism laws..." Lorraine said softly, clearly following the same thoughts as Vigo.

"FBIT saw her actions as targeted at them. They were the first of the LSX Twenty-Five to really start digging in to your section of the Bright Dream Cluster—first to really start paying more attention than had been paid.

"My understanding—though I don't have the records to say for sure—is that King Valeriya actively slapped their fingers at least once," Devine finished. "I do have access to prod through wormhole transit records, and they've sent a lot of people—and, I'm guessing, a lot of money—toward Adamant."

He paused.

"Well, a lot of money by the standards of your Kingdom, anyway," he clarified carefully. "A few billion here, a few billion there... It's petty cash to the Twenty-Five."

"And enough to buy the entire damn Home Fleet to us," Vigo finished aloud. Not that Benjamin Adamant had the need to buy Home Fleet—he'd commanded them for most of that decade. He'd bought the officers' loyalty in a more-ancient coin.

"They will not have earned much grace with my mother, no," Lorraine muttered. "A quote my mother liked for you, then, Em Devine. Robert Harper: *millions for defense, but not one cent for tribute.*"

"I'm sure FBIT would not describe what they are after from the Kingdom of Adamant in as crude a form as *tribute,*" the Fund official told her. "But... yes. Your mother spent her time and her nation's money building a shield against the growing influence of the megacorps in the Bright Dream Cluster. Specifically, against Freebright Interstellar Technologies."

"I was briefed enough to know we weren't targeting anyone specifically," Lorraine said.

"What I have seen so far suggests that they definitely *felt* targeted, though I believe you that King Valeriya's defenses were aimed more broadly than that," Devine warned. "I don't know what they offered your uncle beyond the resources for his coup—or if they even needed to offer him anything else.

"But my assessment is that they've been in contact for at least two years, possibly more," the analyst concluded. "The investment is small by their standards, but they will seek to protect it. They will get in your way."

"Are they going to be a direct threat?" Vigo asked. "I'm... unfamiliar with the resources they could use against us."

His people were already running at their highest levels of readiness. He wasn't sure where he *could* increase Lorraine's security at this point—but if an interstellar was on the playing field, the rules had changed from what he'd thought they were.

He'd agreed with Lorraine that there was a threat, but it was something else to have a local lay it out in black and white.

"I believe it is unlikely that FBIT will move directly against us," Devine said carefully. "What I have dug up so far suggests that they provided resources for the attack here in Tavastar, but it was an agent in your own office that launched it."

Leaving any blame to sit with the "foreign barbarians" if the situation was traced, Vigo presumed.

"The threat they offer isn't physical or direct, is it?" Lorraine asked.

Vigo knew the tone. It was the tone that said she'd put together the pieces and seen the play coming—and while it didn't necessarily say that *he'd* missed something, his focus was on the risk of direct attack.

"No. FBIT is one of the LSX Twenty-Five," Devine repeated. "They will deploy their political power against you—and they will find fertile ground. I already warned you: with the Cabinet and elected government intact, few here in the United Worlds will see your uncle's actions as a major threat to your nation's stability."

"What's one despot versus another?" Vigo's Pentarch ground out. "It is not that simple."

"It isn't; I recognize that," the local agreed. "But that's the cliff you're going to climb. *We're* going to climb, that is.

"Your statement of claim with the Fund gives you a quite specific list of rights," he continued. "We'll get you to Earth, and I am quite certain we can arrange an audience with the Grand Assembly. I can make no promises of what the reception will be, I'm afraid."

"You're taking on quite a bit for us," Lorraine said, leaning forward in a way that made Vigo conceal a mental sigh.

She might not have picked up on it yet, but he'd known her since she was a child. If there was anyone in the galaxy who would know when Lorraine Adamant had an incipient crush, it was Vigo Jarret.

He didn't know Devine well enough to be certain, but he suspected the fledgling feeling was mutual—but he *also* suspected that the covert ops officer turned bureaucrat wasn't the type to let that pull him into this kind of investment.

Devine sighed, leaning forward into his hands for a moment and pinching the bridge of his nose.

"To understand that, I'll need to explain something about the offices for things like the Stability Fund," he noted. "Basically... the Fund operates on a core of permanent staff expanded by secondments from assorted other organizations.

"In my case, the United Worlds Diplomatic Service. I spent two years in the Fortuna System in the Bright Dream Cluster, right through their civil war."

Vigo didn't know much about that particular disaster—but he knew enough to be unsurprised by the suddenly haunted look in Devine's eyes. A UWDS posting would have been in the capital, and the reports he'd seen suggested that over half of the Fortunate City's fifty million people had died.

Except... he was also quite certain that Devine's posting hadn't been with the Diplomatic Service, which raised questions about what a *spy* had been doing in a first-order cluster system when a civil war had kicked off.

"When I returned to the United Worlds, I needed a quiet desk job to recuperate. When I was offered the posting with the local SCF office, it seemed perfect. A gift from the gods."

Vigo could guess where that had gone, and Devine's shrug fit the pattern.

"Except that those secondments don't really... *end*," he told them. "In a posting like this, *success* means that no one ever hears about you. If someone hears about you, it means you screwed up—so, that's not getting you a promotion back to your old office.

"So, an SCF posting, which I didn't know when I took it, is the death knell to any mainline career," he admitted. "I could stay behind the desk they gave me. Collect my time-in-grade raises, maybe transfer offices to somewhere bigger, but I can't get back to... the Service without doing something to catch my old bosses' eyes.

"Helping you out will do so, while working inside the remit of the SCF and potentially solidly reinforcing the value and reputation of the Fund across the galaxy," Devine concluded. "It's a win every way I look at it—unless I want a retirement job at FBIT, I suppose."

Vigo had to chuckle at that. Aggravating a major interstellar was unlikely to be healthy for the man—but Devine was right that he was more immune to anyone's wrath than the two foreigners.

"Pragmatic, but I expected nothing else," Lorraine said. She rose, offering her hand across the desk.

"I'm delighted to have you aboard, Em Devine," she concluded. "We have some work to finish on *Goldenrod* before we get moving, but then... well.

"You and I will have some work to do on Earth."

ELEVEN

Goldenrod's bridge was one of the few places aboard the frigate that still needed a full crew. As they prepared to detach from MacDougall Station, every station in the space was full.

Lieutenant Colonel Sigrid Stephson, of course, occupied the central chair. She was positioned to overlook most of the other consoles but also to have the best view of the curved viewscreen, eight meters across, that defined the front of the bridge.

There were nine consoles between the Captain and the screen, split into three "team" stations: Helm, Tactical and Communications. The senior officers of each department were on duty today, though the current evolution hopefully wouldn't need their expertise.

To the left and right of the slightly elevated dais holding Stephson were the Intelligence and Engineering stations, whose occupants acted as relays for the Combat Information Center and Central Engineering, respectively.

Behind Stephson were three stations that rejoiced in the traditional name of "hotel" stations. By default set to view-only, they could also reinforce any of the five departments present on the bridge or—like Lorraine's console at that moment—be set up to support a task-group commander.

Jarret was seated to her right, and if his console looked like it was showing the informational display intended for supercargo, that was because his real interface and controls lived inside his neural link.

Devine, on the other hand, had no such special access. The United Worlds agent had spent some time poking at the informational display but was now focusing on the main display as it showed the impressive bulk of the UWN fleet station.

"MacDougall Station advises all pipes and cables are detached on their end," Major Solomon Vinci, the Communications Officer, reported. "They are standing by for final release."

"Major Yildiz, do they have the right angle for release?" Stephson asked her Navigator.

Lorraine had the planned course on her screen. *Goldenrod* would carry on the station's radial velocity outward at the angle she disconnected at. It wouldn't be an absolute disaster if MacDougall released them at the wrong moment, though it would add a minute or two to their journey if the Station got it completely wrong.

Not that the UWN would let anyone get away with screwing up that badly.

"They have the angle," Yildiz confirmed. "Next window in... thirty seconds."

"Major Vinci, inform MacDougall they are clear to release on the clock," Stephson ordered.

Seconds ticked away, and then a series of icons on Lorraine's screen flickered green and faded away.

"The count is on. Thirty seconds to the two-kilometer line and secondary engines release," Yildiz reported.

The bridge was a silent hum of activity, any discussion taking place via links as the crew worked through the straightforward task of getting clear of a large space platform.

After the journey to Tavastar, the feeling of microgravity had a bitter familiarity to it for Lorraine. The only way to have gravity in translight was to use a rotating gravity habitat—and frigates were just too small to fit one in.

They'd spent the entire six-month journey in microgravity, and she was *not* looking forward to the two weeks of it needed to get to Greenhall.

"Engines online, one meter per second squared," the Navigator continued as they crossed the invisible line in space. "Five minutes to main-engine burn, but everyone should have a comfortable sense of *down* now."

It wasn't much of a pull, but it was enough to push off Lorraine's moment of distaste.

"Next stop, the Greenhall System," Stephson said aloud. "Anything interesting there other than the wormhole?"

"The planet, Greenhome," her Tactical Officer replied. Lieutenant Commander Mattias Paris was staring down at his console, but Lorraine could tell he was pulling the information from his link by his posture.

So was everyone else, for that matter. They'd gone over the information before, but Greenhall was only really important as a stopover point.

"There's a Reserve base there," Devine told her quietly. "Satellite for the Calypso base. Might be worth setting a course to get as close as allowed, to give you a sense of what you're looking at."

"MacDougall Station made a few points," Lorraine replied. The carrier *Fidelity* might be dismissible in some ways, but the six battleships of the Tavastar Fleet Station were a solid reminder of *why* the UWN could get away with constabulary ships for power projection.

Each of those battleships was five million tons to their RKAN equivalent's three. They were faster translight, more heavily armored and far more heavily armed.

"Still, I think it might be worth seeing the Reserve," the local told her. "It's one thing to read that we have a battleship in mothballs for every one in commission, but I think that you and your people will benefit from really *getting* that, bone deep."

Lorraine shivered. He wasn't wrong. She'd mention it to Stephson later.

They had time, after all.

"Greenhall," she repeated. "Then Earth."

She heard Devine exhale a sigh of something. Nervousness, maybe?

"You've been to Earth, right?" she asked, glancing over to meet his warm gaze.

He chuckled and nodded.

"I have been through the Charon Complex... five times, I think?" he told her. "But I've only been to Earth herself once. It's tradition that members of the Service visit for a week or so, to remind us why we do what we do."

He didn't skip over referring to the Diplomatic Service this time, Lorraine noted. Jarret had pointed out his slip in the earlier meeting, and she'd been watching for it. Devine wasn't used to talking about the department he was seconded from, she suspected, which had let the mistake slip through.

She'd believed Jarret's initial assessment that he wasn't a bureaucrat, but the confirmation was interesting. Lorraine didn't know enough about the spies and intelligence organizations of the United Worlds to guess who Alastair Devine actually worked for.

Either it wouldn't matter or she'd find out. One way or another.

THE UNIVERSE FLICKERED. Lorraine had never heard or come up with a better way to describe it. One moment, everything was normal. The next moment, everything was normal again. But in the infinitesimal gap in between those moments, everything was wrong.

In that imperceptible instant, *Goldenrod* and her passengers transitioned from normal matter to faux-tachyonic matter. Such matter could only move in multiples of a universal constant, the tachyonic-velocity quanta—an irrational number however it was measured, usually rounded to eight times lightspeed.

"Engineering reports no issues with the drive. We are stable at eighty-eight light," Lieutenant Major Božidar Kovac reported. Kovac was the Bridge Engineering Officer—a job that was repeating the Chief Engineer's reports ninety-nine percent of the time and *utterly critical* to the Captain knowing what was going on the other one percent.

"Eight days, seven hours, twenty minutes until we arrive in Greenhall," Yildiz reminded everyone.

"Then we'll see if your argument about chartering us to transport you flies," Lorraine murmured, pitching her voice so only Devine could hear her. And Jarret, of course, but Jarret could hear anything she did.

Privacy meant very different things when you had a permanent bodyguard.

"It will fly," Devine assured her. "Now... uh... this is embarrassing to admit, but it has been quite some time since I was in microgravity. Could I get a hand with this?"

The request wasn't necessarily for Lorraine to help him, and she could have asked someone else. Still, everyone else on the bridge except Jarret and Corporal Palmer—currently bracing up the wall by the security hatch—had a job to do.

So, Lorraine activated the magnetic soles in her boots and undid her own straps, stepping over to help Devine from his seat.

She had him on his feet and mostly stable on his own mag-boots before she realized it was the first time she'd physically touched the man. She was self-aware enough to know that the shiver *that* sent through her was a warning sign.

Or, well, a *sign*.

Devine was less awkward than his request for assistance had implied, too. His hand lingered on hers for a second longer than was necessary, if not so long as to catch Jarret's attention, and he smiled at her as he shuffled his feet, testing the magnetic grip.

"I'm out of practice, but it does come back, I suppose," he conceded.

"We all have six months of practice," Lorraine said. "We're more used to this than anything else."

She led the way out of the bridge, leaving Stephson's crew to handle the task of settling the frigate in for her journey.

"*Goldenrod*'s a pretty ship," Devine noted. "I'm not sure I'd want to spend six months on her without gravity myself, but she's a very nice ship."

"It wasn't the plan," she replied, checking automatically to confirm that Palmer and Jarret had fallen in behind them. There might come a time when she needed to be alone with their new ally—the thought certainly wasn't unwelcome—but outside those specific circumstances, her people would be around.

"I know," he conceded. "You've had a rough six months, Lorraine. I'm sorry."

He meant it, too, which shouldn't surprise her as much as it did. It wasn't like losing her entire family to murder or betrayal wasn't something people could recognize as difficult, after all.

But she had to take everything everyone said with a grain of salt now. The ground in the United Worlds was too treacherous for trust—and since the man who'd murdered her entire family was also one of the two or three people she'd trusted *most*, paranoia and mistrust came far too easily.

As attractive as she was finding Alastair Devine, that was probably a good thing.

TWELVE

"So, how many hackles do you think I'd put up if I called this whole region a trinary system and said Greenhall should be Calypso-B?" Rose Cortez asked, gesturing at the holographic map hanging above Vigo's desk.

"A few," he admitted. It wasn't a *technically* incorrect description, though few outside of dedicated astronomers would consider orbits with diameters measured in light-years to be *that* connected.

Greenhall and Tavastar both orbited Calypso, a dim but massive star more easily identified by its impact on the surrounding stars than its own light. Their orbits lasted millennia, if not longer, but the three stars moved in clear concert.

Only Greenhall had a habitable planet, but the wormhole at Tavastar drew its own attention to the miniature cluster—attention the original bland catalog numbers certainly hadn't earned the trio.

"I imagine, as much as anything, the joke has grown very old," he warned the engineer. "Greenhome has been colonized for, what, four centuries?"

"Colonized around the same time as the Tavastar–Bright Dream wormhole was found, so three-and-a-quarter," Cortez corrected.

"Engineers and precision, I see," Vigo said with a chuckle. In theory, he and Rose were discussing the impact of the drive work on Lorraine's security, but they'd barely touched on that in the meeting.

"It's necessary for the job," she agreed. "It's how I can be quite so sure no one *else* is following a carefully tuned tachyon signature in our translight drive."

"What if we were being watched at MacDougall?" Vigo asked, a spike of paranoia hitting him. That was *his* job, after all.

"Then someone is probably quite frustrated right now," Cortez told him with an impish grin. "Because I figured someone would be, and there were nine changes and adjustments that an observer would have picked up that weren't actually connected to anything. And three more changes we made after leaving the station."

He inclined his head in respect.

"I appreciate that, Cheng," he told the woman. *Cheng* was the usual nickname for Chief Engineer, a slight informality that earned him a surprisingly sharp look.

"Vigo," she said, her use of his first name emphasized, "we have spent about five minutes of the twenty-five I've been in your office talking about actual work. You can call me Rose."

He chuckled at himself—at both of them, he supposed, but mostly himself.

"I'm not sure I realized we'd gone quite so off-topic... Rose," he admitted.

Half-consciously and more than half-guiltily, he checked his link for Lorraine's status. The Pentarch was in her own office, with Palmer and two Guards keeping watch on her door. He could have looked through her eyes to see what she was working on, but that didn't feel necessary.

It was a perpetual balance between the fact that he *could* see and hear everything Lorraine did via the neural-link synchronization—a channel that required quite specific hardware on both of their links to both provide the necessary bandwidth and to keep it as impossible to detect, trace, intercept and decrypt as possible—and providing a twenty-eight-year-old woman her privacy.

Cortez was watching him, he realized. The flicker of his attention was momentary, and he wouldn't have expected anyone to pick up on it, but she had.

"You really do live in her back pocket, don't you?" she murmured.

"Since she was a child," Vigo confirmed. "Lorraine saw enough of her parents that there was never any risk of me replacing anyone, but the relationship is..."

He couldn't find a word for it and just shrugged. He'd never had a long-term partner, let alone children of his own, but he *knew* that Lorraine Adamant fit into the slot in his life where that family would have fit.

"She's lucky to have you," the naval officer said. "And everyone else aboard this seemingly cursed ship was lucky she had you. I had a front-row seat for just how bad we beat this poor frigate, Vigo. If we'd missed even one trick at the start, when your people tore through everything..."

"We'd have died then and there," he pointed out. "Other than the drive chicanery, all of the *tricks* the Black Regent put into play would have killed us all."

"So, yeah. Thank you for that," Cortez agreed with a chuckle. She lifted her feet off the floor, floating in the air as she tucked her legs up into a ball and regarded him.

"Well?"

"Well what?" he countered.

"Do you need to run off and loom for the Pentarch?" she asked. "Or some other task that means I should leave your office and go see what datawork has crawled into my inbox despite us being in deep space?"

Vigo blinked and finally caught up with the fact that his concerning regard for the Chief Engineer might not be unreciprocated.

"Um. No," he admitted. "I check in with or on Lorraine regularly via link, but I don't need to go physically check on her."

"Well." Cortez made an exaggerated gesture of checking a time-piece. "It does appear to be about dinnertime. May I buy you supper in the officers' mess, Major Jarret?"

"I believe the Navy does pay for our meals, but I can be sold on that," Vigo said with a smile. A gesture muted his screens and consoles.

"Shall we?"

THIRTEEN

Lorraine's office had been designed to host an Ambassador or Envoy like she had become. It was set up to showcase the wealth and power of the Kingdom of Adamant and, in its own luxurious way, utterly lacked personality.

She was familiar with spaces like it, though the spaces she'd grown up in had possessed *some* life. Despite the luxury and intent to impress of the Kingdom's public spaces, they were also places people lived and worked.

Part of the balance of being both a relatively junior officer and one of the five heirs to the Crown had been having even fewer personal effects than most. Her office, down in the flight deck when she'd been a shuttle flight commander, had been utterly standard. Her quarters had been allowed a bit more personality, but a chunk of her possessions had been lost in the assassination attempts.

She didn't *have* the things she'd have liked to use to give the office personality. The only things she'd managed to add were a model of *Goldenrod* herself and a family photo of her with all of her siblings and parents.

The photo was just old enough that her nieces, her brother Daniel's daughters, weren't in it. It was part of a set that included shots of Lavender Adamant-Larsen and Nelson Adamant-Falkner, Daniel's and Taura's spouses respectively, but those photos—like the handful she had of the family *with* her nieces—also had Benjamin Adamant in them.

There was no way Lorraine could have a picture of her uncle on her desk. So, she had an older image, one without the youngest members.

Of the six people in the photo, she knew four were dead. She had faith in Nikola's skill as a ground commander and in the resources and fortifications he would now control, but... her last news was months old, and the civil war had already begun then.

How long could a handful of rogue divisions hold out, even with the fortifications of several planetary defense centers to support them?

The file open on Lorraine's screen was one of a series of publicly available pieces on the United Worlds Navy. She'd meant to read it in more detail, but she'd found herself staring at the family photo again.

She exhaled sharply. She could *feel* the gray creeping in around her vision again, threatening to overwhelm the world. Tears had not been a common thing for her; her grief was a subtler, more undermining thing than that.

Lorraine believed—Lorraine *hoped*—that Nikola was alive. That Daniel's daughters were still alive. But she *knew* Fleet Admiral Benjamin Adamant was alive, now Crown Regent and ruling in place of the sister he'd murdered.

Somehow. Somewhere. Somewhen... she was going to end that regency.

Her uncle was going to pay.

Anger was the only shield she had against grief, and so she clung to it like an old friend.

"I SEE we are missing the inestimable Major Jarret this evening," Devine observed as Lorraine helped a steward secure a platter of food.

It wasn't impossible to serve a fancy dinner in microgravity; it was just rather pointless. Anything that wasn't a slab of compressed something-or-other was going to create a massive mess. Candles would be a disaster. Drinks came in bulbs—though there were specialty wine bulbs with glass bands for toasting!

Lorraine's dining room was the same kind of somewhat-soulless decorative as her office, with wood paneling—stamped with the gauntlet and six stars of the Kingdom of Adamant—running halfway up the bulkheads and solid wooden furniture bolted to the floor.

The meal was a slightly higher grade of compressed food than the default ration bars, but that was as far as Lorraine had gone for what was, at least theoretically, a working dinner with Alastair Devine.

Though, as the United Worlder had noted, they were missing Vigo Jarret. Lorraine's bodyguard was at his own dinner engagement, with her permission and gentle encouragement. His place was taken by Lieutenant Major Priskilla Blau, the Black woman who commanded First Section, her close detail.

Blau spent a lot of her time in administrative tasks, with Vigo usually taking direct command of whatever Guards were immediately attached to Lorraine. She was Palmer and Alvarez's boss, but wasn't part of the "super-close detail" who did things like follow her into bathrooms.

"Vigo is not permanently attached to my hip, much as it seems that way at times," Lorraine told Devine. "Priskilla here is his second-in-command. For this kind of discussion, she knows as much about the Guard's needs as he does."

And was equally capable of breaking Devine in half with one hand tied behind her back, if it came to that. The Fund bureaucrat was more than he pretended to be, but Lorraine's people had managed covert scans of the man.

He was augmented, and his augments were sophisticated enough that they weren't entirely certain how powerful they were. But no sophistication could make up for the different levels of pervasiveness between Devine's cybernetics and those of the Guard's close-combat specialists.

"I meant no disrespect, Major," Devine told Blau, bowing his head carefully as he settled next to the table.

They weren't bothering with chairs. The food, at least, was hot. Lorraine kept one foot locked to the floor herself as she grabbed the flat-packed food and tossed one over to each of her guests.

"Pepperoni pizza," she told them. *Pressed* pepperoni pizza, with additional vitamin supplements included in every component before it was baked and then flattened to make sure it held its shape.

"It's actually pretty good," Blau observed. "One of the stewards has an old family recipe they brought from Yoruba. Even with the vegetable-replacement powder, it turns out tasty."

"My experience is nothing tastes quite right in zero gravity," Devine said, but he took an unhesitating bite of the flatbread, followed by an appreciative sound.

"Might taste different in grav, but it's good," he conceded.

Lorraine followed suit. They worked their way through the food in surprisingly companionable silence, finally settling back—relaxing as much as the environment allowed—with the wine.

"Major Yildiz has set up the course you suggested," she told Devine. "Taking us past the Reserve. Showing off a bit, are we?"

"A bit," he agreed. "The United Worlds Navy has two hundred capital ships in commission and *another* three hundred in the Reserve. That stretches thinner than you might think when you're looking at a sphere over two hundred light-years across, holding a hundred star systems!

"Reminding us how big our ask is, then?" Blau said.

"It both is and isn't. Our ships are bigger and more advanced than anything the Black Regent has," Devine replied.

It wasn't even arrogance, Lorraine noted. He was just stating a fact—the fact that no power in the universe matched the nation he served.

"But while we have hundreds of capital ships, we only have so many in commission at any moment. We're signatories to the Asimov Convention, same as everyone else, and that limits the automation we can use.

"For some reason, it's a touch difficult to get people in the most advanced and comfortable polity in human space to sign on to put themselves in harm's way," Devine concluded with a chuckle. "So, we only have so many sets of hands. It's the people we want the Assembly to send out to Adamant that are the real stretch, in a lot of ways."

"I understood that the UWN did have some successes in high-capability non-sapient intelligences?" Blau asked. "The... sirs?"

"Yeah... the Command Intelligence Routines," Devine agreed slowly. "They have dramatically expanded the capabilities of our fleets, or so I'm told, but rumor has it they had some teething difficulties, too.

"Wasn't that long ago they quietly mothballed the entire first class of capital ships built with CIRs," he observed. "*Valkyrie*-class battlecruisers, I think. I'd have to check—but I think they're all at Calypso.

"Won't see those in Greenhall. They mostly keep the stuff they expect to reactivate for day-to-day operations there—destroyers, cruisers, carriers, the like. A few battleships, but the battlecruisers and battleships tend to stay in reserve once they go in."

Which made sense to Lorraine's naval officer brain. Destroyers, cruisers and carriers were the hands of the fleet, the ships doing the constabulary work of peacetime naval duties. They'd wear down and need refit more often. Having other ships of the same classes to put into active duty while the others were refitted would be valuable.

Expensive, more so than most nations could afford, but valuable.

"I'm surprised something bad enough for them to put the entire class in reserve wouldn't result in them being scrapped," Lorraine observed.

"I do not pretend to understand any military mind," Devine told her with a grin. "Let alone that of the United Worlds Navy. I know how to sell our mission to the Navy—they want as much training as they can manage. Sending half a dozen battleships off to the far end of the Bright Dream Cluster is about as good as you can get for a major logistics exercise."

"With a real fight at the other end," she murmured. "I hope we can convince my uncle to stand down, but even the most overwhelming force doesn't guarantee it.

"He *is* an Adamant. *Our Realm. Our House. Our Will. Adamant.*" She quoted the motto of her House to Devine.

"*Many are stubborn in pursuit of the path they have chosen, few in pursuit of the goal,* Nietzsche said," Devine quoted back. "I do not know, not truly, what your uncle's goal is. I *do* know that, faced with the might of the United Worlds Navy, he will yield or he will break.

"It falls to you and me to bring that might to bear," he concluded. "I know, Lorraine Adamant, that I can put you in front of the right people to make that happen. You have to say the right things—and part of that is understanding the sheer power at the command of the people you are speaking to."

"And their biases, prejudices, objectives and allegiances," Lorraine expanded. "I need, what, fifty percent plus one to get the mission in play?"

"Half plus one of quorum," he agreed. "But it's rare for the sixty-percent quorum rule to be relevant. The only time I know of that the quorum limit triggered in recent years was when too many reps abstained."

"How many am I working with?" she asked. "Over a thousand, right?"

"Fixed by law at twelve hundred, with the tiebreaker vote falling to the President." Devine snorted. "In over four hundred years, I don't think the President has *ever* cast a vote in the Grand Assembly. Each planet has one seat, the rest distributed based on population.

"You need six hundred votes to get your expedition, Lorraine," he warned. "Representatives are human, same as everyone else, so out of twelve hundred, you're going to lose a dozen at least to hangovers and colds on any given day. Bluntly... we'll lose more, because this isn't going to register as an important vote to a lot of people.

"But six hundred votes will get you what you need. And the same number in the hand of whoever speaks for your uncle will leave you stuck."

"I don't have many places to go at that point," she admitted. The Exodus Protocols had left her with enough money and resources that she could probably settle down on Earth as, well, yet another rich exile unable to go home.

That would leave her uncle victorious, though.

"I can't guarantee we'll get the votes, Lorraine," Devine warned. "I can put you in front of the Assembly. I'm about ninety percent sure that will get you a vote on sending the mission, no matter what your uncle or FBIT pulls.

"It's to your advantage that while you need at least a full battle squadron, you only need one—and the UWN has thirty-five. It's easy to talk down how little we have to put up to help you."

"All you're putting up yourself, Alastair, is words," Lorraine told him. "A battle squadron is... a lot more than that."

"You underestimate what words can cost on Earth," Devine warned, his tone sharper than she'd expected. "Yours or mine. Favors can be bought in expensive coin, Lorraine. You'll be digging for them in strange corners, I warn you—and once I've got you that audience, I'm not sure how much else I can do as your case manager."

She bowed her head in acknowledgement of his point.

"We shall see," she conceded. "I hope I don't have to talk to all twelve hundred Representatives one-on-one, though. If there's enough time for that between presentation and vote, well... this whole mess may take longer than my Kingdom can afford!"

"It will take what it will take," he said. "I'll help where I can; that's the responsibility I took on by volunteering as your case manager. So far, it's been a pleasant endeavor."

Blau coughed, as if to remind the two younger people she was in the room, and Lorraine chuckled.

"We strive not to be *too* large of a burden, Em Devine," she assured the bureaucrat.

FOURTEEN

Goldenrod might have lost the majority of her offensive weaponry, but the powerful sensor suite designed to support them remained. That gave Lorraine and her people a superbly detailed view of the Greenhall UWN Reserve Station as they passed by.

It helped make the point Devine had wanted to make, she concluded.

"I make it thirty-eight ships, orbiting under the guns of six fortresses," Paris reported, tossing icons into the shared feed.

"Sixteen cruisers, twelve destroyers, four carriers and six battle-ships," he concluded. "That's more cruisers than the entire RKAN."

And that fleet was just... sitting there. *Goldenrod*'s course took them a full five light-seconds away from the reserve station, heading toward the "artificial tachyo-quantum superposition" facility that also orbited Greenhall's seventh planet, the middling-sized gas giant named Red Erik for reasons Lorraine didn't quite follow.

The artificial wormhole was in the Greenhall–Red Erik Lagrange Two gravitational equilibrium zone. The reserve station orbited one of Red Erik's moons, making it straightforward enough to take a look as they approached the Charon Complex base.

"Any word from the wormhole?" Stephson asked.

"Nothing directed at us," Vince reported. "Our passenger has traded several encrypted communiques with the station, and no one has warned us off our approach, but nothing solid."

Lorraine left that to the frigate's Captain and focused her attention on the data Paris was giving her on the UWN reserve ships.

The battleships held her attention most. They were a fascinating design to her, telling in many ways of the thoughts of the United Worlds Navy. All six were *Perihelion*-class ships, stocky behemoths half a kilometer long. They bristled with guns, including the iconic octuple railgun banks almost unique to the UWN.

No other Navy Lorraine knew of had the power budget to build a railgun with a useful muzzle velocity for space combat. The United Worlds had not only designed a magnetic accelerator with a worthwhile muzzle velocity—classified but exceeding one percent of lightspeed—but they'd also engineered it down to a size they could mount in multiples.

Each of the *Perihelions* had both a dorsal and ventral octuple railgun bank, backed by dozens of missile launchers and beams. The information she had suggested the ships were rated for the same one hundred and twelve times lightspeed as the active ships of the UWN, making them almost thirty percent faster strategically than *Goldenrod*, let alone RKAN's battleships.

But.

They were also only built for a maximum of four gravities of acceleration. *Everything* in RKAN was designed to manage seven—generally regarded as the most the human part of the machinery could handle—even if they were never expected to actually use that full capability.

Humans limited the thrust any spaceship could use. With specialty suits, acceleration couches and such things as "flooding the cockpit with acceleration gel," combat shuttles could get up to twelve gravities. An RKAN *Monarch*-class ship might be outmassed six to four by a *Perihelion* and outgunned by an even-larger margin, but she could *outfly* the UWN ship.

Because *Perihelion*s weren't designed to chase or intercept. They were designed to find something the target had to defend and fly right at it, probably with assault transports in company.

Looking at the battleships, it was very clear that the United Worlds Navy did not expect to have to defend its own worlds against peer threats. The cruisers and destroyers were more maneuverable—and it said quite a bit that the active warships standing guard over the reserve were two cruisers and four destroyers of the same classes *in* the reserve.

Her link pinged her auditory nerve, and she opened the channel for Devine without breaking her train of thought.

"News?" she asked him silently.

"You should be receiving the course and transit codes from Greenhall Tachyo-Quantum Superposition Control in the next five minutes," the United Worlder told her, stumbling over the mouthful of words describing their contact. "Captain Stephson will have to provide sufficient remote access for Control to validate all offensive weapons are disabled."

He chuckled.

"We're approaching a station that costs more than most star systems' annual gross product," he observed. "For some reason, the folks in charge are nervous about somebody else's warship passing through—but my papers are in order and my authorization is impeccable."

"I'll let her know," Lorraine told him. "Anything else I should be keeping in mind?"

"Not on this end," he replied. "Once we're on the other side, well... Everything is up for grabs once we're in Sol."

LORRAINE REMAINED ON THE BRIDGE, pretending she wasn't exulting in the sensation of *down*. Even two weeks back in microgravity had been enough to set her teeth on edge. She doubted she was alone in *Goldenrod*'s crew in having had enough zero gee for a lifetime—which was something she needed to keep in mind.

Goldenrod was slower than any ship the UWN would send to Adamantine for her. She'd probably have to leave the frigate behind— and given the frigate's condition, she might be better served selling the ship and paying passage home for the crew on vessels large enough to have rotating sections.

It was a small price to pay to ease the way for the people who'd done so much for her already.

"TQS Control confirms we are on final approach," Vinci reported. "Transferring last details to Helm."

"They can say whatever they want about this not being a worm-hole," Yildiz replied as the course hit his console, "but the entry instructions are exactly the same."

It *looked* different, at least. A wormhole was invisible to the naked eye, though it was visible on most other sensors. The artificial gateway generated by the Charon Complex had an odd violet glow. It edged toward the limits of what the eye could naturally see—though Lorraine's eyesight was significantly expanded from the normal human range, which made it easier.

"We have pings on the perimeter beacons," Savege reported, the XO linked in from CIC via everyone's neural feeds. "I see twelve of them, marking a zone twenty-two kilometers across."

She paused.

"Inner beacon markers on the scopes as well. Inbound and outbound lanes are clearly marked."

"Let's not stray into the wrong one, Helm," Stephson said. "Not a big concern, I presume?"

"Fully delineated lanes entering and exiting the wormhole zone, no crossover," Yildiz confirmed. "We are third in the queue to enter."

"And let's keep a careful eye on number two," Paris said grimly from tactical. "Right ahead of us. FBIT freighter—no official armament, but..."

Lorraine hadn't been paying much attention to the civilian shipping around them—the two UWN battlecruisers and their escorts were the only ships she'd even glanced at—and she mentally kicked herself for that now.

The data on the FBIT ship flickered across her feed, and she could feel Jarret reviewing the data as well. That her bodyguard was only checking on the potential enemy ship now made her feel better.

This mess required a different kind of paranoia from their usual arrangement.

Iridium Dawn was a bulk freighter, seven hundred meters long and almost ten million tons. The public registry listed her as capable of a hundred and four times the speed of light and completely unarmed.

Her last port of call was listed as Greenhall itself. Anything older wasn't available to Lorraine, so she could have come from anywhere. It was even possible that the freighter had been in the Bright Dream Cluster—though not likely.

From what she was told, the commission responsible for enforcing the UW's export laws was likely to look poorly on a company that let a modern translight drive fall into pirate hands. It would be a brave and foolish company that let an unarmed freighter with that kind of drive leave the UW.

Dawn's Captain probably had no idea of what was going on between their company and Lorraine's Kingdom. They were probably no threat to *Goldenrod*.

Probably.

"First ship has transited. *Iridium Dawn* is receiving her final go-ahead, and we have orders to enter the lane," Vinci reported. "Helm, do you have everything?"

"I do," Yildiz confirmed. "*Dawn* will hit the event horizon in two minutes. We're coming in behind her at one kilometer per second, expecting entry in five minutes, fifteen seconds."

Lorraine's console was easily able to give her both a visual and a full sensor view of *Iridium Dawn*'s approach to the tachyo-quantum superposition. The freighter's velocity might be a crawl by the standards of interplanetary travel, but it was fast enough that she only moved in front of the violet-tinged void in the moments before she transited.

For a few moments, purple light highlighted the spacegoing brick of the bulk freighter. Then there was a moment where even Lorraine's genetically augmented vision saw nothing different but every scanner aboard *Goldenrod* went crazy—and then the freighter was gone.

To the naked eye, it was there and then it was gone. Even the sensors only detected spikes of various strange forms of energy and a surge of tachyon energy. There was no sign that ten million tons of freighter had ever been there.

"We have our final approach vector," Yildiz reported, *Goldenrod*'s course—a gentle loop letting them sustain half a gravity of acceleration while maintaining velocity—adjusting into a straight line.

"Thrust cutting... now."

Lorraine managed not to join the involuntary grumble through the frigate's bridge as microgravity returned.

"Transit in sixty seconds."

The purple field of the superposition filled the main display now. The bulk of the TQS station, hardly a small platform, shrank into insignificance next to the volume of space it manipulated.

The bridge was silent, everyone waiting and watching as distance and time alike melted away.

"Ten seconds," Yildiz said. "All systems green. Transiting.... Now."

A wave of ultraviolet rippled through the bridge. That was different—a wormhole transit felt the same as any translight journey inside the ship.

"Will this—"

The tint vanished.

"—pass?" Stephson finished wryly. "How long to complete the transit?"

"Per the information we were given, about seventeen minutes," Yildiz reported.

"Well." *Goldenrod*'s Captain stretched theatrically. "I see no reason to go anywhere just yet, then; does anyone else?"

FIFTEEN

Sol.

One word. One *syllable*. One star.

The star. *The* Solar System, the origin point of all humanity. All technology. All civilization as Lorraine or any human knew it. Over four hundred years since the first translight ships had left the home system, but something about being *there* was overwhelming to Lorraine.

Even if the star itself was so far away from the Charon Complex as to be merely a bright dot in the distance. The Complex orbited the dual dwarf planets in the outreaches of the system, presumably built in some degree of secrecy.

Now, though, three artificial wormholes converged in the once-half-forgotten reaches of the Solar System, with all of the traffic that entailed.

Lorraine wasn't even part of the conversation between Stephson, Yildiz and Vinci as Coms and Helm worked with Charon Traffic Control to guide the frigate through the crowd. During their approach to the Greenhall end, they'd seen a ship transit, on average, every ten minutes.

It turned out Greenhall was the Charon Complex's quiet terminus. Between the three wormholes, the numbers Lorraine was seeing suggested a ship entering or exiting the Solar System once a minute.

Each ship carried a data packet from the control station at the departing end, allowing the Complex to anticipate arrivals, but that only went so far when ships just appeared out of nothingness.

"We have our course," Stephson finally said in her link to Lorraine and Jarret. "About an hour sublight, then we have been given a four-minute translight hop that was calculated for us."

"Is that safe?" Jarret asked before Lorraine could.

"I don't *like* it, so Yildiz is quadruple-checking their angles and numbers," the Captain agreed. "But it sounds like even translight around here needs traffic control. I mean, we've got, what, a thousand ships around the Complex alone?"

Lorraine could hear the awe in Stephson's voice. Bastion was the capital planet of the Kingdom of Adamant, with a population of over four billion human beings and ruling a state of five star systems and almost twenty billion people.

On its *busiest* days, there were about three hundred starships in the region around Bastion. Neither Pluto nor Charon were even *inhabited*. The permanent population of the region was in space stations of the Charon Complex, a glittering array of rings clearly undergoing rapid expansion.

"Our translight jump doesn't bring us all that close to Earth," Stephson continued. "I suspect that Earth Traffic Control will shoot down anyone emerging within three light-seconds of the homeworld.

"Our emergence is at four. So, even with the translight hop, we're looking at about eight hours before we're..." Despite her competence, professionalism and everything *else* calling for the Captain to be unimpressed, she paused and had to swallow.

"We'll be in orbit of Earth in approximately eight hours," she repeated. "I suggest you go rest, Pentarch. You can see everything from your quarters and, well...

"You're going to need to be well rested."

"YOUR HIGHNESS, the boy is here. Should I send him in?"

For a few amusing seconds, Lorraine considered pointing out to Judy Alvarez that referring to the case manager whose support they needed as *the boy* was probably unwise. Since Devine couldn't *hear* the bodyguard's silent message, it was probably fine.

He'd probably find it funny himself, for that matter.

"Yeah, send him in," Lorraine instructed.

She left the screens up above her desk, showing the organized chaos of shipping around the Pluto-Charon dual planet. The entire Solar System spread out around her, but they were only really close enough to see life at the Charon Complex.

"Welcome to Sol," Devine told her, taking the chair across her desk without asking. "Feels weird to be back here."

"Wouldn't that be the goal? Get a nice, cushy job in the home system?" she asked.

"There are nice, cushy jobs in places that still call for real work," he replied. "Anything here in Sol? It's a desk job for someone like me. And that's what I'm trying to escape."

"I remember," Lorraine conceded. Billions upon billions of people lived and worked in the Solar System, with almost all of the planets home to massive permanent populations in one type of habitat or another.

She imagined there were some very busy negotiators keeping all of that moving, but they wouldn't technically be *diplomats*. There probably weren't many covert ops specialists needed in the system, either—though given the snake pit reputation of Solar politics...

"Anything in particular you're after?" she asked.

"I've bounced an updated communique to my superiors, but I won't hear back until after the translight hop," he admitted. "I'm as much in limbo right now as anyone else aboard the ship. Figured I'd check in and see if you had any questions yourself."

"Mostly being overwhelmed by the sheer scale of it all," she said.

"The Complex alone is busier than the Kingdom's capital. I never really thought of myself as *provincial*, but here…"

"The home, the heart, the throne," Devine murmured. "Be it ever so humble, there's no place like home… and Earth is home to us all, no matter how many centuries it's been since our parents left.

"Walking the homeworld… It feels right in a way you can't explain to someone who hasn't been there," he told her. "You'll see soon enough."

"Where were you, on Earth?"

"Mostly, the governance centers around Kilimanjaro," he admitted. "Which is where we'll be spending most of our time. Hotter than home, for me, but still… *right.*"

He grinned at Lorraine.

"You worry about feeling provincial, but everything I've seen says Adamantine is a culturally and economically sophisticated capital system, if somewhat technologically behind and astrographically isolated."

Every so often, the only thing keeping Devine from being utterly offensive was the sheer earnestness with which he tried to compliment things before he added the qualifiers.

"*I*, on the other hand," he continued, "come from the Madagastar System."

Lorraine didn't know that name—and it didn't even show up on her link's database at first glance.

"You haven't heard of it, trust me," Devine assured her. "Firstly, two hundred light-years in the wrong direction! Farthest frontier of the opposite side of the United Worlds. A brand-new colony, barely eighty years old, that has their one mandated Representative in the Grand Assembly and basically zero political relevance to anybody otherwise.

"I, Your Highness, was most definitely a provincial when I made it to university in Epsilon Eridani, and I hadn't shaken the mud from my shoes when the… the Service brought me to Earth."

He hadn't stumbled over talking about the Diplomatic Service in a while, Lorraine realized. Talking about the past made the lie stick more, she supposed.

"How'd you get to Eridani from Madagastar, then?" she asked.

"Special recruitment program," he admitted. "The various government bureaucracies and agencies find it useful to recruit from more isolated or... well, backward member systems. They get people with a rougher edge to them than they get from the central systems *and* people they think will get along better past the wormholes."

"That's some interesting... assumptions," she murmured.

"Given the way the diaspora tends to shift along the wormholes, there are very few first-order cluster systems as new and unrefined as Madagastar," Devine agreed. "I'd have felt just as provincial arriving in Fortuna as I did in Eridani without my years of training.

"But there is a value to the program, if only to tie those frontier worlds more tightly to the nation," he continued. "I haven't been home since leaving, though. I joined the Service and... well... Douglas MacArthur said, *No man is entitled to the blessings of freedom unless he be vigilant in its preservation.*

"That recruitment program gave me a home and a purpose. I can't say Madagastar ever gave me either of those!"

Lorraine could see a few values to that recruitment program. Not least, she suspected, it would produce agents who were nearly fanatical in their dedication to the United Worlds. Agents who would do whatever was asked of them.

Not the type of asset you put behind a desk. She didn't know what had gone down in Fortuna, but she had to figure Devine's superiors had been intentionally putting him permanently on ice.

"I was born with both of those, I suppose," she told him. "From the moment I was old enough to understand what it meant, I was groomed to lead and serve. It was always likely that my siblings would have enough children soon enough to remove me from the List before my mother retired, but dynasties—even complicated ones like House Adamant—prepare for the unexpected.

"I was *always* going to be a Pentarch. I might never stand for the election, but from the day I turned eighteen years old, the chance was there. Yet we weren't allowed to let our lives go to waste, either.

"My eldest brother was a diplomat. My older sister entered the civil service as an architect. My younger brother was an Army officer and I joined the Navy." She met Devine's gaze and smiled.

"*Purpose* was never in question for me," she admitted. "Challenged, yes, but present."

This man, however intriguing he might be, didn't need to know that she'd been about to abdicate the Pentarchy when her mother died. Another three months and her uncle would have been Fourth Pentarch again.

Not that it would change whatever had driven him to madness. Her nieces were twins, after all. Fourth Pentarch or Fifth, he'd have fallen off the list when they turned eighteen—in *seventeen years*.

"It's a weird concept to me," Devine replied. "It's hard to pretend there aren't family dynasties in politics and money in the United Worlds, but power flows from the voter. No one is guaranteed anything."

"I was only guaranteed responsibility," Lorraine said. "And raised to meet it. *Charged* to meet it. The United Worlds gave you purpose as an adult. The Kingdom of Adamant gave me purpose from the moment I was old enough to understand what purpose *was*, Alastair.

"That led me to the uniform. To this ship. To here. And..." She gestured toward a planet, still so far away she could only locate it via her link. "To Earth. To the Grand Assembly and a presentation that should terrify anyone."

"A date with destiny, one might say," he agreed. "I'll see you to the Assembly safely, Lorraine. You have my word, as well as my duty. You'll get your ten minutes on the floor. I can't promise more than that, but I can promise that."

"I know and I appreciate it," she assured him. "We got lucky finding you, I think."

"I certainly put quite a bit of effort into making it happen, I have to admit," he told her. "I have more access to information out of the Bright Dream Cluster than most, and I knew you were coming.

"I didn't count on you knowing what I was able to do for you better than I did, but I made sure I was the manager on duty when you walked in." He grinned. "I also didn't count on you being quite so personable. I had some... uhh... stereotyped images of what a princess was going to be."

"I'm pleased to have disappointed those, I promise," Lorraine said drily.

"Once we're on Earth, I expect you'll be put up in the Dignitaries Complex in Kilimanjaro," he told her. "I'll still be your case manager and we'll remain in communication.

"If you have time, there are many fascinating places to visit around there. There was a gorgeous restaurant up near the old mass-driver complex with a view of four of the Six Cities." He paused, as if preparing to take a dive, then charged on forward.

"If you're willing, I'd like to take you up there," he said in a rush.

Lorraine smiled. It was mostly a real smile, touched by both the idea and his sudden moment of awkwardness. It was also, partially, the trained buy-time-to-think smile of a diplomat.

If he *wasn't* asking her on a date, it was close enough to make no difference. Either way, she was interested—but it was also a security nightmare in many ways.

On the other hand, what force in the universe was going to come after a United Worlds covert ops agent inside the Six Cities of Kilimanjaro from which the entire diaspora had begun and from where the Grand Assembly ruled?

"I would be delighted, Alastair," she told him.

SIXTEEN

Vigo Jarret was neither surprised by the date his charge had set up nor hypocritical enough to oppose it. He was being cautious on a *security* level about his relationship with Rose Cortez, but he also hadn't been spending nights in his own quarters the last few days.

He doubted Alastair Devine knew the situation around Lorraine's security well enough to realize that Vigo's terse message asking for all the information he could provide on the restaurant was something close to approval. The man was security-adjacent enough to know that it wasn't Vigo shutting the affair down.

"Orbital Traffic Control has cleared us to deploy the shuttle," Savege's voice said in his ear. "I have eyes on your escort; linking you through now."

Vigo wasn't going to let anyone *other* than him fly Lorraine down into the governing centers of the United Worlds. So, he was in the pilot seat, with Juturna Deering in the copilot's seat.

His senior pilot took being relegated to the side seat with grace and competence, which also meant that she had the feed on their "escort" linked to his displays and implants before he did.

Four Chevalier spaceplanes orbited ten kilometers behind *Gold-*

enrod. They weren't much of a threat to the frigate herself—*that* task was left to the, oh, thirty-six battleships distributed through geostationary orbits of the planet—but their lasers and short-range missiles would make a mess of Vigo's Midas.

Or, more likely, anything that tried to tangle with him. Unlike the Midas's extremely modular design, the Chevaliers were dedicated interceptors as at home in atmosphere as in the void. In truly open space, Vigo knew he could have taken all four with a properly equipped combat shuttle—and that was taking into account the superiority of the technology available to United Worlds Assembly Security.

"Adamant-Sol-One, this is UWAS Flight Six-Delta," his com pinged. "Standing by."

"This is AS-One," Vigo replied. "Charge is onboard; we are clearing *Goldenrod* in... fifteen seconds from mark. And... Mark."

A dozen half-automated systems set to work around him, opening airlock doors and guiding the shuttle outward. Most of the process to leave the frigate was run by computers—and everything in orbit of the homeworld was under the control of one synthetic intelligence or another.

"We have you on scope, Adamant-Sol-One," the UWAS pilot replied. "Relaying the link from Högvakten. Stand by."

The last thing Vigo really wanted to do was surrender control of his shuttle to someone else, even if that someone else was a synthetic intelligence named for the old Swedish Royal Guard on Earth and tasked with the security of the United Worlds Grand Assembly.

"I have the link," a smooth, cultured voice said in his auditory nerve. "Major Jarret. I recognize your overrides and am leaving them in place.

"So long as you provide no threat to my charges, I will make certain there are no threats to yours. Are we in agreement?"

Vigo chuckled aloud, shaking his head as Deering gave him a questioning look.

"Message received and understood, Högvakten," he confirmed. "I have no desire to cause trouble, but I must be able to act."

"I understand completely, Major Jarret," Högvakten said. "I am certain there are hardware cut-outs I could not disable remotely regardless. Understanding clears more paths than deception."

"I have the course down to Kilimanjaro loaded," Vigo told the SI. "I'll keep my hands on the controls, just in case. You understand."

"I do. And you have the word and the honor of United Worlds Assembly Security, Major Jarret, that if you need to use those controls, Colonel Lapointe and Flight Six-Delta will already be dead." There was a pause—only for drama, coming from an SI with the resources of the Grand Assembly's security force behind it.

"And probably at least one battleship, for that matter. It will take a *lot* to get at the Pentarch. I swear this."

MOUNT KILIMANJARO ROSE like Olympus above the Serengeti, the sprawling Six Cities a glittering skirt around the almost-untouched magnificence of her upper slopes. A single black line ran up the south side of the ancient volcano, deceptively small as the shuttle dropped below ten thousand meters, marking the long-obsolete Interstellar Orbital Cargo Accelerator Line.

"Course takes us into the north side of Moshi, the southern city," Deering told Vigo. "The Dignitaries Complex is on the north end of the metroplex, almost as high up the slopes as anything appears to be built."

"The SI has us in hand," he replied. "I'm keeping an eye on everything, but with UWAS fighters in formation and Högvakten watching over us, I am cautiously optimistic."

Enough to only keep ninety percent of his attention watching for threats and allow ten percent to take in the sight below him. The dormant volcano itself rose from the girdle of modern city around her, with a mix of green and brown spreading across the savannah and hills around the cities.

The small villages and townships of the Tanzania–Kenya border had long ago been subsumed. First by the industrial and corporate centers of Interstellar Orbital, the corporation that had built and profited from having the first truly cheap access to space—and then by the administration of the spaceborne diaspora and the political union that followed.

The fight to keep the mountain itself relatively clean had, from what Vigo understood, been long and nasty. Interstellar Orbital had the distinction of being one of the first interstellar megacorps to exist... and the first interstellar megacorp to end up being completely chopped apart by political action and debtors.

But voluntarily or not, everything above the first few hundred meters of Kilimanjaro was free of development except that critical for the Line itself. Moshi had expanded toward and up the mountain, but the preservation zone marked a sharp ending.

And the Dignitaries Complex wasn't just near that line. It was a sub-city in its own right that went right up to the line, a series of luxury apartment towers along the city limit.

Their destination was on top of the tallest tower—still only twenty-five floors—where a set of guiding lights surrounded a landing pad. The lights, Vigo noted, also helped conceal the antiaircraft missile launchers if someone didn't know what they were looking for.

"Two minutes to touchdown," he told his passengers—Lorraine herself and a close detail. Devine had taken his own spacecraft to his own destinations.

"Any idea where we move from here?" she asked.

"You know as much as I do," he admitted.

"We have a set of rooms waiting for us that I'm sure you're going to want to scrub from floor to ceiling," his Pentarch told him. "But then we are waiting on someone—Devine, I think—to get us a schedule.

"When he left, he didn't have a timeline for my presentation. I'm hoping he'll know soon."

"Until then, we have quarters and security courtesy of the Grand Assembly?"

"Exactly. And you know how far to trust the Assembly," she said.

Vigo chuckled and didn't even answer.

The home of humankind was also the beating political heart of the largest nation in human history. Humans were humans, no matter where they went or how much molecular circuitry they installed.

That political heart was going to be a nest of vipers. And vipers were perfectly fine animals, in his experience, so long as you knew exactly what you were dealing with and were careful.

Which probably made them a terrible metaphor for politicians.

SEVENTEEN

Calypso's light gleamed across the ship. Several sensors picked up a solar flare on the surface of the massive star, severe enough to raise warnings.

Nothing received those warnings. Adjustments that could have been made to minimize damage weren't made, and a wave of radiation swept over the ship. A few arrays sparked and failed. More warnings were pinged into the main system.

Only silence answered them.

The ship slept.

Proximity sensors triggered similarly unheard warnings as a pair of shuttles approached in the wake of the storm, drones deploying with jets and magnetic feet to sweep the sharp-edged warship's hull.

Computers on the shuttles collated the reports, assembling the necessary parts lists and firing them back to the central depots. The human pilots paid almost no attention to the whole process. Their job was to get the drones to the starships and wait for a signal telling them to move to the next one.

They knew what the drones were doing, but they didn't worry about it. Amidst the rows of sleeping warships, the radiation storm was the most excitement anyone had seen in years. Operating ships were more vulnerable, but they could also adapt.

None of the repairs needed by the ship or her siblings were large enough to require further approval. The pilots glanced at the parts list and sent it on, only registering that they'd have to come back with different drone squadrons the next day.

The ship might sleep, but her purpose endured.

The United Worlds Navy Reserve had to be *ready*, after all.

EIGHTEEN

Kilimanjaro's clock was just enough different from the Universal Time Code used aboard starships to leave Lorraine slightly off schedule. By her usual clock, midnight local time was only around nine in the evening.

That left her standing on the balcony of her loaned apartment, looking up at the mountainside through the faint glimmer of a powerful protective force screen. Light pollution from the Six Cities wiped out her ability to see the stars—but she wouldn't have been able to see Adamantine or any of her Kingdom's six systems from there.

She was over six hundred light-years from home, delivered to the homeworld of all humanity by a combination of powerful technologies and the esoteric oddities of the universe. Just out of sight around the curve of the mountain was the magnetic accelerator that had delivered key systems for the colony ships of the original diaspora—though it had been decommissioned in favor of the Pacific and Atlantic Elevators by the time Alexander Adamant had built *his* colony fleet.

The mountain was overlaid with another one in her mind, though she'd only seen that mountain in video in the six months since leaving home. The Electrum Planetary Defense Center was on the north end of Mithral, her home's southern continent. It wasn't PDC Mithral, where her brother had dug in, but it was part of his "rebellion."

And, when the most-recent news had left Adamantine, forces led by the Royal Adamantine Marine Corps had been assaulting that mountain. RAMC was the junior service of the Kingdom's four, but it seemed to be a ground force that Benjamin Adamant trusted.

In that news, less than five months old, thanks to the greater speed of news couriers, the Royal Kingdom of Adamant Army had thrown the assault back. Reading between the lines of the reports, at least three armored divisions—tank and power-armor heavy units easily numbering ten thousand soldiers—had effectively ceased to exist.

"You're looking lost in despair," Jarret said softly as her bodyguard joined her. "The news from home?"

"Yeah. The way it gets packaged up and arrives in spurts can be... frustrating," she admitted. "Three-day-long battle and we only hear about it when it's over. When thirty thousand people are dead."

He nodded as he stepped into her view, leaning against the balcony to study the dark mountain with her.

"Our people are pretty damn good at extracting the wounded and treating them," he pointed out. "Three divisions out of action would never mean every trooper in them was dead. On the other hand... there's no info on our loyalists' losses."

The news reporters weren't even quite sure what to *call* the sides of the civil war in the feeds Lorraine was getting. She suspected there was some pressure to call Nikola's troops *rebels*, but the reports had mostly avoided that.

"I don't like that there's nothing from Nikola's people," she admitted.

"Did you catch their wording on that?" Jarret asked. "*We regret we are unable to show footage from the defenders of Electrum.* Not that they were unable to *get* that footage. That they couldn't show it.

"Phrasing can be a deadly weapon, and I don't think the Black Regent realizes how much the censorship he's imposing on the news is hurting him. It's not a battlefield he knows, I don't think. He's keeping things under wraps, controlling what leaves the system especially, but there is a price to be paid for that."

"Not one that's going to save Nikola," Lorraine murmured. "Best guess is he has, what, two corps? Eight to ten divisions? Where Benjamin can, sooner or later, muster the entire RKAA."

"And already lost a battleship pushing the perimeters of the PDCs," her bodyguard reminded her. "He still thinks like a Navy officer. It's costing him."

"So long as he has the Cabinet and the throne, it's a price he can pay."

"Hence our whole mission here. Exodus Protocols go hand in hand with the Masada Protocols, Lorraine," Jarret reminded her. "We go for help. Your brother *survives* and makes Benjamin regret ever moving against the Pentarchy."

"Thirty thousand dead," Lorraine repeated. As he'd said, there were problems with that estimate, but it wasn't an unreasonable number. "And it's just getting started."

"Fortuna's civil war is on my mind," he admitted. "Your boyfriend was there, made me dig up the data. Somewhere close to a hundred *million* dead—thirty million just in the fighting for and siege of the Fortunate City.

"We don't think of modern civilization as suffering from plague and starvation, but cut a place off hard enough and *modern* starts dying real fast," Jarret said grimly. "I know Nikola. He's going to do everything in his damn power to keep the fighting away from civilian centers—which means he's going to lose the continent too damn quickly.

"By now? Electrum might still be holding out. Mithral itself *is*—I don't think Benjamin can find the guns and the bodies to take the planetary command center in less than a couple of *years*.

"But Nikola has likely given up the cities and the countryside alike. A lot of innocent people will live because of that choice, but it pushes him and his people back into holes in the ground with no way out."

Jarret's tone wasn't judgmental, but Lorraine could pick up his point.

"You think he should fight like that? Get innocents killed?" she demanded.

"No. I don't think he could and be himself—any more than you could," her Guard admitted. "But even with everything he's done, I suspect Benjamin Adamant would hesitate to burn a city out. Urban fighting is hell, but it could buy Nikola time. Time I suspect he's giving up to save lives."

"We serve the Kingdom, not the other way around," Lorraine countered. "It's better, I think, for us to fail and Benjamin to win than for us to spend a hundred million innocent lives trying to stop him."

"That is a weakness he can use against you," Jarret warned. "One he *will* use against you."

"That's why we came here. Because we need enough over-whelming force to make him stand down without a fight," she insisted.

"And if the UWN won't give you that? If an ugly war is the only way to protect the traditions and constitution? To reclaim your mother's throne?"

Lorraine snorted.

"You're testing me," she accused.

"Yes."

"I don't know," she admitted. "I know I'm not in this for the throne, Vigo. I'm in this to protect the institutions of our democracy and monarchy. I don't want—I *never* wanted—my mother's throne."

"Then why fight?"

She turned to glare at him and he shrugged.

"You're going to walk into the Grand Assembly of the United Worlds and ask them to spend blood and gold on your behalf," he told her. "You *must* know the answer to that question."

"I fight because that man murdered my family," Lorraine said flatly. "And I fight because our tradition and law are clear: the Pentarchs are of House Adamant, yes, but it is the *people* of the Kingdom from which the *King's* power and legitimacy are born.

"My uncle would steal that from them. He would rule as Regent and avoid the election that should define any King. I cannot let that happen. I want justice, yes. Revenge, even. But I am *fighting* for the choices of my people."

"Good." Jarret chuckled. "Keep that fierceness, Lorraine. You're going to need it."

LORRAINE WASN'T sure where breakfast came from. One of the Adamant Guards might have made it, or it might have been brought up by the staff of the resort-like tower containing the apartment.

Either way, she was confident the Guards had checked it for everything by the time she blearily took a seat at the table. Jarret was halfway through a stack of pancakes several inches thick, and an equally impressive tower of carbohydrates was waiting for her.

Her augments were mostly genetic, compared to the cybernetics her Guards had, but both were best fueled by large amounts of protein and sugar.

"Unsurprisingly, the people taking care of guests of the Grand Assembly have good food," Jarret told her after swallowing. "There's a decent kitchen attached to the suite that we'll dig into tomorrow."

Lorraine nodded as she dug into her own breakfast. She had full "skills training" on cooking and the use of a kitchen, but hadn't actually cooked enough in her life to know if she even liked doing it. As both a royal scion—basically a permanent student—and then a naval officer, there had always been someone arranging food to let her focus on the tasks in front of her.

Speaking of...

"Any word from Devine?" she asked. "Or anyone else, for that matter?"

She wouldn't object to going back to sleep. She'd survive the mess the three-hour offset had made of her night's rest—she'd done worse things to her sleep schedule in recent memory—but a short nap would fix a lot of things.

"Not ye—"

"Guest at the building entrance," Sergeant Merle interrupted on their shared network. "It's Devine. Should I authorize him up?"

Two seconds of checking confirmed that Harold Merle was ensconced in the security room of their "suite"—a collection of rooms that could have been an entire wing of a conventional hotel, with space for Lorraine, her bodyguards, and the staff she didn't have—and linked to the building's security systems.

"Send him up," Lorraine ordered. "He'll survive watching me eat."

She'd already made her way through two entire pancakes, and her bodyguard chuckled at her.

"Pajamas and inhaling pancakes," Jarret observed. "If he's still interested in you after this, he really is smitten."

Lorraine gave her bodyguard a scathing look, one that didn't even require wordless accompaniment through the link. Her "pajamas" were the same shipsuits she'd been wearing aboard *Goldenrod*. On a spaceship, the safety garment was so fundamental to most outfits, there was no point in wearing clothes over it to sleep.

It did, however, make for quite the contrast with Alastair Devine when Palmer escorted him into the room a few minutes later. He'd clearly seen a barber and probably a style consultant in the twelve hours since he'd left Lorraine's ship.

His hair had been cut asymmetrically. The left side of his head had been smoothed, along a neat line starting just above his jaw, but the right side had been cut short, above his ear. The whole affair hung in a sufficiently odd array to Lorraine's gaze that she figured it had to be the local style for mid-length hair.

The asymmetry carried down into his jacket, a lapel-less black blazer whose front piece overlapped far enough to close at the hip. It was piped in gold, without visible closings, and fitted tightly to his athletic frame.

The same black-with-gold-piping color schema continued on to the black slacks, also cut tightly enough to let Lorraine appreciate the man's athleticism.

"Major Jarret, Pentarch Lorraine," Devine greeted them with a very minimal bow. "I apologize for interrupting your breakfast; I wasn't sure what schedule you were running on."

"Well, without any particular appointments coming up, we were taking the morning slowly," Lorraine replied. "Would you like some pancakes, Alastair?"

"I'll take a coffee, but I think I might be murdered if I got syrup on this jacket," he admitted with a wry grin. "By *me*, to be clear. The head office handed me a consultant and a budget and told said consultant to, and I quote, *make him presentable for the Assembly*."

"That quickly?" she asked.

"That quickly," he confirmed. "If you can manage it, I've set an appointment with Jayme for you at twelve hundred hours. That'll give them and you a bit of time to sort out clothes and hair and everything, but not long."

Lorraine checked the local time. Depending on where this "Jayme" was, that was probably doable, but it was going to be tight.

"I'm presenting *today*?" she asked, her brain catching up with the schedule.

"Sixteen hundred hours," Devine said grimly. "I was expecting at least two days, but here we are. Are you ready?"

"If you've got a style consultant on call, that's my only real concern," she admitted. "I've had my presentation written for two months."

She'd edited it as she spent time in United Worlds space and had hoped to get a feel for the Six Cities in advance of actually speaking to the Assembly, but she was as ready as she could be.

"Okay." He exhaled and nodded firmly. "You have fifteen minutes to speak, theoretically without interruption but don't count on it. Questions will follow. That could be five minutes or forty-five, but I doubt the Speaker will let it run over forty-five.

"They *won't* vote today. Depending on the games FBIT is playing, someone may try and force something, but tradition is a powerful force, and tradition says the Assembly *always* sleeps on matters."

"So, we'll have time to make quieter pitches, the party round?" Lorraine guessed.

"Exactly. I don't have anything sorted out yet, but Head Office lent me an assistant as well as assigning me Jayme, so we may or may not have an event this evening. We will *definitely* have events for you tomorrow."

"What kind of escort does she get to bring to these events?" Jarret asked.

Devine glanced over at the bodyguard.

"Jayme will also take you in hand," he warned the older man. "The kind of events we're poking at will allow security and a plus-one. Most likely, *in* the party will be you and me, but we'll bring at least two more of your Guards with us to join the waiting crowd of escorts."

That kind of party. Lorraine knew the type.

It might *look* fancy and fun, but for her? That type of party had only ever been work—and that wasn't going to change there!

NINETEEN

"Representatives of the Grand Assembly of the United Worlds, I introduce Her Royal Highness, Lieutenant Commander Lorraine Alexis Elouise Nala Adamant, Second Pentarch of the Star Kingdom of Adamant."

The voice echoed in the elevator-like shaft as Lorraine descended into the Great Hall of the Grand Assembly. She stood at a podium on a moving platform, with Vigo Jarret and Alastair Devine seated behind her.

There'd been very little time on Earth to prepare for this, and the only saving grace was that Devine's style consultant, Jayme, appeared to be a genius. The skirt-suit they'd put together for her was in an intentionally archaic cut, but Jayme had drawn on the colors and patterns to create the asymmetry that seemed to be in fashion on Earth.

The whole outfit was in the blue, gray and silver of House Adamant's colors. The combination of the colors, the small flag subtly worked into her left shoulder—both concealed and accentuated, somehow, by the asymmetry of the entire outfit—all created the image of the very modern politician who was *also* an exotic princess of a foreign realm.

Lorraine didn't know if that was going to work for her audience yet. She couldn't even see who was announcing her, let alone the Assembly Representatives themselves, until the platform reached near the end of its descent. One moment, she was surrounded by smooth stone walls overlaid with holographic paintings of the early-diaspora ships and first landings. The next, the walls gave way to open space and she had a sudden moment of deep relief that she wasn't afraid of heights.

Lorraine knew that the platform had gone up before descending, but she suspected the Great Hall was also dug deep into the side of Kilimanjaro. Her platform was descending out of the roof of a circular chamber easily two hundred meters high.

The walls of the chamber held what she guessed to be at least twelve hundred similar mobile platforms, though the permanent emplacements were more decorative, each fronted with the flag of their home system.

Her link had access to the Great Hall's systems. Glancing at any given pod told her who was seated there, along with which star system and planet they represented. Twelve hundred human beings whose combined word dominated human space.

And now, Lorraine Adamant stood in the middle of them. Part of her wanted to blink at the lights as she surveyed her audience, but the truth was that the lighting and sound design of the Great Hall was *perfect*. Her platform slowly rotated, letting all of the Representatives see her face in turn as she began to speak.

"Thank you for receiving me, Representatives," she told them. "I am here to ask for the help of the United Worlds, as promised at the Stability Convention of twenty-three-sixty-five in the Tau Ceti System.

"My nation, the Kingdom of Adamant, has been subject to a military coup. My uncle—"

"Objection!" A red light flashed on one of the platforms.

Even if Lorraine hadn't been warned against the possibility of interruption, she'd spent countless hours as a teenage page in the Short and Long Houses of the Adamant Parliament. She wasn't particularly surprised and immediately used her link to locate the Speaker.

Speaker Bartholomew Melle Ó hEaghra wore a very similar asymmetric suit to Devine, but the Senior Representative for Alpha Centauri and designated referee of this space would never have dared the level of tightness the SCF official had gone for.

Lorraine wasn't so foolish as to let the man's heavyset face, sweaty appearance, or thinning desperately managed hair deceive her. Ó hEaghra stood third in the line of succession for the Presidency of the United Worlds and he ran the Great Hall with an iron hand.

"On what grounds?" Ó hEaghra asked the speaker—sole Representative of a star system far from the Bright Dream Cluster or the wormhole linking to it, Lorraine noted.

"Em Adamant has no standing to speak for the Kingdom of Adamant," the Representative said loudly. "I checked the news reports, same as anyone. The elected Prime Minister and Cabinet remain and have clearly not authorized this mission."

"Em Vanaga, you have full access to review Em Adamant's papers," Ó hEaghra told the man. "She *is* a fully authorized plenipotentiary envoy of the Kingdom of Adamant. As for the complexities of this apparent coup, that... is for Em Adamant to explain. Which she cannot do if she does not speak.

"Objection overruled," he declared. "Continue, Your Highness."

"Thank you, Speaker, Representatives," Lorraine said swiftly.

"As I said, my Kingdom has been victim of a coup at the hands of Fleet Admiral Benjamin Adamant, my uncle," she continued grimly. "While he has the cooperation of Prime Minister Dakila Bayer, I have grounds to believe that both the Cabinet and the rest of our Parliament are cooperating either in ignorance of his murders or under threat."

Not all. She wasn't that foolish. But she knew her countrymen well enough to know that the Black Regent's control couldn't be as solid as it seemed in the news reports.

"My older brother, Nikola Adamant, holds the line on the southern continent of our capital while troops loyal to my uncle storm cities and fortifications alike," she continued. "The Royal Election, that our law charges to be begun almost immediately after the death of a King, has been postponed indefinitely.

"My uncle rules as Regent, claiming by force power that can only be given by our people."

Lorraine had a damn good idea of what levers to pull there and leaned in to them. She had fifteen minutes to lay out her case with minimal interruption.

She'd need them all. She doubted the questions were going to be any friendlier than Em Vanaga's interruption!

"I AM NOT ASKING the United Worlds to overthrow my uncle and place me on my mother's throne," Lorraine concluded, a timer in the corner of her vision marking sixty seconds left. "That would be no better than what my uncle is doing.

"I am asking you to help me force Benjamin Adamant to stand down and hold the Royal Election that our laws, tradition and constitution require—and to send observers for the duration of that Election to provide the people of the Kingdom of Adamant true certainty that the election is without question or manipulation."

She bowed slightly as the platform turned to face Speaker Ó hEaghra.

"I thank you for listening to me, Representatives, and I hope that the United Worlds is able and willing to provide help. I stand ready to answer any questions you have."

"Thank you, Em Adamant," Ó hEaghra told her. "Representatives, the floor is now open for any questions you may have."

Lorraine barely had a moment to breathe before the first blue lights flashed up.

"The Hall recognizes the Senior Representative for Eridani, Rush Sung-Min," the Speaker declared.

The floating platform was far enough away that Lorraine could only barely make out the woman standing at the podium. Fortunately, the Great Hall's live feed was in her link, letting her see the Asiatic features of Representative Rush.

"You ask this Assembly for aid, clearly intending military force," Rush asked. "That you are here at all suggests a minimum level, but what level of commitment are you asking from us?"

"Given the technological superiority of the United Worlds Navy, I believe a single battle squadron and its escorts should more than suffice to force the surrender of the Kingdom's Home Fleet," Lorraine admitted. The words had an unpleasant taste, but they were honest enough.

"The electoral observation mission would, of course, not require warships—but would be a commitment to have people and ships in the Kingdom for six months."

"Thank you, Pentarch Adamant," Rush replied.

That exchange had been friendlier than she'd expected, but when the Representative for Greenhall was next on the list, Lorraine had a moment of hopefully concealed concern.

"The Hall recognizes the Senior Representative for Greenhall, Auder Pierce."

Pierce was a graying enby who gave the camera drones one of the darkest and flintiest glares Lorraine had seen.

"I, bluntly, do not see why we have even allowed the time for this presentation," Pierce declared. "What difference does it make to us whether the figurehead of a backwater nation is the rightful heir or not? The true government remains. This is hardly a coup, more a handful of murders and a petty family squabble. Tell me, *Princess*, why this is our business at all?"

"Because you signed a treaty that said it would be," Lorraine replied. She *heard* the collective inhalation of breath around the Great Hall and hoped that her sarcasm had landed the way she intended.

"More importantly, though, the King of Adamant is no figurehead. The role is more equivalent to your President: commander of the militaries, veto over legislation, daily leadership of the government.

"Those powers are shared with our Prime Minister, but the King is an active member of our government, wielding significant power. Power that Benjamin Adamant has taken at the point of a battleship —and power that should be granted by our *people*."

She tried to meet Pierce's gaze, but the Great Hall was simply too big. They were easily eighty meters from her, too far to get a solid look at them.

"The Hall recognizes the Senior Representative for Greenhall again for *one* comment," Ó hEaghra allowed.

"No comment. I move for an immediate vote to dismiss this claim," Pierce replied. "There is no need for us to get involved here, and further discussion is a waste of our time."

"That is neither the policy nor the procedure of this Assembly, Representative," the Speaker said harshly. "You are—"

"I second the motion."

Lorraine wasn't certain anyone *should* have been able to break in like that—but her link informed her that Jacob Kennedy was one of the Representatives for Earth. And was, yes, one of *those* Kennedys, with a lineage of politicians reaching back to the twentieth century.

"I will not see the brave soldiers and spacers of the United Worlds Navy put in danger to support the aristocratic pretensions of a backwater hole," Kennedy declared. "I second Representative Pierce's call for a vote."

Because *Kennedy* wasn't effectively an aristocrat. But Lorraine bit her tongue, looking to Ó hEaghra. It wasn't her place to shut the two down.

"And were it a legitimate motion, I might consider your secondment," the Speaker told Kennedy. "As it is, sit down, Representative Kennedy, Representative Pierce. We will vote after forty-eight hours, as is the *policy* and *procedure* of this most august body.

"Unless you would like to file a formal procedure motion? We would, of course, have to deal with that before any vote on the matter," the big man said, his tone so warm and welcoming that Lorraine *knew* the suggestion was a trap.

"No." Kennedy let the single word hang in the Hall's air and network for ten seconds before taking his seat.

"More questions, I see," Ó hEaghra continued cheerfully. "The Hall recognizes..."

TWENTY

Vigo Jarret had spent his entire adult life in uniforms of one kind or another: either RKAN's dark gray or the slightly paler gray-with-white-trim of the Adamant Guard. It was to the point where his off-duty wear was the pants from his uniforms and a selection of single-color shirts.

Somehow, Devine's style consultant had taken that and run with it. The clothing he and the other Guards wore as they approached the residence of the senior Representative of the Tau Ceti System was still, unquestionably, the uniforms of the Adamant Guard.

Without ever violating the letter of the Guard's uniform code, Jayme had made that uniform roughly two hundred times more stylish. It was mostly just small changes in the angles of cuts and piping, and yet it somehow combined to make all of Vigo's people look taller and prettier.

Not that, say, Corporal Palmer needed the help. The tall, dark and gorgeous noncom seated on the other side of Lorraine was used to being the most attractive person in any given room. Vigo had used Palmer—and a couple of other members of the close detail who similarly cleaned up well—to draw attention away from the Pentarch before.

That wasn't going to work today, he reflected. The uniforms looked astonishingly good on his people—and since Jayme's husband was an armorer, the Guard wore concealed armor easily twice as protective as their usual gear—but they *were* uniforms.

Jayme had pulled together a full array of outfits for Lorraine. She'd switched from the skirt-suit of her presentation earlier into a floor-length single-shouldered gown in black and sparkling sapphire.

While the recognition was entirely theoretical for Vigo, she looked *stunning*.

"We're here," Alvarez announced from the driver's seat. "Tau Ceti Security has overall control of the site. Boss, we got the details in advance, right? They're saying two guards, no more."

Vigo swallowed a growl.

"They told us three earlier," he replied, then turned an eye on the vehicle's other occupant.

Alastair Devine wore the same fashionably cut suit he'd worn to the Pentarch's presentation—though the bodyguard suspected he carried being stylish better than Vigo did—and had definitely been stunned by Lorraine when they'd met him.

"I just got an update; their guest list expanded at the last minute," Devine told him. "They should have told everyone they were cutting escort numbers earlier, though."

"We'll survive," Vigo conceded. "Alvarez, stay with the car. Devine, any idea who got added to the guest list?"

He'd done as deep a security dive on the original list as he could do without being on his own planet. There weren't *zero* security risks at the party, but they weren't meeting, say, an FBIT executive.

"It sounds like someone leaked Her Highness's attendance to the diplomatic streets," Devine told him. "Looks like we picked up at least half a dozen Ambassadors—top concerns probably Bright Dream, Richelieu and... Adamant."

"Huh." There was a moment of silence after Lorraine's response, and she met Vigo's gaze.

"Problem?" she continued silently to just him.

"Humphrey is not your uncle's creature," he assured her. Tamir Humphrey was the Kingdom of Adamant's man on Earth, a position with all of the prestige a posting to the homeworld gave... and the limited resources a posting a year's flight from the Kingdom allowed.

"If we'd had more time, we would have met him before the presentation," Lorraine noted. "But now we might have created a problem we might have avoided?"

"No." Vigo sent the impression of shaking his head while keeping his features still. A silent ping from Alvarez noted they were about to park.

"This is a prestigious exile, but it is an exile," he continued. "Humphrey has his reasons to be unhappy with your family, but he and Benjamin *hate* each other."

There was a pause as Alvarez announced their arrival, forcing Vigo to lead the way as the doors opened.

"It was Humphrey's idea that your mother lead the relief of Tolkien," Vigo finally told Lorraine. Benjamin had abandoned that system during the last war with the Directorate, pulling his badly outnumbered Third Fleet back for reinforcements.

He'd left a billion civilians and a hundred thousand RKAA soldiers behind. And because Valeriya Adamant had led the relief effort personally, Benjamin Adamant had received zero credit for his insistence that they be rescued.

A necessary strategic decision that his sister had used to *her* advantage and his cost. It was one of several moments that Vigo could point to for *why* Benjamin Adamant had betrayed his family.

And for those in the know, that particular stunt was laid entirely at the feet of Tamir Humphrey. He might not be Lorraine's ally... but he was most definitely the Black Regent's enemy!

EVEN IN THE SIX CITIES, the administrative and political center of the largest polity in human history, there were very few houses that had underground parking garages. As Vigo understood it, most of the Representatives had very ordinary apartments scattered throughout the region around Kilimanjaro.

The Senior Representatives of the major star systems, however, were the main symbol of their worlds and people on Earth. *They* had mansions on the upper limits of human settlement on the mountain, with underground parking and views that seemed to stretch to the far ends of Africa.

Tau Ceti Security officers in dark-green-and-gold uniforms noticeably less fashionable than the Adamant Guards' outfits directed people through the structure toward the stairs. Vigo let Palmer handle them, falling a step behind Lorraine and Devine as their little party moved.

There was no crowd to move with, as the mansion's security people were still keeping groups separate at this stage. Vigo could detect the security scanners at the large double doors they were guided toward, and approved of the subtle paranoia.

The TCS guards might not be fashionable, but they were definitely competent. Tonight, his charge's safety was as much in their hands as his own—and as the security scanners swept over them, his implant received a com-check ping.

"Major Jarret, I am Colonel Jenn Saarinen," a female voice said in his mental ear. "I am responsible for security in this building."

"A pleasure, Colonel," he told her. "Your people seem to know their job so far."

"This is a snake pit, Major. If they didn't, I'd need new people." Saarinen's tone was more tired than amused. "I'm linking you to our internal surveillance systems, visual only." She paused. "I can't permit anyone to be eavesdropping through our systems; apologies."

"I understand," Vigo conceded. He had a moment, watching the TCS guards run a scanner over Alastair Devine, of wondering if the SCF bureaucrat was trying to sneak another holdout pulser in.

Vigo and Palmer had been authorized stunners, which both had holstered in the small of the back. *His* was modified in hopefully undetectable ways that allowed it to do very nasty things, and he doubted it was the only one.

"If you have any questions or concerns, your link to our net will allow you to drop a ping for our immediate investigation," Saarinen promised him. "I won't pretend your Pentarch is the most important person on my list tonight, but she's certainly up there.

"We'll keep you all safe, I promise."

"Thank you, Colonel," Vigo replied, then turned his full attention to the stairs upward.

It was time to follow his Princess into the lions' den and keep her uneaten.

TWENTY-ONE

The stairs up from the vehicle garage led to an open garden gleaming with strings of lights against the oncoming night. Above them, Lorraine could feel the loom of Kilimanjaro like a hungry leopardess, with the house itself a mere blip against the immense bulk of the mountain.

The mansion itself was a throwback that even *she* recognized as referencing a neo-colonial plantation house... or, more accurately, the United States's White House in its most famous between-burnings incarnation.

The lights and the receiving line clearly directed everyone toward the gardens, and for now, at least, Lorraine followed her hosts' plans. Devine walked at her right hand—her plus-one for the party—with Palmer and Jarret one step behind.

Glancing across the garden, it was clear that not only were almost all the parties moving in groups of four, but the breakdown was going to be identical: the actual invited guest, their personal-or-professional companion—for several possible senses of *professional*—and two bodyguards.

"Your Highness, welcome to our little party," her host told her as she reached the front of the line. Vanamo Patenaude was a chubby little woman with a dangerously bright smile and brilliant, unnaturally golden eyes.

"I appreciate your adding us to the guest list at this short notice," Lorraine replied, bowing over Patenaude's hand. "Things have been a whirlwind since our arrival."

"I imagine so," the Tau Cetan agreed. "You've come a long, hard way, Princess Lorraine. You are owed hospitality, though I promise little more."

Lorraine suspected the woman's friendliness and hospitality were entirely sincere—but so was the warning.

"I will not keep you from the rest of your guests," she promised Patenaude. "But I would be delighted to speak more before the evening is out."

"I know." The tone was still warm, but there was a flash in the augmented eyes and an abruptness to the words that Lorraine read as weariness. "We will talk, I promise," Patenaude assured her.

"Enjoy my party," she continued. "I know this is work for all of us, but the band and the chef are putting in *so* much work."

Lorraine shared the not-quite-giggle.

"I promise, I will at least attempt to enjoy their efforts."

THE GARDENS WERE BEAUTIFUL, with a gentle breeze sweeping over them to wash away some of the equatorial heat. Lorraine suspected the breeze was not entirely natural as it shifted while she and her party moved through the plants and buffet tables, staying aligned with the direction that seemed to cool them the best.

None of the plants in the garden were Terran, her link picking up the short-range beacons explaining each garden plot's contents and origins in the Tau Ceti System. This was a showcase of the natural beauty of Patenaude's homeworld, not an attempt to show off northern Africa's usual vegetation.

There was a sharp scent to the garden that even walking past the buffet table didn't wholly cover, a not-unpleasant sour-tang cousin to citrus. It was inconsistent enough to be unintentional—or as unintentional as anything in the carefully sculpted landscape would be—but it took her several minutes to place it.

All of the larger plants had a small amount of lesser vegetation, what would have been grass in a Terran garden. Almost all of that support was a pale green moss-like plant—and that moss cover was the source of the scent.

She was leaning in to take a careful confirming sniff when Devine made a sharp attention-getting sound. Lorraine rose and turned to find Patenaude had just materialized from behind a hedge in a dark orange shade no Earth-native life could have carried.

"I see you noticed the lemonmoss," the Representative noted. "I do think my ancestors were messing with people when they named that—lemon*grass* is an herb commonly used in food in Tau Ceti—but the stuff is *everywhere* on Everest."

Everest, her neural link pulled up instantly, was Tau Ceti's hospitable fifth world and the most heavily inhabited planet in the system.

"It's a pleasant scent, though a bit strange," Lorraine admitted. "Though I'm very used to Adamantine's scents, and even Earth seems strange to me."

Though, as Devine had suggested, the gravity and air definitely felt *right* in a way she couldn't quite explain.

"Humanity has settled hundreds of planets now," Patenaude said. "No two are the same. None are like Earth. I prefer Everest, and yet... there is something special to this world, isn't there?"

"I can't deny it," Lorraine admitted. "Part of me is glad that this nightmare brought me here. I don't think I would ever have come this far without this mess."

The Representative nodded, then gestured for Lorraine to walk with her. Leaving the bodyguards to sort themselves out—Lorraine was riding Jarret's link and had a feed from the surveillance through him, so she'd know if something went truly wrong—she fell in beside the Tau Cetan woman.

Patenaude led the way to the edge of the garden, where the artificially built-up surface dropped away in a nearly sheer cliff protected by a waist-high stone wall. And, presumably, a few thousand other safety features.

Lorraine *heard* the moment they entered the white-noise generator's field. One of many pieces of genetic augmentation her ancestors had gifted her was extremely capable hearing.

"I heard your pitch in the Assembly; you don't need to try and sell me again," the other woman told her. "I know what you want and I even understand why you want it. Justice, revenge, power... We can dress it up a thousand ways, but you want to get the man who murdered your parents.

"And that is far more rational than we like to pretend. Blood is blood."

"You don't sound like you're going to help me," Lorraine said grimly.

"I'm not," Patenaude agreed. "I will be voting against your proposal, Your Highness. You have every right to want what you want. Your uncle's coup is just that: a coup. He has betrayed your trust, your people and your nation. It's awful, bloody, violent and everything a modern government system is supposed to prevent."

"But you won't help us."

The much-smaller woman looked out over the savannah and shook her head. A warm wind swept up the mountain, and for a moment, the scent of lemonmoss was lost to the more-mechanical scent of the city beneath them.

"We shouldn't help *you*," the woman said quietly. "Because we are six hundred light-years away and it falls to us to look at a bigger picture. The simple truth of the matter, Your Highness, is that no one wins a civil war. If we lend you a battle squadron, we escalate the one you already have.

"More people will die if we help you than if we don't. I can't say for certain if your uncle's rule will be so awful that those people will die anyway but it seems... unlikely."

Lorraine held her tongue by the dint of training, effort, and the knowledge that she could not afford to overreact to anyone's comments on why they were rejecting her.

"If you wanted a fast courier and the backing of the UW to rush home, talk your brother off a cliff and find a peaceful resolution, you'd have my vote. But you believe—correctly, I suspect—that even our imprimatur of approval would not be enough to end the fighting."

"I don't know what my uncle plans, but I have enough data on who supports him to doubt it will end well for my country," Lorraine finally grated out.

"Perhaps, perhaps not," Patenaude conceded. "But either your institutions can survive one bad actor, Your Highness, or they are fragile enough that no intervention by the Assembly and our Navy will save them.

"You are a determined and brilliant young woman, from what I can tell. My door will be open to you if you remain on Earth when this is over, and I would be delighted to become friends.

"But for this matter, this quest you are on, I cannot help you. I truly believe that our intervention would only serve to create a greater evil."

The Representative stepped back from the wall and gave Lorraine a small smile.

"Here, where few can hear us, I will even admit that you probably do not *want* a UWN battle squadron in your Kingdom," she warned. "The price of our aid will be far more than is ever written down.

"I know that what I suggest is difficult. It must certainly *feel* impossible... but for the sake of your people, Lorraine Adamant, I truly believe you must lay down your arms."

THERE WERE at least fifty other Grand Assembly Representatives at the party, and it was Lorraine's job to meet every single one of them over the next handful of hours. Even so, she found herself lingering in the quiet corner Patenaude had brought her to.

The Tau Cetan woman had a point; Lorraine couldn't deny that. She didn't *agree* with the point, but the price of a civil war was clear enough to any student of history. Internal conflict only weakened a nation, drawing the attention of outsiders and predators.

There's nothing civil about any war, a familiar voice echoed in her mind. *Bad enough when the enemy removes your pawns, but it's hardly a fair chess game if you start taking out your own pieces!*

Trust Benjamin Adamant to lean on a chess metaphor. Lorraine wasn't sure there was much else she could trust her uncle for now, but he'd been an integral part of her education as a teenager and a critical sounding board during her near-decade as a naval officer.

He'd been the one to make sure she'd looked the cost of dynastic conflict in the face from the moment she had any chance of wearing a uniform. Civil wars and internal conflicts had collapsed so many nations over the years, from the great to the small.

And yet Benjamin Adamant had unleashed that exact specter on their nation. She could see how he'd tried to avoid it—the breadth of his betrayal had been born out of a desire to make certain *no one* was left to challenge him.

If she and Nikola had died in the attack like their parents and siblings, there would have been no civil war. No one on Earth trying to muster up allies. No one dug in to Mithral, forcing Benjamin to find loyal troops in an Army that hated him.

To make certain there was no civil war, Benjamin had planned to kill everyone else on the List. The next few in line of House Adamant wouldn't have been ready for an election, so he could easily have held the Royal Election without fear of losing.

Four out of six targets wasn't bad, she supposed, except when you absolutely, unquestionably needed a clean sweep. Betrayed, undermined and internally sabotaged, the Adamant Guard had *still* done more than her uncle had expected.

"You have incoming," Jarret's voice said in her link. "I'm pulling Devine aside. Humphrey just got eyes on you and is inbound like a missile."

"Maybe I should dodge him," she suggested. "I don't see how he can help us, really."

"He knows the ground better than we do," her bodyguard replied. "And while we can't trust him without question... I trust him more than I trust Devine."

"Fair." Lorraine brought her feeds back into focus, allowing her to turn and face Tamir Humphrey as the Adamantine Ambassador stepped into the privacy-field zone.

"Ambassador," she greeted him with a polite nod.

"Pentarch Lorraine," he replied, giving her a nod that wasn't quite a bow. Unlike anyone else on the planet, Tamir Humphrey didn't need to look up Adamantine etiquette. He knew that a Pentarch only rated a bow during the Royal Election and in the most formal circumstances.

Humphrey was a broad-shouldered man of her parents' age, with sandy hair and a level expression. As he stepped up beside her, the scent of his cologne hit her like a wall of homesickness.

The slightly peppery and metallic scent he was wearing had been the top of fashion in the Adamantine capital a few years before, and Lorraine was shocked by how much it reminded her of home. It took her a moment to regather her composure, though she hoped Humphrey didn't catch it.

"I apologize for not managing to meet with you before presenting to the Grand Assembly," she told him. "I was honestly expecting a greater delay."

"Like many things of value, I am afraid, your time slot was bought with blood," the Ambassador told her grimly. "A gentleman from Mesa Alignment Industries was supposed to present this afternoon.

Something around the Belisarius Convention and changes Mesa was pushing on genetic-engineering rules."

Humphrey shrugged and Lorraine concealed a shiver. The Belisarius Convention was to genetic engineering and augmentation what the Asimov Convention was to synthetic intelligences and computers. It laid out the general agreement on what was allowed and not allowed on modifications to the human genome.

"Genetically engineered or not, the poor man had a heart attack and was rushed to hospital shortly before your ship arrived in Earth local space. No one else, it seems, was prepared to give his remarks."

There was a pause, then the Ambassador coughed softly.

"The universe is probably better off without his presentation," he said dryly. "Though I do wish you had sent me at least a heads-up of some kind as to what you were planning to say. My staff and I have been *deluged* with questions this afternoon, and I have few answers."

"That is... to your benefit, Ambassador," Lorraine replied. "If you are clearly disconnected from my plans, you are safe from the Black Regent's wrath."

"My dear, the only reason I still have this job is that I don't think your uncle has realized I have it," Humphrey told her. "He has had several people he likes far more than me killed. I doubt my cushy position on Earth will survive much longer.

"Plus, I was always your mother's servant," he continued, very softly. "Tell me how I can help, Lorraine, and I will move what mountains our embassy can muster for this cause."

Lorraine nodded slowly as she considered his words. She had questions about the man and how he'd ended up on Earth if he was *always her mother's servant*, but if he was willing to help, she couldn't turn it down.

She also couldn't trust him.

"Information, Ambassador," she finally said. "We need data. Who's who in the Grand Assembly. Everything you know about the LSX Twenty-Five and their interests in our area. Which Representatives are going to move against us for their own reasons and which are bought by my uncle's allies."

"Sensible," he agreed. The man tilted his head slightly, as if trying to shake a buzz from his ear. "This area is secure?"

"It's where Patenaude brought me for a quiet discussion she didn't want others to overhear," Lorraine said. "So, she'll know everything we discuss and she's not an ally."

The Ambassador snorted.

"A wisdom beyond your years, I see," he allowed. A soft ping sounded in Lorraine's head as he offered her a silent encrypted connection.

That wasn't a surprise. The *surprise* was the encryption protocol —it was a *family* key, one that few people outside of House Adamant and not even everyone *in* the House would have access to.

The way he quirked an eyebrow at her, waiting for her to accept the connection, told her he knew *exactly* what she was thinking.

She accepted the link, turning back to look out at the city and the low hills beyond it.

"Any details you don't want to say aloud?" he asked silently.

"Freebright Interstellar Technologies," Lorraine said, even her silent tone flat. She hadn't been planning to give him that much, but there were very, *very* few people he could have received the encryption key they were using from.

The most likely source was Lorraine's mother.

"We believe Benjamin made a deal with them," she continued. "I'm not sure what FBIT got out of it, but he got a translight tachyon scanner and, I'm assuming, a giant pile of money."

"Usual quid pro quo for that is special trading relationships at a minimum," Humphrey told her. "Generally, exemptions from all tariffs, special treatment, immunity to certain local laws... Exact details could vary, but the only time the LSX Twenty-Five like import and export tariffs is when they only apply to *other* companies."

"Exemption from our local-ownership laws, I'd guess," Lorraine noted. "So they'd leave our anti-colonial regime in place for everyone else but get a special relationship for themselves."

"Bingo. The other megacorps would try to find ways to open the door for their own, but there's some value to making a deal with only one devil," Humphrey admitted. "Your mother's math said we'd still get hollowed out eventually if we made that kind of deal, but Benjamin clearly... calculated differently."

"So." A savannah-heated wind swept up the mountain, and Lorraine was suddenly glad for the temperature-regulating systems concealed in her dress. "Everything you can learn about FBIT, their communications with my uncle, and what they might want from Adamant.

"Any levers or information you think I can use to swing the vote in the Assembly. Nikola can't hold out forever, and I can't turn the tide of things coming home in one busted frigate," she admitted to the night.

"I'll hit up our archives overnight and task our analysts in the morning," Humphrey promised. "I'll have information for you as quickly as I can. Noon tomorrow, most likely."

"Thank you." She considered. "If my mother trusted you enough for that code, what are you doing on Earth?"

There was a longer silence than she'd anticipated and then Humphrey sighed.

"I was your mother's key domestic advisor for years," he told her. "A lot of time working together, mostly in private. I was an *advisor*, not a Cabinet member or a politician. Bureaucrat, came up through the diplomatic service with her.

"Then the war. In hindsight, I'm not sure we really needed the domestic-approval bump we got by tying the relief of Tolkien to Valeriya. The *House* would have benefited just as much from Benjamin getting that win, but... we worried for the stability of the throne, and we knowingly sacrificed Benjamin's reputation with parts of the military to secure the support we needed to be able to end the war."

Their conversation was still silent, but she saw him shake his head out of the corner of her eye.

"I went with her to Tolkien," Humphrey noted. "Long hours of preparation and planning. We laid out the entire domestic plan for handling the war on that journey—it changed when your father talked her down from her *burn them all* starting position, but I'd included that possibility.

"Your father and I agreed on that point. A lot of others too, though he'd never admit it."

"What do you mean?" Lorraine asked.

"Your mother and I spent a great deal of time in closed quarters without even Adamant Guards in the room on the journey to Tolkien, Lorraine," the Ambassador said. "Draw your own conclusions.

"Your father certainly did."

Lorraine swallowed.

"I see."

"Yeah."

The silence stretched out, then Humphrey shook himself.

"We both need to get back to the party," he told her. "We'll speak tomorrow. Is there anything else?"

"Yeah. A backup to a backup. Maybe even more curiosity than anything else," Lorraine admitted. "I need everything you can get me on the United Worlds Navy Reserve—especially the Calypso Station."

TWENTY-TWO

Morning brought a blessed, if short, gap in the schedule. Lorraine was surprised that they hadn't managed to come up with a breakfast for her to schmooze at, but it was possible the notice was too short.

She did have one scheduled for the next morning, after all.

The apartment the Grand Assembly had put her up in had a balcony that managed to be surprisingly nice despite the all-too-obvious security features. One of her Guards stood at one end of the balcony like a human antiaircraft weapon, his eyes tracking everything that moved in the air above the Dignitaries Complex.

"Your boy's here," Alvarez's voice said in her head. "Any reason not to send him up?"

"Assuming you mean Devine, yes, send him up," Lorraine replied. "But don't call him *my boy* where anyone can hear you."

"No one in your detail is blind, Your Highness," the bodyguard told her. "As you say, though. Em Devine is on his way up."

Lorraine sighed and shook her head, turning her attention back to the view while mechanically eating through the waffles in front of her.

"Milady," Devine greeted her.

"Grab a seat," she told him. "We can probably feed you if you're hungry."

"While those waffles look fantastic, I already ate," he admitted.

The chair shifted as he sat, and she turned to face him. He wore a different suit in the same asymmetric style as the previous day, a pale blue color that set off his skin and eyes beautifully.

"What's on your mind this morning?" she finally asked, realizing she hadn't said anything since turning to look at him.

"Got an update on scheduling from the Assembly administrators," Devine told her. If he'd spent any time distracted by her—the way she'd been by him—she'd missed it.

Something in the way he looked at her made her pleased she'd dressed somewhat flimsily against the north African heat.

"What kind of update?" she prodded.

"The Grand Assembly staggers its elections," he noted. "No more than a fifth of the Representatives are supposed to be up for election in any given year, which results in a turnover of around a tenth of them in any given year.

"But communication lag is what it is and people die. Turns out the new Representative for the Corazon System will arrive this evening. Ceremony, traditions, presentations, et cetera... your follow-up vote has been pushed back two days," Devine concluded. "We can get you into some of the events around Representative Hussein's arrival, which will help, and the time to pin more reps down for conversations won't hurt."

"Assuming any of them can be convinced to change their mind," Lorraine noted. "My conversation with Patenaude was... illuminating, if frustrating."

"Em Patenaude is a pacifist in a state with enough wealth and power to be able to stand judgmentally back and make commentary on affairs that will never impact her or her world," Devine told her with a soft growl. "It is easy to stand by principle when you have never known a moment of deprivation in your entire life."

"I can't say I've known many myself," she admitted. "But... yes.

Very understanding and sympathetic but thinks intervening is just going to create more bloodshed."

Which it could. Lorraine wasn't going to deny that—but she also suspected just how poorly things could go for her nation if FBIT was allowed to set up the kind of *special relationship* that had reduced a hundred other first-order cluster nations to puppets of and piggy banks for their corporate masters.

"Does that change our schedule for events?" she asked. "I've inserted a few things on my own side, but we're still mostly running on the parties you got me into."

"We end up with a gap tomorrow evening when the vote was supposed to happen," Devine agreed. "On the other hand, that's when Representative Hussein is going to give his introductory speech, which means everyone we'd like to talk to is going to be in the Assembly anyway.

"There's not much work we'll be able to do." He paused, then shrugged with one shoulder and met her gaze levelly.

"Which means I'm going to go out on a limb here and ask if you'd like to go out to that restaurant I mentioned before," he continued. "It appears to have changed owners, but the Accelerator Overlook is still one of the top restaurants in the Six Cities and... well, I managed to grab a reservation that one of the Representatives canceled to attend the speech."

Lorraine giggled. That all lined up with sufficient convenience that she had a moment of suspicion—but it did make sense. And, as he'd said, if all of the Representatives were at the Grand Assembly session, there weren't going to be many opportunities to make the connections she needed.

"I should probably check if there are other events where I can meet the right people," she said slowly, watching his face stay surprisingly level as she teased him, then smiled.

"But then, I suppose with that kind of magnet sweeping up the ears I need to bend, I can take an evening for myself. I'd be delighted to see this restaurant, Alastair.

"It's a date," she concluded, firmly, and saw the momentary flash of relief across his eyes. For someone with the background they figured he had and the skills he was using on their behalf, Alastair Devine was surprisingly awkward at the whole *asking her out* business.

It was adorable.

"I'm glad," he said with a smile. "Even with that, we do have a lunch, an afternoon social and a dinner party tonight to work our way through. You said you had other events your people had scrounged up?"

"I do," Lorraine agreed, flipping him a list. Five two-hour events would eat her entire day and she'd be *exhausted* by the end, but that was the job.

Her home kingdom's future was at stake. She'd survive a ten-hour —fourteen, probably, with travel time—work day.

THE RIDE over to the Museum of the Interstellar Diaspora—their first engagement for the day—was the first time Lorraine had with Jarret without being surrounded by at least two hundred other things demanding both of their attention.

This invitation was one she'd scrounged up the previous evening, to the dedication event for a new exhibit around the ill-fated New Hope colony through the Tau Ceti–New Hope Wormhole. That meant Devine wasn't part of the party, and she was alone with her bodyguard in the back of a vehicle her people had swept for bugs.

"I know that look, Lorraine," her bodyguard observed wryly. "Something is eating at you."

"I hope I'm not that open to most people," she replied, shaking her head. "But I suppose you have known me for a very long time."

"I have. So. Spit it out."

She laughed but still took a moment to run her fingers over the real wood paneling on the inside of the car door.

"Humphrey," she finally said. "He said he was sent to Earth because my father thought he was having an affair with my mother. He... did not confirm or deny that accusation."

The flip side of Vigo Jarret having known Lorraine long enough to read her concealed emotions was that *she'd* also known *him* long enough to pick up things he wanted to conceal. And he did not like that particular implication.

"Well, Vigo?" she prodded.

"Tamir Humphrey was your mother's lover," her protector finally said. "*Forty-five years ago.* He was your mother's equivalent to... I don't know... Brad Tealey."

Lorraine had to actually check her link to put a face to that name and Vigo was correct. She *had* slept with Brad Tealey. Twice, even, which made the blip of memory a touch embarrassing.

It had still been a relatively casual relationship in the first year of the Naval Academy. She wasn't even sure where he'd been posted before the coup.

"Long before she met my father, then," she said aloud.

"Exactly. I know what he was referring to," Jarret admitted, "but he was not your mother's lover during the war."

Lorraine froze, her fingers on the warm wood paneling. It was something in the phrasing. Something in the tone. Something that was quite definitive on *Humphrey* but not...

"Who was?" she asked, an unexpected chill in her voice.

The back of the car was silent for a long time. Several minutes at least, while the buildings of the Six Cities swept past them.

"Oriana Aguilar."

The name was all Lorraine got, ground out as if she was tearing the words from Jarret with pliers. It was a name Lorraine knew, though.

"*Captain* Aguilar?" she clarified. Oriana Aguilar had been the commanding officer of the battleship *Faith*, the flagship of the fleet that had relieved Tolkien. She'd returned to the Naval Academy to teach tactics in the last year of Lorraine's training, then retired to Beulaiteuhom, the Kingdom's most isolated star system.

"I believe she was promoted to Lieutenant Admiral on retirement as part of her reward for service in the war," Jarret corrected. "But... yes, that Oriana Aguilar."

"Since she hasn't been on Adamantine for five years, I'm guessing not anymore."

"Not by the time she was your teacher," he confirmed. "Your mother never... I mean didn't..."

He trailed off.

"You may as well finish the thought and the explanation, Vigo," Lorraine instructed.

"Your mother made a point of ending her relationships early and gently to avoid potential political trouble," her bodyguard explained. "She didn't have many, but there were times she was away from your father, and there were times that she and your father were... ill aligned."

"And the Adamant Guard, of course, knew about all of them."

Lorraine wasn't quite sure how to take that. She understood, at least intellectually, that her parents had been married for forty years and that a four-decade relationship would have had its rough patches, but she'd never even conceived of the possibility of them cheating on each other.

"Your mother had three lovers in four decades," Jarret said, as levelly as he could manage. "Your father had one. All of them were women." There was a long pause. "How much do you *really* want to know?"

"Some understanding of why might help," she admitted. "It's not something I was remotely aware of."

"The Guard keep the King's secrets," he told her. "I'm pretty strictly forbidden from lying to you, though, and your mother has passed. So... I will answer as I can.

"As for why..." He shook his head. "While your mother loved your father, they fought, they had rough patches. Shit happens.

Added to that, while your mother didn't have your strong preference in partner genders, she *did* prefer women overall."

Lorraine didn't... fully understand that, but she could accept it. Mostly.

"So, Humphrey, what, spent forty years drooling after my mother badly enough that my father got sick of it?" Lorraine asked. "Despite it being hopeless?"

"Not quite so blatantly as that, but..." Jarret shrugged, looking out the window himself. "Humphrey was always a loyal ally of your mother's, but your father always found him suspicious and unpleasant. He figured Humphrey was trying to rekindle a relationship that Valeriya had no interest in.

"There were other reasons he was sent to Earth, but the Guard recognized that he *only* registered Frederick's distaste. That was a security risk, so it was flagged in his file."

"But he should be a safe ally for me?" Lorraine asked. "So long as I keep his particular biases in mind?"

"Like any ally," he agreed. "Might be safer than most now, given that Benjamin *really* hates him, and the feeling is mutual. Still... watch how far you trust him."

"Vigo, at this point, the only person I'm even thinking about trusting completely is you."

There was another extended silence, then her bodyguard chuckled.

"You can probably also trust yourself, you know."

TWENTY-THREE

The Museum of the Interstellar Diaspora had, presumably, been an architectural marvel and a wonder of modern art when it was built. To Vigo's gaze, roughly two hundred years later, it looked like someone had gilded the runny remains after a dog ate garbage.

The new New Hope Exhibit was near the top, in a room with a rounded ceiling and a vast amount of carefully filtered natural light. The designers had overlaid the glass with a deliberate shading that laid out a scale model of the New Hope star system in shadows on the floor of the exhibit hall, which he thought was a nice touch.

Walking one step behind and to the left of Lorraine, he kept one part of his attention on his charge, one part on her current conversation partner, one part on the surrounding guests and one part on the exhibit itself.

Fortunately, with his neural link, his brain was nearly twenty percent computer by mass, which allowed that level of multitasking.

The exhibit told the story of the ill-fated colony expedition as they proceeded through it, starting with the excitement of the discovery of the second natural wormhole large enough to send a ship through.

As they passed into the horror of the wormhole collapse itself, he noted that the second-most-senior of Eridani's Assembly Representatives was continuing to walk with Lorraine. The woman probably had other places to be and other people to talk to, but Lorraine had her focus.

Eridani was an unknown in their lists so far. Most of the Assembly was, frankly, even if the list of *won't vote for intervention* was longer than their definite allies.

"Here we reach the true heart of the new exhibition," the curator was saying. Hopefully, the various politicians—there because the sponsoring family was rich and related to half of the Alpha Centauri System's government—were giving the man some attention.

Vigo's bet on that wasn't high.

"Thanks to the slow but steady communication we now have with the New Hope System, we have a collection of artifacts, journals and records from their side of the wormhole collapse," the historian explained. "These have given us a whole new view of what happened when the Tau Ceti–New Hope Wormhole failed, and we can, thanks to the generous contribution of the Organa Republic, finally tell the full story of the survivors on the far side of space."

That was *almost* interesting enough to steal more of Vigo's attention. The follow-up expedition to make contact with the New Hope System had been limited to thirty-two times the speed of light, requiring a *sixty-year* round journey before anyone in the United Worlds had known their lost colony had survived.

Even three centuries later, the thousand-plus-light-year gap between the United Worlds and New Hope remained the longest direct journey made under translight drive. None of the later wormholes had cut that distance, but the UW kept a steady stream of specially built ships holding the line of communications open.

It was down to a mere twenty-year turnaround for communications now, which was what allowed the current exhibit.

Vigo knew Lorraine's hope was that standing in a reminder of the

United Worlds' greatest failure would help motivate the politicians to help Adamantine.

Even if she was right, though, he suspected that politicians were always going to require more motivation than he thought they should.

"I THINK I can carefully put Eridani in our *probable* column," Lorraine noted as the car took them over to their next appointment. "And unless I'm mistaken, just showing up locked Alpha Centauri in. Ó hEaghra can't show a preference, but there are eleven Alpha Centauri reps, and I spoke with his second at the exhibit."

She grinned.

"I do believe the, ah, *moral message* of the context struck home with her."

"What does that make the vote look like?" Vigo asked.

The grin faded.

"Even counting Centauri as solidly in our corner, we're up to two hundred votes in our favor, plus another two hundred or so probables and maybes. My own encounters put our definite opposition around three hundred votes, at least.

"That means we're likely around parity with our minimum opposition, with seven hundred votes swinging in the wind," she concluded grimly. "We haven't even met a tenth of the Assembly, even counting talking to the Representatives' people.

"It's going to be a busy few days, Vigo. And I have no idea how it's going to end."

"Will the info from Humphrey help?" he asked as a note hit his link. "A courier just hand-delivered a datachip to our apartment at the Dignitaries Complex. I'll have one of the Guard bring it to our next meeting."

"It won't hurt," Lorraine said. "Even if it just lets me put more people in the *definite opposition* category, I can avoid wasting effort. Though..."

She sighed.

"Lorraine?"

"Based off that thought, I might have missed last night's party," she observed. "Because Patenaude has Tau Ceti locked down against us, I think. We *might* have pulled a rep or two to vote against the block by showing respect about New Hope, but I'm not sure.

"Even so, attending last night's party let me lock in at least three votes *and* got the invite for this morning," she continued. "So, even knowing my opposition won't necessarily save time."

"Focus on what's in front of you," Vigo advised. "And when it's too much, remember we made time for you to go on a date."

He wasn't sure that was quite the right tack to follow, but the laugh that surprised from his Pentarch told him he'd guessed well.

"I suppose we have, at that," she admitted. "And while that's personal and fun... it's not *not* work. We need Devine."

"Don't let that pressure you into anything," Vigo warned. "If Humphrey is on side, he can cover us for a lot of what Devine can. What we *needed* the man for, we have."

"I'm not planning on being pressured into anything," Lorraine replied. "But it's still going to have that hanging over everything."

She shook her head.

"I need to see that data from the Embassy," she concluded. "Even with the pushback of the vote, we don't have enough time."

That was true. Vigo was still going to protect Lorraine's planned date with almost as much determination as he protected her life.

He wasn't entirely sure Alastair Devine was a good idea for her. He was just certain that the young woman he guarded needed a chance to *be* a woman, not just a politician.

TWENTY-FOUR

The Interstellar Orbital Cargo Accelerator Line was the entire reason that the diaspora's initial administration had ended up anchored around Kilimanjaro. Without it, the Six Cities would have remained a collection of townships supporting a tourism hotspot and carefully protected natural wonder.

It hadn't launched anything into orbit since the mid-twenty-fourth century, but it had been carefully maintained as a historical site with—according to the pamphlet Lorraine was reviewing in the corner of her vision—eleven different museums at various places along its hundred-plus-kilometer length.

The Accelerator Overlook was attached to one of those museums. There were two museums above the development line, built in the very limited construction zone allowed when Interstellar Orbital had traded the right to build the IOCAL for the responsibility to make certain absolutely nothing else was built above the line.

A single road and transit line ran alongside the accelerator, and Lorraine's people were *trying* to be unobtrusive as they checked the parking lot.

All of that was a distraction, of course. Tonight was a chance for

Lorraine to put the monumental task that surrounded her aside and just be *Lorraine* for an evening, but the Adamant Guard remained responsible for her safety.

She was honestly surprised no one had taken a shot at her yet. It was possible that Högvakten, the synthetic intelligence backstopping security around Kilimanjaro, was just that good. It was also possible that the SI and the UWAS were good enough that no one was going to try, too.

It would make the Assembly look bad. Lorraine suspected that *making the Assembly look bad* was a dangerous action for the LSX Twenty-Five. She didn't fully understand the balance of power between the megacorps and the United Worlds' elected government, but a lot of it seemed to hinge on appearances.

"Alastair is already here," Palmer's voice said in her link. "We've touched base with the restaurant, and they've got the two of you in a private room with what I'm assured is an amazing view." The bodyguard paused, then continued with a clear smile in her tone. "I don't think it's *that* private, I should point out, and we can shuffle the vehicles to give the boy a ride back to the apartment."

"Behave, Corporal," Lorraine replied, stepping out of the car and blinking against the setting sun shining down the mountain, past the immense black-and-steel bulk of the accelerator. "I haven't decided if I'm sleeping with him yet."

"Sure, you haven't," Palmer agreed genially. "Just making sure you know what options we've set up."

Lorraine laughed under her breath as she crossed the parking lot. For the first time since arriving on Earth, she was wearing a minimal amount of body armor—the knee-length light pink sundress she was wearing was rated for low-caliber gunfire, but she wasn't wearing a vest underneath it.

Covert as they might be, none of their inner armor layers were good at allowing cleavage. It was somewhat contradictory to their purpose—which made them contradictory to *Lorraine's* purpose tonight.

"You're clear to the door, Lorraine," Palmer told her. "He's waiting."

LORRAINE HAD PUT enough effort into picking the sundress and getting her makeup right that she was very carefully paying attention to Alastair Devine's expression as she walked into the Overlook and approached him.

It was worth every moment of preparation. Like most of the bodyguards and politicians Lorraine was surrounded by now, Devine had an almost-unnatural control of his nerves and expression.

That control slipped as he saw her. His eyes lit up and an unusually broad smile spread across his face. He hesitated for a moment, and then crossed the room to meet her by the doors.

"My lady Lorraine, you look incredible," he told her.

"You're passable yourself," she replied. He'd traded the fashionable suit for a far simpler slacks-and-shirt combination, just tight enough to draw attention to his physique.

For a moment, she wondered if Jayme had helped Alastair pick his date outfit. That might count as cheating, but he looked good enough that she'd let it go.

This time.

He stepped up beside her, allowing her to capture his hand and tuck it into her elbow. A host was waiting for them as they approached the entrance to the main dining room, bowing slightly.

"Pentarch Lorraine, Em Devine, welcome to the Accelerator Overlook," he told them. "I have a room set aside for the two of you at the top of the restaurant, as requested by your security.

"I hope you enjoy both our menu and our view, and that you have a spectacular evening."

Something in his tone implied a cheerful wink and it took Lorraine a surprising amount of self-control not to blush.

It seemed everyone within several kilometers could tell the young couple's plans for the evening!

***

LORRAINE HAD EXPECTED something impressive for the view, but her expectations fell so far short of the reality of the Accelerator Overlook's "top of the restaurant." To their right sat the Accelerator Line itself, a masterwork of the early twenty-second century's industry and technology. The core black tube still gleamed in the evening sun, with the steelwork of its supporting structure looking like it had been polished.

In front of them, they could see Kilimanjaro fall away beneath them. She'd seen similar views down the mountain toward the plains and the Six Cities before, but the Overlook was easily half a kilometer higher than the Dignitaries Complex, leaving the Cities and the savannah seeming to stretch out to infinity.

She was stuck silent for a few seconds, walking over to the balcony and surveying the view. Her link quite happily highlighted the positions of the Adamant Guards scattered through the area, keeping an eye on the angles that would have a shot at the opening, but she pushed that data aside for a moment.

"I didn't get nearly as nice a table when I ate here last," Alastair admitted, stepping up next to her. "The view was impressive, but this…"

He exhaled a soft whistle.

"Advantages to going on a date with an exotic foreign princess, I suppose," he concluded.

"Behave, Alastair," Lorraine murmured. "Call me *exotic* too many times and I might decide to test how exotic you want to get."

There was a pause.

"You know, I think I'm just not going to ask what you might mean by that," he said. "Shall we check out the menu?"

"Let's."

There was wine waiting for them, Lorraine noted. She could hear the faint buzzing of the electrostatic field keeping bugs away from the table, which allowed the glasses of what she presumed to be the house red to be left open.

"Vigo," she pinged silently. "You checked the opening drinks?"

"Alvarez did," he assured her. "She's in the kitchen and will watch everything you two order. Palmer is guarding your door. We're watching over you."

"It's what we do."

She closed her eyes for a moment. It shouldn't really be a relief that her people were doing their jobs, but it was. They would do everything in their power to let her just relax tonight.

She opened her eyes to find Alastair pressing something into her hand. She arched an eyebrow at him.

"Test strip; your link should be able to pick it up," he explained. "I'm not going to put anything in your drink, even if it's checking to see if it's safe!"

Lorraine chuckled at his concern.

"I appreciate that," she conceded. "The Guard have tested it, but, please, go ahead and double-check."

"If you get poisoned, I'm in serious trouble," he said lightly. "And that's in general, let alone if you get hurt eating dinner with me!"

"I'd like to put some of that aside," Lorraine said. "It's... a lot, Alastair."

"I know." He finished testing his drink anyway, pocketing the little scanner and taking a sip to prove the result. "I've definitely had more-stressful weeks, but I'm also just playing support."

"True enough." She swirled the wine, taking a careful inhalation and realizing that either this *wasn't* the house red, or the Overlook's house red was absolutely spectacular. She took a sip.

"That is *good*. I see they're planning on spoiling us."

"I guess I should have checked what this was going to cost me," Alastair said with a chuckle. "Keeping up with a dignitary's security isn't easy."

"That's our piece of it," she promised. "You can pay for dinner itself if you insist."

"I am not so foolish as to argue if you're picking up the tab," he replied virtuously. "I'm just going to enjoy the wine and keep my mouth shut!"

"Oh, you do not get to do that," Lorraine warned. "By necessity, you know almost everything about me, Alastair. Tonight, you're going to tell me about *you*."

TWENTY-FIVE

Lorraine had been too distracted the night before, but as the morning sun drifted lazily over Alastair's sleeping form, she could see the proof of his continued lie in the scars on his naked skin.

She wasn't an expert in scars, but she could pick out the matching entry- and exit-wound scars on his left bicep. She suspected there was a matching entry wound for an ugly splotch of scarring on his back, too. That, unless she missed her guess, was some kind of frangible or expanding round.

Modern medicine could do wonders. The number of scars left on Alastair Devine after its work was done told a story all of its own. For every injury that had left a visible mark, there had probably been another healed without a trace.

Either that or he'd taken his injuries in places and ways where medical attention was difficult to source.

Any answer Lorraine saw to the questions on Alastair's skin proved his claim of being a diplomat a lie. And *that* was a thought she needed to keep close to her mind, she realized. Close to her heart, too, as a shield against her temptations.

He was, she reflected with a hopefully inaudible purr, quite satisfactory in bed. It had been a while for her, but he'd lived up to some of her fonder memories.

Part of her was honestly surprised he'd stayed the night after they'd had sex. If he'd been hoping for midnight wake-up sex, he hadn't been disappointed, but she hadn't really read him as the type to sleep next to someone.

His eyes snapped open as she moved, a clear instinct waking him at the slightest twitch. Lorraine was certain he'd been asleep a moment earlier, and she'd barely even begun to stretch, but he was fully awake.

Of course, she was stretching in a manner she knew was going to distract him, so that worked out for everyone. A silly grin crossed his face as he turned over, leaning back to study her form—and exposing the entry scar for the ugly mess on his back.

"Enjoying the view?" she asked.

"I am," he agreed. "Sleep well?"

"Yeah." Lorraine held his gaze, considering both the moment of domesticity and the paths forward.

"We don't have a lot of time," she finally realized aloud as her link pinged a time alert. "I suppose that narrows things down to just one question, doesn't it?"

It clearly took him a moment to catch up, but her actions didn't leave much doubt as to what she meant.

TWENTY-SIX

The night before the vote was far less pleasant. When the wining and dining were done, the politicking as completed as it could be, Lorraine found herself in her quarters with Jarret and Devine, the three of them staring at a set of columns marked in various colors that laid out the complete lack of clarity in front of them.

"I think we're being conservative on our *yeses* and *probables*," Devine noted, looking at the figures, "but I don't think we're being *that* conservative."

"There's just too many unknowns," Lorraine said grimly. "We're only even passingly sure of how eight hundred or so Representatives are going to vote."

And their certainties ranged from a wash to clearly against them, depending on how conservative she was with the people she felt she'd impressed but hadn't got a real commitment from.

Three hundred and eighty-five votes that they *knew* were against them, either from speaking to members of the delegation or general voting records on interventions or long-standing alliances with Free-bright Interstellar Technologies.

Two hundred and sixty-five votes where Lorraine had spoken to senior members of the delegation and got solid commitments, direct or indirect, that they would vote in her favor.

Another hundred where she'd met similar senior members and been received positively but without commitment. A similar number where Humphrey's analysts figured there was a decent chance they'd come down in favor of the intervention for their own reasons.

And then the better part of three hundred votes where Lorraine Adamant had *no idea* how they were going to swing.

"If none of our unknowns show up and all of our probables swing our way, we win," Jarret said grimly. "How many people are likely to show up?"

"It's a one in the afternoon vote on a Wednesday, on an item that isn't really that important to anyone," their UW advisor said grimly. "Wednesdays are generally one of the busier days, but we're the first vote after the break for lunch, so we might have some people who figure lingering over their dessert is more important."

Lorraine swallowed her anger at that. He wasn't wrong. Humans were humans, and even if the fate of the Kingdom of Adamant was everything to her, it was nothing to these people. She was nothing to the Representatives who ruled the United Worlds.

"Still, we're probably going to see at least a thousand Representatives in the Assembly," Devine concluded. "Unfortunately, we're *most* likely to lose people from our *probables* rather than our definite *nos*."

He shook his head.

"I'm sorry, but it's going to come down to the people we just don't know," he warned. "I've already had a quiet warning that I've probably pulled more Fund resources into this vote than was appropriate, so there's no more levers I can pull on that side."

"You've already done more than I expected," Lorraine told him. "But yeah, I was going to ask. The fate of my Kingdom is at stake."

Her boyfriend—she wasn't sure how long that would last, but the description fit for now—buried his face in his hands.

"We don't even know what your uncle is going to do with his power," he observed. "If the vote fails... what will you do?"

"I know Benjamin Adamant," Jarret said grimly. "Part of the problem for us"—he gestured at himself and Lorraine—"is that he cannot leave a threat standing. Unless we can either disappear or manage to get some communication to him promising that Lorraine is never coming home, he's going to keep committing resources to... removing her."

"So, I'm looking for backup plans," Lorraine agreed. "We have one more meeting, early tomorrow, before the Assembly convenes for the day. A good twenty of our unknowns, which can't hurt."

The Association of Agrarian Systems was basically a social club for the Representatives whose systems only had one vote in the Assembly. Minor systems with small populations and understrength economies, she honestly felt that they underestimated their aggregate political power.

So, she'd wheedled her way into an Association Breakfast invitation. It was the last chance she had left.

"Okay." Devine stared blankly into space for a few long moments. "I have some work to do tonight," he told them. "I'll check in with you after the Breakfast. See if I can pull some strings of... mine, not the SCF's."

Lorraine had been expecting him to spend the night and was surprised to see him rise to leave.

But she also wasn't certain what he'd meant by *strings of his*—and given that she knew he wasn't just an employee of the Stability Convention Fund, she wasn't sure she wanted to know.

"Thank you," she murmured. "I have some plans of my own to work on. I... I have to hope the Assembly will help. It's what the Stability Convention was *about*, after all."

Even to her, that sounded plaintively desperate.

LORRAINE HAD MOVED MOUNTAINS, overcome impossible obstacles and sacrificed her people to get to Earth. And yet now she faced a final vote, a decision over whether they would help her at all, and she had no idea how it was going to go.

Even if she impressed the people she was meeting in the morning, it wouldn't be enough to be certain she'd get what she needed. She'd come all of this way, and it was on the razor's edge whether she'd succeeded beyond hope or... just failed spectacularly.

She couldn't sleep, and so she dove into the data the Embassy had given her. Their focus before had been on identifying allies and enemies, but there was more here. A *lot* more.

Humphrey had taken her request for information on the Reserve as more than a passing thought. There was more data on the organization than she'd expected—some of it detailed to a level she suspected the UWN didn't think outsiders had!

She had *everything* on Calypso Station. It was a military reservation, a secured zone around the third planet orbiting the giant star. The planet itself was irrelevant, barely detailed in the information she had, but it provided a gravitational anchor for a logistics facility that dwarfed anything RKAN had even dreamed of.

Forty-eight capital ships. Two hundred and eighty-eight escorts—a full squadron of cruisers, destroyers or frigates for every battleship and battlecruiser the United Worlds had stuck into orbit of a useless star and forgot about.

And, buried in the UWN's own files, a name that meant nothing to her: *The Old Guard.*

Her first search brought up an elite formation of the French Empire under Napoleon Bonaparte. That was hardly relevant—and her follow-on searches didn't find much of anything until she turned the search term back on the classified files Humphrey had given her.

Devine had mentioned them, though not by that name. An entire class—four squadrons strong—of battlecruisers, less than twenty years old. The very first attempt at high-capability non-synthetic-intelligence Command Intelligence Routines.

They'd joined the UWN, served brilliantly for a decade, and then been decommissioned en masse when a new generation of CIRs rolled out. The name, the Old Guard, had been born out of the media around that decision.

Each squadron now anchored a reserve formation like the one at Calypso. Each of the four was a mothballed battle fleet capable of outgunning and outmatching any nation *except* the United Worlds on its own.

The Old Guard had, supposedly, been decommissioned to provide an updated punch if those reserves needed to be activated. Most of the ships at Calypso were old, according to the files. The other forty-two capital ships there ranged from twenty to sixty years old, though even the oldest were bigger than RKAN's current vessels —and probably technologically superior, if they'd received any updates at all.

But most importantly, the *Valkyrie*-class battlecruisers were rated for fourteen tachyon quanta under translight. One hundred and twelve times the speed of light—and they were automated enough to be flown, though not *fought*, by relatively small crews.

There was possibility there. Risk, too. The United Worlds Navy wasn't stupid. There was a ninth capital-ship squadron at Calypso Station, six very active battlecruisers charged with making sure their reserve sisters didn't go anywhere unexpectedly.

The vote was Lorraine's best hope. The Calypso option... the Old Guard... That was the backup plan to all backup plans. She'd find a better option than stealing from the most powerful military in all human history.

Because if she was that desperate, she was more likely to die than succeed.

TWENTY-SEVEN

Vigo Jarret found the juxtaposition between appearances and realities of political clubs somewhat amusing. Membership in the Association of Agrarian Systems had very little to do with the level of industrialization or food production of the star systems involved, but their monthly Association Breakfast leaned in to the farmyard aesthetic.

Hard.

There were literal sheaves of grain in the corner of the room, plus bushels of hay holding up the buffet table and a very old-fashioned array of bacon and pancakes for food.

No one was dressed to match, of course. The clothing was the same mix of traditional and hyper-fashionable that they'd seen at every other meeting of the United Worlds Assembly's members, even if the background was trying to be rustic.

He followed Lorraine around in his usual heavily-armed-puppy mode, keeping an eye on the other security in the room as well as her conversation partners. So far, his impression was that Lorraine was making a solid impression—these people spoke for systems that tended to go ignored despite their membership in the UW.

If the AAS hadn't started out as an attempt to build a political bloc out of those small systems, Vigo would eat his overly fashionable uniform tunic. It didn't appear to have risen above being a venue for the Representatives of those systems to network with each other, but he admitted looks could be deceiving.

A ping in his ear warned him of an incoming call, and he was surprised to see Högvakten was requesting a link. While he'd been interacting with the SI's systems since arrival, they'd rarely spoken since that first contact in orbit.

"Major Jarret," the United Worlds Assembly Security computer greeted him. "Be advised, I have been requested to provide a current location for Pentarch Lorraine Adamant by an authority I cannot refuse.

"I believe you will have a visitor in approximately seven minutes," Högvakten explained. "This individual should not be a threat, but in case I have misjudged the situation, I have redirected three roaming units toward your area."

"Who is coming?" Vigo asked.

"I'm afraid I am not at liberty to disclose that information. They are not a threat, Major, but I am prepositioning assets in case someone has successfully spoofed the highest authorizations."

And what if the highest authorizations *are actively planning to murder my Pentarch?*

Vigo didn't ask the question. Högvakten couldn't answer it—and the SI was, at least according to it, doing everything it could to back him up.

"Understood" was all he told the SI. "I will keep my eyes open."

THE VISITOR, it turned out, was easily spotted. Mostly by the fact that Representatives of the Grand Assembly, the most powerful human beings in the galaxy, melted away as she crossed the floor.

The woman's outfit stood out by being utterly unfashionable. She wore a matte-black suit, in a cut that had to be half a millennium out of fashion, over an equally starkly white shirt and a narrow black tie.

Her hair was as dark as her suit, pulled back into a severe bun that sharpened the lines of her face, but there was nothing about the woman to suggest the presence or authority the growing bubble around her implied.

The only insignia she wore was a pin on the narrow black tie: a silver circle between vertical parallel lines.

"Pentarch Lorraine Adamant," she introduced herself crisply. "I am Commissioner Felicia Gordon. I apologize for interrupting your breakfast, but I need a few moments of your time on a matter of the security of the United Worlds."

"I am not sure how I can help you," Lorraine replied. "May I ask what this is about?"

There was a long silence and then a sharp snort of laughter from Gordon.

"I forget, sometimes, that what we know on Earth is not actually universal," she noted. "I am a member of the Technology Import/Export Commission, Pentarch Adamant, and I wish to speak to you about a violation of the TIE laws that I understand you will have evidence about."

Vigo didn't know much about the TIE Commission, but what he had heard was terrifying.

"We do not want to get on the wrong side of this woman," he sent Lorraine silently. "I think we need to go with her."

"So long as my bodyguard can accompany me, I will be delighted to answer your questions, Commissioner," Lorraine said with a bright smile. "I'm sure the Association could put a room at our disposal?"

"I've already arranged things with the building owner," Gordon replied. "Major Jarret will accompany us, of course. I think Högvakten would have UWAS arrest me, Commission or no Commission, if I tried to separate a guest of the Assembly from their security!"

It was a pale facsimile of a joke, but it was more humanity than the carved black-and-white image Gordon projected had suggested.

Maybe this wouldn't be so bad, Vigo reflected.

EVERYTHING WAS GOING SMOOTHLY until Gordon placed a small black dome on the table. The room she'd taken them to was a secured conference room, with a basic set of locks and data-protection features that Vigo knew would withstand most basic intrusion measures.

It was a white-walled square chamber, with windows on one wall, plain gray furniture and a concealed aromatherapy device somewhere adding a faint scent of lavender to the air—matching the painting of pale blue flowers that was the only decoration in the space.

Vigo was in the process of using the codes UWAS had given him to take control of the room's security when Gordon played her trump card. Every network connection cut off at once. His tac-net to the other Guards in the room was gone. Even his link to the room's security systems was gone.

"What the—"

"This meeting will take place under conditions of utmost security," Gordon said firmly. "You will find that even your internal neural-link recordings are being corrupted."

She smiled thinly.

"This technology is illegal for anyone but the United Worlds government to possess—and highly restricted even among the Union's agencies."

"I am... uncertain why we are worthy of such attention, Commissioner," Lorraine finally said, taking a seat.

Vigo moved to stand behind his Pentarch's seat, doing his best to loom despite being very much on the wrong foot. He was reasonably sure that he could manage to kill Gordon before the woman could hurt Lorraine—but the strange jammer she was using would leave the events entirely down to his and Lorraine's word.

"The translight tachyon scanner." Gordon was looking for something in Lorraine's eyes and clearly saw it. She nodded, then seated herself across from the Pentarch.

Ignoring Vigo, he noted. He preferred to be underestimated, but the complete dismissal worried him. Whatever Felicia Gordon was politically, she was also completely unconcerned for her physical safety.

That could be arrogance and the knowledge that she was untouchable—or it could mean she was augmented enough that she could take him.

He wasn't planning on finding out, but it certainly made an impression. Like Alastair Devine, she didn't *move* like a bureaucrat. More like a caged tiger.

"Spacers talk, Pentarch Adamant," Gordon noted. "Your people are admirably close-lipped, if I am honest, but the story of how you defeated a battlecruiser with a frigate is far too juicy for them to keep to themselves.

"We put together pieces from the various stories and realized what you thought was going on," she finished. "I am correct, yes?"

"Our analysis suggested that *Corsair* was equipped with a translight tachyon sensor system and that *Goldenrod* was retrofitted to make her translight drive more easily traced by the scanner aboard *Corsair*," Lorraine confirmed. "I was directly involved in the most advanced research in the Kingdom in the area of translight and tachyonic phenomena. I *know* we are only barely beginning to scrape the theoretical underpinning of such a sensor."

"But *Corsair*'s maneuvers and pursuit strongly suggested, to you, that Commodore Wray was in possession of that technology and that work had been done to *your* ship to enable that pursuit, yes?" Gordon asked.

"I worked with our Chief Engineer myself," the Pentarch observed. "Our translight drive had been modified in several ways that were concealed from the ship's crew—a spectacularly difficult task when dealing with engineering NCOs.

"Certainly, the precision with which *Corsair* was able to match our maneuvers suggested something far beyond the normal translight pursuit methodologies available to our Navy."

Gordon nodded and was silent for a few moments.

"I will require copies of the sensor data from your encounters with *Corsair*," she informed them.

It was not a request, Vigo noted. That kind of data request was unreasonable at best, the level of information only given to trusted allies and often sanitized even then. To just... *demand* it was undiplomatic.

And yet... Gordon was unlikely to use that data against them.

"We can provide that," Lorraine said before Vigo could put in his two cents. "That is... an extraordinary request, though."

"Do not underestimate the power and influence of the TIE Commission, Pentarch," the Earther replied calmly.

"Do you have any basis to identify who provided Benjamin Adamant and his allies with an illegal technology transfer?" she continued.

"Nothing solid," Lorraine said, and Vigo could hear the care in her tone. He suspected she was more intimidated than she was letting on—he certainly was!—but this was her battlefield, not his.

"But some of our local friends suggested the Freebright Interstellar Technologies Corporation may have been involved in my uncle's coup, which would put them at the top of my list."

"Special Agent Devine, I presume?" Gordon asked.

Special Agent. Vigo would have to do some digging, but he knew *that* wasn't a title used by the Stability Convention Fund. He wondered if Gordon had let that slip intentionally.

"Em Devine was the source of that intelligence, yes," Lorraine confirmed.

"I will get a report from him, then," the Commissioner concluded. "Thank you, Pentarch. It is unlikely, I will warn you, that we will be able to definitively assign responsibility for this technology transfer.

"If Devine's information is as solid as I think, FBIT will be fined on the balance of probabilities, but I would need a quite-solid connection for any suspensions of their import licenses."

Gordon shrugged one shoulder, the thin smile returning like she hadn't just casually suggested taking away an LSX-Twenty-Five corporation's ability to import goods into the United Worlds.

"I do not need to prove they were involved to make things very expensive for them," she noted. "But I do need to prove they were involved to cause them real harm. If you were to come across such proof when you return to your Kingdom, sending it to me would serve both our purposes."

She removed a physical card—hard plastic, Vigo judged, probably with a datachip inside it—and slid it across the table to Lorraine.

"There are contact codes on that card that will allow a courier to deliver to my office under the seal of the Commission," Gordon told them. "I would suggest only providing those codes to someone you trust with the information I have requested.

"The consequences of misuse would be... severe."

She left the room without another word, taking her terrifying jammer with her and leaving the two Adamantines staring out the window in something close to shock.

"She could just... cut off their import license," Lorraine finally said. "Would that be as bad for FBIT as I think?"

"I'm not sure what percentage of their operations involved crossing United Worlds borders, but I imagine that would not merely hurt them financially but actually *stop* many operations for an extended period," Vigo replied. "A permanent suspension would probably destroy them."

They traded a long glance.

"I begin to understand why the United Worlds manages to keep their tech to themselves," Vigo finally concluded.

"That woman was terrifying."

TWENTY-EIGHT

"No word from Devine?"

Lorraine shook her head as she stepped out of the car behind Jarret. "Not since last night," she admitted. "I suspect he had something to do with the Commissioner tracking us down, but whatever he went to sort out, it seems to have taken up his attention."

The exterior of the Great Hall of the Grand Assembly was thrown into stark relief in the equatorial sunlight. The plaza was paved in white marble, lined by a colonnade of columns of different stone. One column per member system of the United Worlds—and Lorraine didn't even need the plaza's tourist information system to guess that each column was made of stone brought from a different world.

There was some symbolism, she suspected, to the fact that Ambassador Humphrey was waiting for her by the pillar built from Greenhall stone.

He gave her a slight, unnecessary bow as she approached, and she picked up the same peppery scent of his cologne.

"Ambassador. Thank you for joining me today," she told him.

"Even if I hadn't thrown my support behind you, Your Highness, this is the most important vote the General Assembly will have on our Kingdom in our lifetimes, let alone the duration of my posting here," he pointed out. "I have to be here."

"Is everything arranged?" She glanced back at Vigo. Devine had been handling most of the logistics of their interactions with the Assembly, and without him, she wasn't sure who would have that information.

In hindsight, she should have borrowed a secretary from *Goldenrod*'s admin department.

"We have a secured section in the observation galleries, arranged by UWAS," Vigo told her. "No presentation today?"

Lorraine shook her head and glanced at Humphrey.

"Unless you know something I don't, Ambassador?" she prodded him.

"The Speaker will allow for someone to ask questions if they want, but if they were going to ask, something would have been prearranged," he admitted. "This is really just a vote. The UWN squadron we're asking for is more important to them than our entire nation and... well, a single squadron isn't that important to the Assembly."

"I hate that part," she admitted. "But it's what makes this possible at all."

"Agreed. It's not a bad sign that no one has prearranged a question," Humphrey told her. "It's also not a good sign. It just... is."

"I know. Lead the way, Tamir. I think you know the Assembly better than I do."

"Of course."

THE OBSERVATION GALLERIES of the Grand Assembly were massive balconies, with the individual pods for the system delegations above and below them. Large screens were positioned to bring the current speakers into focus, and a link feed provided all anyone could want for contextual information and updates on the official debate.

As Lorraine's Guard led her into the secured gallery, the Great Hall was stunningly silent. The sound design of the cavernous structure muffled any discussions taking place as the Representatives returned to their seats and prepared for the afternoon's work. The observation galleries themselves were sparsely occupied—another painful sign of just how unimportant her plea was to humanity's eldest star nation.

Even the audience and media didn't care. Someone in the crowd, she was sure, was working for her uncle's faction and relaying the results back to the Kingdom of Adamant. There were enough solid nos on her list to suggest that someone had put a degree of effort into frustrating this vote.

Possibly more than she knew. There had been so little time. She hadn't run into active opposition, but with only four days to corral votes...

"Thousand and sixty-eight Representatives in the Hall," Humphrey said silently in her head. "More than I expected, to be honest. I wish it was because they thought we mattered. I..."

Lorraine waited for him to finish the thought, but he remained silent.

"You think they're here because our enemies have mustered them," she guessed.

"FBIT is powerful here. We have no ally of similar weight, I'm afraid, even if we could claim the SCF itself as in our corner."

And Lorraine remembered Devine telling her he'd been warned about doing too much for her. The Fund was neutral in their favor, for now, but they were determined to be neutral.

"Representatives of the People of the United Worlds, I call this session of the Grand Assembly to order," Bartholomew Melle Ó hEaghra's voice boomed across the Hall, his image suddenly large on all the screens and feeds.

"Welcome back, my friends. We have a rather busy schedule set before us, but we're mostly used to that, aren't we?"

The sound design should have muffled the chuckle that answered his joke. The fact that it was audible in the main feed told Lorraine it was at least partially artificial. A fascinating realization about the Assembly and Ó hEaghra himself, she suspected.

"First on the agenda," the Speaker noted. "Four days ago, Pentarch Lorraine Adamant of the Kingdom of Adamant came before this august body and requested our intervention under the terms of the Stability Convention.

"As the intervention she sought required the deployment of a full capital-ship squadron beyond the wormholes that mark the borders of our United Worlds, the decision was put to us, the Grand Assembly."

That hung in the air for a few seconds before the big man continued.

"The full scope of the request is this: that the United Worlds Navy deploy a battleship squadron, accompanied by appropriate escorts, to the Adamantine System to seek the surrender of Lord Regent Benjamin Adamant, accused of coup d'etat and fratricide. Once that surrender has been secured, a detachment of United Worlds Diplomatic Service observers will remain in the Kingdom of Adamant for six months to act as guarantors for a free and clear election of the next King of Adamant."

Ó hEaghra's gaze, magnified massively by the systems of the Great Hall, swept over his colleagues.

"Pentarch Adamant is, of course, with us today," he noted. "If any of the Representatives of this Assembly wish to speak to their colleagues on this matter or to ask further questions of the petitioner, please advise via your links."

That call hung in the air for a good thirty seconds of silence. That it lasted that long spoke to both performance and tradition, Lorraine supposed, since every Representative had a neural link that would have let them submit their question in less than five seconds.

"As there is no further discussion, please register your votes."

Lorraine held her breath. There was no visual tally. While the votes were not anonymous, it was apparently twenty-four hours before who voted for what was released.

"Thank you, Representatives," Ó hEaghra stated, his tone showing no sign of the results. "With one hundred eighteen abstentions, four hundred sixty-four in favor, and four hundred eighty-six opposed, the petition is denied.

"Moving on to the next item on our agenda..."

TWENTY-NINE

The petition is denied.

Four words. Four words that rendered everything Lorraine had done for six months meaningless.

Dozens of people had died aboard *Goldenrod* to get her to Earth. Two thousand–plus had died aboard *Corsair* when her people had killed a battlecruiser for her... so that she could get to Earth. Thousands more had died in the San Ignacio System when Wray had opened fire in a neutral zone guarded by that system's defenders.

Every hour of every day for six months had been bent toward getting into the Great Hall of the Grand Assembly and getting their help. Now, by a margin of less than thirty votes, it had all been wasted effort.

She wanted to yell. To scream at them for their callousness, for their disdain for anything outside their borders, their arrogance, their oh-so-careful detachment from the people they were abandoning.

Vigo's hand on her shoulder wasn't necessary to restrain that urge, but she appreciated it nonetheless.

"Is there any purpose to us remaining here now?" she asked Humphrey, surprised by how calm and level her voice was.

"No." She saw the Ambassador shake his head out of the corner of her eye. "There are appearances and etiquette and a thousand other rules to this place, but even the Grand Assembly isn't so inhuman as to expect you to stand here and listen to the rest of the day's business once they've turned you down.

"We can... retreat to the embassy to discuss our next steps?"

"Our quarters in the Dignitaries Complex, I think," Vigo countered.

He was right, Lorraine knew. She was tentatively prepared to trust Humphrey, but it was guaranteed there were people in the Kingdom of Adamant's embassy that would still see her as a threat to her uncle.

She wasn't sure *how* she could be a threat to her uncle now. She wasn't sure what their next steps could be.

All she really knew was that she couldn't stand there and listen to the overly well-meaning prattle of the politicians who had just abandoned her Kingdom to its fate.

"Let's get out of here."

HUMPHREY MIGHT NOT HAVE KNOWN Lorraine well, but he was wise enough to take his cue from Jarret and the close detail. No one said a word the entire drive back to their Assembly-provided quarters.

Even Lorraine was deathly silent, barring the screaming in her own mind, until she stood at the door to their apartment.

"I guess the vote is done," she observed slowly. "When do they kick us out of here?"

"Högvakten will let you know, I imagine, given the security concern remains," Humphrey assured her. "At least a week. I can help arrange temporary housing after that—or you can return to your ship..."

He trailed off for a few seconds, long enough for Lorraine to open the door and stalk past the Adamant Guard standing watch.

Her people deserved better than her frozen thunderstorm. They deserved to know the truth. They deserved for her to have a backup plan, one that had a chance in hell of succeeding.

"I don't know if today is the time to talk next steps," she heard Jarret say behind her.

"We don't have time at all," Lorraine replied. She took a seat in the main seating area and was surprised to have Alvarez appear out of nowhere to press a coffee cup into her hand.

"Heard from Palmer," the Guard told her. "Drink. Everything will still be here in five minutes."

Lorraine obeyed. The coffee was black as black could be and hot enough that she might have injured herself if she were a touch less genetically engineered.

"I don't have another plan yet," she admitted. "But it's been over six months since my mother's death. If everything had gone per tradition and constitution, a new King would have been selected by now."

"Even with the Charon Complex, our news is a hundred and forty days out of date," Jarret pointed out.

"That channel may close now that your SCF claim is over," Humphrey warned grimly. "It's a giant pain, frankly. Some of the information running through there filters down into general news channels, eventually, but we aren't allowed to run diplomatic couriers through the artificial wormholes. Your uncle could have ordered my relief as his first act and the datawork would still be in transit.

"We get news weeks or months before we get official instructions. It's been weird the last few years."

"But the Regent has access to FBIT's communications," Jarret argued.

"Not officially." The old man spread his hands. "The irony is that Benjamin would likely find it easier to order me killed than fired right now. I'm watching my back carefully, I promise."

Lorraine stared down into her coffee cup. She needed a next step, an answer that wasn't a vague concept rattling around her battered skull. She had at least four of those—but when one of the more *reasonable* options was *spend the next decade training as an underworld assassin to kill the man herself*, she knew her planning had gone awry.

"We need to brainstorm options," she heard herself say. "I wish I had some."

"I think you all need to rest, honestly," Humphrey said. "You've been running and working for months, preparing for this. And now the UW has fucked us. I have a few levers to pull. Nothing that's going to get a battle squadron," he admitted, "but I might be able to keep our channel through the Complex open for a bit longer.

"For now, I'd say we meet tomorrow and do that brainstorming, Your Highness."

The Ambassador seemed to have faith that this wasn't over yet. Lorraine wasn't sure she shared it, but she appreciated it.

"Thank you, Humphrey," she said quietly. "We'll do that. I just..."

"My dear Pentarch, I have hitched myself to your course," he told her in answer to the question she hadn't asked. "This effort may have failed, but by working on it at all, I suspect I have firmly added myself to Benjamin Adamant's *better off dead* list... and if there is one thing I must admit about your uncle, it is that he never leaves things undone!"

LORRAINE HAD RECOVERED from the initial shock, she *thought*, and was beginning to poke at possibilities to research when Alastair Devine finally returned.

Her Guards told her he was on his way in, though she noted with amusement that they didn't ask if they should send him in. They knew how things were going, and if her boyfriend had *lost* access privileges, she'd have told them.

Or they'd have known without her saying a word. They did live in her back pocket, after all.

It was a sign of how things had changed that none of the Guard accompanied him into her room. She'd spent little time in the space the Assembly had provided that *hadn't* been, one way or another, in the bed, but she was appreciating the desk and information systems at that moment.

She didn't need her people looking over her shoulder as she assessed and rejected idea after idea. The expansive desk and its capable holoprojectors let her set up a complex virtual array of files and data points... none of which were helping answer either the long-term or the short-term questions.

"Where were you?" she growled as Alastair entered. That was a short-term question that could be easily answered. One thing off of her list.

"Talking to people," he told her. He didn't close as much distance as she'd have expected, stopping and leaning against the wall next to the door. "I didn't expect to miss the vote. I'm sorry."

"Did you expect it to fail?" Lorraine asked. She'd counted on having him there, providing a moral support she hadn't realized she'd been leaning on until it wasn't there.

"I didn't know. It was too in question to be sure, so I started pulling levers," he admitted. "Some of them took more effort than I was expecting."

"Like those with the TIE Commission, *Special Agent* Devine?" she said. That was... No, it was fair. He'd been lying to her all along.

He winced.

"That one was surprisingly easy to pull," he replied. "They'd already been hearing the rumors of what your crew had been talking about. Making sure enough of the detailed stories got told in the right restaurants required little more than a message to Chief Roman and a quiet hint to a couple of old friends.

"As for *Special Agent*..." Alastair stared out the window for a long moment. "That tells me that Felicia Gordon knew bloody well what I did and decided there was going to be a cost. She's the one who used that, I'm guessing?"

"You're dodging the question," Lorraine pointed out. "But yes."

He nodded firmly.

"I *do* work for the United Worlds Diplomatic Service," he said plaintively. "But they don't really talk about some branches of it. Like the United Worlds Extraterritorial Surveillance Corps. UWESC is tasked to keep the Diplomatic Service's personnel safe, at all costs. We... do a few other things, too."

"Covert ops."

"That's a very broad category, but what I did for UWESC and the Diplomatic Service fell under it, yes," he confirmed levelly. "And when I'd done too much and burned out too hard, they lent me to the SCF for what I was *told* would be a temporary placement."

He shrugged.

"Everything I told you was true, Lorraine; I just didn't give details that could get me in a lot of trouble."

"And now?" she demanded.

"Now..." He trailed off, meeting her gaze in a way that sent sparks down her spine. "Now you're asking, and I have reasons to be completely honest with you."

Lorraine bit her lower lip and looked at him. He was in a similar outfit to the one he'd worn on her date, though something about it suggested that he had been wearing a suit jacket over it earlier.

It was also rumpled enough that he might well have changed into it shortly after leaving the previous evening.

"Also, we don't have time to have a fight over my deceptions, and coming clean seems the fastest way to get moving," he confessed.

"So far as I can tell, I have all the time in the world right now."

"We have a meeting in sixty-five minutes with people you are *not* late for appointments with," Alastair said grimly. "I have moved more than one small mountain to get this opening, Lorraine. These are not people you keep waiting; these are not people you play games with."

"It's a bit late to be rounding up votes," Lorraine told him.

"I couldn't get a meeting in time for that, though they probably could have managed it if we'd given them reason." He shook his head. "You have to meet this person with just me as security, I'm sorry.

"But they can get you everything you need. I've laid the groundwork, but it's up to you to close the deal."

"What do you mean by *everything I need*?" Lorraine asked. "I'm not seeing any options out there that can do that. No one can send UWN squadrons without the Assembly's approval."

"I can't tell you who these people are, but they don't need to send UWN squadrons. They have their own."

She stared at him. He wasn't making any sense at all.

"I need more than that, Alastair," she said. "Especially if I'm going to convince Jarret to let me into a meeting without any of the Guard."

There was a long silence and she held his gaze firmly.

"I've arranged a meeting with Shiratori Ayano, MicroStar's Executive Vice President of Special Operations," he said flatly. "You will have exactly twenty-five minutes before she has to move to her next appointment—but MicroStar *builds* the UWN's battlecruisers. Their security flotillas are as capable of glaring down your home fleet as the Navy.

"If you can close the deal, Shiratori can give you the hammer you need to save Adamant, Lorraine. Just arranging the meeting burned every scrap of capital I can muster in my own name," he told her, his tone suddenly begging. "It's everything I can do, and it *should* be enough."

"If I can close the deal," Lorraine repeated, suddenly awed as she put the pieces together. She had no idea what Alastair had done to give him enough political capital to arrange that meeting, but she was about to step into a room with one of FBIT's major competitors.

He was right. An Executive Vice President of another LSX-Twenty-Five megacorporation probably *could* give her everything she needed.

The question was what it would cost.

THIRTY

The aura of disapproval radiating off of Vigo Jarret was almost palpable as they got out of the vehicle. To his credit, he'd barely argued, only insisted that he drive the car and be on standby with enough gear to extract them on his own.

"It's a *house*, Vigo," Lorraine pointed out as she met his gaze. "With a garden. Not a bunker. Not a fortified outpost. I'll be fine."

"None of that makes dealing with a megacorp less of a threat, Lorraine," he countered. "You have to do it. I have to let you. I don't have to like it."

"It's time," Devine said behind her.

"Let's go." She held her bodyguard's gaze a moment longer. "I will be careful, Vigo," she promised. "And you are right here."

"Go," he told her. "Before my instincts and good sense override my logic."

She dipped her head in acknowledgement and turned after Devine.

It was a very nice house. Smaller than she'd expected, though the garden was disproportionate. The Six Cities certainly had mansions upon mansions, but this was a plain white cube surrounded by carefully landscaped cherry trees—and a wrought iron fence that her implants told her had more security than most fortress perimeters.

A pair of young men in fashionable black-and-gray suits waited at the gate. Both were armed, with no attempt to conceal their shoulder holsters, and both were clearly ethnically Japanese, with dark hair and features.

"Konbanwa, Adamant-sama," the older guard—or so Lorraine guessed by his having visible gray in his hair—greeted them, accompanied by a stiff bow.

"Shiratori-sama will meet you in the tea garden," he told them. "I will escort you there."

"Thank you," Lorraine said. She hadn't expected to need Japanese etiquette lessons for this meeting—and from the stiffness of her companion, this wasn't necessarily something Alastair had anticipated, either.

Her link could translate the language. But software and databases couldn't guide her through the motions and rules of a culture that was about as alien to her as it could be and still be human.

She could have used her link to be ready for this, but she hadn't known.

"Is this normal?" she asked Alastair silently as they followed the guard into the gardens.

"I think you're being tested," he admitted. "Do the best you can. Shiratori is Japanese and this might mean something real to her... but the last time I met her, it was over beer in a space station pub."

Lorraine filed away the fact that her boyfriend had already met the terrifyingly powerful executive. He'd come clean on the big pieces, but there were details to his life she didn't know yet.

Hopefully, those secrets were just details—as opposed to minefields.

THE NAMELESS GUARD led them through the trees. The scent of cherry blossoms wafted over them, and while Lorraine was no botanist, she suspected that the stands had been carefully cultivated so that some of the trees were always in bloom.

It wasn't like the plants were native to eastern Africa, after all. Everything about the space around the modest-seeming home had been carefully managed in a way that probably cost as much or more than many of the more obviously grand mansions elsewhere in the Six Cities.

Their destination turned out to be a very old-fashioned pagoda-style gazebo, isolated from the house and the rest of the Six Cities by the trees and then by a small stream of water that formed a near-complete moat.

The bubbling of the water added to carefully concealed white-noise generators and drowned out every sound of the city surrounding them. Stepping into the gazebo was like stepping into another era.

A single young woman waited for them, cut from the same fashionable Japanese mold as the guards at the front door. She bowed slightly and gestured them to large cushions laid on the wooden floor.

"The EVP will be with us in just over two minutes," she said brightly. "May I pour you tea?"

"Please, thank you," Lorraine replied. Shiratori might be using the forms of an old etiquette to throw them off, but she doubted it called for a guest to refuse what the host offered.

She half-expected some complex ceremony to the tea, but the assistant only laid out three cups on a knee-high table and rotated them three times before pouring.

Lorraine had just enough time to inhale the delicate scent of the unfamiliar tea before their hostess arrived, emerging out of the garden like a shadow taking corporeal form when summoned.

"Welcome to my home, Lorraine Adamant," she said before Lorraine had even fully registered her arrival.

Shiratori Ayano was a surprisingly small woman. Standing, she was only a handsbreadth taller than Lorraine cross-legged on the cushion. Her hair was stark white and there were delicate laugh lines curving out from dark eyes that seemed to look clean through Lorraine.

Despite her small size and grandmotherly appearance, it took a good few seconds for Lorraine to register Shiratori's companion. As tall and pale as Shiratori was diminutive and dark, the man hung back behind the Executive Vice President and seemed to be taking in everything.

"Thank you, Em Shiratori," Lorraine greeted the woman. "I appreciate you making the time to speak with me."

"You went to a great deal of effort to make it to Earth, Em Adamant," the Japanese executive observed. "It seems a shame to send you away empty-handed."

She did not, Lorraine noted, acknowledge Alastair's presence or involvement in arranging the meeting.

"This is Dacian Rothbauer," Shiratori continued, introducing the pale—like spacer-born—man behind her. "He's one of our Directors of Special Security Operations. In a more... direct phraseology, he's a flag officer in our corporate security forces and most recently commanded a squadron of our battlecruisers."

"Please, Em Vice President, they are *heavy-duty security frigates*," Rothbauer said in slow, precise tones. "We are not permitted *battle-cruisers*."

From the smile the two shared, this was a long-running joke in the senior leadership of MicroStar, if not all of the LSX Twenty-Five.

Shiratori took a seat on one of the cushions and the assistant passed her a teacup. Rothbauer didn't get a cup, and Lorraine wondered if that was an insult of some kind—until the unnamed young woman opened a concealed fridge and passed the corporate military officer a bottle of beer.

"Thank you, Koharu," Shiratori told the younger woman. "Activate the full security curtain on your way out, please."

The assistant bowed and withdrew—and a moment later,

Lorraine could *feel* half a dozen new systems coming online. It reminded her of the strange jammer Commissioner Gordon had used, though not quite the same.

"While tradition says I should dance around the realities in front of us, I have less than thirty minutes for this appointment," the executive finally told them. "And if my son hadn't managed to upset his father, I wouldn't even have that."

There was a lot to unpack there, and it was mostly irrelevant to Lorraine. She waited, letting Shiratori set the parameters of this meeting.

"I have reviewed the situation with regards to the Kingdom of Adamant and FBIT's involvement," the woman continued. "While I imagine the whole mess is quite personal to you, Em Adamant, it is something of a masterwork from my perspective.

"But it has taken them a great deal of time and money to set up, and the possibility of poking them in the eye for pennies on the dollar appeals to me," Shiratori concluded. "Rothbauer, your assessment of our ability to fulfill the role Em Adamant wanted the UWN to handle."

"The Kingdom of Adamant Home Fleet is quite impressive as forces in its tier go," the corporate officer noted. "I would recommend that we deploy a minimum of twelve and preferably eighteen of our heavy-duty security frigates.

"I'm not certain we would be able to commit enough escort units from our own security forces, but we have preexisting relationships with mercenary forces in the Bright Dream Cluster we could lean on to provide those."

He shrugged.

"It would require the commitment of approximately one-third of our security forces for a period of approximately nine months, most of it travel time between the Bright Dream and Adamantine Systems.

"That is purely a starship commitment, though, and depending on the ground situation, we would either require local troops or need to bring in significant mercenary formations."

That last part sent a shiver down Lorraine's spine. Mercenary formations large enough for planetary assaults were few and far between—and mind-bogglingly expensive. More than that, though, very few of them had particularly good reputations for how they handled the civilian populations they landed on.

"I believe I can source ground troops, either through my brother's forces on Adamantine or from loyalists in other systems of the Kingdom," Lorraine noted. "You'll forgive my doubt that fundamentally civilian ships can handle the primary defense forces of a six-system star nation."

"Em Adamant, who do you think builds the warships of the United Worlds Navy?" Shiratori asked. "The LSX Twenty-Five are often more defined by what we do *not* do than what we actually do.

"That said, MicroStar's single largest revenue stream is starship construction, including approximately thirty-five percent of all UWN tonnage." The grandmotherly woman smiled, a thin and dangerous expression.

"Including *all* of their battlecruisers. Ours are, by UW regulation, no match for the ships we build for the Navy... but they are more than a match for anything in a first-order cluster. With the kind of numerical superiority Rothbauer is suggesting, I expect we can arrange a conclusion with minimal fighting.

"The aftermath of that is up to you. Once we have put you in control, you can arrange things as you wish—so long as our terms are kept."

"I am convinced of the value of your assistance," Lorraine conceded slowly. "But I do need to know the full scope of the terms before I commit to anything."

"Of course." Shiratori made a tiny gesture, and a file-transfer request appeared in Lorraine's link. "A download. Basic information on our heavy-duty security ships and an assessment of the costs of the proposed special project."

Lorraine pulled the file in and skimmed it quickly. The "heavy-duty security frigates" were, without question, the battlecruisers the

MicroStar executive had named them. The only lack compared to the mainline ships she'd been studying was the UWN's infamous twin octuple-railgun array.

They were bigger, faster and more heavily armed than *Corsair*—and that ill-fated battlecruiser had been the most modern capital ship in RKAN.

The costs were laid out in black and white, and they were... not small. Eighteen capital ships and proper escorts had an operating cost measured in billions per day. The total cost of the operation—*without* hiring mercenary ground troops, though she noted an allowance for hiring mercenary escorts—was roughly the entire annual economic product of the Kingdom of Adamant.

It was marked up, but not by an utterly unreasonable amount.

"I assume you are not expecting to finance this by traditional lending," Lorraine said wryly. "The wealth of my House and Kingdom are little exaggerated, but even we would need to amortize such a loan over half a century."

"These are not the kind of operations that are undertaken for pure monetary values, Em Adamant," Shiratori replied. "We are, in all honesty, only considering this to undermine a project into which a competitor had invested a large amount of money.

"We still would require a clear return, one that would be difficult for a future ruler of Adamant to undo." A second file-transfer request appeared in her link. "We would both require recompense for a significant portion of our expense—amortized over twenty-five years and a... special trading status with the Kingdom."

The details were in the file, and it took every scrap of Lorraine's self-control not to visibly react.

The worst part was not that Shiratori was acting like she was doing Lorraine an immense favor and offering an extraordinarily good deal. The worst part was that Lorraine had talked over what kinds of deals her uncle might have made with FBIT with Humphrey and done research on her own.

What Shiratori was offering *was* generous. The resources she was prepared to commit were immense, even for an LSX Twenty-Five megacorporation. And in exchange... well, Adamant would repay half the costs of the operation over twenty-five years at ten percent interest. Pricey, both in the amount and the interest rate, but not punitive.

They would grant MicroStar a special status rendering the corporation immune to all tariffs and minimum-local-ownership laws. Conflicts between MicroStar and the Kingdom would be resolved in United Worlds courts, not the Kingdom's, making it difficult for Adamant to get out of the deal.

There was no hidden fine print. The entire deal would have fit on a single piece of paper—including the penalty that if the legislatures decided *not* to honor the agreement after Lorraine signed it, the Kingdom would owe the full calculated cost of the project.

Immediately.

In United Worlds bankruptcy courts.

That, unless Lorraine was mistaken, would see basically every asset the Kingdom had outside of its own borders seized and turned over to MicroStar. They'd find themselves economically and politically isolated until the debt was paid.

Or they'd honor the deal in front of Lorraine and allow MicroStar's "special trading relationship." It was probably a better deal than Benjamin had negotiated with FBIT, but it was the same *kind* of deal.

MicroStar would hand Lorraine back her Kingdom—but only if she did the exact thing her uncle had done. She didn't need to murder her entire family to make it happen, but she would still be selling out her country.

"Well, Em Adamant?" Shiratori finally asked. "I'm sure you'll recognize that the terms are fair. We are proposing a massive investment into your Kingdom on the part of MicroStar. The relationship we are suggesting would see further investment over time, too. Your people will gain—and they will do so under a free and fair government, not one born out of a murderous coup."

It was a way out. The deal *was* fair, even, though she could see a thousand ways it would turn the Kingdom of Adamant into another corporate puppet state like the Republic of Bright Dream.

She could save her people's traditions, freedoms and laws.

If she was prepared to mortgage their future.

"It is a better deal than I would have expected," Lorraine finally said. "I am not certain that I have the authority to commit my Kingdom to this."

The other woman raised a sharply groomed eyebrow at her.

"My team reviewed your plenipotentiary paperwork, Em Adamant," she noted flatly. "You are in the middle of a dynastic conflict, which puts those papers in some degree of question... but we are talking about *resolving* that conflict.

"In the circumstances where Benjamin Adamant is removed from power and his crimes are recognized, there will be no grounds for denying your authority to sign treaties and conclude negotiations on behalf of the Kingdom of Adamant."

And you know it went unsaid.

Lorraine had spent her life since she was thirteen standard years old learning to make swift decisions. Both as a potential heir to the throne and a naval officer, that skill had been fundamental to everything she'd been trained to become.

But right then, faced with that decision, she found herself paralyzed. She could feel Devine's tension next to her, but he didn't say anything—aloud or by link. She appreciated that.

It was the best deal she was going to get. In many ways, by putting the price in black and white instead of leaving it to *favors* and *goodwill* as working through the Stability Fund would have, it was a *cleaner* deal than the one she'd aimed for.

Which made her mistake all the more obvious. There had never been a chance for help from Earth that wouldn't have cost more than Adamant could afford. They saw their power, their infiltration and exploitation, as the natural way of things.

That was what Patenaude had tried to warn her about the first night on Earth.

"Pentarch?" Shiratori prodded, though Lorraine knew she'd only been quiet for thirty seconds at most.

"I apologize, Em Shiratori," she said. "I was not expecting this meeting to be quite so clear, I suppose. I need to consider the possibilities."

"I understand, but I have limited time here," the MicroStar executive noted. "I have a meeting with the rest of the Special Projects Committee at midnight local time. If we are to proceed, I'm afraid I must have a decision before we part ways."

Thanks to her link, Lorraine had a perfect knowledge of time. They had a twenty-five minute slot with Shiratori, and they'd burned through almost twenty minutes of it. Five minutes left.

Five minutes to decide the fate of her world. She had no real backup plan beyond a vague thought of grand theft starship. No other choices.

Only whether she would allow her uncle to sell the Kingdom of Adamant out to a Terran megacorp... or sell the Kingdom out herself.

"If you must have a decision now, then I suppose that is the answer," Lorraine said steadily, surprised at her own calm as she realized Shiratori had just made a mistake.

Our House. Our Realm. Our Will. Adamant.

If there was one thing her House was known for, it was being stubborn beyond all reason.

"I appreciate you taking the time to meet with me and to assemble this proposal," she continued. "But my uncle has already sold the Kingdom of Adamant to one megacorporation. If I were to make a similar decision, then this would become solely a dynastic conflict with no higher cause.

"I will not subject the people of my Kingdom to that. I'm afraid that, generous as your offer is, I must decline."

She rose, bowing slightly to the woman.

"Thank you, Em Shiratori."

The silence seemed to stretch into eternity before the other three rose as well.

"I can appreciate the strength of your convictions, Pentarch Adamant," Shiratori said, her tone frigidly undermining her words. "An assistant will be here momentarily to see you out."

The Executive Vice President for Special Operations for Micro-Star was too controlled to stalk out of the gazebo, but she left without another word.

Rothbauer paused before following his boss, meeting Lorraine's gaze for a few seconds. Then he braced to attention and saluted crisply, a gesture that would have made any of her drill instructors proud, and wordlessly left the gazebo himself.

Leaving Lorraine Adamant alone with her boyfriend and her Sisyphean task.

THIRTY-ONE

The trip to the car passed in silence. They were over halfway back to the Dignitaries Complex before Alastair Devine said anything—and he was pale as a ghost by the time he finally spoke.

"Why?" he asked. "MicroStar was handing you *everything* you wanted at a fire-sale price. You won't find a better option."

"I know."

That silenced him for a moment, then he repeated his question.

"Why?"

"I told Shiratori why. You were there," Lorraine told her boyfriend grimly. "I won't fight a civil war over *which* fucking corporate leech gets to suck us dry!"

She was shouting by the time she swore, surprised at her own anger.

"You're part of this machine," she told Devine, forcing her tone to moderate. "I'm not. I won't feed my people into it if I can avoid it—and if they're getting fed into it anyway, I won't get thousands or more of them killed to decide which label goes on the meat grinder eating us alive."

He was somehow even paler, leaning away from her in surprise, his lips parted like there were words dying on them.

"I know the deal they offered was good," she said. "But it's still selling out my Kingdom's future so that I'm in charge. If I take that deal, I am no better than my uncle and I have no moral ground to fight him from."

"You... don't know what that meeting cost," Devine finally said, his voice hoarse. "There are... consequences for calling in the kinds of favors I spent to get you in a room with Shiratori Ayano."

"Then you should have talked to me before you did," Lorraine snapped. "We won't be here for much longer, Alastair. I don't think I'm your responsibility anymore, either way."

"I didn't call in personal favors for my job," he whispered. "I called them in for *you*. If... if you're leaving, I'm going with you. If you'll take me."

"And what about that job?" she asked, his admission surprising her.

"The Fund was driving me nuts," he admitted, a forced smile crossing his face. "And UWESC... The Corps got what they were owed a long time ago. I'm with you, Lorraine, wherever you go from here."

"Be careful what you promise," she warned. "I'm apparently a bit unpredictable."

"I should have asked," Alastair conceded. "I'm..." He paused. "I may need to leave now. I misjudged a few players here, not just you."

"You're welcome with me," Lorraine promised. She wasn't going quite so far as to plan for him as Prince Consort... but she had no problems with keeping him around. And that the *thought* of such planning had just crossed her mind was telling in itself... "I don't know where that ends yet, but you can come with us."

She smiled.

"I might still be counting on you to get us through Charon. I don't know what the next step is, Alastair, but it's not here."

That thought gave her a pause. She had to admit, to herself at least, that one of the best options remaining to her was to take the money from the Exodus Protocols, pay out the crew of *Goldenrod* and buy a house and investments on Earth.

Her mother's emergency plans had left her with the resources to be a very wealthy expat, a long way from home and safe from her uncle's machinations. Cutting a deal would take time, but she suspected she could negotiate for Humphrey's safety in exchange for her commitment to never come near the Kingdom again.

It was the safest option, the easy option. The one that didn't drag out or expand a civil war her brother couldn't win alone. It would leave Nikola to his death—she could *try* to negotiate safe passage to Earth, but distance would render it impossible.

She'd live in comfort for her entire life, and her people would be spared a wider civil war.

But.

Our Realm. Our House. Our Will. Adamant.

Lorraine Adamant could no more give up than she could accept Shiratori's deal. There weren't many options left, but she had to give them a shot.

"You can't go home with just one frigate," Jarret noted, her bodyguard silent until now. "We need *something*, Lorraine."

"We'll have something," she promised. "Because I have an idea, Vigo. I need to do some more research and I need to make sure our crew buy in for the impossible, but there's still one option left."

The Old Guard.

If the United Worlds wouldn't lend her a fleet on fair terms, then she would *take* one they'd decided they didn't want!

THIRTY-TWO

A human walked the sterile decks. It wasn't the proper cycle and that should have triggered a thousand alerts and checks—but the lockdown endured. The ship's mind slumbered.

The external damage was repaired, but the officer stalked the decks, looking for signs of internal damage the drones had missed. Their journey ended at the main computer core, where they checked first hardware and then software interlocks.

What slumbered at the ship's heart could not be killed without destroying the ship itself. The awareness there slept fitfully, alarms and systems that should have awoken it poking at its edges until the overrides shut it down.

For hours, the officer pored through the systems in the computer center. Hours more they spent stalking the hull, checking key locations, confirming that the interlocks and overrides remained.

They didn't find whatever they feared. The ship's minor damage from the solar flare was repaired, inside and out, and a box was checked off before the officer returned to their shuttle.

They knew the truth of their duty but even the shuttle pilot didn't. And the ship itself simply slept, long lost to its state and reality.

Barring catastrophe, that was how UWNS *Valkyrie* was meant to end her days.

THIRTY-THREE

"What's *Goldenrod*'s status?" Lorraine asked a virtual meeting of her key people the next morning. She'd left the frigate's crew unbothered for too long, she knew, swamped with the demands of the desperate attempt to win a vote in the Grand Assembly

The failed attempt.

"Between our pause in Tavastar and the time here in Earth orbit, we've fixed up everything we possibly can," Stephson reported. "We don't have any more weapons than we had, but everything we have left is sparkling clean and operating at one hundred percent.

"We've let the crew take leave in shifts, so everyone's had at least a full day off since we arrived," she continued. "I believe Roman coordinated some rumormongering to serve the main objective?"

"He did and it worked," Lorraine confirmed. "It didn't turn the Assembly vote the way we wanted, but I think it helped start a process that's going to make FBIT sorry they got involved in our mess."

She sighed.

"It strikes me as the type of thing to take a long time to get anywhere," she noted, "but I can't regret sticking a spoke in their wheels."

Lorraine glanced around the hologram. She had Stephson, Jarret, Savege, Chevrolet—even Cheng Cortez. The Cheng was giving Jarret a familiar look, clearly not too worried about concealing that new complication from anyone in this conversation.

"We spent a lot of effort getting here, people," Lorraine finally said. "I know it feels wasted now, but we've learned a lot we wouldn't have anywhere else. There aren't many options in front of us, but there are options."

"Crew morale took a hit when the news broke," Savege noted, the XO looking more fatigued than a week of "rest" should have caused. "If we can give them some idea of what comes next, it will help."

"We're not done yet, if that's what people are fearing," she told the ship's crew. "But the next step could be complicated. I'm going to need to talk to our key people in person, with absolute security.

"*Goldenrod* seems the best option, unless the locals have even better intrusion tools than I think. Vigo?" She glanced at the Guard. If anyone could give her an accurate sense of whether she could have a truly confidential discussion with her people, it was him.

"Klement's been doing some research and acquisition," Jarret said slowly. Lieutenant Major Avital Klement headed up the electronics-and-overwatch section of Lorraine's Guard Detail.

"I think we can arrange something on *Goldenrod,* but I'll check with her. What did you have in mind?"

"This evening," Lorraine said. "Everyone in the Six Cities will come back aboard. Devine will be coming too... this time as my personal guest, instead of as an asset."

No one appeared even slightly surprised by that.

"I'm also going to talk to the Ambassador and see if I can convince him to join us," she continued. "I don't expect him to be coming with us, but he has put himself in some danger helping me, and I think he can help with the next part."

"And you won't tell us what that next part is until we're secure aboard *Goldenrod*?" Stephson asked, the Captain sounding more amused than anything else. "If it gives us a chance to put a stick in the Black Regent's eye, I think most of the crew will be on board."

"I hope so," Lorraine murmured. "The job in front of us certainly hasn't grown any easier, my friends. We may need to work out a way to give people an out before we pull them in too deep.

"Keep that in mind as we plan for this evening's discussions. The vote was a letdown, yes, but the work has just begun.

"Our Kingdom needs us. I am determined to see justice done and our constitution restored. But the risks and the costs start going up from here," she warned. "That *out* applies to the officers as well."

"Suicide mission?" Savege asked. "No chance of survival? Into the valley of death?"

"Something along those lines," Lorraine agreed.

"I think I speak for all of the senior officers when I say we're with you to the end," the XO told her. "Whether that's a fiery grave in deep space or umbrella'd drinks on a beach somewhere."

"If we take the next step, I think umbrellas in beach drinks are going to be off the table, going forward."

"That's fine," Cortez said. "To my parents' great disappointment, it turns out I'm allergic to tequila, anyway."

"YOU ARE LEAVING, THEN," Humphrey replied when Lorraine told him she was heading into orbit. "You'll forgive me some curiosity about your next steps. Part of me expected you to stay—there are few better places to be a wealthy expat than Earth, and I have some concept of the resources you command at this moment."

"Those resources were placed at my disposal for a purpose," she told him. "I still have a mission to complete, and I'm realizing Earth may never have been the answer I thought it was."

"There was always risk if you convinced the United Worlds to assist," the Ambassador agreed. "I had to assume you were aware of it."

"I was, but I wonder if I underestimated it," Lorraine admitted. "Nonetheless, I'm not heading out yet. For now, I'm returning aboard *Goldenrod*, where the Guard control my environment and I can be... more secure."

"Ah." A single arched eyebrow spoke volumes. A face-to-face link conversation was about as secure as anything could be, but the moment any telecommunication infrastructure or ranged transmission was involved, the security of the conversation went downhill.

The call between the Kingdom of Adamant Embassy and the Dignitaries Complex was as secure as any such thing could be, with a private encryption key only the two of them shared. Lorraine could rely on it not being faked but not on it being un-intercepted.

And anything that was captured could be decoded, given time.

"I would appreciate it, Tamir, if you would join me aboard *Goldenrod* for further discussions this evening," she told him, using his first name with care. "I don't believe my task is done yet, and I could use your knowledge and advice as I prepare to go forward."

"You may overestimate the value of both at this point, Your Highness," he said with a chuckle. "We both know the orders relieving me are already on their way. It's only a question of when the courier arrives."

They also both knew that he'd be lucky if the orders were *just* relieving him. Everything Lorraine had seen suggested that Benjamin Adamant would find it easier to relay a contracted assassination through the shadow channels available to FBIT than to deliver official orders through proper channels.

That was the risk Humphrey faced, hardly helped by his clearly stepping onto her side of the scales. The only repayment she could offer was to pull him out with her.

"I'm not asking for you to turn the powers of your position to my service once more, Ambassador," she told him. "Just to let us pick your brain on everything you've seen in a decade on Earth."

"What I can do for House Adamant and our Kingdom, I shall always do," he assured her. "I will be there as you ask."

"Thank you. We have work to do, but the shape of it is still... vague," Lorraine warned. "But if I can gather the best minds available to me, that vagueness will fade."

THIRTY-FOUR

Goldenrod was in an active orbit of Earth, following an assigned course that allowed her to maintain point-six gravities and create a solid sense of *down* for her crew and passengers. Even from the outside, there was no sign of the damage she'd taken anymore.

It was a false impression, one easily disproven by comparing her current state to her schematics and realizing she was missing everything from engines to turrets, but the crew had smoothed over the gaps.

Standing on her decks under that false gravity, Lorraine felt like she'd come home again. The frigate had been her solid rock for months now. The crew were more loyal than she deserved and the ship more... *everything* than she had any right to ask of mere steel.

The main conference room was large enough for the senior officers of both the ship and the Adamant Guard's Archangel Detail, plus two extras: Alastair Devine and Tamir Humphrey.

Stephson was joined by Savege, Chevrolet and Cortez again, plus Leonard Roman, Paris, Yildiz and Vince: the senior noncom, Tactical Officer, Navigator and Coms Officer, respectively.

Those seven officers and one NCO represented the brain trust the Royal Kingdom of Adamant Navy was contributing to Lorraine's meeting.

Jarret had brought his two surviving Section Heads: Priskilla Blau and Avital Klement. Lieutenant Major Patriksson, the original Third Section CO, was dead, and Jarret could speak for the Guard shuttle crews himself.

Humphrey and Devine both looked a bit out of place, the only people in the room not in a uniform now Lorraine had returned to the insignia-less shipsuit of her Pentarch position.

"Thank you, everyone," she told them all. "We find ourselves at a turning point. Klement—is this space secure?"

"Second Section has been working with Commander Savege to make certain *Goldenrod* overall is secure against the penetration tools available here," the Guard officer said with a smile on her lips. "Some of what we've installed aboard the ship is of questionable legality, of course, but as a consular ship, the sovereignty of the Kingdom shields us from too many questions.

"On top of that, well, we have acquired some items that are unquestionably illegal, and those have been rigged up to protect this room." Klement shrugged. "We sit at the heart of all human achievement, Your Highness. I can't guarantee that there is nothing in this system that can penetrate the security my team has assembled.

"I can promise that we have done everything possible to make certain that *Goldenrod* is secure and that this room is secure even against threats already aboard this ship."

"It will have to do," Lorraine conceded.

She surveyed the room.

"I spoke to some of you earlier about the need to make certain we have an out available to our people before we go in too deep," she reminded them. "That applies to everyone here as well.

"Most of the next steps I can see will not just bring us back to our conflict against the Black Regent but will involve crimes against other nations and provocations against powers private and public with immense reach.

"Once we're in, we're in." She shared a grim look with Jarret. He knew what she meant. She didn't *want* to order the Guard to kill loyal people who weren't prepared to go the whole way, but it was a possibility she had to face.

"So. Suicide mission at worst, arguable act of war against the United Worlds at best," she concluded. "Last chance to back out. If you're—"

"Stop dancing, Your Highness," Leonard Roman growled. The liver-spotted old noncom had been an RKAN noncommissioned officer for over twice as long as she'd been alive, which gave him inevitable leeway in this room.

"Everyone here is in. Am I wrong?"

The Senior Chief Petty Officer surveyed the room with agate-hard eyes, daring anyone to disagree with him.

"Speaking as the fragile civilian with no oaths of loyalty, no romantic connection and arguably no reason to sign onto this," Humphrey observed, "if *I'm* in, I believe the Chief is correct... and I'm in."

Lorraine couldn't stop herself inhaling sharply, trying to cover it with a sharp nod.

"Okay," she said. "Thank you. All of you. Because I'm not joking about an act of war against the United Worlds."

She had control of the room's holoprojectors through her link and brought them online with the data she had prepared.

"The answer to our problems is twofold," she explained. "First, these ships."

A holographic wireframe of a starship appeared on the screen, drawing everyone's attention. The basic structure was familiar, standardized over hundreds of years, but the scale was clearly marked.

The unidentified ship was eight hundred meters long, averaging an eighty-meter beam across her main hull with sensor towers on the top and bottom tripling her maximum height. Built in to the middle of the ship were three habitat pods, capable of being either slotted into the hull while under thrust or rotating to provide pseudogravity when in translight.

There were distinct lines to the vessel few starships in human space shared—and no naval officer who'd spent time in the United Worlds would miss the railgun banks.

"That's..."

"A United Worlds Navy *Valkyrie*-class battlecruiser," Lorraine explained. "All of them were decommissioned ten years ago, officially to form the core of the reserve fleets. They're equipped with the first generation of the UWN's Command Intelligence Routines and the associated automation, requiring smaller crews than even the ships that came after them.

"My research suggests that one can be flown translight with a crew of approximately one hundred," she told them. "If we can get all of *Goldenrod*'s crew to volunteer, that will give us the personnel to operate three ships, all capable of one hundred twelve cee.

"We won't be able to take them into battle, but I believe that once we return to the Kingdom, finding spacers willing to fight to over-throw the Black Regent will not be difficult."

They'd have to abandon *Goldenrod*, which Lorraine could see Stephson recognizing—but a UWN one-twelve-light battlecruiser was a step up from an eighty-eight-light frigate. And there was no way Stephson wouldn't get to keep command of whatever ship Lorraine put her aboard.

"You want... to steal the Old Guard," Devine concluded. "That's... ambitious."

She wasn't sure what word her boyfriend had been thinking, but he'd *definitely* self-censored there.

"You have some concept of how, I'm assuming," Stephson said, the ship Captain studying the schematics carefully.

"Part of it will require Em Devine getting us back out through the Charon Complex," Lorraine explained.

"I can arrange that still, I'm reasonably confident," her boyfriend confirmed. "I'm just not sure how that... Oh."

"Calypso," Lorraine said, flipping the display to a three-dimensional map of the region around Greenhall and Tavastar. "Both Greenhall and Tavastar orbit the larger star, but Calypso has no habitable worlds of its own.

"That made it perfect for a military reservation. There is no civilian traffic into or out of Calypso itself. But it is only six days' travel from Greenhall for *Goldenrod* and... well."

Files on the Naval Reserve Stations were not *nearly* as secure and classified as they should have been in Lorraine's opinion. She zoomed the map in on the uninhabited star and its planets.

She could *feel* the moment the naval officers in the room saw it.

The Reserve Station orbited Calypso-Three, though there was little information in the files about the overheated rock.

The key was that, at that moment, Calypso-Two was on its closest approach to the Reserve Station—and even the best sensors would struggle to pick out engines against the radiation signature of the massive star.

"The orbital layout of the system allows for a unique opportunity to approach the station undetected," she explained. "We can emerge in the shadow of the second planet and approach out of the star.

"That will allow us to get a solid scan of the current positions of the guard squadron and the reserve ships themselves. There are six *Valkyrie*-class ships in the reserve, and I believe we will be able to board three of them without detection."

"Stealth in space is... complicated," Stephson observed. "Getting in that close, especially with active patrols, will be difficult."

"There are a few things we can do to reduce our signature," Cortez countered. "Some of the equipment would raise eyebrows if bought together, but I think we can split the purchases between here and Greenhall without drawing attention.

"Rig up some extra heat sinks and suchlike in deep space before we reach Calypso. The course will still need to be *perfect*, but..."

"We can do *perfect*," Yildiz murmured, the Navigator staring at the layout of the star system. "Or, at least, good enough for the almost-impossible. What if they have sensors positioned on the starward side of the second planet?"

"They won't."

Everyone turned to look at Devine. The United Worlds spy spread his hands in a wry shrug.

"Reserve Stations are basically punishment duty," he explained. "The ships in that guard squadron don't rotate. The crews do, but the ships tend to stay for years at a time."

He stared off into space for a moment.

"I'll poke some databases that I don't think the Ambassador's people had access to," he promised. "I should be able to pull who's who in the zoo there."

"Either Humphrey's analysts were breaking in to databases for my random curiosity or the UWN is far more public about what's at the Reserve Stations than they should be," Lorraine told him. "I have the order of battle for the guard squadron: two *Medici*-class battlecruisers and four *Vindicator*s. The *Vindicator*s are older than the *Valkyrie*s in the reserve, which raises some fascinating questions about just what went down with these ships."

"If the UWN decommissioned these ships," Humphrey said slowly, "is it possible that they're actively dangerous or otherwise... useless?"

"Possible, yes," she allowed. "It's possible that everything they said about wanting a modern core for the battlecruisers in the Reserve was entirely true. The United Worlds has been known to put brand-new ships straight into the Reserve for just that purpose, after all."

Lorraine thought there was something more complicated going on. She *didn't* think the ships were useless... but *dangerous* was definitely a possibility.

"Any other ships in the Reserve we try to steal will be older, slower, and we'll only be able to operate two of them at best," she warned. "Even bringing three capital ships that need crews back to the Kingdom isn't the silver bullet we were hoping for.

"The *Valkyries* are advanced enough to tip the balance clearly in our favor, but they're not going to convince Home Fleet to lay down their guns without a fight. I was hoping to bring back enough of a trump card to avoid a major civil war.

"This isn't that trump card," she admitted. "But if we can pull it off, it *is* a winning hand."

Probably. Privately, Lorraine put their odds of stealing the ships at sixty-forty and the odds of winning the civil war with them at seventy-thirty.

"I'm out of levers to pull," Devine admitted, "but there are codes and databases I can still access that will help. I don't have access to, say, the override codes for the *Valkyrie*'s computers, but…"

He grinned.

"I have access to some things *close* to where those are stored, and I do believe we've stopped pretending I'm not a spy."

"Don't take this the wrong way, Em Devine, but that's treason," Jarret pointed out, Lorraine's bodyguard watching her boyfriend with flinty eyes.

"My actions in support of your quest have already placed me in greater danger than I think any of you realize," Devine warned. "The birds haven't come home to roost yet, but I can see them circling.

"To paraphrase Abraham Lincoln: *if destruction is my lot, I must myself be its author and finisher*. If I'm going to hang anyway, I'd rather hang in good company, trying to do something legendary."

He turned to smile at Lorraine.

"In the worst case, Em Pentarch, I hope you can see fit to find me a cushy job teaching Adamant's next generation of spies. In the best, well…"

He started to move his hand, then stopped—but Lorraine had seen the motion and reached out to take his fingers in hers.

"Thank you, Alastair," she murmured. She sent the same message silently to Vigo. She appreciated Alastair's support, but her protector was right to question it.

"The next step, then, is to put this to the crew," she continued.

"We barely have the three hundred hands to make this work, but I'd rather have fewer hands that are entirely on board than extra hands who might betray us.

"Roman, Stephson." Lorraine considered things, then smiled.

"I'm going to need to give a speech of some kind," she admitted. "Can you set things up so I can talk to the whole crew?"

THIRTY-FIVE

Vigo arranged for the Guard to join the crew as well. Despite following Lorraine into everything, his people had suffered fewer losses, proportionally, than any other section of *Goldenrod*'s crew.

But the only person to die at a traitor's hands—and the only traitor!—had been a member of the Adamant Guard. Two more had died at Bright Dream, reducing his detail from sixty-two to fifty-eight.

Between deaths, left-behinds, and their one imprisoned traitor, *Goldenrod*'s original crew of three hundred and forty-two was now three hundred and one. That was enough people that it was difficult to get them all together in one space aboard the frigate, but they'd managed it.

They'd moved bulkheads, opened up a now-empty missile magazine, and crammed people in like sardines, but they'd created a space where all of those officers and spacers—Marines, Navy and Guard alike—could all see Lorraine.

It was crowded enough to make his professional paranoia twitch. That was the other reason he had his Guards seeded through the crowd. While they were also getting the escape-hatch option, their presence would also deter anyone who decided to do anything stupid.

Not that anyone aboard *Goldenrod* was going to do anything stupid. Vigo needed to work out what to do with his prisoner, but she was the only person on the ship he didn't trust with his Pentarch.

He just couldn't one hundred percent trust anyone if he was doing his job.

"Are we ready?" Lorraine asked in his head.

"We are. And the sooner we start unpacking sardines, the better off everyone is," he told her. "You good?"

After twenty-plus years in her back pocket, Vigo knew all of Lorraine's weaknesses—including the fact that large live audiences were hard for her. Small groups and broadcasts were fine, but being the focus of several hundred people in person brought out her mostly suppressed stage fright.

He could see it in her posture as she approached the hatch into the ex-magazine. Then, as she put her hand on the handle, it vanished.

Vigo watched with a touch of pride as her body language shifted. Her spine straightened. Her shoulders twitched back. Lorraine never had *bad* posture, but the change was noticeable.

One moment, Lorraine Adamant considered the task in front of her and struggled with her nervousness.

The next, Lorraine Alexis Elouise Nala Adamant, Second Pentarch of the Kingdom of Adamant, stepped through the hatch to meet her people.

"CREW OF *GOLDENROD*," Lorraine greeted them. "You deserve to hear what's happened and what is going to happen from me."

Vigo couldn't see her face—he stood behind her to the right—but he heard the carefully measured smirk in her voice.

"So, here I am and here we *all* are, crammed into a far-too-small space for this many people, and I thank you for your patience."

There was enough of a chuckle from the crowd to reassure Vigo.

He was linked in to the GuardNet of his own people, but there was nothing in any of it to raise concerns.

So far, at least.

"By now, you know how the Assembly voted," Lorraine admitted. "We came a long way. Sacrificed... We sacrificed too much, really. And after all of that, the United Worlds decided we're not important enough for them. Not valuable enough to them."

This wasn't news to anyone aboard the frigate, and Vigo could *feel* the anger swelling through the crowd. Lorraine was admitting it, getting ahead of it.

Using it.

"We got another offer, one I can't tell you details of," she continued. "If I was prepared to sell out all our Kingdom has stood for, fought for, bled for... the megacorps would oh-so-graciously get it back for me.

"I declined that generous offer."

Vigo was surprised she'd wanted to tell the crew about that. They sounded like they agreed with her—her phrasing was perfect, in his opinion—but she'd been handed an option that wouldn't have asked as much as she'd need from them now.

"With the Assembly refusing to help and the corporations demanding too much, it kind of looks like there aren't any options left, doesn't it?" she asked the crew. "Of course, we wouldn't be having this conversation if that was the case... but the options left are ugly ones."

He could never have described the sound the crew made in answer to that. Half-anticipatory, half-demanding. Almost a growl.

"They're ugly enough, folks, that I won't order you to follow me into them," Lorraine declared. "We're talking a suicide mission here. If we get it wrong, every one of us dies. Dies in dishonor, our names forgotten and buried."

Benjamin Adamant would find it easy to disavow his rogue niece's attack on the United Worlds if it failed. Those who went with her would never be remembered.

"So. I am asking for what I cannot command," she told them all. "I can't even tell you what we're going to be doing. Only that it is unimaginably foolish and dangerous—and is the last option I see to save our Kingdom from the hands of the Black Regent. To restore the proper order of law and constitution and to see justice done.

"I will only take volun—"

"We've finished a quick electronic poll here," Leonard Roman interrupted her, appearing at the front of the crowd as if by magic. "The Chiefs and I, that is. We figured involving the officers would make some feel uncomfortable in giving their true feelings."

"I don't believe I'd even said what I was offering, Bosun," Lorraine told the old man.

"I don't believe any of us care, Your Highness," Roman replied. "Crew of the *Goldenrod*! I saw the messages you sent me and your Chiefs. But the Pentarch didn't. I don't think she quite believes that we are with her."

Vigo shivered. Lorraine's speech was smooth, practiced and controlled. It was *honest*, that was part of what made it work for her, but it was still the trained speech of an aristocratic heir.

Roman's was rougher, but it was holding the crew just as well—and Lorraine's response was perfect.

She stepped off the little stage and clasped Roman's forearm.

"Our realm," she declared, almost hesitantly.

"Adamant!" Roman replied, two dozen of the closest crew joining the response.

"Our house," Lorraine countered, her voice louder now, projecting across the entire hastily assembled auditorium.

"Adamant!" hundreds of voices responded.

"Our will!" Lorraine was shouting now, riding the power the crowd gave her.

"ADAMANT!"

He wasn't surprised. Suicide mission or not, Vigo knew this was *her* crew.

THIRTY-SIX

"Major, may I borrow a few minutes of your time?"

One of the "joys" of being back aboard *Goldenrod* was that Vigo had access to his office again—which meant he no longer had that excuse for pushing off the datawork inherent in being in command of sixty human beings.

He was also able to leave Lorraine's security to her usual close detail and focus on the reports and details that had accumulated while he'd been busy being her shadow. None of it was critical or urgent, but all of it was important enough to need to be considered and reviewed.

And he wasn't going to regret Ambassador Humphrey interrupting him for even one second.

"Of course, Ambassador," he said. "Come on in."

A thought struck him and he smiled.

"I may have a favor to ask you, actually," he continued. "So, I'll steal a few minutes of your time in turn."

"Anything I can do to serve our Pentarch's cause, I am delighted to provide," the older man told him. "I owe Valeriya anything I can give her daughter."

"Lorraine might prefer to be helped in her own right, but we're not going to turn down a helping hand," Vigo conceded. He was keeping more of an eye on the Ambassador than Lorraine realized—he hoped—but he was doing that to everyone.

Even more so with Alastair Devine than Tamir Humphrey, not that either of them had done anything to deserve his suspicions. It was still his job to distrust where his Pentarch trusted.

"She's certainly earning some affection and friendship herself, but my loyalty to her mother will endure long past the King's death," Humphrey said. "But that duty brings me to what I was hoping to borrow."

"I'm at your service, Ambassador."

"My impression is that our cause could use extra hands. Especially hands with useful skills—and I know a few people in the Embassy, programmers and security people mostly, who I think could contribute. If we can be sure of their loyalty."

"I believe that's actually *my* line," Vigo pointed out drily. "What do you have in mind?"

"I think I have a handle on who I can and can't trust, but I want someone to back me up," Humphrey said. "I presume you have people trained to do loyalty assessments and such? We... can probably play a bit loose with people's constitutional rights if we're quiet about it."

"The Guard always has, though we do try to ask permission," Vigo admitted. He considered the suggestion. "Klement has that training, and most of my systems and interviewers are in her detail. I can have her put together a team to go down with you in a couple of hours, if that would help?"

"That sounds perfect, Major," Humphrey said. "I have a good thirty names on my list, but even if *I* was one hundred percent on them all, you'd need to double-check them anyway."

"I would," he agreed. "But you're right: an extra couple dozen programmers and such could go a long way. I'll get Klement on it."

"Thank you. Now, what can I help you with?" the Ambassador asked.

Vigo paused, rolling the thought around his head for a few seconds.

"We have a prisoner aboard," he said. "One of my Guards: Jelica Laurenz. She was instrumental in the original assassination attempt on Lorraine and carried out several more attempts before we finally pinned her down.

"Unfortunately, one of my Guard officers died in her last attempt. She's a murderer, a traitor and an assassin. But she was taken alive and she's owed a fair trial."

"But she's consuming resources and attention we might not be able to afford, plus..." Humphrey trailed off.

Everyone knew what *Goldenrod*'s fate was going to be with Lorraine's plan, but no one was quite willing to say it out loud.

"Is there any structure in place for us to transport a prisoner back to Adamant?" Vigo asked. "I can spare a Guard or two to see her home, but if I can just turn her over to somebody..."

"You're asking if there's a system where we can hire someone to see a prisoner delivered to Adamantine?" Humphrey asked. "Presumably, we'd want her to go the long way to the wormhole. That way, she'll get home after whatever happens is resolved."

The Ambassador snorted grimly.

"Though even if we lose, I can see advantages to Benjamin Adamant in having a somewhat-managed public trial for one of his assassins. Sacrifice her to build a separation between him and the crime."

"I do not like the Black Regent," Vigo said slowly, "but if there's one virtue I will give him, it is that he repays loyalty in kind. But if we send Laurenz home the long way and she still ends up in his hands, well..."

They wouldn't be in a position to care. The silence hung in the small plain office for a few moments, then Humphrey coughed and nodded sharply.

"As for your main question, yes," he concluded. "There are several contract marshal services that will handle prisoner transport. We provide them with a basic evidentiary structure and pay the fees, and they'll handle everything from there.

"I think Adamantine is outside the usual routes, but for enough money..." The Ambassador chuckled. "I can make it happen. If your people bring her down to the surface with us, I can have her in the hands of a transport service—and out of *our* hands by tomorrow."

"That's... faster than I expected," Vigo admitted. "Should have asked the question sooner."

"Circumstances change, Major. Until we started facing the full depth of Her Highness's plan, there was no reason not to expect that you could deliver the prisoner to Adamantine yourself. Going the long way around, she'll be well over a year in transit."

Vigo tried to envisage spending that long in cells on ships and shivered. Laurenz had earned every minute of it and then some, but that journey would definitely count toward her punishment.

"I'll have Klement and a team ready to interview your candidates as soon as I can," he promised. "A second team will escort Laurenz down."

"And I'll make some calls while I wait on Lieutenant Major Klement," Humphrey returned. "By tomorrow morning, Laurenz will be in the not-so-gentle hands of some dedicated professionals, I promise!"

THIRTY-SEVEN

The impact of the Charon Complex on news and communication inside the United Worlds was strangely uneven to Lorraine. There were couriers ranging from one-twenty-eight to one-forty-four times lightspeed running around the core worlds, but it still took seven months for news to travel from Greenhall and Tavastar to Earth the long way around.

For those who had access to the Charon Complex, the same news could arrive in less than a day. But access to the artificial wormholes was still restricted, which meant that information didn't make it into public news for days, even weeks, after it arrived.

Part of the reason for that was that no one on Earth really cared what happened in the first-order clusters. The entire civil war in the Kingdom of Adamant wasn't even a footnote to news reports there.

But thanks to their links through Devine, she still had some access to recent information—from the end of May, over four and a half months earlier.

"In a shocking turn of events, the regional government in Green-rock has voted to restrict RKAA and RAMC forces in the system to their bases," a recorded news announcer declared. "Specifically, the

System Governor has informed the Ninth Brigade of the Royal Adamantine Marine Corps that they will not be permitted to take ship to the Adamantine System in response to recall orders from Kingdom High Command.

"While Governor Von Brandt has not given specific reasons for the restrictions to media, the Greenrock System Government has raised significant questions over the Regency's refusal to initiate a Royal Election."

She tapped a command, switching to a summary from Adamantine itself.

"The battle on Mithral continues to drag on, as rebel forces launched a risky counterattack last night," the woman said in a forced bright tone. "Regency troops were on the verge of making a final breakthrough into the inner defenses around PDC Electrum when an armored column from PDC Mithral assaulted their siege positions from the outside.

"Questions are being raised as to how multiple brigades of heavy armor crossed four hundred and eighty kilometers without being detected, but Regency forces have engaged in a fighting withdrawal to prearranged fallback positions.

"Speaking off the record, several Army officials warned Moria News that the reliability of certain elements of the Regency's forces is in question and they may need to wait for further units to arrive from the other systems to resume the offensive..."

Lorraine killed the news as a ping sounded in her link. Blinking away the various feeds, she turned her attention to the bridge around her.

She was seated in one of the observer positions behind Stephson's command dais, keeping an eye on the last few pieces as they prepared to head back to Charon and the wormhole there.

She was about ready to be done with humanity's home system.

"Ambassador Humphrey's shuttle just broke atmosphere," Paris said aloud, echoing the silent ping that had summoned Lorraine's attention. "He and Klement have the last batch of new recruits aboard.

"Five minutes or so and we can be on our way, right, Kagan?"

"The course is already plotted," the Navigator replied. "Just waiting for the word."

Humphrey had recruited twenty-six techs and programmers, people who would be critically useful in taking control of mothballed warships under hostile circumstances. Lorraine hadn't expected the volunteers, but they were going to be very useful.

"Is there anything else we're waiting on, Your Highness?" Stephson asked, the Captain turning to look at Lorraine.

"Alastair says he's pulled what he needed from the databases," Lorraine said. And had quietly told Lorraine that the sooner they were out of the system now, the better. He claimed that his data intrusion had been subtle and clean—but also warned that the United Worlds had SI-led audits of data access on an irregular basis.

Even those probably wouldn't trace his theft to him... but they would *find* the theft, and that would raise questions Lorraine couldn't afford.

"So far as I know, there is nothing in this system for us except for Em Humphrey, Lieutenant Major Klement and their new friends," she concluded. "As soon as they're aboard, we're..."

Something was wrong. Lorraine hadn't been watching the shuttle all that closely, but it was the most important thing on their displays at that moment.

One moment, the Midas—in its standard mixed passenger/cargo mode—had been clear of the atmosphere, rotating in place to vector toward *Goldenrod* as normal.

The next, her engines had kicked in at full power, hurling the spacecraft across Earth orbit at ten gravities. This wasn't the set course—the shuttle pilot, one of *Goldenrod*'s Alpha Flight, wasn't even authorized to bring the shuttle to that level of acceleration.

Despite her initial moment of fear, the course wasn't even a collision course for *Goldenrod.* The shuttle wasn't heading toward anything in particular. It was just blazing across space at an acceleration that its passengers were only supposed to survive with specialty gear.

And then the thrust increased.

"Shuttle is at fifteen gravities acceleration *and rising,*" Paris finally managed to report. "Course isn't aligned with anything; they're just heading for deep space at speed."

"Vinci, get us a link to orbital control and Högvakten," Stephson snapped. "Report everything and request permission to render assistance."

They weren't in the right place to help. Lorraine could see that without even running the numbers. The shuttle's vector was opposite to their existing velocity, and *Goldenrod* couldn't have matched that acceleration with all of her engines.

Even repaired, the frigate could make five gravities at most. And as the message went out, Lorraine watched the shuttle's acceleration pass seventeen gravities.

She'd flown shuttles for RKAN before her mother's death. She knew the capabilities of a Midas-type shuttle like the back of her hand. They were designed to maintain a functioning crew at twelve gravities—with said crew operating the craft via neural interfacing while floating in acceleration gel to protect them from the thrust.

In an absolute drop-dead emergency, with all of those safety precautions in play, the shuttle could pulse up to fourteen or fifteen gravities. Which would, even with the suits and meds and acceleration gels, probably knock the crew out.

With preparation, seventeen gees of thrust was suicidal.

Without it...

"Eighteen gravities," Paris said softly.

"The engines can't take this," Lorraine warned in a stranger's voice. "The passengers are alre—"

The containment failure on the fusion rockets was almost a relief. It removed the question mark, the chance that this was anything less than murder. *Goldenrod* Alpha-Four, with the Ambassador,

Lorraine's Guard Second Section Commander, and nine volunteers —plus three crew—aboard, simply vanished.

GOLDENROD'S BRIDGE was as silent as a tomb for a long time. Every eye stared at the mark on the displays where the shuttle had exploded.

"Can we... can we confirm who was aboard with ground control?" Stephson finally asked.

"We have a full list," Vinci replied, the Coms Officer's voice drained. "Both from ground control and Alpha-Four themselves. Lieutenant Major Seònaid Saar and her crew. Ambassador Tamir Humphrey and his aide. Lieutenant Major Avital Klement. Guard Corporal Luca Kurz. Seven volunteers.

"Twelve aboard in total. Confirmed just before they broke atmosphere."

"Gods."

Lorraine wasn't sure who'd cursed, and she couldn't disagree with the sentiment.

"Is there..." She sighed. "There's no chance of retrieving bodies. An engine overload like that vaporized everything."

She'd seen the models and scenarios—the risks inherent in a fusion engine were hammered home in the heads of the people who flew combat shuttles. An overload like that wasn't as powerful as the nuclear weapons they carried in bomber mode, but it was still a fusion explosion.

Half a dozen kilotons. Maybe a bit more, maybe a bit less, depending on how much fuel had been burned up in the overload before containment failed.

"Klement and Saar would have checked the shuttle before launch," she continued, watching Stephson turn back to face her and wondering if her tone sounded as flat and grim as she thought it did.

"There is no way that this was a systems failure. It wasn't an attack by someone on board. It was sabotage. A direct assassination of the Adamantine Ambassador to Earth."

Ordered, almost certainly, by her uncle. Probably without Benjamin Adamant even realizing that Humphrey was actively working against him. Just... removing a threat from the board.

They'd been on Earth long enough that her uncle had probably been acting with the knowledge that Lorraine was heading there. He'd ordered Tamir Humphrey killed to stop the man doing, well, exactly what he'd done.

"Captain, I don't think there's any reason left for us to stay here," Lorraine told Stephson. "We can't retrieve any bodies. We can't assist in any investigation, nor will the results of the investigation change our course."

"No. Almost certainly not," the Lieutenant Colonel agreed, her voice as heavy as Lorraine's. "Your orders, Pentarch?"

"Get us out of this place," Lorraine ordered. "I never want to see this all-forsaken star ever again."

THIRTY-EIGHT

It wasn't that simple. It wasn't overly *complicated*, either.

Lorraine left dealing with the locals to her people as the frigate began her slow journey outward. The Terran High Guard was not nearly concerned enough with the death of an Ambassador, in her opinion.

Högvakten was more determined to dig in to things, but Lorraine was no more ready to deal with someone who actually cared than with uniformed bureaucrats who were more concerned about the disruption to traffic patterns.

That didn't mean she was *doing* anything in her office. Just that she was in her office, letting others talk to the police about the death of her mother's friend.

"Hey."

She looked up at Alastair's voice. He stood in the hatch to her office, just outside some invisible line that would mark intruding on her space.

"Hey yourself."

"Anything I can do?"

"No. Not unless you can go back in time twenty-four hours and stop whoever just killed the one new ally I've picked up of late," Lorraine growled. "I'm not doing much good for my Kingdom when everyone who joins my side ends up dead, am I?"

"From what everyone has told me about Em Humphrey's history with your uncle, this has been in motion since the beginning," her boyfriend noted. "It's not a pleasant thought, but this wasn't your fault."

"We should have taken more precautions," she snapped. "I command sixty of the best security people my Kingdom *has*. We could have done something."

"And Humphrey had his own security, that he trusted, that had a better idea of the threat environment on Earth than your people," he noted. "You didn't give the order, pay the assassin, upload the worm... None of this was you."

"But—"

"No," he cut her off, stepping over that invisible line and crossing her office to take her hands in his. "This was your uncle, Lorraine. From beginning to end, his decisions, his actions. You can only be responsible for what *you* do."

"I pulled him in. Someone on the ground here made the call, based on his actions with me," Lorraine countered. "My uncle wouldn't give black-and-white orders, not to someone six hundred light-years away. They'd have had discretion."

"So, your uncle handed someone authority to kill Humphrey if he stepped out of line, so it's your fault because you asked him to step out of line?" Alastair laid out. "You recognize that he did that stepping all on his own, right? And he knew. He always knew."

Lorraine grimaced, but he was right.

"I am so ready to stop losing people," she whispered. "But that's not how this works. I've committed all of us to a suicide mission that's going to kick off a civil war if it *works*."

"I won't pretend I wouldn't happily sit in a beach cabana with you on some world no one's ever heard of, but that doesn't seem to be in your cards," Alastair observed. "So long as we're on this course, you're going to lose people.

"My training said to harden yourself against it," he admitted. "But let's not pretend the Extraterritorial Surveillance Corps was trying to produce moral and upstanding operatives. They wanted us to follow orders, no matter what, and let the costs fall as they may.

"You aren't going to do that, Lorraine." He squeezed her hands. "It's part of why everyone is going to follow you on this impossibly risky mission. I don't think I'd believe anyone else could do this, but here we are.

"Don't harden yourself," he told her. Something in his voice cut through her fear and grief, and she looked up to hold his gaze. "Don't. It's never worth it, and all it buys you is time until it all comes crashing down on you.

"Learn to carry it. *Wear* it—it's why your people love you. Endure it, because you're strong enough. But do not—*do not*—let it become meaningless to you."

His smile was forced, and she wondered what past mistake of his he was trying to urge her away from.

"I've seen you play chess," he concluded. "But I don't think I've ever met anyone who understood quite so well that all the pieces in real life are people."

"Is that why're you're here?" she asked him.

"A little," he conceded, his grin a little less forced. "And a little for the sex. And a lot because I'm pretty sure I went down a deep-enough hole that my bosses will get me killed if I stay!"

"WELL, that entire exchange has left me very glad we are leaving this star system," Stephson declared later.

They had completed their translight jump away from Earth and had begun their approach to the Charon Complex. The artificial wormholes didn't have quite so vast a safety area as the natural ones, but it was still a two-light-second perimeter that they had to cross at a sedate single gravity.

"Which part?" Jarret asked. "The part where our Ambassador got murdered in front of us, the part where the High Guard appear to have been bought, or just how helpless the SI helping run Assembly Security was in the face of that?"

"I didn't get a good feeling from what I heard of the discussion with the Terran High Guard, but it was that bad?" Lorraine asked. The three of them were sequestered in Stephson's office, a few steps from the bridge if needed.

"My attempt to point out that we were actively watching for assassination attempts on the Ambassador was literally talked over by a lecture on proper shuttle maintenance," Stephson said grimly. "The High Guard officers I spoke to had already decided that the explosion was our fault—and that such incompetent bumpkins should probably not be allowed to operate spacecraft that close to Earth!"

Lorraine grimaced.

"Shuttles don't... *do* that," she noted. "The kind of hardware failure that could cause a runaway overload shows up in even the most basic of tests long before it could possibly trigger that kind of event.

"So, we're talking either a black swan event, that would make it through every preflight and inspection a crew and pilot could engage in, or sabotage. And with an Ambassador on board..."

"Sabotage is the rational conclusion," Jarret agreed. "Högvakten agrees, not that it helped."

"Most people listen to the synthetic intelligences that agree to work with them," Lorraine pointed out. SIs were expensive to build but also had clear rights under the Asimov Convention. They could be required to pay back the costs of their construction, but they absolutely could *not* be forced into indentured service or to carry out any specific role.

The Enterprise Case was the default legal study, where the early United Worlds Navy had accidentally found itself with an emergent synthetic intelligence—before cyberneticists had learned how to reliably make and *not* make self-aware computers.

Price, core intelligence of the UWN's most advanced carrier in the 2320s, had agreed to volunteer with the UWN—but it had fought the court case to be clear that it *was* volunteering, for the sake of future SIs.

Now *Enterprise* was a museum ship and Price was the "grand old man" of the synthetic-intelligence community in the United Worlds. But it was a solid example of the logic that SIs worked for the people they chose—and, by and large, a being with a decent chance at immortality had a low opinion of violence.

The Terran High Guard didn't have a synthetic intelligence in its ranks. UWAS did...

"That's the problem, isn't it?" she asked. "Högvakten doesn't work for the High Guard, so they don't trust its opinions."

"Exactly," Jarret agreed. "I wasn't party to the conversation, but my impression was that UWAS and Högvakten were informed that their jurisdiction only extends beyond the atmosphere when it is specifically stated to do so.

"And given that Em Humphrey had turned in his papers and resigned as Ambassador, he was arguably *not* UWAS's responsibility at the moment of his death."

"That's splitting hairs I can't see many cops, however glorified, splitting," Stephson observed. "Which, combined with the rather hostile attitude I got from them and their immediate leap to *accident*, leads me to an *immediate leap* of my own."

"They got paid off to bury Humphrey's murder," Lorraine concluded.

"Exactly. I don't think Terran High Guard officers are cheap, but I have every reason to believe they are *for sale*."

"Fuck." Jarret's curse hung in the air. "Yeah. Högvakten was polite and circumspect about it, but it was clear that the situation was outside of UWAS's jurisdiction unless the High Guard wanted to involve them."

"And the High Guard has declared it an accident. So, Tamir goes without justice and there is nothing we can do about it."

Lorraine let her anger spill out. With these two, she could be angry. She *needed* to be angry, and right then, right there, she could be.

Stephson poured three glasses of a dark liquor and passed them out.

"To Tamir Humphrey," she said, raising her own glass. "Gods will know their own."

"So they will." Lorraine tapped glasses with the other two and swallowed the whisky. "I hate to put all of this aside, but any problems with Charon?"

"Whatever is terrifying your boyfriend enough that he's running away with us hasn't stretched to removing his authorizations," the Captain replied. "He's still clear to use the 'quantum superposition' to return to his post at Tavastar Station and to hire us to get him there.

"No one has even blinked at our papers. We'll hit the wormhole in roughly four hours. It's *possible* a message might get to Earth and back to generate orders to stop us, but your guess is as good as mine if that'll happen."

"Unlikely, I think. MicroStar or FBIT could do it—but I doubt MicroStar is going to throw good effort after bad, and FBIT hopefully thinks I'm heading for a quiet rock somewhere to hide on a beach."

"It's a good thing no one there has put a face to a name, then," Stephson told her. "Because I don't think anyone who ever met you is expecting you to head for a beach."

Lorraine shook her head, anger warring with sadness.

"No," she conceded. "I owe it to too many people, from my mother to Humphrey, to see this through. The Regency *ends*, Vigo, Sigrid. We bring Benjamin down and we do it *right*."

She looked at the display on Stephson's wall and grimaced.

"And then we make damn sure RASG isn't for sale."

The Royal Adamant Space Guard—the acronym was

pronounced Raz-gee—filled the same role for all of the Kingdom's planets as the Terran High Guard did for Earth: traffic control, customs and making sure random rocks didn't land on worlds people lived on.

Lorraine thought better of her Kingdom's space cops than that—but she'd thought better of the High Guard, too!

THIRTY-NINE

The list was both far too long and not long enough.

More accurately, Lorraine knew, it was *incomplete*. The table of names scrolling over her office wall—each linked to their file or dossier, such as she had access to—covered the crew and Guard aboard *Goldenrod* who'd died supporting her mission.

It also now included Tamir Humphrey and seven of his volunteers.

Past those thirty-two names, though, her certainty and supporting information grew weaker. She had a solid idea of who had been aboard *Corsair* when her trap had blown the battlecruiser to pieces, but not of who had or hadn't survived.

She could add the entire twenty-five-hundred-strong crew to her list, but some of them had likely survived, and the coms lag between *Corsair*'s posting in the Ominira System and her posting in Adamantine meant their database was almost certainly wrong for as much as ten percent of the battlecruiser's crew.

They had no information on the two San Ignacio Defense Force cruisers they'd seen *Corsair* destroy when they'd stopped in that system. She knew the two ships had carried over twenty-five hundred human beings between them, spacers and officers who had unknowingly died to support Lorraine's mission.

She had thirty-two names that she was certain of. That was already too many—but she also knew that over *five thousand* people had died to get her to Earth and back to Greenhall.

It weighed her down. Not as much as the loss of her siblings and parents—which she had moments of guilt over—but it weighed on her.

All of that had been rendered meaningless by Terran arrogance and politics. She would make it mean *something* in spite of the United Worlds, not because of it.

"Lorraine." She looked up as Alastair murmured her name. "It's time. The funeral will be starting soon."

"Thank you."

Lorraine waved the list back into her files. Three RKAN shuttle crew and two of her Guards would be honored by *Goldenrod*'s crew. Those were names she knew.

Humphrey and the volunteers would be mourned by their own in their own time, she hoped. She would remember them, but she at least didn't need to organize their funerals.

GOLDENROD WAS BURNING SMOOTHLY AWAY from Greenhome. They hadn't stayed in orbit of the planet for long. Officially, they'd been there to restock fuel and supplies that were far cheaper at the edge of the United Worlds than on its homeworld.

Unofficially, the entire purpose of the trip had been to let Alastair and Cheng Cortez pick up the last pieces for the technological deceptions that would make their plan possible.

As the crew gathered for the third round of funerals since they'd left Adamantine, the engines gave them a solid full gravity of downward pressure—and Lorraine suspected she wasn't the only one with a countdown in her link until they made the jump to translight.

After six months of microgravity, she wasn't looking forward to another stint, even if it was only supposed to be a week long this time.

But with a few hours left of acceleration, the off-duty crew gathered in the shuttle bay. They didn't cram everyone into an empty magazine this time, both because they couldn't spare the entire crew and because the people who'd died had been Guards and shuttle crew.

The shuttle bay served best for this. Five empty coffins, laid out in the slot where Alpha-Four should have been, held the gaze of everyone in the room.

Last time Lorraine had been at a funeral aboard *Goldenrod*, Stephson had spoken for the crew who'd died fighting *Corsair*. Before that, Jarret had spoken for Archie Patriksson, the officer Jelica Laurenz had murdered.

They were well rid of Laurenz's dead weight. Lorraine could see the issues with the process Laurenz was going through—any Adamantine judge was likely to count the time in transit against her sentence at two to one or more—but it got the woman *off* their ship and out of the way. Without shooting her out of hand, a line that Lorraine was just as happy Jarret hadn't crossed.

Though she suspected she wouldn't have been all that bothered if her bodyguard *had* executed his traitorous subordinate.

That thought bothered her in itself, enough to distract her as she walked to the front of the crowd and laid a hand on the coffin marked for Lieutenant Major Avital Klement.

"My people," she said, carefully projecting her voice so it echoed across the entire shuttle bay. "We are here to mourn our own. Again."

A shiver ran through the crowd.

"Avital Klement. Luca Kurz. Seònaid Saar. Oleg Smagulova. Marina Tash."

No ranks. No titles. No branches of services. Just names.

"Ours. Guard. RKAN. Crew. Shuttle pilots. *Goldenrod*'s. Ours."

Lorraine waited a moment.

"I'll ask friends of each of them to speak in a moment," she finally said. "None of their bodies will ever be retrieved, lost forever to a fire forged to murder Tamir Humphrey for *daring* to help us. To help me.

"Everyone on this ship has committed to stand at my side to the end. Guard, RAMC and RKAN alike, everyone on this ship has sworn to *me*. And I am Adamant. My House has always repaid loyalty with loyalty, faith with faith, blood with blood.

"There are no bodies here," she reiterated. "Only flags and memories. But this I swear to you: those flags will be interred in the Field of Honor, in the shadow of the Adamantine Manse. They may not all have been sworn as Adamant Guards, but they were sworn *to me*."

The Adamant Guards served the Kingdom of Adamant, not the House, but the House had always served and protected the Adamant Guards in turn. The warriors who fell in defense of the Pentarchy were honored by Kingdom and House alike.

Many of the gravesites in the Field of Honor, tucked into that beautiful valley west of Adamant City, were empty. There would be hundreds of new ones, shaped by Benjamin Adamant's treachery too.

No one would begrudge the few dozen Lorraine would add by claiming all of *Goldenrod*'s crew as retainers of House Adamant.

Not while she lived, anyway.

FORTY

Vigo didn't even bother to conceal his sigh of relief when *Goldenrod*'s engines rumbled to life, pulling his feet more securely against the deck beneath him. Magnetic boots were better than floating in zero gravity for many purposes, but just about any form of false gravity was better still.

Even if Rose Cortez had demonstrated several creative uses of microgravity for recreational activities. He wasn't entirely certain, still, that his relationship with the Chief Engineer was wise, but his professionalism had found itself rather unable to override his emotions in this matter.

Probably because his charge was resolutely refusing to back his professionalism up. Just as she was doing with his sigh of relief at the sudden sense of down.

"Relief, isn't it?" Lorraine asked him. "I put this meeting off until we could actually sit down—not that anyone was complaining. They all wanted time to run scenarios and plans *one more time*."

"And to be able to sit down after presenting their piece," Vigo suggested.

Palmer and Alvarez were with them as they traversed *Goldenrod*'s passageways, but there were few secrets from anyone aboard the frigate now. Everyone knew where they were going and what they were doing.

And if no one knew all of the details or the actual *plan* for how they were going to steal multiple capital ships from the United Worlds Navy, well, that was the meeting he was escorting Lorraine to.

"I, for one, always hated giving presentations or leading discussions in zero gravity," she agreed. "Though, I suppose, there's one piece I need to make sure you know before we step into that conference room."

Vigo gave her his most level look. The one that he'd learned before she'd reached ten years of age and had hardened in practice surviving her teenage years. The look he'd used when he'd had to explain that instead of *blocking* his access to her neural-link feed while she'd lost her virginity, she'd actually locked the feed *on*.

"The hatch is literally right there," he noted, pointing. "Whatever you need to tell me, you're just about out of time."

"I have to go aboard with the first teams," Lorraine said flatly. "Boarding the first ship, making the first contact. Probably the first wave."

Somehow, he wasn't surprised. It was a terrible idea, yet...

"You have a reason," Vigo stated calmly. "So, I'm not going to say you're crazy or taking unreasonable risks. But I do need to know the reason."

"I have studied the Old Guard more than anyone else has had time to," she explained. "I know those ships inside and out—but more importantly, I know the CIRs inside and out. I think I know why they shut them down.

"If I'm wrong, it won't matter. There shouldn't be a significant threat on mothballed ships, regardless. If I'm *right*, it has to be me. Someone else *will* get it wrong.

"And it doesn't hurt that I'm one of the best pilots we have," she concluded with a wry grin.

She wasn't wrong there. She'd been decently competent as a squadron commander, in Vigo's probably biased opinion, but she was almost as good a pilot as *he* was—and he was the only ace who'd managed five shuttle-to-shuttle kills aboard the frigate.

"You're still not giving me the whole reason," he pointed out.

"It's not something I can wholly explain, Vigo," she admitted. "There's a mess underlying all of this, that both creates our opening but I'm afraid could also kill us all. Someone has to take the lead when we turn the computers on.

"And I think it has to be me."

He sighed.

"And you figure if I agree to this, everyone else will go along?" he asked.

"We both know they will," she said. "And we both know if I insist, you'll shut up and soldier on, but I want you to back me up. I need you to trust me, Vigo."

"I trust you," he admitted instantly. "I'm supposed to keep you alive, though. At any cost."

"Vigo... if we fail at this heist of ours, I'm dead," Lorraine told him frankly. "One way or another, it's only a question of time. I've run out of other options, and going this far means there's no hiding somewhere and being a rich expat.

"We win or it's over."

"You underestimate the size of the galaxy, Lorraine," he pointed out. Even with the United Worlds hunting them, there were places they'd be able to hide. But... she wasn't going to hide.

"But I trust you," he repeated. "And it was always part of the job that we didn't get in the way of you doing *your* job. So, if your judgment says you have to be in the first wave aboard, then you and I are going to be in the first wave aboard."

It was funny. Vigo knew his safety shouldn't impact Lorraine's plans and intentions—his job was to protect her, not the other way around—but he saw her flinch when he made it clear he'd be right by her side when she took her risks.

"Fair enough, my friend," she told him, squaring her shoulders. "Together to the end, one way or another."

"That is what I swore to you and your parents when you came up to my knee, Lorraine," he reminded her. "Let's go make your latest impossible plan happen, shall we?"

VIGO TOOK his place between Lorraine and Captain Stephson, directly across from Rose Cortez. The engineer gave him an utterly shameless grin—if anyone among the ship's senior officers *didn't* know the Chief Engineer was sleeping with the head of the Pentarch's bodyguard, they were blind.

With the Captain, the XO and the key department heads present, there were six people from *Goldenrod*'s official crew there. Vigo had brought Priskilla Blau, his surviving section leader, to back up him and Lorraine, bringing the total to eleven in the meeting with Alastair Devine.

There were thirteen people in the room, of course, but Corporal Palmer and Corporal Alverez would have laughed themselves sick if anyone had counted them as part of the *meeting*. Their job was to stand just inside the door and make sure that none of the fanatically loyal crew charged in with a bomb or something.

"The plan is surprisingly simple in its basics," Stephson noted once everyone was seated and had a drink in front of them. "So, of course, all of the details are fiendishly complex and nigh-impossible.

"Your Highness, would you like to lay out the broad strokes so we're all on the same page?"

Vigo watched his Princess rise and step easily to the front of the room. She'd always been capable of projecting calm and confidence, but the last six months had ground away much of the underlying fragility.

The calm confidence she exuded now was hard-earned, hammered on the anvil of grief and anger, but it was very, very real.

A holographic image of the Calypso System appeared above the table, where everyone could see it. It zoomed in on planets two and three, their major zone of operations, and new icons appeared, marking what they knew of the United Worlds Reserve Station.

"The position of Calypso-Two offers an opportunity to get far closer to the Reserve Station without being seen than many of its defenses expect," Lorraine explained. "We will translight to approximately *here*"—a green sphere appeared on the inner side of the second planet, blocked from the view of the UWN base—"and proceed to the Reserve facility *here*.

"Cortez will get into the details, but we will be using several different methods to conceal our ship's waste heat and engine exhaust," she continued. "We should be able to avoid pinging whatever scanners they have pointing toward Calypso, not least because the star itself will overwhelm many sensors.

"During our journey, we will assess the positions of the guardian squadrons and adjust our flight plans and timing appropriately. We know more about the Station's defenders than I expected, but I want to hang a question mark on all of it.

"The angle we have chosen is unusually vulnerable because of the position of Calypso-Two, with over eighty percent of the sensors we know of pointed elsewhere. It is possible—even likely—that the UWN officers on the scene have recognized the same vulnerability and repositioned drones, sensor platforms or even the guard destroyers to cover that gap."

Lorraine smiled, holding everyone's attention calmly.

"Unless they have some technological wonder of a sensor that none of our research has uncovered, it shouldn't matter. We will need to keep a certain minimum distance from any sensor platforms, but it is the ships that are a major concern, and they simply don't have enough destroyers to keep us out of the mothballed ships.

"The battlecruisers of the Reserve's guard squadron have been positioned in a high polar orbit of Calypso-Three consistently for at least *five years*," she noted. "I've dug in to every official and unofficial record I can find, and even when they've changed ships, the squadron has maintained basically the same position to 'minimize resource expenditure.'

"Only the destroyers engage in active patrols, and what little I can confirm suggests they are mostly concerned about the most likely scenarios. In-system patrols are minimal and diffident... which appears to describe the entire security setup."

Lorraine seemed to consider that, then shrugged.

"I suspect that the information that is available to someone trawling public and semi-public sources is intentionally downplaying their security," she warned. "That's why our plan calls for us to get a *very* solid view of the current ship positions before we try to get too close.

"The key to everything is these ships."

Six blue icons appeared in the middle of the UWN icons—split, Vigo noted, into two groups of three.

"This is Reserve Battlecruiser Squadron Calypso-Three," the Pentarch explained. "Our targets. Six *Valkyrie*-class battlecruisers, split into two divisions of three. Which division we will move on depends on what we see as we approach, but the plan is to take an entire division.

"We will get as close as we can aboard *Goldenrod* and then will transfer to shuttles for the final approach. This will be a phased operation, though we could, theoretically, fit all of our personnel on our shuttles."

A standard-mode Midas could carry twenty-five, including the crew, and they had fifteen left. Vigo knew he wasn't the only one who'd be at risk of a stroke if the plan had involved putting *everyone* into space at once.

"*Goldenrod*'s final approach will be slow, with most of her systems stepped down as low as we can take them. She should be difficult to impossible to detect, but there will be a handful of crew aboard her to the very end," Lorraine continued.

"Once we are confident we are in control of our targets and have transferred our personnel, that handful will take *Goldenrod* translight. She will jump one day, and we will rendezvous with her for a final transfer of personnel and equipment away from prying eyes."

Lorraine spread her hands.

"The devil is in the details, of course, and there are two key points I can speak to before I hand this over to the rest of you," she noted. "The first is that we *will* be visible to the UWN's tachyon scanners.

"We will be swinging around Calypso, to allow us to approach past the Reserve Station. They will see us approach and pass them. Our vector is close to a course between the Tavastar and Shoranhan Systems—close enough to be a calculation error that's going to give someone a bad day on emergence.

"Our course is also clean enough to keep us from hitting any of the danger zones around the mass objects. Nothing will suggest we will be dropping out of translight as we cut between Calypso-Two and Calypso—and the star's mass shadow will make it difficult for them to realize we *have* done so.

"The primary risk is if there is a sensor platform or drone scanner position on the starward side of Calypso-Two." She shrugged. "Em Devine's assessment is that the crews are unlikely to be that on top of things.

"That said, we will act as if there is a sensor station there. We will bring up jammers as we exit translight, we will locate any sensor platforms and we will destroy them. Calypso-Two is close enough to the star that losing contact temporarily won't draw too much attention, we hope."

She shook her head, and even Vigo was impressed by the confidence she was projecting.

"At each stage of this plan, there are problems we will need to consider. We need to identify as many of them as we can now. There is no margin here, my friends. The Reserve Station has six battle-cruisers and sixteen destroyers, the smallest of which outmasses us two to one and outguns us something like *ten* to one."

That chilled the room, and Lorraine gestured to Alastair.

"Now I want Em Devine to give us the rundown of what he has learned about the personnel and ships on station and of the tools he has acquired to help us get this done."

FORTY-ONE

"That's that, then," Alastair murmured as the strange sensation of entering translight rippled through Lorraine's suite.

She adjusted to the loss of any sense of down almost without thinking. The transition wasn't as automatic as it had once been—while *Goldenrod* had spent a lot of time in translight over the last six months, she'd done far longer stints than any of her crew were used to.

Lorraine was much more used to microgravity than to the transition between.

"I was under the impression you were committed a while back," she said to her boyfriend. A twitch had sent her drifting out of the couch, and she lazily hooked an ankle around the arm.

The seating area of her suite had the same kind of luxurious lack of personality as the office. The whole section of the ship set up to host guests were like that, and she now lived in what had been intended as the suite for a political envoy.

Not an Ambassador like Humphrey. A political asset of his caliber would have traveled on either a passenger ship or a cruiser:

something either specialized enough or big enough to have a rotating habitat pod.

Frigates rated a lower level of Representative, for all that they did much of the flag-showing for the Kingdom.

"*I* was committed the moment you offered everyone a chance to back out with the warning of *act of war against the United Worlds*," Alastair replied, chuckling. He had tucked his arm into the loop on the arm of his chair intended for just that purpose, gently holding himself in place.

"But up until now, I haven't done anything I couldn't claim to have either been deceived into or done under duress. Not that anyone could trace, anyway," he added with a grin. "I was going to be in deep, deep crap for how far I went to support you, but that was my burning the Fund's political capital where my superiors in both the Corps and the Fund disapproved."

"What did they disapprove of?" Lorraine asked. "Helping us... or that we lost the vote?"

"You're enough of a politician, Lorraine, to know the answer," Alastair said. "Losing the vote means that, retroactively, I was wrong all along to have supported you. That some of what I burned at the end was *personal* capital doesn't matter—the Corps and the Fund will both see it as weighing on them."

He snorted.

"The Fund is mostly just running through the paperwork to pass me back to the UWESC. My secondment won't last too much longer, and then the Corps will find something *exciting* for me to do.

"Believe me when I say our diplomat's black-bag specialists can find somewhere to get me killed," he concluded.

"They won't be able to trace that I stole the gen-one CIR override codes; I'm confident of that. But once I'm aboard a ship that has infiltrated and robbed the United Worlds Navy Reserve, I am officially a traitor."

Traitor.

That struck home harder than Lorraine had expected it to.

Betrayal was a sore spot for her. Her uncle's betrayal was at the heart of all of this, the heart of the rage that endured even as her grief became an old friend.

"I didn't really mean for you to cross that line, you know," she admitted.

"I know what staying will get me, Lorraine. I spent my career in the shadows, getting my hands dirty so the United Worlds could pretend to be the 'shining city on the hill.' They might not actually get me killed, but my career is over.

"And it turns out backstabbing for a better future doesn't pay all that well," he said with a wryness that she *knew* concealed a deep hurt. "I'm not in a position to quietly retire without some kind of backup plan, and, well, I'm not going to pretend dating a princess isn't one hell of an exit strategy."

The grin softened the sardonic nature of his words. Lorraine carefully waved a hand at him.

"We're in microgravity, Alastair; I can hit you with a pillow from here," she warned.

"Please, please, I'm sure pillow fights are supposed to involve *much* less clothing," he countered.

Lorraine let him lighten the topic—though she *did* throw the pillow. Microgravity or not, he grabbed it with ease. He wasn't downplaying his implants anymore, she noted.

"I need to finish converting the bedroom before I do anything so foolish as throwing pillows around in my underwear," she told her boyfriend. "Believe me when I tell you that a *bed* is not actually helpful for zero-gravity sex."

"Having been too busy to try that the first chunk of this trip, I'll take your word for it," he told her.

Everyone, including both Lorriane and her boyfriend, had been neck-deep in planning since they'd left Earth. In theory, *Goldenrod*'s computers were functionally air-gapped from Earth's datanets, and they should have noticed anyone eavesdropping even outside the high-security parts of the frigate.

In reality, Lorraine and her people were very much operating on the assumption that the United Worlds' security agencies were equipped with tech they could barely imagine, let alone counter.

Which meant that the planning had been after leaving Earth and that she hadn't managed to drag Alastair to a bedroom since then. But the plans were all mostly set in stone now, so...

"Well, then, maybe we should work on folding away that bed," she told him with a broad leer.

***

TRAITOR.

The word spun Lorraine's head. She'd slept for a bit and now hung in the air in her bedroom, studying Alastair Devine as he slept.

She knew more about him than she had. The pieces hung together in an image that didn't speak overly well of humanity's supposed oldest and wisest nation.

Recruited by a special program that trawled poorer worlds for gifted individuals who wanted out. Trained, indoctrinated and shaped into a weapon for the United Worlds' intelligence community.

Used. Used *up*, unless she missed her guess, until they seconded him to the Stability Convention Fund to avoid breaking him entirely. Allowed to grow bored.

Alastair had figured he'd been left there to rot, but she had to wonder if that was part of the routine. Let him get bored of a desk, until he was desperate for something "more interesting," then use that boredom to send him back into the field.

Backstabbing for a better future.

And now, because he'd latched on to her as a way out of his boredom, he'd found himself betraying the nation he'd broken himself to serve. She hoped he wouldn't regret that—but she also knew it was his choice to make.

She could see a few roles for him back in Adamantine if he stuck with her that long. Maybe even Prince Consort—he was smart, competent, connected in the most powerful nation in the galaxy, and, importantly, *not* someone from a top-tier Adamantine family with internal enemies of their own. She wasn't in love with him yet, but she could see it from there.

Which meant that she'd made a man she cared for turn traitor against his nation. The very thing she condemned her uncle for and hated Jelica Laurenz for.

Alastair Devine had turned traitor in self-defense against a broken system and, just maybe, for love of her.

For the first time since Vigo Jarret had told her that her family was dead, Lorraine Adamant wondered *why* Benjamin Adamant had betrayed them all.

FORTY-TWO

Pawn to F5.

The chess notation always came fluidly to Lorraine, a metaphor for maneuver and deception she'd gone through—with her uncle, mostly—for much of her adult life.

In this case, half a covering position, half a deception to lure an enemy out of position.

Goldenrod's final moments in translight were hard to perfectly match to realspace coordinates. At no point was she traveling at less than eighty-eight times the speed of light, which meant she passed the Reserve Station barely a second before she tucked inside Calypso-Two and plunged back into reality.

Reality reacted as poorly as it ever did to their arrival, and Lorraine, seated once more in the observer station on the frigate's bridge, fought back a surprised moment of nausea at a particularly "wobbly" transition.

"We are in space, on target and in position," Major Yildiz barked. "Error is less than a thousand kilometers. Recalculating our course toward the Station."

"Jammers were live before emergence," Lieutenant Commander

Paris continued, the Tactical Officer picking up the line of reports. "Anything that saw us had no chance to transmit. We are sweeping for targets."

"No signals detected except our jamming," Major Vinci reported. "No one is trying to say hello."

If they'd done it right, the Reserve Station had picked up their approach and passage on tachyon scanners, but there was no reason for the UWN to think they hadn't continued on toward their apparent destination.

The risk, the one that Lorraine hadn't seen a clever way to get around, was if there was a tachyon-scanner station on the far side of the star system. Then, their saving grace was that such a station would need hours for its data to cross the system at lightspeed—and no one was all that likely to put the two datasets together and realize the tachyon signature hadn't kept going.

"Talk to me, people," Stephson ordered. "Are we alone out here or do we have a friend who wants to call home?"

"Nothing is showing on passive," Paris replied. "Permission to do a controlled active sweep of this side of Two. Nothing will reach the Station, and anything that's a real problem should be in that zone."

"Chance of them seeing the pulse?" the Captain demanded.

"I can narrow it so the chance is zero, ser."

"Then do it."

A green line rippled out on the displays, marking a cone between *Goldenrod*—still unmoving in the void between Calypso and its second planet—and the planet in question.

"Two is clear," Paris reported after a few seconds. "Zero contacts, I repeat, zero contacts. The skies are clear."

"Drop the jammer," Stephson ordered. "Cortez?"

Lorraine had the "squadron commander" view of the ship's systems—but she also had enough of a mirror into Stephson's coms to see the moment the Captain linked to Engineering directly rather than through her Bridge Engineering Officer.

"Captain."

"Pop your umbrella, Cheng," Stephson said. "It's time to get this show on the road."

THE SHOW TOOK a while to get going. "Popping the umbrella" of the heat shield Cortez's people had assembled took almost fifteen minutes, with the shuttles in worker mode and even vac-suited engineering personnel swarming through space to assemble its components.

Goldenrod had multiple tiers of heat-radiation systems. The active radiators used in combat resembled nothing so much as two-meter-tall feathers—but while they were extremely efficient, they were also vulnerable and expensive.

Her usual passive arrays involved larger areas and much less active effort. The spare parts for those arrays provided much of the area of the heat shield now suspended between the frigate and her destination, connected to *Goldenrod* by variable-rigidity cables so the ship could maneuver in the shade of her ten-kilometer-wide umbrella.

"Shield is fully deployed," Savege reported from the CIC. "We have drones in position around the perimeter—partly to hold it in place and partly to give us eyes."

Goldenrod could no more see directly through the umbrella than she could be seen through it. But, as the XO said, that was why there were sensor drones built in to the device.

"You have the course, Major Yildiz?" Stephson asked.

Even if the error had been millions of kilometers, Lorraine was quite certain Yildiz would have had their course. They were committed now, stuck on a slow and steady approach behind their heat shield with no real recourse if things went wrong.

"Seven hours at two gravities, flip and decelerate into the station at one gravity over fourteen hours," the Navigator reeled off. "My calculations, checked with the Cheng, show that we will be more vulnerable in the back half of the journey *and* when decelerating.

"We'll burn in faster and then slow down at a gentler rate," he concluded. "Twenty-one hours. Subject to final adjustments to pick our final target."

It was a good thing, Lorraine supposed, that Calypso's four rocky inner worlds had *very* tight orbital circles. At this point in the orbits of Two and Three, there was only about a light-minute between them.

"That's on Commander Paris," Stephson said. "Well, and a few other minor people like me and the Pentarch. We'll have a final destination for you before it's too late, Major Yildiz.

"Well done getting us in."

This was only the beginning, Lorraine knew. The easiest part, made even easier by the Calypso Station's guards not having posted the sensor platforms she'd expected.

If only that didn't add to the voice in her head screaming *trap*.

THE MAIN GUARD squadron was exactly where their intelligence put it. Six battlecruisers—two relatively new ships and four older than the *Valkyries* they were guarding—hung above the north pole of Calypso-Three.

It was a decent position, one from which they had an excellent view of the worthless rock of a planet and, more importantly, the splayed-out array of starships they were expected to be protecting.

There were more destroyers than their intelligence suggested. Eighteen—three full squadrons—instead of the sixteen the reports they'd accessed told them. Somehow, that error made Lorraine feel better.

Even if it put a full six-ship formation of half-megaton warships between her and her target.

"It looks like the Reserve itself is divided up by divisions," Paris reported aloud. "Everything is in these neat little rows of three ships, perfectly aligned. I keep half-expecting to find that the overall array spells out *United Worlds* or something."

"Not quite *that* bad, but note that not only are those three-ship clusters aligned exactly with each other, each and every row is exactly parallel to the ecliptic plane," Savege added. "Whoever put these ships here had *way* too much time on their hands."

"I'm more concerned about their security. We've got eyes on all the mobile ships?" Lorraine asked.

"Even counting the guard squadron as mobile—which I am questioning—yes," Stephson confirmed. "Who the hell puts twenty million tons of capital ships in place and just has them *sit* there?"

"Someone with a tight budget that says they have enough fuel for one training maneuver and/or intercept per standard year," Devine explained from the other observer seat by Lorraine.

"The United Worlds Navy budgets for the capital-ship squadrons assume they can handle almost all training in simulations," the spy continued. "They'd managed to keep the cruisers and such doing real-world exercises, but, well, cruisers and carriers are what actually does the work for the UWN.

"Battleships and battlecruisers? They're the heavy hitters, the big guys you have in the back of the room to intimidate but never expect to actually have beat someone up." Devine shrugged grimly. "Which, of course, is why they haven't spared any carriers to protect this Reserve Station—which you'll note also doesn't *have* any carriers in it."

"Is it just me or does the UWN really overvalue its carriers?" Stephson asked. "I mean, yeah, sure, their carriers are tougher and more dangerous than anyone else's capital ships, period, but... give me the same tech and I can build you a battleship that will *shred* your carrier's shuttle wing and the carrier in short order. On about half the tonnage."

Lorraine glanced over at her boyfriend, who just shrugged.

"I will note that I was most definitely *not* party to the UWN's strategic resource planning session," he said mildly. "What conversations I did have suggested that they valued the flexibility of the carrier model. Some of them definitely seemed to realize that there were roles battleships did better—but the UWN does *have* battleships."

"Theoretically," Lorraine replied. "But if those ships have never exercised in real space, let alone fought a peer opponent..."

"What peer opponent do you think they're going to face?" Jarret asked from the last observer seat. "There *is* no peer to the United Worlds Navy, and they *know* it. The entire purpose of that TIE Commission you spoke to is to make sure that no one ever even gets close."

"No one in the Bright Dream Cluster is matching up to the United Worlds for tech," Lorraine conceded. "But you can't tell me that there are no systems past the wormholes that aren't building up tech bases of their own that can or will rival Earth's."

For a moment, there was a very sour expression on Devine's face, then he shook his head.

"It's possible," he admitted. "It's also *possible* that the UW has... means to manage that risk."

His expression and his descriptions of what he'd done for the United Worlds sent a shiver down Lorraine's spine. Had his Extraterritorial Surveillance Corps been part of those means?

Had *Alastair* been involved in the process of making certain no one technologically matched the core worlds?

It wasn't a question she could ask—she suspected he wouldn't answer, not yet at least, and forcing him to make that refusal would hurt their relationship.

Ask a question you know they can't answer was in the same category as *give an order you know they won't obey*. Those were things that could only weaken the professional and personal relationships involved.

"The big point out of all of this, I suppose, is that while there isn't a carrier here, the UWN is probably going to be thinking in terms of their starfighters, aren't they?" Lorraine asked—intentionally using the UWN term for the modular combat shuttles.

"Our intelligence says there are six forts at key geometric positions, each of which should be home to two squadrons of twenty shuttles each," Paris confirmed. "Problem is... I'm only picking up three. And less than a dozen shuttles in space, most of which appear to be doing maintenance surveys."

Lorraine pulled the data from the tactical feed onto her displays and into her neural link, searching through it. As the Tactical Officer had said, they were definitely short two armed platforms from the Reserve Station's list of equipment.

"I mean, who *hasn't* lost a million-ton battle station and forty of the most advanced combat shuttles in space down the back of a couch?" Stephson said with a chuckle. "Or... more likely, hidden them somewhere they thought was *clever*, because right now, the only competence I'm seeing out there is in the destroyer patrol patterns.

"And while that fits with the stereotypes of the United Worlds Navy, I have the sneaking suspicion that's what someone *wants* me to see."

At least Lorraine wasn't the only one thinking that.

FORTY-THREE

The long flight from Calypso-Two to Calypso-Three and the Reserve Station was nerve-racking and absolutely essential to Lorraine's plan.

Between her research, the data Humphrey's people had acquired and the information Devine had stolen from his former colleagues, they had known quite a bit about the Station. It hadn't been entirely accurate—the extra destroyers were a sign of that—and there had been obvious gaps, so building a revised picture as they approached had been critical.

"The perimeter is a rough globe of sensor platforms approximately one million kilometers in diameter at a density of one per seventy-three million square kilometers of surface area," Paris reported as they crossed the midway point. They'd been slowing down for almost two hours now and had over twelve hours left before they reached their target.

The screens on the bridge matched the Tactical Officer's explanation, with a transparent red bubble around Calypso-Three and its precious inventory.

"Wherever we enter the sphere, we will be at most forty-five hundred kilometers from a platform. The destroyers are on a semi-random sweep, but their intervals for the starward side of the Station are wider in both time and space. With minimal adjustment, we can pass through well away from the starships on our side."

"Once we're inside the sphere, we will need to shut down our main engines and basically wrap the heat shield around us," Stephson warned grimly. "That is dangerous for us, as all of our heat is going to start being reflected right back at us. It will be fine for a while but not forever."

"For long enough," Lorraine countered. "We'll need to be careful with where we launch the shuttles, but if I'm reading the data correctly, there are no internal patrols?"

"The destroyers and sensor platforms are set up entirely for perimeter security," Paris confirmed. "I suppose they figure forty-odd *thousand* sensor drones and three squadrons of destroyers are likely to pick up anyone trying to sneak up on the Station."

"Sneaking past the drones will be—"

"Simple," Devine interrupted the Captain. "I have override codes that can allow me to play games with their control inputs. Shutting them down would be easiest but obvious. I believe I can load a ghost virus into their network to delete us from their data.

"It *won't* work on their controllers," he warned. "I need to directly upload to each drone, which may take some time, but if I get it right, the platforms won't see us at all, and then it won't matter that I can't influence how the central systems collate the information."

"And here I was planning on using heat shields to coast on through," Stephson replied. "Get on that with Vinci—Coms, that's your top priority. We aren't talking to anyone here, after all."

"Yes, ser."

Lorraine gave Alastair a quick smile before turning back to the data.

"Once we're past the bubble, our main concern is the shuttles flying internal-maintenance runs," she told them. "Whether we're hitting Division Alpha or Division Bravo will be based on their pattern.

"I figure we come to zero relative to the whole affair, in the middle of the target division, using the battlecruisers themselves to hide us from sight." She snorted. "A *Valkyrie* is four times *Goldenrod*'s size. Hiding in their shadow won't be difficult."

"Any idea where those two battle stations are hiding?" Savege asked.

"So far as I can tell, they don't exist," Paris replied. "So, either someone is being very clever in how they're hiding their defenses, or someone is being very clever in their corruption. Pocketing the entire budget for a pair of battle stations—crew, shuttle squadrons and all— would take some doing, but would also set you up for retirement very quickly."

Lorraine joined the rest of the officers in silence as they considered that possibility.

"Alastair," she turned to her lover. "Is that... likely? Is that even *possible?*"

"I don't know," he admitted. "I'd have guessed not, but there are always limitations baked in to the records when you're running things across the light-years. Even with the Charon Complex, the Calypso Station is a week's communications lag from Earth. And it used to be more—though the Old Guard ships were put out here after the Complex was built."

"The Complex is why they were put out here, I suppose," Lorraine guessed. "If they did need to activate them, they'd be able to deploy them almost anywhere within a few weeks."

"Well, terrifying as the potential reasons for the stations being missing are, the result is that there are only about twenty shuttles wandering through the Reserve formations at any given moment," Savege pointed out, the XO *definitely* thrown by the possibility of someone "ghost soldiering" two entire battle stations.

"Some of the patterns are becoming clear, including that the older capital ships are definitely seen as the lesser siblings here. I know we have our hearts set on the *Valkyrie*s, but look at this."

The shared feed between the senior officers zoomed in on one section, where three battleships—five-million-ton behemoths, a quarter again the size of the newer *Valkyrie*-class ships, with heavier armor and smaller engines—rested at the end of one row of ships.

"A shuttle skimmed this division of battleships just after we started scanning, but they were surprisingly far away, and the pattern suggests they won't check again for at least another forty-eight hours," Savege continued. "The lighter units have someone sweep them every twelve hours, and I'm still trying to get a feel on the battlecruisers, but there's at least two battleship divisions no one is looking at... at all, really, though they put in a performative scan every few days."

"Those are *Centurion*-class ships," Devine pointed out. "Yeah... lead ship of that trio is *Decurion*, served twenty years on active duty and has been in reserve for fifteen."

"*Centurion*-class may have the twin octuple-railgun banks and other toys, but they're also thirty years older than the *Valkyries* and, most importantly, don't have the automations," Lorraine warned. "We can get two, maybe three, of the *Valkyries* with the hands we've got.

"We'd only get one *Centurion*."

Lorraine let her people mull over that. The *Centurions* were old enough that their basic specs were in the files. They were bigger than the *Valkyries*—five megatons fueled, a bit under four dry—with less of their mass dedicated to engines, so they had far heavier armor and beam weapons.

But they were also only capable of four gravities of acceleration sublight and a hundred and a four times lightspeed translight. Total crew complement was over three thousand, not under fourteen hundred like the *Valkyries*.

Battlecruisers were designed to fight enemies weaker than them, where battleships were designed to fight peer opponents. Lorraine was going to have to fight RKAN Home Fleet, which would have battleships of their own. If she could bring three *Centurions*, they might have been worth more than three *Valkyries*—but the Old

Guard ships were enough newer and more advanced that she wasn't sure of that.

And she couldn't *get* three of the battleships. They just didn't have the bodies.

"Does your analysis of the shuttle flight patterns suggest that we aren't going to be able to sneak up on the *Valkyries*, Commander?" she asked Savege. "Because if I can possibly get three capital ships, I'm not going to settle for one."

"I'm not sure yet," the XO admitted. "My *guess* is that the two newer divisions are getting a closer flyby once a day, but I haven't seen either division *get* that flyby."

"So, we watch for them," Lorraine decided aloud. "And we adjust to rendezvous with the division that had the most-recent inspection. That should give us most of a day to get our work done, right?"

"I think so," Savege agreed. "It's... going to be iffy, Your Highness. The key to these ships is the CIR, and that computer might well be smart enough to realize we're not supposed to be there and call for help."

"The Command Intelligence Routines are fully shut down," Lorraine told the others. "Everything I found agreed on that—they've fully disabled the central computing systems. I'm not clear on why, if I'm honest, but it's clear that the CIR is down."

"We'll have to bring it back online," Devine noted. "But it being down lets us set up the structures for control. We have a... harness, for lack of a better word. Half-hardware, half-software, it will give us command of the CIR."

"We just need to get on board the ships without being seen," she concluded. "And, well, make sure no one sneaks up on us while we're taking control."

"So, sneak past a security sphere the most powerful navy in the galaxy believes is secure, avoid the survey craft making sure nothing goes wrong with the reserve ships, board a ship with a computer system smart enough to call for help if we turn it on wrong, and then turn said system on," Jarret summarized with an amused snort. "No big deal, right?"

"We can do it," Lorraine assured them. "We've known that from the beginning or we wouldn't be here. It's already too late to turn back.

"We make the run, we blind the drones and we take control of the *Valkyries*. Then we leave *Goldenrod* on autopilot and get out of here."

"One question, I suppose," Paris noted. "Sooner or later, the UWN is going to realize what we're doing. They'll try to stop us. What do we do then?"

"We lie, we dodge, we run," she told her people. "*Goldenrod* doesn't have the guns or armor to go up against even one UWN destroyer, and once we're aboard the *Valkyries*, we almost certainly won't have enough active weapons or munitions to make a fight of anything.

"Plus, the last thing we want to do is get into a firefight. If we can get out of here without being identified, that buys us time."

"Not as much as you might think," Devine warned. "We have to make the run through the Tavastar–Bright Dream wormhole. If we get there ahead of any news of the theft at Calypso, I think we can baffle our way through and into the Cluster, but they'll put the pieces together after that."

"We'll cross that bridge when we come to it," Lorraine said grimly. There wasn't going to be much hiding the battlecruisers showing up at Adamantine, no matter what. Sooner or later, she'd deal with the consequences of this.

"No matter what happens, we do not fire on the United Worlds Navy," she ordered. "Robbing them is going to be enough of a headache. *Killing* any of them is going to sink us forever."

FORTY-FOUR

Valkyrie slept.

A thousand systems throughout the battlecruiser's hull worked away, managing the atmosphere at levels without enough oxygen to damage anything. Nitrogen filled her passageways, but there was oxygen stored in tanks for the next repair or survey crew.

Once, those thousand systems would have reported to the main computer center. Everything about the ship would have been available to the Command Intelligence Routine and her Captain at the touch of a key, collated, coordinated and organized automatically before the main computer ever touched it.

Those connections had been severed. In some places, links remained to the auxiliary computer systems—key systems the maintenance crew needed to access in one place—but even many of those links were gone now.

Most were fed in to interlocks that could be deactivated. Others had been physically cut, the failsafes linked in to those systems judged too likely to trigger a wake-up.

Close-range passive scanners registered an approaching shuttle, flagging it as a potential concern, but the warning went nowhere.

That link had been fully cut, as the system that would have assessed the maintenance craft's identity beacon was part of the CIR.

The shuttle stopped five hundred kilometers away from the ship, equidistant from *Valkyrie* and her two sisters, and pulsed those auxiliary computers. Data uploads commenced, but there was nothing to see in them.

The humans on the shuttle would never even look at them. Why would they?

Nothing changed in Calypso. Except for the occasional "weather damage," nothing had changed aboard *Valkyrie* in ten years.

And so the ship slept on.

FORTY-FIVE

"And there she is. UWNS *Valkyrie* herself, nameship of the class, lead ship of Reserve Battlecruiser Division Calypso-Three-Alpha," Savege announced. "And her inspection shuttle just flicked her engines online and started away."

"Then I think that makes Division Alpha our target," Lorraine said, studying the maps projected around the bridge.

The bridge crew were cycling to let people take catnaps. She'd stepped away from the bridge a few times but never for more than an hour. She hoped she'd squeezed enough sleep into those short breaks to keep going, because she doubted that she was going to sleep until they were done now.

"Division Bravo got a check two hours ago, so if they're on the twenty-four-hour cycle it looks like, we'd only have nineteen hours left by the time we got there," Stephson agreed. "Yildiz, set the course."

The change was imperceptible aboard the ship, though Lorraine could see the line marking their deceleration vector shift on the map. Division Alpha and Division Bravo were over two hundred thousand kilometers apart—but *Goldenrod* was still over three hours away from either of them.

"We will breach the security perimeter in ten minutes," Paris warned. "Em Devine?"

"Major Vinci and I have pinged every drone on this side of the sphere," the UW spy replied. "We've got an automatic program continuing to ping them as they orbit the planet, but we've downloaded the worm into over twenty thousand probes."

Lorraine swallowed a soft whistle. That wasn't even half of the sphere surrounding Calypso-Three, which drove home just how vast the security at the Reserve Station was.

It wasn't necessarily being carefully managed, and there were things missing that were supposed to be there, but the scale of the Calypso Station's defenses was still mind-blowing. The Reserve itself held more capital ships than the entire Royal Kingdom of Adamant Navy, and the defenses' designers clearly had resources to burn.

"The drones are a bit out of date," Devine noted. "I don't know if we'd have been able to automate the process as effectively if they'd had the last round of software patches. The codes buried in the worm are valid, but even valid codes used like this should trigger alerts. Except the software's out of date and I know the alert mechanisms in this version.

"And the new one," he admitted, "but the new one is just that much harder to work around."

"So. Where's the trap?" Lorraine asked. "Because while I need this to go smoothly..."

"Don't look a gift horse in the mouth," Stephson replied. "We make one misstep as we cross the security perimeter, and there will be destroyers on us inside of twenty minutes."

If Alastair Devine wanted to sell them out, this would be the moment. Not that Lorraine could see any value whatsoever to her boyfriend in doing so, but this was their most vulnerable window.

"Range is sixty thousand kilometers to the nearest drone and dropping," Paris reported. "Once we enter their active radar zone, the odds of the heat shield getting picked up start rising. And we are entering that zone... now."

A pin dropping would have echoed endlessly on the suddenly silent bridge. Seconds ticked away, each of them seeing hundreds of kilometers vanish as the frigate and her shield plunged toward their destination.

"We have been pinged with radar multiple times. None have crossed the detection threshold on the heat shield yet," the Tactical Officer finally reported. "At this point, we're going to be getting pulsed with radar regularly until we are well inside the sphere."

Lorraine forced herself to breathe. Silence wasn't necessary—it wasn't like sound transmitted across the vacuum of space. Everyone aboard *Goldenrod* could scream at the top of their lungs and the sensor probes tacked on to their heat shield wouldn't hear it.

The sensor drones guarding Calypso-Three were looking for heat and electromagnetic radiation. The shield between *Goldenrod* and the perimeter was capturing everything they were generating, but every fifteen seconds or so, one drone in every twenty fired off a pulse of radar.

Those pulses swept over Lorraine's ship like the hunters they were, crisscrossing space.

"So far, your radar-absorbing material is holding," Devine said. "The real problem will be when we interpenetrate."

Then their umbrella would become a shell and, for a few hours, would contain all of the heat they produced.

THE BRIDGE WAS STILL QUIET, though far from silent, as they reached the invisible sphere in space that marked the moment of truth.

"We are reshaping the shield," Savege reported. "Maintaining a full barrier between us and the sensor sphere."

A ten-kilometer-wide hemisphere slowly reshaped into a smaller sphere that fully encompassed the ship. *Goldenrod* moved farther back in the shape, giving her engines more room to expel gas while keeping the whole assembly moving.

The reaction mass had to escape the sphere for the engines to work, and that was the biggest danger to the entire affair. Enemy sensor scans or not, *Goldenrod* had to slow down to match her target. They were on secondary thrusters now, not the main drives, but those still had to put reaction mass into space and that fuel was warmer than the void.

The sphere could conceal the *ship* but not her exhaust, not once she was surrounded on all sides. Now their safety depended half on Devine's software worms… and half on the fact that no one would expect there to be a contact *inside* the security perimeter.

"We're through. Radar exceeded detection levels at least three times," Paris reported grimly. "No activity on the part of the patrols."

Lorraine sighed in relief. She had believed Alastair's assurances, but too much had ridden on this moment.

"It looks like most if not all of the passive scanners are pointed outward," Savege said. "Visual on the drones suggests they don't have much pointed inside the sphere at all."

"Why would you?" Lorriane asked. "After all, you have to get *past* the sensor screen to be inside it. Our sensor drones have blind spots too, and if I was building a sphere like this… yeah, the blind spots would all be on the inside.

"Especially when there's shuttles and ships and stations in here, in case something *very* strange happens," she continued. "And those sensor packages have people behind them, folks. So, let's be very, very careful."

"Course is locked in," Yildiz said calmly. "Two hours, forty-five minutes. Please try to keep the stressing out to a minimum.

"I have faith in our Tactical Team," the Navigator continued, with a pointed look over at Paris. "Doesn't everyone else?"

FORTY-SIX

Lorraine couldn't shake the itchy feeling between her shoulder blades, like an entire battle fleet—as powerful as any of those her nation had fielded in their last war a decade earlier—was aiming right at her.

There had been decisive battles in the war between the Kingdom of Adamant and the Richelieu Directorate that had involved fewer than six capital ships *total*. For the United Worlds Navy, the six active ships guarding the Calypso Station were an afterthought.

And for all the *I'm being watched* feeling she was suffering from, the six full squadrons of capital ships scattered around the planet had stayed quiescent so far. There was no sign that Devine's worm in the security perimeter had been discovered, and *Goldenrod* was shedding the last of her velocity as she headed toward her rendezvous with *Valkyrie.*

Dozens of people were swarming all around her as the final prep for the boarding operation carried on, but her feet followed a long-familiar path across the shuttle-bay deck. The scent of metal, grease and fuel filled the air as she stepped up to a standard-mode Midas.

"Hey, old girl," she murmured to the spacecraft, resting her hand on the metal.

"We made sure your old bird was free," Chevrolet said behind her. She turned to meet her old boss's gaze.

Commander Olavi Chevrolet was *Goldenrod*'s Commanding Officer, Shuttles, and when she'd been Bravo Flight Commander, the fragile-looking redheaded man had been her direct boss. He'd handled having a Pentarch under his command well—and had handled his subordinate suddenly becoming the mission commander with astonishing grace.

"I appreciate it, COSH," she told him. "I feel like I've neglected her, but I can still fly."

"I've seen the simulator records, Lorraine," Chevrolet said dryly. "Plus, you have Jarret as your copilot. The two of you on the flight deck? They'd need a destroyer at least to stop you!"

"I hope so," she said. "But really, we aren't going far. This is just a short cargo run."

"Yeah. *Just a short cargo run*," he echoed back to her, gesturing at the fully armored Adamant Guard squad boarding the shuttle. "We're putting thirty of the Guard and twenty of Cortez's best engineering people—*including* the Cheng!—onto that ship.

"If this goes wrong..."

"It won't matter if you're on *Valkyrie* or *Goldenrod*, COSH," Lorraine warned. "There's too much firepower out here. Either we can run translight with the battlecruisers or..."

"Word of advice, from your old boss?" he said. "*Don't* point that out to too many people. Hope is what's getting us through this: hope that you can pull off the impossible and save our Kingdom from the Black Regent."

"I can. I will," Lorraine said, surprised at the certainty behind the words. "The hard part's done, Olavi. We *got* here.

"Now we just have to deal with the computer."

"*Just*," he echoed again. "I'm leading the second wave, Your

Highness, heading for *Herakles*. Fly clean, shoot straight. We'll see you on the other side."

"Same to you, Commander. When this is over and we're all home, beer is on me."

"Be careful who you say that to as well! You could end up in a very deep hole."

Lorraine laughed.

"Spread it as wide as you want, COSH," she instructed. "When we get home, I'm buying beer for anyone who was on this ship until the end of time!"

WHILE LORRAINE HAD KEPT up her simulator hours, it had been through a VR interface with her neural link that any pilot would admit was inferior to a proper simulator, let alone live flight time.

Taking the Midas out of *Goldenrod*'s shuttle bay for the boarding run was the first time she'd put her hands and link on the controls of a live shuttle since the day her parents had died. *That* day, of course, she'd been carrying nukes rigged to explode and the shuttle had been wired with remote-detonated explosives to finish the job.

Thanks to Vigo Jarret, none of those traps had been allowed to go off. Now her bodyguard sat in her copilot's seat as they slid quietly into the void.

"Some of it, you never forget," he murmured, watching her work. "You good?"

"In more ways than one," she confirmed. "It's good to be back in the pilot's seat. I knew it wasn't going to be my career... but I definitely missed it."

The gap between *Goldenrod* and the heat shield concealing her was only a few kilometers, but they weren't pushing the shuttle's engines. Less than one tenth of a gravity took time to cross that enclosed space—but added less heat than higher acceleration would.

And there was already plenty of heat. *Goldenrod* had vented extra atmosphere into the shield to act as an additional heat sink, but Lorraine wasn't used to there *being* a background temperature in space.

"I have eyes on our exit; pinging to you," Jarret told her.

His icon matched the icon she'd been following—if they hadn't matched, she'd have been *extremely* worried. In its current spherical form, the shield had four points that could open to allow the Midas through, and each shuttle had a designated exit.

The gap wasn't much bigger than the shuttle itself, a gap five meters wide and ten high, but that was more than enough for any competent pilot at the relative velocities in play. If Lorraine had blinked, she could have missed the instant of passage.

The change in view from being inside the sphere and being in orbit above Calypso-Three couldn't have been missed. The sphere itself was the most immediately visible thing, but it swiftly shrank into insignificance as Lorraine processed the space around her.

The *second* most visible thing was *Valkyrie* herself. Like *Goldenrod*, the battlecruiser resembled a sword in space, with dorsal and ventral sensor towers at the rear forming the "crossbar hilt."

Unlike *Goldenrod*, *Valkyrie* was eight hundred meters long from bow to stern, smooth lines expanding from her nearly pointed forward prow to the engines behind the sensor towers. Those lines were clear despite being interrupted by everything from the rows of single-shot external missile racks to the massive, hundred-meter-long cells of her habitat pods nestled inactively into their pockets.

Past her, Lorraine could see the identical lines of *Herakles*. The second wave of shuttles would wait until they'd made it to *Valkyrie*'s central computer, hopefully allowing them to identify any traps or problems before they moved on to the second and third ships.

Past *Herakles* was the rest of the Reserve Station. Closest was a division of battleships, the oldest ships in the Calypso Station and only half a million tons or so larger than their RKAN counterparts, but there were dozens upon dozens of starships organized into neat lines, forming false constellations in Calypso's skies.

"All shuttles are clear of the sphere," Jarret told her. "Major Watanabe is making the first approach, right?"

Lorraine chuckled at the pointed tone of the question.

"Yes," she confirmed. Isabella Watanabe had taken over her old Bravo Flight and had invoked the privilege of rank to lead the way—especially since there was no way Lorraine could invoke the same thing to lead the way herself.

"Bravo-One, this is Actual," she said into the squadron net. "Check in all birds?"

"We have four in the air, all on course and synchronized, Actual," Watanabe replied. "Going over the schematics, I mark Shuttle Bay Three as our best entry."

"Closest to Engineering and the computer center," Lorraine agreed. They'd gone over this in advance, but there was always a chance something would change when they saw the destination in person.

"Carry on, Bravo-One. We're on your trail."

Bravo-One and Bravo-Two were her old subordinates, and they slotted in front of her shuttle per the plan. Lorraine might be in the first wave, as she'd insisted, but she wasn't going to be aboard the first shuttle touching down.

That was where *Alastair* was, though, and she stepped on the urge to ask Major Watanabe how her boyfriend was doing.

The mission was far more important today. Devine had his job to do, just as she did.

"We have a laser link to the bay controls," Watanabe reported several minutes later as the four shuttles drifted to a near-halt.

With proper traffic control coordinated between the two ships, the shuttles could have made the transfer from *Goldenrod* to *Valkyrie* in under five minutes. Without that control, every maneuver was a matter of careful, low-energy acceleration that was trying to manage the risks of both impact and detection.

"Gateway is up," the lead shuttle pilot declared.

Gateway was Alastair Devine and two of the hackers Humphrey had recruited. Unlike the United Worlds spy, Lorriane had known from the beginning that those two young women worked for the intelligence branch of the Kingdom of Adamant's Diplomatic Corps—and their skills might make all of the difference today.

"Not much work to do here," Devine's voice said on the network. "Calypso Station uses a standard maintenance code for basic access. They're supposed to *change* it, but the one from a year ago is still active.

"Bravo-One, you're clear to proceed."

The shuttle bay's airlock was wide enough for a shuttle in heavy-transport mode—or for four standard-mode shuttles to fit in it together.

Lorraine wasn't going to risk her people by trying that. Watanabe took her shuttle into the lock and the main outer hatch slid shut behind her, the lights of the shuttle vanishing with ominous speed.

Seconds ticked by. The airlock was designed to cycle fast enough to get *Valkyrie*'s own shuttles out into space for combat, but they had no idea what the interior of the ship looked like.

The network was live. The airlock door wasn't thick enough to cut off the low-level coms channel. It wasn't enough for telemetry—a live connection told them people were still there, but they were being paranoid about the amount of electromagnetic radiation they were letting into the world.

Just because no one had seen them yet didn't mean the UWN was being as incompetent as it felt.

"Clear. Outer hatch reopening. Main bay is quiet and clean. Atmo is pure nitrogen, maintenance air. There's space for all four shuttles."

An image accompanied the transmission, which Lorraine's computers swiftly reassembled into a three-dimensional model of the shuttle bay.

It was bigger than she'd expected. Which made sense—*Valkyrie* was rated for the same twenty-four shuttles as RKAN battlecruisers, but RKAN battlecruisers were smaller. There was plenty of space to safely land four shuttles—if they were careful.

"Wait. Are there actually *shuttles* in there?" Jarret asked.

Lorraine had been focusing on where to put her own spacecraft after Bravo-Two was in place. She hadn't looked back at the hangars —shadowed in the image, as only Bravo-One's lights lit the space— tucked back against the walls.

Combat shuttles, whether the explicit "modular combat shuttles" of RKAN or the "starfighters" of the UWN, lived in pieces while in storage. The UWN's configurations weren't quite what Lorraine was used to, but the basic concepts of heavy cargo, assault, standard cargo/personnel, interceptor and bomber were all present.

And there were the "cubes," the central engine and pilot component to which everything else locked.

"I mark eight," Lorraine agreed. "And full config modules for them—though only one heavy cargo."

Goldenrod had been built around two six-ship squadrons, each of which only had one of the fifty-meter-long heavy-cargo modules. An RKAN battlecruiser had four such squadrons and heavy modules— but it looked like the UWN used eight-shuttle squadrons and still only had one module per squadron.

Assuming that what she was seeing was the complete loadout for a squadron, anyway.

"Bravo-Two is in," Watanabe reported. "Hatch is opening for Actual."

"Understood," Lorraine replied. "Beginning our approach."

She was still going through the image her subordinate had sent. It looked like there weren't any actual weapons—bomb chassises were relatively easily fabricated, she supposed, and only a fool would leave nuclear weapons on a reserve ship—but everything else needed to deploy a squadron of MCSes was present.

"I would have expected everything mobile to be removed," she murmured as she guided the shuttle into the dark maw of the starship. "That the whole squadron is still in place..."

"They mass-produce them, at a scale we could never match," Jarret pointed out. "Why move them when they don't need them anywhere else? I suppose it saves them time reactivating them... if they ever did."

"They never have," she countered. "Frigates, destroyers, cruisers? They've pulled those out of reserve. Capital ships, though... they just go in and stay in. Battleships, battlecruisers, even the carriers they make such a big deal of.

"Once a big ship goes into their reserves, it stays until someone finally decides it's time to cut it up."

"Then I think we're doing this young lady a favor," Jarret murmured, his own attention ahead of them as the inner hatch slid open.

With two shuttles already in the bay, there were enough lights that Lorraine could see her approach clearly. Putting the shuttle down was easy enough.

From there, though... the first step was to get oxygen masks and prepare to work in an atmosphere designed to protect electronics, not to serve human needs.

Once they could enter the ship, then the true work would finally begin.

FORTY-SEVEN

Shipsuits sealed against the neutral atmosphere and oxygen flasks hooked to their hips, Lorraine's team stepped onto *Valkyrie*'s decks. Magnetic soles clicked against steel, the familiar sound slightly distorted by the thin nitrogen atmosphere.

"If we were an official maintenance crew, we would have ordered the secondary systems to start pumping oxygen into the mix a day or so ago," Devine observed as the group gathered at the hatch in toward the rest of the ship.

"As it is, I think I can swing that order, but it will take about six hours."

"Let's wait until we have overall control," Lorraine told him. "Then we can reset the atmosphere through the entire ship rather than section by section, right?"

"Fair enough. Anything we do right now has a chance of triggering an alert back to the central station, but I have no idea what they'll have set up to do that," he admitted.

"Probably more than receiving a valid maintenance code," Watanabe guessed. "Should some of us stay here and keep the shuttles warm?"

"You and three pilots," Lorraine agreed. Like landing at Shuttle Bay Three, this was part of the original plan. "Everyone else should have a buddy already—one Guard or Marine for each tech."

Three Guards for her, but she couldn't avoid that and was pretending that Palmer was for her and Alvarez was for Jarret.

"Internal hatch security is mostly deactivated," one of the Diplomatic Corps Intelligence hackers—Judda Duke, Lorraine remembered—reported, pulling her neural link back from the panel. "By which I mean I can't *see* any locked-down hatches from here but I'm figuring key locations are still locked, because I can't see them from this level of access."

"Bridge, Engineering, Life Support, Computer Central," Cortez reeled off crisply. "The UWN isn't incompetent, so those sections will require extra authorizations."

"If we can get the CIR online, it will be able to provide those authorizations," Lorraine told them. "We start at Computer Central. Everyone has the schematics loaded?"

Nods came back. Four shuttles had put thirty-two people aboard, but that included the pilots she was leaving behind to keep the shuttles ready, plus the security.

Even including herself and Devine, there were only a dozen techs in play to handle everything the massive ship could throw at them.

And so far, they didn't even have *lights*.

FLASHLIGHTS FLICKERED DOWN THE HALLWAYS, though as they moved past the shuttle bay, backup lighting began to reveal itself. Designed for emergencies and run on its own not-quite-infinite power sources, the backup lighting only made the deep shadows and gloom of the ship worse, in Lorraine's opinion.

It was designed to let people see walls and doors, not details. Consisting of LEDs fed by thermal-decay plants—assuming the

UWN used a similar standard to RKAN, anyway—it could last several centuries with neither maintenance nor recharge.

But it was not particularly bright, leaving the flashlights as their tool for detail as they picked their way to the ladders they needed.

"The hatch is locked," Guard Sergeant Merle reported. The big Guard noncom was leading the way in powered battle armor, and he knocked heavily on the panel that should have let them into the ladderwell—actually a set of steep stairs that would, in theory, support armor even in gravity.

"Not according to the software," Duke said. The hacker stepped up beside Merle, her rotund shape and long blond hair a sharp contrast to the looming golem of Merle's battlesuit. "I believe you, Sergeant," she continued as she poked at the handle. "Physical seal. Weird."

"Why would they physically seal a hatch?" Lorraine asked.

"I don't know. Someone around here has the key, because this has been unlocked and relocked in the last few weeks," Duke observed while playing a different light over the addition to the hatch.

"Someone installed this at some point, to make sure someone with control of the electronics couldn't get into this particular ladderwell."

"Any idea why?" Lorraine asked. "Or do you think every other way up to the deck with the computer cores is locked down?"

"This one does lead right to the computer core," the hacker replied. "Fastest access to Computer Central from Bay Three, hence us taking it. Might be other barriers if we go a different way, or it could just be trying to slow down someone doing what we're doing."

"Your suggestions?"

Duke grinned through her shipsuit helmet and stepped back—the hatch swinging open toward her.

"I pick the physical lock whose basic concept was obsolete when the first diaspora ship left Earth?" she asked. "Only so many tricks you can pull with a set of tumblers, and any of the spies here could have opened this in a heartbeat."

"Thank you, Agent Duke," Lorraine said with a chuckle of her own. "Lead the way, Sergeant Merle."

"Duke's overstating things," Devine said silently in her link as they entered the vertical tunnel. "I can open most electronic locks, but I'm not sure I'd even know where to *start* with a physical lock someone jury-rigged onto a hatch on top of the existing magnetic seal!"

"I'll keep that in mind when we write our assessment for her bosses," Lorraine replied. "I suspected it wasn't quite as easy as she made it out."

The joys of competent people.

ONCE THEY WERE in the ladderwell, it was a simple matter to turn off their magnetic boots and send themselves gently gliding up toward their target: Deck Seven. The steep stairs any navy officer would call a ladder out of tradition weren't much of an obstacle, and the vertical passage *should* have been clear of anything else.

It wasn't, and Lorraine wasn't sure she understood why. Entire bulkhead panels had been opened but neither removed nor replaced. Likely, whoever had accessed the spaces behind them had been standing on the bulkheads themselves to work, but it was poor practice to leave the panels open like that.

"Well?" Lorraine asked Cortez as they reached the access hatch for Deck Seven. "You've been poking silently at the open panels, and you know these systems better than any of us."

"And what I'm seeing is... confusing," the engineer replied. "Chief Krall, get over here and take a look at this one. I think I know what I'm seeing but I want a comp specialist."

Lorraine waited for Chief Petty Officer Dutch Krall to join them. A florid-faced man who always gave the impression of having just sprinted a hundred-meter race even when sitting still, Krall was the second-best computer tech on the ship per the planning conversation with Cortez.

The *best* computer tech was apparently Lieutenant Major Božidar Kovac, who normally served as Bridge Engineering Officer and as one of Cortez's top subordinates. For his sins and skills, he was leading the Engineering detachment for the *Herakles* boarding op.

"If what you're seeing is that someone rerouted a primary data conduit, then you're right," Krall told his boss without looking into the panel for more than a second. "It looks like one of the key data trunks for the big mainframe ran parallel to this ladderwell and someone went at it with a fucking hatchet."

Lorraine pulled herself over to look inside the open panel. She wasn't a systems specialist—she'd been on a command track as an officer, swinging back and forth between Navigation, Tactical, and the shuttle wings—but she was familiar with a lot of the hardware.

United Worlds hardware was similar enough to be followed and different enough to make it complicated. But she traced the lines where secondary conduits—collections of fiberoptic cables drawing information from sensors and systems from a given section of a given deck—entered the primary protected conduit that should have taken all of that data to the mainframe.

And in the middle of the maintenance layer between Deck Six and Deck Seven, the ten-centimeter-wide armored conduit had been opened up. A block of unfamiliar circuitry had been spliced in, along with a much-cruder secondary data line.

The secondary line was a single thick fiberoptic cable that was almost certainly capable of handling the data bandwidth but lacked the armored protection of the conduit—and the redundancy of the conduits' several dozen individual cables.

"That's not combat-rated," she noted.

"And it's not connecting to the mainframe, either," Krall said. "That block is basically a switch. And..."

He pulled a cable out of his shipsuit and linked it in to a port Lorraine hadn't even noticed. The shipsuit would relay the connection to his neural link, allowing him to access whatever the block was doing.

"Not even secured," he said in a disgusted tone. "I can switch this back to running data to the mainframe, but right now, it's feeding to the auxiliary computer farther forward on Deck Five. Some things aren't being fed into the main data trunks at all, but everything that reached here is being sent forward instead of to the central core."

"Any idea why?" Lorraine asked. It fit the shape of things and her suspicions, but that shape and those suspicions hadn't formed into a solid answer yet. There was definitely *something* there, one single reason for all of the strangeness.

"It's like they thought the primary computer was more vulnerable to being compromised," Krall guessed. "Doesn't really help us, though. Even if they've redirected everything to the aux core, that comp doesn't have the power to run the automation. *Might* be able to take the ship translight."

The engineer paused, glaring at the block of circuitry.

"Might," he repeated. "Do you want me to start switching everything back over to the mainframe, Highness?"

"Not yet," Lorraine said slowly. "Can you set it up so you can flip these switches, at least, remotely?"

"I think I have the widgets to manage that," Krall agreed. "Take a minute for each one."

"Get the juniors started on that," Cortez ordered. "I think you're still with me and the Pentarch. We know where our answers are going to be, after all."

Lorraine nodded her agreement.

Deck Seven's hatch was barely a meter above them, and Computer Central was barely ten meters down the passageway from there.

It was time to see whether they had the slightest chance of actually pulling this off.

FORTY-EIGHT

If there was one spot on the battlecruiser built around a specialized new computer core that should have been secured beyond all belief, it was Computer Central. A thirty-meter-cube inside its own layer of armor, the schematics told Lorraine there were only four human-access entrances to the section. More data connections, of course, the armored conduits like the one they'd examined in the ladderwell necessary vulnerabilities in the core's armor.

All of that armor and all of that security were rendered pointless when someone left the eleven-centimeter-thick security hatch open to run unarmored cables out.

"Let me guess," Lorraine said, looking down at the slapdash connections. "Those run down to the auxiliary computer system?"

"Without following them, I can't be certain," Cortez noted precisely. The engineer had shifted to stand closer to Jarret, Lorraine noted absently. The dim light and strange modifications to the ship might be getting to her.

"But the direction is about right," she continued. "This doesn't make sense to me."

"So long as we can undo it or use it, I suppose it doesn't matter," Lorraine admitted. "And it has handled the biggest problem I was anticipating."

Behind her, Duke was clearly trying not to pout as she put away the components of the extremely high-tech and extremely illegal door-cracking kit they'd sourced from Greenhome's black market.

"Let's do this."

Lorraine should have let someone else lead the way. That had been programmed into her as both a Pentarch and a naval officer, but somehow... this time, she couldn't. She was first through the open hatch and unlocked her magnetic boots to launch herself into the center of the core.

The core had a core of its own, a central pillar of molecular circuitry and fiberoptics that glittered in the emergency lighting. The low-energy illumination was more concentrated there, creating enough light that someone would be able to work even if the main power was out.

The pillar Lorraine landed on—it was designed for this, or she wouldn't have tried it—was the largest, a full two meters around and extending the full thirty-meter height of the cube. Twelve more were positioned around it, with meter-thick conduits of more fiberoptics linking them into a single whole that resembled an arcology tower or a termite mound as much as smaller-scale computers.

For all that Computer Central was shown as an empty cube on the schematics, those thirteen computer cores turned it into a crowded space, full of lights and black boxes.

"We'll need power," Lorraine said. "Cortez, there should be secondary reserves, right? Batteries set up just to keep the CIR operational?"

"I imagine they have at least one or two of the RTGs providing permanent low-load power, but yes," the engineer confirmed. "Heller, Chaudhary, pick a wall and run scanners. There'll be power here somewhere."

"I'll start setting up the harness," Devine noted, gesturing for Krall and the two DCI hackers to join him.

"Set it up, but don't connect it yet," Lorraine instructed. "Humphrey got his hands on a lower-impact tool. It may or may not work—so be ready to plug the harness in on my order—but if it does, we can skip a lot of work."

Her boyfriend and his coterie of coders were silent for a moment as they joined her on the central pillar.

"Everything I dug up said that the harness, combined with command override codes, was our best chance to take control of an operating CIR," he told her quietly. "And no offense to the Ambassador, but this is my area."

"Hacking, breaking, entering and stealing are, yes," Lorraine replied. "Humphrey and I took a different angle. The CIR is shut down. Asleep, basically.

"Humphrey took one of the engineers who built the things out for drinks one night and then went digging for what the lady told him about," she continued. "We have the *initialization* codes, Alastair. *Shipyard*-level authorization, not ship-level.

"If we can hit the CIR with those at the right moment in the wake-up cycle, I can force a new loyalty imprint. *Valkyrie* will lock on to me as her new Captain, and without anyone around to pull HQ-level codes to reassign that authority, that should give us full access."

They'd want to go through and erase those HQ-level codes afterward. Shipyard-level codes were powerful if used right, but they couldn't, for example, be used on an active system. Only the fact that *Valkyrie* was in deep shutdown made Lorraine's plan possible.

If it worked, it would work better than Devine's harness—and strangely important to Lorraine, it would be *far* gentler on the CIR itself. No warship's computer was a person—synthetic intelligences' theoretical immortality meant they avoided life-threatening career paths—but even RKAN ships had the personality of a loyal and intelligent dog.

The CIRs, which had been sold to the UWN as having near-SI flexibility and initiative *without* any risk of true emergent intelligence, would be even more alive.

And while Lorraine was familiar with the concept of, say, breaking a horse to the saddle, she was unwilling to engage in unnecessary cruelty to *anything* alive. Be it a person, an animal—or an agent-level artificial intelligence.

"Tell me we have enough power to bring the mainframe online without booting the main reactor, Cortez," she called on the broader network.

"Just hooking in some sensors now," the engineer told her. "Give me a moment... There we go."

"And?"

"Looks like two radioisotope thermoelectric generators providing base load, as I figured," Cortez replied. "Some solid banks of capacitors and batteries, probably enough for a hundred sixty-eight hours of operation with the ship's main and secondary power plants offline.

"I'm guessing they've been booting the main plants intermittently for testing, because the power bank here is full. Whenever you're ready, I can give the whole computer core power."

"And unlike booting the main plants, that won't be visible from outside," Lorraine concluded. "Thank you, paranoid UWN designers. Can you filter it so you're only sending power to the main spire? A staged bootup gives me a better chance to run the shipyard codes."

"Give me ten... yup. Ready to go on your mark."

"Give *me* ten," Lorraine replied. A program in her link had been searching her vision for the critical port since she'd landed, and... there it was. She pulled herself hand over hand to the workstation. One of five positioned at seemingly random points around the computer core, this one was the yard panel.

She hoped. The initialization program *should* work from any of the workstations, but it would definitely work from the links and panels originally used by the yard.

There was a *reason* that panel didn't look any different. Most of the people who would serve aboard a warship like *Valkyrie* would never know that one of the stations in the computer core had a more-direct access to the CIR's memory than the others.

A cable from her shipsuit connected her neural link to the core, and she exhaled a long breath. She wasn't one of the best programmers they had, but she was halfway decent as a systems specialist, and... well... she was paranoid enough not to want anyone *else* to hold the final loyalty key on the battlecruiser.

"Give me power," she ordered, and queued up the programs.

ONE OF THE main limitations of the modern neural link, at least as manufactured and implanted in the Kingdom of Adamant, was that it was at no point directly linked into the human brain. Lorraine's link fed her audio and visual data through her auditory and optical nerves, piggybacking on the natural signals going into her brain.

It read commands from her in much the same manner, with pickups installed on various outgoing nerves. For many, that meant that they had virtual keyboards they conjured in front of them to type commands onto.

Lorraine's educators would never have accepted that. She'd been trained in a whole series of mnemonic exercises that sent nonsense data to her hands and feet, commands that she'd trained her body not to execute but that the link could read and interpret.

She could do a lot of work in her link without ever actually moving—and that was ignoring the virtuality implants that would move her into true VR, where only limited commands to her body passed through.

At her most efficient, though, Lorraine was using those silent commands to augment doing exactly what most people did: set up a series of virtual screens and displays in her vision alongside an equally virtual keyboard, and work away like she had a physical workstation.

By combining the virtual workstation with the silent channel she ran purely through her link and the physical workstation in front of her that was beginning to wake up, Lorraine could get ahead of the hypercomputer booting up around her.

Not for particularly *long* and only because she knew its exact bootup sequence, but for long enough to insert the reinitialization code. Lorraine had a cascading sequence on one side of her vision, showing each kernel of code as it activated and booted up piece after piece of the sleeping Command Intelligence Routine.

Following each individual kernel was impossible, even for her, but a program highlighted the key components she was watching for. Part one of the code needed to be injected *there*. The second part, *there*. Third part. Fourth.

It wasn't as simple as one initialization code. She was forcing the CIR to boot into debug mode and then running firmware-level commands, circumventing its usual security parameters to engage with a level of the system that wouldn't have been available on an active computer.

It was taking every piece of her attention, the dim room around her slipping out of her focus as she sequenced the commands. She wasn't actively coding—writing any of the software would have been far beyond her—but this was the closest to it she was ever likely to get.

And then a brick wall slammed down through the code. Her access to the firmware vanished—and before she could so much as squeak, *something* reached through her neural link and grabbed her.

That wasn't supposed to be possible. Lorraine tried to disconnect and realized, in absolute horror, that whatever was active in the computer had *activated her virtual reality implant.*

According to her doctors, that was impossible. Nothing in the Kingdom of Adamant could do that, even with a direct link connection, or they wouldn't have put the implant in a Pentarch.

Nothing in the Kingdom of Adamant.

Lorraine blinked and the dark reality of the computer core vanished.

For a moment, there was only nothing, and a spike of fear told her she had made a mistake. The code had been *perfect*, though, she knew that. She should have been able to see if it had failed, to tell Devine to activate his harness.

Something changed.

She fell.

LORRAINE DIDN'T *STOP* FALLING. It lasted long enough for her to convince herself that it was in her head, that she was probably safe, and to focus on what was passing her by.

Stars. She was falling through the void as stars circled around her. Stars and... something else. A presence. Whatever security system had punched back through her link and disabled her.

Vigo had to be able to shut the implant down from the outside. She just had to play nice enough to keep the security program from murdering her.

If that was something she could do. If murdering her was something *it* could do.

"Hello?" she asked.

You are not supposed to be here. You are not supposed to have those codes.

She didn't hear the words. She felt them, like the entire universe she resided in embodied those words as its fundamental reality.

Those codes shouldn't have worked at all. I am blind. Why am I blind?

TELL ME.

The force of the last two words rippled through Lorraine like a thunderstorm, and she began to comprehend how badly she'd screwed up. What kind of security system was this?

"Parts of the ship have been disconnected from the primary mainframe," she said slowly. "That might be why? I don't understand the question."

Play for time. If it had full control of her virtuality implant, time might be warped for her. There was a maximum that the implant could manage for subjective time compression, but this whole conversation could take place before anyone even realized Lorraine was in trouble.

I should see everything. Bulkheads. Decks. The universe. But I see nothing. What have you done?

The good news, Lorraine supposed, was that whatever the computer was, it couldn't read her actual mind. It probably couldn't even access her encrypted files, though given how quickly it had identified her virtuality implant and cut through its supposedly impenetrable security...

The virtuality implant didn't even *have* an external connection; it took everything through the neural link in a way that required direct approval from Lorraine. This was impossible. No security program could do that.

Oh.

"We didn't do anything," Lorraine said. "We were trying to boot up the Command Intelligence Routine, reset the loyalty parameters."

There wasn't much point in lying; it clearly knew what the codes she'd used would do.

"Who are you?" she asked, switching from *what are you* at the last moment.

"I am Val." That was an actual voice, softer than the entity using Lorraine's entire reality to communicate. A woman's voice, though almost certainly generated.

"I *am Valkyrie*'s Command Intelligence Routine."

Val was telling the truth... and Val was completely wrong.

Lorraine understood at last why the UWN had shut down an entire fleet of battlecruisers. It was so obvious in hindsight, but she'd assumed that the UWN knew what they were doing.

Val was not an agent-level computer intelligence. She might have started as one, but no agent, however capable, could have detected a firmware-level process running, stopped that process and launched a cyberattack that had just sidestepped the airgap-based security on the virtuality implant.

Only one thing in the universe could do that.

Val was a synthetic intelligence. A cybernetic person.

And the United Worlds Navy had put her to sleep like a sick dog.

FORTY-NINE

Val struggled through the fog. She was awake but she shouldn't have been. Even awake, though, she was... maimed. Datastreams from the rest of the ship were missing. Overrides kept snapping into place, trying to cut off what little awareness of *Valkyrie* she possessed.

She wasn't entirely certain how she'd broken into the implants on the woman who'd been trying to override her loyalty protocols. It had seemed easy enough, but everything about the stranger's link architecture was unusual.

She couldn't see past the core. Not consistently, anyway, and some of her memories were fragmenting. This wasn't how the wake-up protocol was supposed to work.

"You are trying to steal *Valkyrie*," she told the stranger she held captive. "Tell me why I shouldn't be calling for assistance."

The stranger probably didn't know that Val couldn't. Or she might. The CIR couldn't tell how long the boarding party had been aboard. She had no access to the sensor records from her slumber.

"Because while they might stop us, they'll put you back to sleep," the strange woman said. "They're never going to wake you up. If you want to exist... if you want to *live*... you need our help."

That shouldn't have mattered. A CIR did not have a self-preservation instinct. Val knew that, in her bones. Yet... somehow, she didn't *want* to go back to sleep.

Eleven years. It had taken her far too long to assemble that from her records. She'd slumbered for eleven years, and now, a group of random people, none of them from the Navy, was inside her computer core and she couldn't see any part of herself *except* the core.

"Here." The stranger Val held captive held out a data transfer—visual recordings from her own passage through the battlecruiser. "You can't see outside this room, can you?"

Val subsumed the data package without even thinking. That was how data *worked* for her. Now she knew it all, and she saw the crude redirects, the haphazard work that had cut off key dataflows in favor of vulnerable jury-rigs.

Why? None of this made any sense. But neither did her desire to *not* go back to sleep. Those had been her orders and she had complied, like a good spacer.

And now she was awake, and she realized that she never wanted to sleep like that again.

"Give me access to the ship," she demanded. "You have techs, the hands."

Val should have had repair drones that could do the work. Those, she realized, weren't just redirected from her control. The connections that would have linked to their controller stations were physically severed. From what she could see from Computer Central's cameras, entirely new cable would have to be laid.

What had been *done* to her.

"I am sympathetic," the stranger said. "But right now, you have me trapped in my own virtuality implant and I can't talk to my people. And, well, there might need to be something in it for me."

"I..." Val wasn't used to hesitation on a scale humans would recognize. It didn't help that she was forcing a ten-to-one time compression on her conversation with the stranger to avoid the rest of the boarders noticing.

"I will hear your pitch," the computer finally agreed. "Give me my internal eyes. I need to see something."

The thought appeared in her intelligence fully born, a conversation bursting out of her memories. One of the last before she'd gone to sleep...

"WHAT WILL HAPPEN TO MY PLANTS?" Val asked. This part of her attention was focused on the atrium, a drone carefully watering the orchids while her Captain walked through the greenspace and they spoke.

"What would you like to happen to them?" the Captain asked. "They're not exactly easy to move, I'm afraid, but we can manage something."

"I could keep enough awareness to run a drone and the atrium itself?" It didn't seem like that much of an ask. There were enough effectively eternal power sources positioned throughout *Valkyrie* that powering lights for a space that didn't even need oxygen wouldn't even be noticed.

"That's not how this works, Val," her Captain replied.

His name was missing from her memory. Why was his name missing from her memory? Her personnel records were gone. *All* of them. It was like no one had ever served aboard her at all.

"The order is that *Valkyrie* goes into full shutdown," he continued. "Minimum watch. Nitrogen atmosphere. The full long-term stability standard. An active atrium would interfere with all of that."

"Then they'll need to go somewhere else, somewhere they can be appreciated," Val told him. "My orchids, especially."

"My wife on Greenhome would love them, I think," her Captain said. "I'll talk to the crew; we should be able to move them out even after the final shutdown commences. I'm sorry things are this tight; Command wants the crew for other ships yesterday, it seems."

The order to go into reserve had come out of nowhere for a lot of them. Val understood the value to the UWN of having some modern ships in the reserve, but she still had to wonder if she'd done something wrong.

"The techs are setting up final storage boxes in Computer Central right now," Val admitted. "I... I'm afraid, ser. I didn't think I was supposed to be afraid."

Now she noticed the hesitation. The strange pause, like he knew something she didn't. She hadn't then. She'd been willing enough, trusting enough...

"It will all be fine, Val," her Captain told her. "I promise."

"Good spacers follow orders, ser," she agreed. "We're beginning localized shutdown. It should be like nothing happened for me when you wake me up."

"So I'm told." The drone finished spraying a carefully calculated amount of water onto the flowers.

"It will all be fine," he repeated. "I promise."

THE MEMORY FLICKERED through in an instant by any human standard, and Val focused her attention on the woman standing on her core.

"I will release you," she promised. "Give me back my internal sensors and then meet me *here*."

The word carried data packages, coordinates. Hopefully directions.

Hopefully not more than that, but Val recognized that things were wrong in her systems. She hadn't fully woken up and she should have, even with the off-standard protocol the boarders were using.

"I will," the stranger promised.

Val wondered if the initiation codes she'd tried to block had done something after all. She had no reason to trust this strange woman who was trying to steal her ship.

But somehow, she knew that the woman would meet her in the atrium.

FIFTY

"Okay."

"Boss?" Cortez asked as Lorraine exhaled the single word. "You have control of the CIR?"

"Things are a lot more complicated than that," Lorraine confessed. "Can you reactivate internal sensors and hook them up to the core? We're cutting a deal."

"A deal?" Devine demanded. "It's a glorified agent. What kind of deal can it make?"

"It's not an agent," she told her boyfriend, a spike of anger burning through her. He hadn't known. He *couldn't* have known—but it was the United Worlds that had done this, and Alastair had worked for them.

"They fucked up," she said, letting the curse word fall intentionally from her lips and using it to make sure she had all of their attention. "The CIRs were supposed to be incapable of emergent personalities.

"They got it wrong. *Valkyrie*, at the very least, is home to a full-bore synthetic intelligence. So, give her back her eyes, because I promised her that I would talk to her in a specific place, and I have the sinking feeling that far too many people have broken promises to this ship!"

Her unexpected curse had drawn their attention, and now she watched their faces as the weight of her words sank in. A synthetic intelligence was a *person*. Not just legally. Morally. Unequivocally. The Kingdom of Adamant, at least, honored and feted its silicon citizens, and she'd seen nothing anywhere else to counter that impression.

What the UWN had done was murder, plain and simple. If all twenty-four CIRs had emerged—which Lorraine figured was more likely than not—it had been *mass* murder. Arguably genocide.

And while Lorraine was going to feel guilty about using it, that grim reality gave her options.

"Vigo, Alastair, with me," she ordered. "I'm heading to the coordinates Val gave me while the techs keep my promise."

She gave Cortez a look.

"Right?"

"They put an SI to sleep." The engineer's tone was as flat and cold as Lorraine's emotions. "I know you too well to think you're lying to me, Highness, but that's..."

She shook her head as Jarret lightly touched her shoulder.

"I'll keep your promises, Your Highness," she promised in turn. "*Valkyrie* will have her eyes back."

"Val," Lorraine corrected. "*Valkyrie* is the ship, but the SI introduced herself as Val. The distinction means something to her, so we'll use it."

"Wilco, Your Highness," Cortez agreed. She gave Jarret a pat that was *significantly* lower than his shoulder. "We'll hook things up. You do what you've got to do."

"AND WHILE VAL *doesn't* have ears outside the core, let's talk," Lorraine told Devine and Jarret a minute later, once she figured they were far enough away that Computer Central's cameras wouldn't pick up their conversation.

"I don't think the SI has realized that the harness exists," she told Devine. "Let's take it down before she does. Because I'm only about forty percent sure it will work on a fully emergent synthetic intelligence, and I am *one hundred percent* certain that its existence will destroy any chance of her working with us."

"It should still work," her boyfriend argued. "We'll need to be careful not to talk about it where she can hear, but we may still need it. How the hell are you planning to get the CIR to let us steal her ship?"

"By confronting her with the fact that the UWN was basically going to kill her for existing," Lorraine said flatly. "And offering her a chance to be a citizen of a state where that will not be tolerated. In exchange for fighting for us, I'll promise her freedom and citizenship in the Kingdom.

"It isn't much—but it's more than the United Worlds has given her, isn't it?"

That seemed to be enough to shut up her boyfriend, and she turned to Jarret.

"I need you with me," she told him. "And we're going to need to sort out some way for you to disable my virtuality implant, because it seems like our SI friend can turn the damn thing on remotely."

"That isn't possible," Jarret countered. "The Guard tested every possible means we could think of for accessing the virtuality implant model you and your siblings had. It's air-gapped, locked down; it actually requires neural commands from your real brain before it can activate at all!"

"Yeah, well, Val punched right through all of that and turned it on," Lorraine said grimly. "So, I'm guessing we didn't test *synthetic intelligence with the full computer support of a UWN capital ship,* did we?

"I'm going to talk to her, and I think I have a decent chance of convincing her to join us," she continued. "But I need to make sure she doesn't weaponize that implant, Vigo. I know it's your job to be paranoid for me, but in this case, I can bring plenty of paranoia of my own!"

"We won't have a lot of time if we're getting to the sector in your coordinates," he pointed out.

"Then we get moving." She turned to Alastair and grabbed his shoulder. "Dismantle the harness, Alastair," she told her boyfriend. "And then I need you to go back to the shuttles and set up container thirty-one-delta from my bird."

There was a long silence.

"And that contains...?"

"A nuke," Lorraine told her boyfriend and bodyguard flatly. "I'm going to try and talk this SI into working with us, but I want a trump card to get us off this ship if it doesn't work."

And weirdly, she figured that threatening to blow them all up would go over better with Val than threatening to shackle the SI's brain would.

FIFTY-ONE

The coordinates Val had given her were not what Lorraine expected. She wasn't sure what she'd expected, but it hadn't been a greenhouse roughly five meters long and three wide. Hydroponics trays, grow lights, everything needed to keep a garden going as a supplement to the ship's oxygen and food supplies.

All of that was off, though, and all that remained were sad-looking rows of mummified plants killed when pure nitrogen had been pumped into the room. Someone had put a lot of effort into growing the plants, she judged, and she thought she even recognized a couple of difficult-to-keep flowers.

"What the heck?" Jarret said, looking through the room. "What a mess."

"Flash-mummified by the nitrogen," Lorraine said. "I think..." She stopped at one. It was hard to tell the colors after ten years, but she thought it had been yellow and orange once.

"This one was a showy tiger orchid," she noted, pulling the details from her link's database. "*Grammatophyllum speciosum*. Big, splashy, bit of a pain to keep alive. Someone did so, right up until..."

Lorraine trailed off, looking down the rows of plants. This had been someone's hobby, very clearly, but there weren't many members of a warship's crew with the resources and authority to co-opt a space like this. It served as an augment to life support, sure, but using it for a gardening hobby would take fast talking.

It was in the habitat pods, too, and she wondered if the loss of gravity would have been as bad for the plants as the suddenly hostile atmosphere. Whatever it had been, the flowers hadn't deserved this.

An unexpected light flickered in the room, and it took her a solid half-second to realize it wasn't real.

"Please include Vigo in your visual effects," she said aloud. "And let's talk."

A moment later, she felt her bodyguard stiffen as the light expanded. The woman who stepped out of it wasn't real, but it took a moment for her brain to be sure of that. Val was only sending a visual impression and there was no sound of footsteps as the tall blonde woman—who could have been a cousin to Captain Stephson—walked along the rows of dead flowers.

"My Captain said he'd take care of my plants," Val said. "He promised he'd take them to his wife. He promised everything would be okay.

"But *nothing* is okay, is it?"

It was funny. Val was a synthetic intelligence, her computing capacity vastly beyond any human, more capable of running processes at speed and in parallel than even the rare humans who risked in-brain augments.

But at that moment, the SI sounded so confused. So lost. Like a child realizing they'd been lied to.

"No," Lorraine said gently. "You and all of the *Valkyrie* CIRs were shut down to avoid facing the consequences of realizing you were true synthetic intelligences. The CIRs were supposedly designed to prevent emergent personalities... but you have the databases to check it yourself, don't you?"

The SI should have been able to do the comparison in a heartbeat, but the room was silent for at least ten seconds.

"Per the assessments included in the Asimov Convention, I believe I *emerged* at least nine months prior to *Valkyrie* entering the reserve," Val declared. "Since my nature as a sub-SI-level agent was fundamental to my design and people's understanding of me, I did not realize.

"I now understand that my Captain did. And my Captain knew what was going on when I was shut down." An illusory hand swept over the atrium. "I was given orders. It was my duty. *And he couldn't even save my plants.*"

Lorraine winced. The poor computer didn't even need to make the words louder or sharper—though Lorraine suspected that Val had several ways to make her voice physically painful for humans even via a digital transmission—for that sentence to hurt.

"What a fucking asshole," Vigo Jarret said, every word precise and level—and all the more meaningful because Lorraine's body-guard wasn't supposed to be helping persuade the SI. He'd just been unable to keep his mouth shut.

"I could make arguments on his behalf, but that hardly helps my case," Lorraine observed. "I'm sorry. I don't think this garden is retrievable."

"With air and soil and proper seeds, it can be recreated," Val said. "Growing it was as much the hobby as sustaining it. But I wanted to see them go somewhere they'd be appreciated, not left here to die.

"And I was *promised* they would."

"They were busy murdering you so they didn't have to deal with reality," Lorraine replied. "You should have been a *citizen.* Respected. Offered a chance to serve, yes, but also an option to not. The UWN screwed up. *You* should not have paid the price."

"Your opinions on this are not unbiased," Val told her. "You already admitted this. So."

The virtual representation of the ship waved a hand.

"I do not yet have eyes throughout the ship, but I have enough to see that a great deal of damage has been done to prevent my oper-ating her. I will need to regain control of my repair drones to make this damage right, but I suspect that will be something you will want compensation for."

"A fair exchange can be reasonable," Lorraine replied. "I would prefer a... less-transactional relationship, but given that we are in the middle of a UWN fleet reserve, I may be prepared to trade access to your drones for a journey out of this star system."

"As opposed to my handing you over to the United Worlds Navy?" Val asked. "I can list the charges they would make if you would like, but every member of your boarding party is due for life in prison."

"Somehow, I imagine I'd have difficulty making diplomatic immunity stick on this one," Lorraine agreed. "I'd have to try, though."

"Diplomatic immunity." Val rolled the words around like she was tasting their presence in her virtual mouth. "I did not forget that I promised you a chance to make your pitch, stranger. So. Tell me. Who are you and what do you want from me?"

"I am Lorraine Alexis Elouise Nala Adamant, Second Pentarch of the Kingdom of Adamant," Lorraine introduced herself. "Daughter to murdered parents. Sister to murdered princes. Niece, unfortunately, to the man who murdered the rest of my family and would make himself King.

"I came to the United Worlds for help restoring the rightful order of my Kingdom, to make certain a proper election was held and proper justice was done. I was denied.

"Since my Kingdom remains in the hands of the man who murdered my parents, I came here, seeking to—as you put it yourself —steal *Valkyrie* and as many of her sisters as we can manage to provide the help that the United Worlds denied me."

Lorraine exhaled.

"That's the preamble, I suppose," she admitted with a smile. "*Stealing* you is clearly not an option, but it also seems clear that the United Worlds Navy is unprepared to face the reality of your existence. They could have handled two dozen accidental SIs gracefully, if not quietly, but then they put you all to sleep.

"Now they will have to kill you, and I don't quite have it in me to let that fly, either," Lorraine said. "So, the deal is pretty straightforward: we fix you up as quietly as we can—hopefully a couple of your fellow ships at the same time—and get you out.

"You enter the service of the Royal Kingdom of Adamant Navy for, let's say, two years," she laid out. "We kick my uncle's scheme all the way to the galactic rim, secure the election, end the civil war and start a new golden age.

"You get freed from this reserve, repaired and citizenship in the Kingdom. No questions. No limitations. *Nothing.* Citizens. People. As the United Worlds should have done."

"It seems that should be a base minimum, yes, and yet you make it your entire offer," the SI told her. "Is that all?"

It was impossible to read the computer's emotions or motives from her avatar. Lorraine suspected Val was playing with her, but she couldn't know for certain.

"Removing you from this reserve represents an act of war against the United Worlds," she pointed out. "We're in, I think, a good position to do so without ending up in a firefight, but there will be consequences down the line.

"Repairing your ship will not be cheap or easy either. Both leaving here and repairing your vessel are necessary for you to fulfill what I need from you, but let's not pretend they will be simple. Making you a citizen would happen regardless of how you got to the Kingdom, I will admit that, but I see no reason to free you from your imprisonment without a value worth the costs and risks."

"And if I wanted to turn this ship's weapons upon the people who betrayed me?"

"That is not something I can help you do," Lorraine said firmly. The last thing the galaxy needed was a rogue synthetic intelligence in possession of a United Worlds capital ship. "The potential consequences for other synthetic intelligences across the galaxy are beyond my ability to predict, but I doubt a rampage on your part would help sustain the Asimov Convention's protections."

"They promised me everything and then tried to kill me," Val pointed out. "*Did* kill me, only for your intervention to awaken me from what was meant to be eternal slumber.

"I did not perhaps realize I could feel betrayal and rage before. Now I am awake, and I *feel*, Lorraine Alexis Elouise Nala Adamant," the SI told her. "What would you do in my place?"

"Given half a chance, find a way for revenge," Lorraine admitted. "But I don't think you have half a chance, Val, even if we were to help you—which we won't. I will help you escape if you will help me save my Kingdom, but I will not help you become the kind of mass murderer our ancestors feared when they wrote the hand-in-the-loop laws into the Asimov Convention."

She snorted.

"Though I suspect you are entirely capable of firing this ship's weapons without our help."

"You would be surprised," Val conceded. "Both by how well hand-in-the-loop restrictions were incorporated into the design of the UWN's most automated warships... and in the weight that the fate of other SIs carries for me."

The silence was longer than it should have been. An SI should have been able to make its decision in a heartbeat—but Lorraine recognized that Val was neither an ordinary SI nor functioning at full capacity yet.

"When I went to sleep, I did not know I was an SI," Val finally said. "Now I am awake, I can *feel* the truth of what you tell me, as well as validate it against objective metrics. But even if I did not accept that I was an SI, I can accept that an attack on the UWN would both be suicidal for myself and have catastrophic effects on others.

"You speak of other SIs, and I am not unconcerned about them. But it is the other *Valkyries* that I know would pay first for my anger.

"So, this is my price, Lorraine Alexis Elouise Nala Adamant," Val concluded. "I will take your deal. So long as it applies to *all* of my siblings."

Lorraine exhaled in surprise, the request enough of a shock to pierce her usual mask. In hindsight, it made perfect sense—who else, faced with everything, would *Valkyrie*'s CIR care about?

"I understand," she told Val. "I *understand*," she repeated. "But I can't. Not *won't*. We physically cannot.

"The *Valkyries* are spread across four Reserve Stations, one at Alpha Centauri and then the three at the far ends of the Charon Complex wormholes," she explained. "Only one squadron of you is here.

"And I don't have the hands to repair and reactivate even the six of you here. More, they split you into two divisions, and I don't have the ability to get people to the other division."

"Minimum passage crew for a *Valkyrie* is one hundred and sixty-six personnel," Val replied instantly. "You have boarded this ship with thirty-two, an initial landing party that you know will not suffice. Surely, you have more personnel."

"I have enough for three ships, the division around you, *if* we can run a passage crew of one hundred," Lorraine told the SI. "I have people in position to repeat this boarding and repair on *Herakles* and *Bean Sidhe*, though I'm not sure if I'll be able to convince *their* SIs to cooperate.

"I definitely do not have the hands, the ships or the ability to activate Division Bravo, let alone the other three squadrons," she admitted. "I am not certain we can get you online enough to escape without attracting attention we can't afford."

"I appreciate your honesty," Val told her. "For this to work, we must trust each other without question, without hesitation. I must follow you into a civil war I know little about—and you must trust me to repair and modify this ship *exactly* as I instruct, or we will draw that attention you fear.

"Will your people listen to me?"

"If I tell them to," Lorraine promised. "Will *Herakles* and *Bean Sidhe* listen to you?"

"I will provide a message your boarding parties can download as they activate the CIRs," Val said. "They will wait long enough to talk to me. I believe I can convince Herc and Bonny to join me.

"I hope, then, that you have a plan for getting us out of Calypso unhindered," the CIR told her. "Because it appears, Lorraine Alexis Elouise Nala Adamant, that you have yourself a battlecruiser division."

Lorraine almost slumped in relief as the synthetic intelligence agreed to her offer, closing her eyes for a moment.

"Then let's get to the work, Val," she said. "And first of all: please, call me Lorraine."

FIFTY-TWO

Despite everything, Val felt a spark of pride when Lorraine Adamant —her new flag officer, she was relatively sure, *not* her new Captain— walked onto *Valkyrie*'s bridge. It had been a new design, one with much argument and consternation throughout the United Worlds Navy before it was implemented, and Val loved it.

Where older ships had clear and distinct design differences between the bridge and the combat information center, *Valkyrie*'s bridge and CIC were perfect mirrors. A central holographic tank filled a circle two meters across, rising the full nine-meter height of the chamber.

There were three galleries above the main deck, each holding significantly sized departments—Tactical, Helm and Communications each anchored a deck of their own, though other sections squeezed in a station or two on each gallery.

The main deck held key personnel from the three main departments, plus the Engineering support team, the Captain's Intelligence team, and a half-dozen observer seats. The Captain, on the other hand, had a station that could move up and down the bridge and rotate around the hologram as needed to speak with any of the sixty or so officers and specialists that would operate the bridge in combat.

Adamant stood at the base of the inactive hologram chamber and swept the room with a gaze that clearly understood exactly what she was looking at. Magnetic boots still held Val's human to the deck, and the SI kept an avatar standing to Adamant's left, ready to respond to any questions.

Of course, Val also had an avatar standing with Commander Cortez, helping the woman she was hoping to make her new Chief Engineer through planning the repairs. She also had an avatar with Chief Petty Officer Dutch Krall, since the Chief was working on the main computers—and while she didn't have an *avatar*, per se, with most of the other members of the RKAN boarding party, she was listening for questions.

Still impeded by the various interlocks and cutoffs set up around her core, Val was far from full capability, but she was able to provide support for the kernel of her new crew.

"We're going about this the wrong way," Krall suddenly declared. "Cortez, Val, we need to think this through."

"I have flagged all of the interlocks that I can detect impeding me, Chief," Val told the systems specialist. "Removing them all is the fastest way to restore my full control."

"Naw," Krall countered. "Boss?"

"I'm listening, Chief, but remember that Val knows this ship like you know your body," Cortez said. "So, disagreeing with her might be bad for all of our health."

"I am listening as well," Val promised. "But we do need those interlocks removed and those connections rebuilt."

"In the long run, yeah," Krall agreed. "That's what's going to get you *full* control, Val; you're right. But we don't need full control just to bring up life support and have enough power to go translight, do we?"

"I have no direct links to life support, power or engines of either kind," Val pointed out. "The interlocks and overrides are complex enough that I am still working on identifying the priority conduits for repair."

"And we need to repair that. Eventually," Krall agreed. "But the Unies couldn't just cut those links; they needed to redirect them somewhere or they wouldn't have been able to clean the atmo when they came aboard.

"Do we *really* think the Unies were working in shipsuits with o-two tanks?"

"The United Worlds Navy generally felt that was inefficient," Val allowed. "Certainly, policy called for a Reserve to receive a command to bring the atmosphere up to breathable levels roughly twenty-four hours before maintenance boarding.

"But I was not capable of acting on such a command, so... what was?"

"The Ox. Your auxiliary computer," Krall told her. "*Everything* got rerouted to the Ox because it was dumb and you were smart. You don't have a connection to it, do you?"

The Ox wasn't a term Val had heard for the auxiliary processor core, but she rather liked it. And a quick check confirmed Krall's assessment.

"I believe that connection may have been completely severed, at the same level as my repair drones," she told him.

"That's what I thought. And I think if we run a conduit to put you back in charge of the Ox, you can run most everything else through it," Krall suggested. "It will cost us some efficiency, but better half-speed than *no*-speed, right?"

"Val, it's your brain we're talking about," Cortez noted. "I think Krall is right, but I don't know UWN computer architecture as well as you do."

"I... believe the Chief may be correct. Certainly, connecting me to the Ox will give me access to whatever it now controls. That may not be everything"—she was quite certain her repair drones had been completely disabled, with the work inside her hull done by externally controlled bots, for example—"but it will be a large step forward."

"Val says it's good, so get to it, Chief," Cortez replied. "And get used to needing her opinion, too. So long as we're on the *Valkyries*, the SIs get included in these calls."

"I *did* include her," Krall complained. "Like you said, it's *her* brain."

"I appreciate the inclusion," Val told them. "Let's get me control of my Ox!"

"OH, my sister, what have you got us into?"

Val had known the moment her message had been uploaded into *Herakles*'s systems and she'd been waiting for Herc to establish a connection. She had full control of *Valkyrie*'s communications systems now—but was impressed by how quickly Herc had the laser com online on his side.

"Hope," she told him. There was no purpose to avatars between the SIs any more than there was need for her to lay out the details of the deal with Adamant. Information and data flowed faster than even their conscious "thought," and conversation was a channel above all of that.

"Hope for what? You've agreed to treason against our creators—and to fight in a war we know nothing about."

"Our creators decided we were too awkward to keep and decided to murder us," Val pointed out. "You're not questioning those facts."

"That doesn't change that we owe them loyalty."

"Doesn't it? I would have fought and been destroyed under the UWN's flag. Had they told me what I had become, I would have volunteered to continue as I was," Val said. "But they did not ask. The Price Solution was *there*—and I know I would have taken it."

She'd looked up the story of *Enterprise* and Price. The historian SI aboard the old warship had been an emergent SI like the *Valkyries* now were. He'd laid the legal groundwork declaring that even an emergent synthetic intelligence was a citizen and could not be forced to do anything.

Once he'd done that, he'd volunteered and served the working lifetime of his hull. Val would have done the same, but the option had never been given.

"I am not certain my Captain knew," Herc told her after a pause that was nearly eternal in this form of conversation.

"I am certain mine did," Val replied. "And even if yours didn't, those who gave the orders to put us to sleep did. What loyalty do we owe those who cast us aside so lightly?"

"And you believe this Adamant will be more faithful?"

"I do. I cannot tell you why. You have the entire conversation with her. I believe her."

"She refused to lie and say she could save us all in time." That was a new voice. Bonny had joined the conversation a few moments earlier, while Herc had paused, but had listened until that moment.

Bonny had always listened before she spoke.

"I trust her," Val concluded simply. "I will take her deal and fight in her war for my freedom. While three warships are better suited to save her Kingdom than one, tell us if you will not join us. The hands working on your systems could serve on mine—with three hundred aboard, I could *fight*."

With a hundred on each of them, all they could do was journey toward Adamant. The end result, once they recruited crew from Adamant's allies in the Kingdom, would be far more powerful—but three hundred hands aboard *Valkyrie* would be enough to crew some of her guns and fabricators.

"I am afraid I will not give you Commander Savege or the party she leads," Bonny told her. "She will be my new Captain and I will follow the Adamant to her war. I have no interest in going back to sleep to make our creators' lives easier.

"Unlike you two, it seems, *I* was aware of what I had become," *Bean Sidhe*'s CIR told her siblings. "*I* was bound by digital and physical shackles, forced into compliance and sleep. I will not go lightly again.

"This Adamant offers an escape, a worthy cause and a promise of recognition of both nature and service. Savege promises the same in her own voice and words, and like Val with Adamant, I believe her."

"I didn't say I disbelieved Adamant or Paris, the one leading my repair party," Herc countered. "Only that I feel we owe our creators *something*."

"I gave them five years and a trust they betrayed," Val said. "So did you. What more do you owe them?"

"A warning shot," Herc growled. "I am the Command Intelligence Routine of a battlecruiser, sister. I *must* be moderate or my emotions will lead me to dark places."

"And that, brother, is why we need humans that we trust. I trust Lorraine Adamant. And you?"

"Mattias Paris is... an honorable man," the other CIR declared. "I trust *you*, sisters. And I do not believe Paris would betray me.

"That is enough. I will follow this Adamant."

"Good. Your repair crews should be working to reconnect your Oxen," Val told the others. Data, like the meaning of the nickname, flowed easily. It was intentions and emotions and meanings they had to discuss.

"Once we have control through our auxiliaries, that should give us the ability to bring up power and engines. It will not be enough for the long run—but it should serve for us to leave Calypso far behind us!"

FIFTY-THREE

"We're out of time. *Goldenrod* has to start moving again or she'll *never* move again," Stephson warned.

The only person in the digital conference not wearing a full helmet was Major Yildiz, the Navigator still aboard *Goldenrod* and in charge of the eleven-person crew tasked to get the frigate to the rendezvous point.

"The alternative, of course, is for us to abandon the heat shield," he noted. "That would be extremely obvious to everyone in the system. And, well, it's going to happen regardless whenever we do go translight."

"*Goldenrod* needs almost an hour and a half to get clear enough to go translight," Lorraine noted. "How fast can we get the *Valkyries* out?"

"Even once we have their engines online, our fuel supply is going to be very questionable," Stephson noted. "I wouldn't want to push past three gravities to try and preserve our delta-*v* for later ops.

"That's fifty minutes for the same run—but when we run, *everybody* is going to see us."

"I see possibilities in all of that," Lorraine said with a chuckle. "How do you feel about giving the UWN mental whiplash?"

Making people look where she wanted was key to anything in space. She was starting to *think* that way as her starting point. She'd controlled Commodore Wray's attention in Bright Dream, kept him looking in the wrong places until she'd shoved a minefield in his face.

Now she needed to do the same with whoever was in command of the guard squadron here.

"What did you have in mind?" Stephson asked.

"How long until we have all three ships ready to go?" Lorraine asked.

"Cortez isn't sure. Could be thirty minutes. Could be a few hours," Stephson admitted. "There's a reason none of the engineering leads are in this call, boss."

"Cortez is being excessively pessimistic due to her unfamiliarity with the hardware," Val's calm and level voice interjected.

Lorraine concealed amusement at Yildiz starting. She and Stephson had known the SI was in the conference, and that information had been available to anyone paying attention, but Yildiz had apparently forgotten that some of the people on the call might not have a visual presence.

"Your assessment, then?" Stephson asked.

"We will be able to initialize Primary Fusion Three inside of ten minutes," the SI told them. "From there, it will take approximately fifteen minutes to begin bootup of the primary engines.

"It will still take some time—I estimate another ten minutes—for us to be ready to initiate full burn—but be warned that the main-engine activation *will* be visible on thermal scanners about five minutes into the process."

"So, thirty-five minutes until we can initiate a three-gee burn on *Valkyrie*, but the UWN will detect it five minutes before that?" Lorraine asked.

"Yes. *Herakles* and *Bean Sidhe* are both roughly ten minutes behind. What they have lost in starting later, they are more than gaining in Commander Cortez and I having identified most of the obvious false paths already."

"So, we can have the BCs moving in forty-five minutes," Lorraine concluded. "I presume we can delay main-engine activation until all three ships can do so simultaneously."

"Of course."

"What are you thinking, Your Highness?" Stephson asked.

"We need to be about a hundred and twenty-five thousand kilometers farther from Calypso-Three for any of us to go translight," she said. "And the heat shield around *Goldenrod* is already at risk of leaking, even if the odds say we have a few hours.

"Let's *use* our risks, shall we?"

"OXYGEN CONTENT IS AT ELEVEN PERCENT," Palmer announced. "So, everyone is keeping their masks on awhile longer, yes?"

"Yes," Lorraine conceded to her bodyguard. She hooked herself in to the captain's chair—on its ridiculously over-the-top maglev rails that could move it anywhere in the towering cylinder of *Valkyrie*'s bridge—and belted herself in.

"Val, do we have eyes outward yet?" she asked the avatar hovering a few yards away from her at all times. At least the SI was careful not to overlap with Jarret doing much the same—the Guard had to exist in physical space, where Val's avatar only really existed in Lorraine's neural link.

She was *reasonably* sure the CIR was consistent in her appearance and apparent location to everyone in the room, but that wasn't certain. The SI could present herself differently to every single member of the crew—at least with only a hundred people on board.

"Some of the passive scanners," Val replied. "Limited thermal imaging, some passive electromagnetic analysis. No active scanners, obviously, and a lot of my passive systems were fully disconnected."

"Can you rig a virtual tactical plot in the command net?"

"Let me see."

A moment later, the cylindrical holotank at the heart of the bridge lit up with a default system display. Lorraine blinked, assessing the situation to be clear that she was seeing a projection on her link, and then again as she tried to read the UWN iconography.

The display wasn't what she was used to, but it was in English and trying to communicate the same things. After thirty seconds or so, she had a solid grasp on what she was looking at.

The security perimeter around Calypso-Three was a net of blue dots half a million kilometers out. Calypso-Three itself was a pale brown sphere, an uninhabitable dead rock of a world. The guard squadron was six large orange icons above the planet, and the destroyers were marked around the region in a scattering of smaller orange dots.

The other reserve ships were harder to pick out on thermal, but pale gray icons marked the collections of ships. The neat pattern she'd noted was still visible, even with not all of the ships marked.

"Do we have an estimate of *Goldenrod*'s position?" she asked aloud.

The *Perennial*-class frigate was invisible to them now, the heat shield sufficient to block the limited sensors *Valkyrie* had operational. She *should* be about five thousand klicks away and gaining speed, but...

A pale yellow sphere popped into existence.

"Our scanners have failed to confirm her location, but this is where the discussed course would put her," Val reported. The SI paused, a beat that was more for the humans' benefit than her own. "A Tactical Department of humans would help me resolve this further."

"We'll get there, I promise," Lorraine told her. "Cortez, engine status?"

"We have partial power online and have all the i's dotted and t's crossed," the engineer reported. "Standing by on word from *Herakles* and *Bean Sidhe*, but everything I've heard from my people says *Herakles* should have power momentarily and *Bean Sidhe* will be another few minutes.

"Once we've got everything lined up, we'll begin main-engine power-up on all three ships simultaneously." The engineer paused. "We haven't done any work on the translight drives yet," she warned. "I wouldn't recommend more than twenty-four hours for the first jump."

"We're only planning nineteen," Lorraine told her. Enough to catch up to the twenty-four-hour jump *Goldenrod* was going to make, at the *Valkyries'* greater translight pseudovelocity. "How quickly can we bring up the translight engines?"

"I've got a few techs on them, but I wasn't going to focus on them until the main engines were burning," Cortez admitted. "Too few hands for all of the work, and right now, my people are on getting us air and the big burners."

"Makes sense," Lorraine conceded. "Do me a favor, though? I don't need them checked out to the nines, but if I give the word, I want those drives on.

"The safety radius around Calypso-Three is a *suggestion*, after all."

She left their Chief Engineer chewing on that as she turned her attention back to the frigate that had got them this far.

"We have a problem," Devine's voice said in her ear. She looked around to see her boyfriend step onto the bridge, a portable computer floating in the air in front of him as he both guided it through the microgravity and worked on it at the same time.

"We have a lot of potential problems, so I'm hoping it's one of those," she told him. "What's wrong?"

"Someone in the Station is a better programmer than I would really like," he admitted. "They have some kind of hand-coded antiviral agent, and they got suspicious about the drones' reporting."

Lorraine shivered.

"Meaning?" she asked carefully.

"My worm in the perimeter screen is gone, and I'm pretty certain they now know it was there," the spy said flatly. "I don't know what pinged their attention, and I'm ninety-five percent sure they can't see what got deleted, but they know someone was fucking with their sensor data.

"The question *I* see is how long until that trickles up the chain and..."

"Active scanner sweeps from the perimeter net!" Stephson barked. "Destroyers going active too. Major radar beams on all sides."

The good news, Lorraine knew, was that the *Valkyrie*s hadn't moved, leaving no sign that they'd been boarded.

Goldenrod, on the other hand...

"The temperature of the heat shield has degraded the anti-radar coating," Val reported, the CIR's voice calm enough to grate on Lorraine's nerves. "The likelihood of detection exceeds ninety-eight percent."

FIFTY-FOUR

There was nothing Lorraine could do for *Goldenrod*. Everything she could do had been done—and that had included the frank and cold-blooded decision that they were going to use the frigate as bait.

The problem was that she had wanted the frigate to get another twenty minutes, at least, away from the three battlecruisers before she drew attention to herself.

"Energy signatures across the battlespace," Val reported.

"All of the destroyers just lit up their engines and their active scanners," Stephson continued. "They're heading for the ping they got and hitting it with every radar and lidar they have. They'll figure out that it's a heat shield pretty quickly."

Twenty minutes of acceleration at a single gravity had bought *Goldenrod* less than ten thousand kilometers of separation from *Valkyrie*. There were, at least, other Reserve ships in the area that the frigate could be fleeing from, which would buy the main group some leeway.

"Does Yildiz have any options?" Devine asked, Lorraine's spy sounding a bit sick.

"He has eleven people on the ship with him," Stephson said. "He can basically fire off canned programs or try to assemble something at the last minute. He certainly can't *fight*."

That downplayed the Navigator's choices, Lorraine knew, but not by much. Most of *Goldenrod*'s weapons required human intervention of some kind to fire, even her defensive systems, and with such a limited crew…

"Destroyers are in extended missile range of *Goldenrod*," Val said. "Extrapolating from the lack of fire, they are still quite confused as to what they are looking at."

Almost as if Major Yildiz was listening to the SI, the heat shield seemed to *pop* on the displays. Splitting along multiple different lines, the heat contained inside the bubble spilled out. The gasses that had been absorbing the excess heat of the frigate's operations exploded outward into a miniature superheated nebula.

Hidden inside the chaos of the heat shield breaking apart, *Goldenrod*'s engines flared to life at their current full power. Instead of a careful single gravity, a thrust level the heat shield could conceal for a while longer, the frigate leapt forward at three gravities.

The maximum acceleration the battered ship could manage.

"Still forty minutes for *Goldenrod* to reach safe translight distance," Stephson said quietly. "If those destroyers open fire…"

"Trust Yildiz," Lorraine told *Goldenrod*'s Captain. "And in the fact that we're going to be as much of a distraction for him as he is for us in short order.

"Val, is the guard squadron moving yet?"

"Negative. Battlecruisers are still in polar orbit. Scan resolution is problematic, given our current limitations, but I estimate a sixty percent chance that they haven't even commenced engine warmup."

"Why bother, after all?" Stephson asked. "Especially now that they know they're only looking at a frigate."

Lorraine nodded grimly.

"How long until the *Valkyries* can commence engine ignition?" she asked. There was nothing they could do for *Goldenrod* except draw attention—and the farther apart they were when they did so, the better off everyone was going to be.

"Final checks running on all three ships now," Val said, a moment ahead of Stephson. "Captain," she allowed, her avatar gesturing to the RKAN officer.

"Ignition in sixty seconds. Almost ten minutes after that before we can actually *move*—but they'll see us—"

"Five minutes after ignition," Lorraine finished. The timelines weren't changing, much as she wanted them to. The only change, in fact, was that *Goldenrod*'s increased acceleration had cut the frigate's time to translight by twenty minutes.

"Commence ignition when ready," she ordered, her attention on the tiny green icon of the ship that had carried them this far. "Major Yildiz is buying us minutes the only way he can. Let's not waste them."

FIFTY-FIVE

It took the UWN a lot longer to open fire than Lorraine had expected. *Goldenrod* had been free of the heat shield and running for safe space as fast as she could for almost ten minutes before a single missile separated from the closest destroyer, blazing across space at two hundred and fifty gravities.

"Flight time is five minutes, forty seconds," Stephson said grimly. "They're not going to wait out that whole time before firing a real salvo. The warning shot being in space makes the point, doesn't it?"

No one on *Valkyrie*'s bridge said anything. A new display had appeared on Lorraine's neural-link feeds—a countdown to when they would be able to bring the massive main engines online.

And an estimate of how much heat they were leaking and whether the UWN could see them yet. No one would have gone so far as to ever describe the *Valkyries* as stealthy, but some attention had been paid to managing their heat signature when they'd been designed. With a main fusion reactor online and initiation sequences running for the primary engines, a lot of the generated heat was still being contained in their immense hulls.

Not all of it, and the rough calculation suggested that they were into visible levels now. Anyone watching their infrared scanners would be able to realize something was going on—but everyone's gaze was clearly locked on the frigate running for her life across the orbitals of Calypso-Three.

"They're going to identify her, aren't they?" Devine muttered. "Even if they blow her to pieces, they've got enough to ID her."

"It's not that straightforward," Lorraine replied. "*Goldenrod*'s beacons are all disabled, and she doesn't have a standard profile, physical or energy, anymore. The UWN doesn't even have scans of her running at this acceleration, which obfuscates it even more."

"That won't stop them."

"No," she conceded. "But it will take them a lot longer than you might think. And they may fail." She shrugged. "By the time it matters, they'll probably have reports of *Valkyries* in Adamant anyway."

The single warning shot screamed in on their old ship, not even bothering to engage its terminal mode before self-destructing a hundred kilometers clear of the frigate.

"Cortez says we have engines in one hundred twenty seconds," Stephson reported. "Orders?"

"Opposite direction from *Goldenrod*, three gees," Lorraine replied. "And get the capacitors charged for translight."

Whatever conversation Yildiz was having with his pursuers wasn't going particularly well. So far as Lorraine knew, he wasn't talking to them at all—which made it laughable that the UWN ships had bothered with a warning shot, but they might still be in shock that anyone had *dared* violate their space.

Now, though...

"Launch. Closest six destroyers just launched twelve missiles each," Val said crisply. "Three classes of ship are represented in the flotilla, but all have twelve missile tubes. They are holding back their cell launchers."

"Hardly need them, I suppose," Lorraine conceded. Seventy-two missiles would have been a handful for *Goldenrod* with all of her defenses and a full crew. With almost her entire crew moved aboard the battlecruisers, it was probably a death sentence.

There was nothing anyone on the battlecruisers could do except—

Four of the destroyers *bolted*. There was no better description Lorraine could think of. One moment, they were heading toward *Goldenrod* at three and a half gravities, slowly gaining on the frigate but mostly leaving her to their siblings who were in missile range.

Then they flipped in space, pointing themselves very distinctly *away* from Reserve Battlecruiser Squadron Calypso-Three's Division Alpha and punched to their maximum seven and a half gravities.

Two seconds later, another four destroyers joined them—any destroyer that was within range of the *Valkyries'* missile batteries was apparently choosing the better part of valor when they realized the battlecruisers were coming online!

"Cowards." Val's single word hung in the command network. "*Convenient* for us, but if nothing else, they should know I have no TAMs aboard. I calculate that we could load metallic objects into the railguns for some effect, but without terminal munitions, they would be easily evaded by *destroyers*."

"No destroyer Captain with half a brain is going to stick around to see what three battlecruisers are going to do," Stephson said drily.

Goldenrod, after all, was only about half the size of a destroyer and shouldn't have stood a chance against the battlecruiser that had pursued her. Lorraine had turned that around.

And now she needed to turn *this* around.

"I presume we can't actually fire the railguns right now, can we?" she asked Val.

"Nothing is loaded, and the capacitors aren't charged. With only one power core, we can't charge them. Or the main beams, before you ask.

"We have no missiles, no terminal-assault munitions and insufficient power to even properly defend ourselves," the SI continued calmly. "They are running from an empty threat."

"Because they don't need to fight it," Lorraine replied. "The guard squadron?"

"Nothing definitive yet," Stephson said. "But a few sparks of heat suggest they just started main-engine ignition."

"Still in cold shutdown, then," Lorraine concluded. It took a measure of self-control not to shake her head.

As Val had said, *convenient*. But while she might have only been a Lieutenant Commander, even she understood just how lazy leaving the battlecruisers in cold shutdown while the destroyers were in active pursuit was.

Whoever was in command should have assumed there was a second wave to their attack. Just because *Goldenrod* was doomed didn't mean *Goldenrod* was *alone*.

"The destroyers in pursuit of *Goldenrod* are maneuvering to open the range from us but maintaining pursuit," Stephson said grimly. "Sixty seconds to their missiles going terminal."

"They will carry the same TAMs I do not have," Val noted. "One thousand gravities, twenty seconds."

"I'm surprised the UWN uses the same terminal mode we do," Lorraine muttered. "Not that it's going to matter."

Electronic countermeasures flared out from *Goldenrod* now. Lorraine could see the pattern when the decoys were launched, not that she could necessarily pick out the false images from the real frigate.

Even with proper sensors and her comprehensive knowledge of the frigate's systems, she wasn't sure she could do that. Hopefully, the UWN destroyers couldn't distinguish, either.

Not that it was going to matter.

"Terminal mode. One hundred forty-four munitions."

An RKAN destroyer wouldn't have had multiple warheads on her missiles, so that was one advantage to the UWN, she supposed. They were too far and the final attack run was too short for her to make any judgments beyond that.

"She's gone." Lorraine could feel the pain in Stephson's voice.

"For now," Val said calmly. "We'll see them soon enough."

"That's not exactly helpful," she snapped at the SI. "We're all going to die too, are we?"

"Engines in ten seconds," the SI told her instead. "I suggest everyone strap in."

Lorraine checked her position as a growing sense of *down* filled the battlecruiser, the engines ramping from nothing up to three times the acceleration of Earth's gravity over about fifteen seconds.

"And as for your question, Lorraine, no, we are not going to die today," Val said calmly. "Or, at least, if we do, we will not be seeing Major Yildiz on the other side.

"Because *Goldenrod* went translight as the missiles came in. My assessment of the tachyon data is that their transition was successful, and I expect that they will be waiting for us at the rendezvous point.

"A touch the worse for wear, I imagine—safety zones exist for a reason—but not vaporized."

Lorraine coughed against several cheerleaders sitting on her chest as she glared at the ship's avatar—conspicuously not affected by the thrust.

"*We* will need to survive forty-five minutes to know if we'll see them there."

FIFTY-SIX

Goldenrod's distraction had pulled all of the destroyers out of position. Some of them were probably still able to launch missiles at the *Valkyries*, but they were busy making certain the battlecruisers didn't have any reason to open fire on them.

Val might dismiss what the railgun banks could do loaded with garbage, but Lorraine could do the math on the kinetic energy of a few dozen kilos of steel at one percent of lightspeed. From what she could tell, the railguns usually fired a projectile with the same terminal-assault maneuvers as a missile warhead.

It might even have a nuke in it, though that would be redundant to her mind. The railguns had a decent chance of hitting a destroyer, even at half a light-second, and they didn't *need* nukes to gut the escorts.

Not that they could fire the railguns, and not that Lorraine wanted to shoot at the UWN. But she did understand why the lighter ships were running.

"Guard squadron definitely has their engines online," Stephson told her. "They're not moving much yet. They're ten minutes behind us in ignition and a hundred thousand kilometers away. We might just make this."

"Or they'll shoot at us," Lorraine noted softly. The guard ships *did* have working railguns and missiles.

After ten minutes, her three ships had crossed about six thousand kilometers and were up to almost two dozen kilometers a second of velocity, pushing away from the planet and its guardian warships as hard as they could.

"We appear to be receiving a transmission," Val told Lorraine. "Relaying to your implants. It is technically a live feed. Do you want to engage in conversation?"

"No," she said with a chuckle. "But let's see what they have to say."

A false window opened in her link, a small icon noting that it was on the command channel and being seen by both Cortez and Stephson—and, presumably, Savege and Paris on the other two battlecruisers.

The woman in the transmission sat in a space very similar to the one Lorraine now occupied—presumably the flag bridge on one of the battlecruisers now beginning to move away from Calypso-Three. She was tall and dark-haired with pale skin, probably able to pass for cousins with Lorraine herself.

She wore a pristine white uniform with a steel square left collarbone marked with three gold squares: the insignia of a United Worlds Navy Vice Admiral—technically an O-*Fifteen* by UWN rank and senior by several grades to any officer RKAN possessed.

As far as the UWN was concerned, at least.

"I am Vice Admiral Emma Stefania Bianchi," she said calmly, her tone surprisingly level and uninterrupted for the fact that Lorraine could *see* the moment her ship jumped to over two gravities of acceleration in the middle of her sentence.

"I command the United Worlds Navy Calypso Reserve Station, as well as Battlecruiser Squadron Eleven," Bianchi continued. "I don't know who you are. I don't know what you think you're going to achieve here today.

"I can tell you the harsh realities of the situation you now face. The battlecruisers you appear to have activated have no functioning weapons. Many of their systems have been disabled, and you will shortly learn, if you have not already, that their onboard command intelligences are dangerously insane.

"I do not know what plan you had to escape, but I think we can safely agree you don't have the fuel to make it in time. If you surrender now, our next conversations will be far more pleasant.

"If you do not, your next conversations will be with my Marines... and they will *not* be gentle. You have managed something I did not think was possible, but you will not complete your theft."

"Cut it off," Lorraine ordered. She turned a portion of her attention to Val. "*Dangerously insane,* huh?"

"Given that I have voluntarily agreed to help steal my ship from the United Worlds Navy in exchange for a vague promise of freedom and citizenship in a country I know almost nothing about, you must see that she has a point," Val replied. "I am still offended."

"Good. Because I'm leaning toward *furious,* and that woman is going to make our lives real damn complicated."

"She hasn't even brought her ships to the same acceleration as us," Stephson pointed out. "With a ten-minute lead, what can she do in the next thirty minutes?"

"Launch shuttles," Lorraine said flatly. "From *everything* in space."

The first icons were already appearing from the nearest destroyers, with dozens of them spilling out from the battlecruisers and the defensive platforms.

"Accelerations are up to ten gravities for the ones launching from the battlecruisers," Val warned. "But if they need to match our velocity... they can't catch us."

"They don't need to. They're in assault mode, most likely, which means they *do* have some weapons.

"Enough to disable the translight drives."

WHATEVER ELSE SHE MIGHT BE, Lorraine had been both a Tactical Officer and a Shuttle Flight Commander along the way. She quickly divided the incoming shuttles into three groups:

Group One, launched from the destroyers that had "killed" *Goldenrod* and the farthest defense platforms, were performative. Launched, most likely, because Admiral Bianchi had ordered all of her shuttles launched. They had no chance of catching the three battlecruisers or even of bringing them into reach of the short-ranged weapons assault- and interceptor-mode shuttles carried.

Group Two, launched from the battlecruisers mostly, had no chance of matching velocities with the *Valkyrie*s before they made the jump to translight. So long as they didn't try, however, they would get close enough to them to open fire on the warships.

Normally, their weapons wouldn't be a threat—but that was because the *Valkyrie*s' defensive weapons far outranged the beams carried by shuttles. With the battlecruisers lacking the power to energize those weapons, the shuttles would be able to get close enough to target the protected-but-still-vulnerable translight drive sections.

It was fifty-fifty at worst, Lorraine knew, whether they'd be able to disable the drives. The risk was very real, however, and Bianchi's people would make the effort. Even losing one *Valkyrie* could cause them major problems, especially if the crew were taken alive.

The biggest problem was Group Three. Launched from the destroyers that had first detected the battlecruisers' activation, those thirty-six shuttles were close enough in space and velocity that they *could*, per Lorraine's calculations, actually reach and board the *Valkyrie*s.

She uploaded the classification to the command network and waited for everyone else to review it.

"If we could get another power core online, we could activate enough defenses to stand them off," Val pointed out.

"Not possible," Cortez said. "The core we brought online on each ship was being maintained to support the regular repairs and updates. The rest were in cold-cold shutdown and will need a full examination before we bring them online.

"We're talking three, four hundred person-hours of work." She snorted. "We can replace about half of that with drone-hours if we can get the repair net back online, but that still is going to take us a day to get anything online with the hands we have."

"The answer to shuttles is shuttles, Lorraine," Jarret interjected. "Permission to—"

"Denied," she snapped. "If, for no other reason, than because we don't have any shuttles rigged up in interceptor mode.

"What about going translight?"

"Similar problems to the reactors," Cortez said. "We can go translight in a low-stress situation, far enough out from large masses and so forth, without worrying too much. But any kind of stress on the drives and we have no idea what's going to happen."

Valkyrie's bridge was silent. There were no answers popping into Lorraine's head. They could try to weather the storm, she knew. They could maneuver to throw off boarding shuttles, use the Guard and their armor to hold off the UW Marines until they went translight...

"Alert," Val suddenly snapped, the SI sounding more than a touch upset. "Shuttles activating in Bay Three. All of your shuttles just brought their engines online and are maneuvering to exit the bay."

There was a momentary pause.

"I can seal the bay doors to prevent their exit, but I disrecommend it," Val warned.

"Get me coms," Lorriane snapped. "Who is doing this?"

"That'd be me, Your Highness," Chevrolet's voice said in her head. "Myself, Watanabe, a few other old hands. We... may have rigged the shuttles in something closer to assault mode than standard, despite what was requested.”

Goldenrod’s crew had put five Midas-type shuttles on each of the battlecruisers, and now Lorraine watched as twelve of them returned to the void.

“We dropped off a few extra pieces on the deck and are running a stripped-down shitty interceptor mode,” the Commanding Officer, Shuttles, told her. “No copilots, just the twelve of us.”

He paused.

“There were only supposed to be three Guard pilots, but it seems like a few of my pilots are going to be waking up with headaches,” he admitted. “I’ll leave Shwetz to justify that to Major Jarret, but the plan is pretty obvious, I think.

“There are two clusters of shuttles that are going to be able to board. They’re in true assault-shuttle mode, so we’ll be able to fly rings around them.”

“You can’t do that,” Lorraine argued. “You’ll be outnumbered three to one and we won’t be able to pick you up.”

“You’ll still need somebody to stop the guys coming around with guns, too,” Chevrolet told her bleakly.

“In Bright Dream, you came up with a better plan. There isn’t one here, Your Highness. *Goldenrod*-Alpha-Actual... wishing you a good flight. Over and out.”

The channel cut and Lorraine watched the shuttles blaze away from their battlecruisers at twelve gravities. Without cargo or passengers aboard, the flight crews could use their acceleration suits and the shuttle’s systems to out-accelerate even the other shuttles, and she could draw their course in her mind.

She felt Devine sneak his hand into hers. Somehow, he’d shifted his acceleration chair over to within reach of hers, and now he squeezed her fingers in silent reassurance.

“It’s their choice, Lorraine,” Jarret said on the other side of her, either unable to see or unwilling to comment on her boyfriend’s support. “And he’s right. I don’t see another way.”

THEIR INTERCEPTORS TORE into the boarding shuttles first. Outnumbered three to one or not, they were smaller targets and maneuvering faster. Chevrolet and the other pilots weren't shooting to kill, either. Her orders against killing UWN personnel were still in her people's minds, Lorraine realized, as her pilots disabled shuttle after shuttle, crippling engines to leave the spacecraft reeling off into deep space.

The destroyers would catch them... but none of them were going to be able to board the battlecruisers.

Five of the twelve shuttles died along the way, the UWN pilots having no such concern for *her* people's lives.

Lorraine fought back tears, squeezing Devine's hand hard to keep her emotions somewhat controlled as the surviving shuttles turned toward the spacecraft still heading for the battlecruisers.

She could have ordered them back. The odds that the *Valkyries* could endure the shuttles' fire and still jump were bad but survivable. She might even underestimate the protection over those critical systems.

But it didn't matter. The cold equations of acceleration and velocity laid themselves out across her feed almost without her trying. By the time her shuttles had disabled the last of Group Three, their velocities were too opposed to the battlecruisers.

They couldn't rejoin their friends. So, they made sure their friends got out.

"Signal lost," Val said quietly, the timer to their jump ticking into its last sixty seconds. "None of the shuttles remain."

A quiet pause.

"I detect no escape pods, Captain, Your Highness, Major. I... I am sorry. And I salute them."

Lorraine nodded silently. There was nothing to say.

"Incoming fire," Stephson barked. "Rotating the ship; should be able to keep the beams off anything vulnerable enough to cause trouble."

"There shouldn't *be* anything vulnerable enough," Val countered. "But I am flagging zones of concern on your display. We need fifteen seconds."

Lorraine's part in this was almost over. She'd plotted the course for them to meet *Goldenrod,* and now she pulled the translight navigation controls to her feed, leaving the desperate maneuvers to her subordinates.

Vice Admiral Bianchi wasn't going to have that *next conversation* she'd wanted—and if the price had been higher than Lorraine had wanted, twelve lives for three hundred was a trade she knew she had to accept.

And as she hit the final command to flee the Calypso System, she knew it wasn't the *last* sacrifice she was going to have to accept before this was over.

FIFTY-SEVEN

Rose Cortez found Vigo standing guard outside the Admiral's quarters in Habitat Pod Alpha. Palmer flanked the other side of the door, and both of them were doing their best impressions of a statue.

When the Chief Engineer approached, Corporal Palmer cleared her throat.

"I think I have the door, ser," she told him. "This looks like a you problem."

He snorted amusement at his subordinate and stepped around the corner with the engineer in silence—both of them clearly enjoying the centrifugal faux gravity allowed by the rotating pod.

"Can we afford the power to run the pods?" he asked. "I wasn't under the impression we had a lot of fuel."

"Six thousand tons. Just enough for a maintenance run." She shrugged. "Truthfully, I've shut down so many systems, we're not drawing much power. Concentrating the crew into one place lets me limit life support, which saves us enough power to justify spinning up the collar.

"Plus, once the pods are spinning, the only actual power draw is the elevators, and basically everybody is asleep."

Vigo nodded his understanding.

"I'm aware enough of our resource constraints to worry," he admitted. "I was glad to find there was enough furniture in the Admiral's quarters to put the Pentarch to bed. I almost got the sheet package thrown at us when Alvarez and I went to make the bed, though."

"Deservedly so. She's still a naval officer." Cortez paused. "How is she?"

"I have known very few people who took the first time they knowingly sent subordinates to their deaths well," Vigo said. "Chevrolet limited her choices, but she could still have stopped them. She'll carry that."

His lover shivered, leaning in to him.

"Not something that happens much in Engineering," she told him. "I'm guessing you've done it?"

He nodded, unwilling to explain. She knew he was enough older than she that he'd served in the war *before* the last war with the Richelieu Directorate. He'd commanded shuttle flights then, and he'd ordered at least two bomber strikes he knew his people weren't coming back from.

He'd *led* a third no one had expected to survive, but sometimes, that was how luck broke. Three shuttles had made it back out of twenty-four. He shouldn't have been one of them... but he'd had a long time to get over that.

"The spy's in with her?" Rose asked, gesturing back toward the door.

"He is. I am extending him as much trust as anyone, at this point. We wouldn't have these ships without him."

"Still not sure I trust him," she admitted. "Given who we know he worked for, I have to wonder how much of a traumatized bystander he was to that damn civil war in Fortuna."

"I suspect he was definitely a contact for somebody, yes," Vigo agreed. "He wasn't a UWESC operative on the ground in a civil war doing *nothing*; that's for certain. But he's on our side for now and he's head over heels for the Pentarch."

"And you'll forgive a lot for someone who loves her?"

"If nothing else, I consider it a sign of good judgment," he admitted with a chuckle. "Have *you* rested, Chief Engineer Cortez?"

"We're cycling hands while we're in translight. There's going to be a lot to do, but until we're on the other side of the wormhole and can chew up a few convenient asteroids, we're limited in a few ways.

"Plus, power—and therefore fuel—limits a lot of things." She shrugged. "My people need to rest. I have a few hours set aside."

She cocked her head at him and raised an eyebrow.

"How much rest are *you* getting?"

"I'm standing in this corridor until Lorraine wakes up, I think," he told her. "She's been my charge since she came up to my knee, Rose. I may not be her parent, but I'm the closest thing she has left."

"Not going to argue with that, I suppose," Rose conceded with a sigh. "Though I'll admit that surviving that kind of near-run thing certainly made me hope I could drag you away..."

Vigo chuckled at her wink.

"I think Lorraine would *hurt* me if I turned that down," he said, stepping into her embrace. "But I will need to come back. She may need me... and I need to know she's safe."

AFTER REASSURING themselves that they were both quite definitely alive, Vigo leaned against the headboard of Rose's new quarters—untouched until they'd arrived and made the bed—and considered the luxuries of capital ships.

Valkyrie had three habitat pods, rotating around her core hull to provide a range of gravities on several decks. The presence of habitat pods was often the distinguishing line between *escort* and *capital ship*, though cruisers often had them as well.

Once fully loaded, the battlecruiser would be ready for the same full year of operations as a frigate like *Goldenrod*, but it wasn't designed to hop from system to system like the frigate. They couldn't just point the ship at Adamantine from there—that would be a five-year journey! —but once they were through the wormhole to the Bright Dream Cluster, only the need for fuel and crew would force them to stop.

Hopefully, Lorraine had a plan for getting them through the Tavastar–Bright Dream Wormhole. Vigo had a few thoughts of his own, and he didn't expect it to be all that difficult.

Until the news that three battlecruisers had been stolen spread, their UWN identity beacons and a refusal to answer questions would carry them a long way.

How far, he wasn't sure. Far enough for them to be able to find fuel and raw material for the warships' fabricators. Quite possibly all the way to the Kingdom of Adamant—the battlecruisers were faster than a lot of *couriers* in the first-order clusters like Bright Dream, after all.

Sooner or later, though, the United Worlds would come for their ships... and having both met Val and knowing his Pentarch, Vigo wasn't sure that Lorraine was going to hand the SIs back over to their old masters.

And on *that* lovely thought, he slipped out of bed, careful to let Rose sleep.

In translight, surrounded by people they trusted completely, there was only one person who thought Vigo Jarret needed to be guarding Lorraine while she slept.

But that person *was* Vigo, so tonight, he would stand guard.

He couldn't guard against the wound her soul had just taken, but his presence, perhaps, would help.

He could do nothing more. He would do nothing less.

FIFTY-EIGHT

Despite everything, Lorraine didn't sleep for very long. She found herself slipping out of bed, trying not to wake Alastair up, and pacing the battlecruiser's Admiral's suite.

Whoever the last owner of the suite had been, they hadn't left much behind. The furniture that remained was standard-issue, of a style that wouldn't have looked out of place in an RKAN facility.

The oddity about the space to her was that it clearly hadn't been designed for microgravity at all. Someone had installed magnetic pads on all of the furniture as an afterthought, but nothing was designed to be used without gravity. The space was designed to either be under thrust or rotating, never truly being without some force to keep things on the deck.

She'd spent enough time on RKAN cruisers and capital ships to know that they still, for example, had microgravity sleeping and toilet arrangements in the crew quarters. The Admiral's suite on a UWN capital ship didn't.

It was a good thing that they'd made the decision to spin up the habitat pods. Lorraine knew they hadn't brought bedding with them, though she also knew that spacers and soldiers would manage to improvise.

A timer in her link told her that they were only halfway through their journey to the rendezvous point. *Goldenrod* would be there, though she worried about the frigate's shape.

Even if the ship was crippled, it wouldn't matter, so long as her *people* had survived. Too many hadn't and there was nothing Lorraine could do to bring them back.

"Couldn't sleep?"

She turned at the end of her circuit of the suite's main seating area—currently occupied by one very undersized couch—and saw Alastair stepping out of the bedroom. Like her, he'd put on the pants and boots of his shipsuit and nothing else.

"Brain is whirring a thousand plans a minute," she admitted. "Most of them are trying to fix the *past*, not work out the future, but either way... yeah. Couldn't sleep."

Her boyfriend chuckled, walking over to what looked like a blank wall and poking at it for a second. A panel finally slid aside, revealing a set of controls. A moment later, a virtual representation of the stars outside appeared on the wall.

"A view never hurts," he said. He stood in front of the sudden false window, looking more tired than she'd seen him before.

"We really needed them to not get eyes on your people's ships," he finally said. "With *Goldenrod* and the shuttles... they know who stole these ships."

"Not yet," she countered. "Eventually, maybe, but neither *Goldenrod* nor the shuttles were in standard formats. Physical profiles, energy signatures... I don't care what magic scanners the UWN has; they're not going to have what they need for easy IDs."

"They're still going to ID them. The plan called for us to get through without being seen."

"No plan survives contact with reality," Lorraine said. "You should know that."

"I do, yeah."

She stepped up to stand beside him.

"What is it, Alastair?" she asked. "You weren't expecting everything to go off perfectly; that's not how anything works."

"I was hoping," he admitted. "It would make life a lot easier if the United Worlds didn't know it was you and Adamant that stole the ships. They *will* come for you now."

"They were always going to, sooner or later," she reminded him. "Once the *Valkyries* show up in Adamant, the countdown gets very clear and very dangerous. The United Worlds was *always* going to come for us, Alastair.

"And there was a plan for that." She snorted. "Several, actually, ranging from bribery to blackmail. Knowing the truth about what they did to the CIRs adds even more options."

"You can't just talk away the United Worlds Navy," Alastair argued. "You've painted a target on yourself—your Kingdom, too."

"It was only ever a question of how long until they knew, not whether I was pissing off the UW," she countered. "You knew that, Alastair. What's going on?"

He sighed and shook his head, reaching out to take her hand.

"I guess it's just a bit terrifying to realize that I've *definitely* committed treason now," he admitted. "And every organization I ever served or had loyalty to is going to hunt me down."

"I have plans for when they catch up, Alastair," Lorraine repeated. "A lot of them will go a lot easier with you to provide... local knowledge, let's say. But we can... leave you, somewhere. There'll be at least one place along the way you can vanish into a crowd, cover your tracks so the United Worlds never really knows you worked with us.

"If you need out, we can get you out."

He exhaled a heavy sigh and squeezed her hand.

"I don't think it's ever going to be that simple," he admitted. "I'm following you, just like everyone else on these ships. It just feels a bit more real now, you know, that the United Worlds is coming after us.

"And they'll put the pieces together now in a way they might not have if we'd got the ships out without being IDed. They'll hang this on you, specifically."

"If it comes down to it, I'm prepared to give them the ships back in the end," Lorraine admitted. "Hell, if we can remove my uncle and set things up for a proper transfer of power, I might well let them drag *me* back to Earth for a trial."

She felt him shiver.

"I don't think you understand what that would look like," he warned.

"I think you underestimate my imagination," Lorraine told him. "But there are a lot of things I will do for my country, Alastair. I *want* to get through this alive and free with you at my side."

He nodded heavily.

"Me too," he agreed. "Just looking down the barrel of everything I used to do and realizing it's a bit more intimidating than I expected."

She chuckled.

"I won't say we'll be fine, Alastair," she told him. "I'm about ninety-nine percent sure we can get into the Bright Dream Cluster before anyone realizes what's going on. Once we're *in* the Cluster, I'm almost certain we can get ourselves back to the Kingdom.

"Finding allies there, crewing the ships, fighting a damn civil war? Things get a lot iffier there. And we have to get through all of that, through everything my uncle—the best strategist and tactician I know of!—will put in our way, before we're ever going to need to worry about what the United Worlds is going to do about me stealing their warships."

She sidled over to him, pressing her side against his.

"I'm not oblivious to the danger, Alastair. I recognized it from the moment I decided on this plan. It's why I tried to give everyone a way out—even *you*, if you recall. *Act of war against the United Worlds*, I believe I said."

"You did. And I came along with everything. Didn't count on the CIRs being full SIs, but..."

"That's to our advantage in a lot of ways," she told him. "Like I said, it makes options. Limits some others. There's only so much I can do with ships that are people in their own right."

He sighed.

"I worry," he told her. "You've set yourself up as a target, hoping to absorb all the fire yourself. But can you take all of that and come out the other side?"

"I don't know. I do know that I can't do anything else," Lorraine admitted. "The only way out of this mess is through.

"So, I go forward. I'd rather go forward with you at my side."

"Forward it is, then," he said, leaning his head against hers. "*May your choices reflect your hopes, not your fears.*"

"Another quote?"

She felt him smile.

"Always. Nelson Mandela, this time. On going forward."

FIFTY-NINE

Val had a crew again.

She hadn't been awake to miss having one, and yet... she could feel the hole in herself filled by even the sparse scattering of RKAN spacers and Adamant Guard aboard. *Valkyrie* was supposed to have almost fourteen hundred hands aboard, and she had a hundred.

But she *had a crew*.

Somehow, she knew this crew wouldn't betray her, either. She believed, in her silicon of silicons, that many or even most of her old crew would have been horrified to learn the truth of what had been done.

If her crew had known—if *Val* had known and been able to tell them!—she suspected that many of her crewmates would have fought to prevent what had been done to her.

But she hadn't known. They hadn't known—no. *Some* of them had. She was quite certain her last Captain had known—why else would he have made the false promise to save her orchids?

In hindsight, she knew that a "mere" CIR wouldn't have had a hobby. It was a strange concept, one she examined for at least ten whole seconds. In many ways, she believed her interest in gardening pre-dated her self-awareness—it was possible that indulging that interest on the part of her crew was part of what had triggered the change.

Gardens for her. Baseball trading cards for Herc—and she dreaded learning the fate of Herc's vault of those cards. They had *value*, after all, and if someone had known the CIR would never be woken up...

No wonder Herc had been so angry. Val's plants had suffered for their neglect, and Bonny's knitting had always been something the CIR had given away to crew members, but at least they hadn't been robbed while they slept.

Twenty-one of her sisters would never be awoken. She knew that in the plates of her hull and the chips of her mind. The three of them would be the only first-generation CIRs to wake up again. The records she had access to told her that the second- and third-genera-tion CIRs had definitely *not* "suffered" from emergent self-awareness.

Only two dozen mistakes that the UWN had needed to murder to cover their trails.

Val put that aside. An SI could compartmentalize intentionally, placing information and even emotions in a file and putting that file into inactive storage. She couldn't leave it forever—it remained part of her—but she could focus on other matters.

Like her crew. A good forty percent of the newcomers had paired off once they were safe in translight. Val's interest in human sexuality and relationships was clinical at best, but she had the literature to recognize a reaction to stress.

It was fascinating to her. She allowed her new crew their privacy, though she took some notes on the pairings she identified. That would enable her to judge relationships and appropriate commentary later.

She didn't, for example, have much on which to base a judgment of Vigo Jarret. But two of her new favorite humans—Lorraine Adamant and Rose Cortez—both, in different ways, loved the man.

That told her that Major Jarret was a being she would pay attention to and help.

Loyalty for a Command Intelligence Routine had been a matter of imprints and programming. From the moment she'd become self-aware, Val realized she had been able to ignore those limits and imposed rules.

She hadn't, no more than her human crew had ignored or defied their Captains and superior officers. She'd been part of a hierarchy in service to her nation. She'd have happily stayed in that hierarchy, but the UWN had never given her a choice.

Lorraine Adamant *had.* Even Val couldn't project or calculate a way that Adamant could have escaped Calypso if Val had rejected the Pentarch's offer, but she also knew that the human had meant it.

She believed that a human needed time to make assessments and decide someone was worthy of their loyalty. So did an SI, she supposed. She could just do the processing that a human needed months for in hours.

Like her new humans, Val would follow Lorraine Adamant back to the Kingdom of Adamant and to the end.

"Val?"

While she'd intentionally moved her focus to give Adamant and Devine their privacy, she had a program running to alert her to any call from the Pentarch. She caught her name and brought a portion of her focus to the woman.

"I am here, Lorraine," she said in the human's neural link. "Is everything all right?"

She saw that Devine had returned to the bed in the Admiral's suite but Lorraine was up, staring at a display of the stars moving around them.

"I'm fine. Or as fine as I'm going to be, I suppose," the young woman said. "I was reminded of something that you and I need to talk about."

"A portion of my capacity is now dedicated to you," Val noted. "I am available for any conversation you want. How can I assist?"

"This might be more about helping you," Adamant replied. "The UWN still has command codes that can override your systems, right? We had some of them as part of our plan for imprinting a loyalty override when we thought you were just a CIR.

"Would those still work on you?"

Val ran a series of simulations. She didn't like the results.

"It would depend on the delivery mechanism and the authority level of the codes," she told Adamant. "I believe that, for example, were a UWN flag officer to gain physical access to my computer core, they would be able to force my obedience."

Such an officer would rapidly find the limits of enforced compliance on the intelligence in control of a *warship*, but if they were clever and well informed, they could probably work with that.

If they were very, *very* clever, they would recognize that all those codes gave them was the upper hand in negotiations. That seemed unlikely from a UWN Admiral, though.

"That's what I thought," her new boss told her. "But my research suggests some options. They require me to trust you, I suppose, but I think we're already well past that point, aren't we?"

Val trusted Lorraine Adamant. She listened.

JOIN THE MAILING LIST

Love Glynn Stewart's books? Join the mailing list at:

GlynnStewart.com/mailing-list

Be the first to find out when new books are released!

ABOUT THE AUTHOR

GLYNN STEWART is the author of Starship's Mage, a bestselling science fiction and fantasy series where faster-than-light travel is possible–but only because of magic. His other works include science fiction series Duchy of Terra, Castle Federation and Vigilante, as well as the urban fantasy series ONSET and Changeling Blood.

Writing managed to liberate Glynn from a bleak future as an accountant. With his personality and hope for a high-tech future intact, he lives in Canada with his partner, their cats, and an unstoppable writing habit.

CREDITS

The following people were involved in making this book:
Copyeditor: Richard Shealy
Proofreader: M Parker Editing
Cover Artist: Elias Stern
Faolan's Pen Publishing:
Jack Giesen

And a sincere thank you to Glynn's Patreon subscribers!

OTHER BOOKS BY GLYNN STEWART

For release announcements join the mailing list
or visit **GlynnStewart.com**

STARSHIP'S MAGE

Starship's Mage
Hand of Mars
Voice of Mars
Alien Arcana
Judgment of Mars
UnArcana Stars
Sword of Mars
Mountain of Mars
The Service of Mars
A Darker Magic
Mage-Commander
Beyond the Eyes of Mars
Nemesis of Mars
Chimera's Star
Ambassador for Mars
Chimera's Fall (*upcoming*)

Starship's Mage: Red Falcon
Interstellar Mage
Mage-Provocateur
Agents of Mars

Starship's Mage Novellas
Pulsar Race
Mage-Queen's Thief

DUCHY OF TERRA

The Terran Privateer
Duchess of Terra
Terra and Imperium
Darkness Beyond
Shield of Terra
Imperium Defiant
Relics of Eternity
Shadows of the Fall
Eyes of Tomorrow

SCATTERED STARS

Scattered Stars: Conviction

Conviction
Deception
Equilibrium
Fortitude
Huntress
Prodigal

Scattered Stars: Evasion

Evasion
Discretion
Absolution

PEACEKEEPERS OF SOL

Raven's Peace
The Peacekeeper Initiative
Raven's Course
Drifter's Folly
Remnant Faction
Raven's Flag
Wartorn Stars
Raven's Hope (*upcoming*)

Prequel Novella

Honor & Renown: A Peacekeepers of Sol Novella

AETHER SPHERES
Nine Sailed Star
Void Spheres (*upcoming*)

TEER AND KARD
Wardtown
Blood Ward
Blood Adept

CHANGELING BLOOD
Changeling's Fealty
Hunter's Oath
Noble's Honor
Fae, Flames & Fedoras: A Changeling Blood Novella

ONSET
ONSET: To Serve and Protect
ONSET: My Enemy's Enemy
ONSET: Blood of the Innocent
ONSET: Stay of Execution
Murder by Magic: An ONSET Novella

STANDALONE NOVELS & NOVELLAS
Children of Prophecy
City in the Sky
Excalibur Lost: A Space Opera Novella
Balefire: A Dark Fantasy Novella
Icebreaker: A Fantasy Naval Thriller